Prisoners of Silence

Patricia Beaton

ISBN 978-0-9587289-4-2

Published by Multilingual Music

Cover design: John-Pierre Favre

Prelude

In this box, his eyes adjust to the gloom
Like being shut up in a coffin. Surely his penance
He draws back the curtain enclosing him. Just a sliver
Dark to light

He peers at the penitents in the pews, silhouetted like the shadows of evening
Patiently waiting their turn to confess. Heads bowed. Anxious to cleanse their souls of sin
Unaware he can see them
Dark to light

He slides back the screen, catching a fleeting glimpse of each one entering the confessional
With time, he learns to recognise voices. Make out profiles from behind the grille
Unless they try to hide with their hands in votive position like this one
The one he saw at communion. Elfin almost. Like a pixie
Fourteen or fifteen years of age. Just blooming
She tells him she's been stealing
From whom, he asks

From my father, she says, embarrassed, head bowed low
He puts his head closer to the grille and gently asks her why
He's got plenty of money and never gives us any, she says shyly
Ah! Vulnerable. Age of innocence
He gives her no counselling

A penance of three Hail Marys to be said before the statue of the Blessed Virgin Mary
He slides the screen across, turns and pulls back the curtain an inch. Slowly
Dark to light

He watches her walk up to the statue to kneel near the altar rail
A little thin, perhaps, but innocent and beautiful in her blue summer dress
Wedges of colour from the stained-glass window merge to illuminate her face
Dark to light

1

Molly

Eight years I've been living for this day. The day I pack my suitcase for the last time to leave this dusty town that grew out of a goldrush. I'm too excited to feel a hint of sadness as I say goodbye to my friends. The teachers I liked. Most of them, I suppose.

Through the grimy window on the train, I glimpse the pipeline that carries water from the reservoir to the town. It's carried *me* many times, that pipeline! As it recedes into the distance, I'm treading carefully on it like a tightrope walker, arms flailing, counting my steps, determined to stay on longer than anyone else before overbalancing onto the cracked clay below. I'll miss those Sunday walks through the bush with the girls. Outside any convent would have to be better than inside. A chance to devise your own games, your own competitions. The possibility of an adventure. I could find a gold nugget. Come across smoky campfires under red river-gums, swirling eddies and rapids, or the creeks and deep mountain valleys pictured in our school readers.

Snakes and goannas are the only wildlife in the St Arnaud bush. The only humans I've seen are prospectors panning for gold in a trickle of water from a nearby billabong, or swagmen squatting by a campfire with their burnt black billies, often the same ones who beg for handouts at the back door of the convent. Remnants of machinery and relics from goldrush days – carts, crushers and puddling machines – rust away among old mines barricaded by mounds of dirt. We test their depth by dropping stones down the shafts and counting the seconds.

Matriculation maths, so don't bother thinking about it, one of the nuns said when someone asked her why. One second is 16 feet. Two seconds, 64 feet. Three seconds, 144 feet. We listen for the faint thud as the stones hit the bottom. Listened! I keep reminding myself that it's all in the past now.

My last train trip from St Arnaud! *Our* last train trip, I should say, seeing that my two younger sisters are with me. For eight years I've been pleading with my father not to send me back to boarding school, but every year he's ignored me. Just as he did when he drove me there the first time as a five-year-old in 1945. During that long journey, his responses to my questions were abrupt and evasive. Where are we going? To St Arnaud. Where's that? In the bush. Why isn't Mum with us? No answer. What about Brigid and Veronica? No answer. Where's Tony? Away. His dismissive manner frightened me. When a grey slate roof and a tall red brick building loomed into view at the end of the drive, I thought it was a church. I remember him parking the car in front of it. Ringing the doorbell. Handing me over as though I was just another piece of luggage. Abandoning me. No explanation about why I'd been taken away from my family. No hug or kiss goodbye. Finally, after eight years – a week before the Christmas of 1952 – I was leaving boarding school behind forever. In 1953 we would all be day-scholars!

Brigid and Veronica were as excited as me. I had a shilling in my pocket to cover our tram fares for when we arrived. I was so eager to alight when the train pulled into the station, I almost fell onto the platform. The tram seemed to take ages to arrive. My instructions were to alight at the Sir Henry Barkly Hotel, where Dad would be watching out for us. I counted seven hotels between the station and the hotel we'd been directed to, all the while trying to quell my excitement; trying to imagine living with my family permanently; never returning to boarding school again. The best Christmas ever!

The sharp smell of beer hit me first as I stepped off the tram clutching a suitcase, Brigid and Veronica trailing behind me. The public bar was overflowing with men, mostly standing, their raucous laughter and conversation swirling around with clouds of smoke from their cigarettes. A few were perched on stools, one or two slumped against the bar, their heads almost on the counter. Behind it, my father was pulling a beer. When he noticed us, he gestured towards another entrance further along the footpath. The beery smell and men's voices penetrated the rooms and passages, their swearing and blasphemy a shock to my thirteen-year-old convent ears, although I soon became immune to it.

We found our way to a small kitchen where Mum was stirring something in a bowl. Despite not having seen us since the beginning of the year, she greeted us as though we'd never been away. If she was pleased to see us, she kept it to herself. There was little warmth in her smile. No questions. No kisses. No cuddles. Her eyes were more dead than alive. We were strangers rather than her children. That's how it's always been with Mum since I left home for boarding school eight years ago. It's not that she's cruel or nasty. More that she's indifferent. Uncommunicative. Something inside her seems to be frozen. Something that says she's not always coping with the world. 'The three of you are sleeping in the room at the end of the passage past the piano room,' was about all she said after we greeted her. We scuttled past the customers to a bedroom so small that we had to climb over the bed-ends to get to our three beds. We didn't mind. Anything was better than a dormitory! The hotel with its poky old rooms looked like it was on its last legs, but I didn't care! I was going to be living with my family.

Going to a new school. A day-scholar for the first time in my life!

Having been shuffled around Victoria between friends and relatives for most of the school holidays, I knew my brother Tony little more than I knew my parents. I found him in an outdoor bungalow fiddling with a crystal set. He picked up almost immediately that I was anxious to know if we were going to be all living together permanently.

'We're old enough to help out now,' he reassured me. 'That's why you're staying. I've been here the whole year. I'm a day scholar at St Bernard's now.'

And here was I thinking my parents had only just moved into the pub! Dad did his duty by writing to us once a term at boarding school, but at no time did he tell us they'd moved into a hotel. The first I heard of it was when one of the nuns told me the day before I left St Arnaud for the last time.

From Tony's bungalow, I saw men fumbling with their fly buttons as they returned from the outside toilet. In the yard, they were hoicking and spitting. One vomited into a gully trap. Another shock to my senses was the noise that built up in the late afternoon, Fridays and Saturdays the worst. Every evening a sharp hand-bell echoes through the hotel to signal the start of the six o'clock swill. The stampede. A buzzing crescendo and frenzied rush to the bar. Time for the last round to be lined up on the counter. Time to top up before staggering out the door fifteen minutes later. Six o'clock at boarding school was the deep clang of the Angelus bell to signal the nuns' *knell of parting day*. Black curtains swishing along the corridor to the chapel. Veils billowing. Rosary-beads rattling in rhythm with their footsteps as they murmured *Angelus Domini nuntiavit Maria...*

I'm not complaining about my new life. Just comparing. After eight years of boarding school, this shabby little pub is paradise.

Suddenly I'm free. Free to get up in the morning and go to bed when it suits me. To get my own breakfast. Go to the picture theatre on Saturdays. Walk around the city, the lake and botanical gardens. No daily Mass or reciting the rosary every evening. Now I can become an individual. Not confined by the restrictions and regimentation of boarding school. Having scarcely handled money, doing the shopping was a bit of a shock. I suppose it was a gradual realisation for the four of us that Mum never left the hotel, despite the shops being within a few minutes' walk down Main Road.

I met Gabby when we were trying on our St Martin's College uniforms in Myers after Christmas. We managed to sit together for Form 2 and become good friends. The first day at my new school was a bit of a shock. There were about forty girls in the class. So much quieter without boys! Our teacher, Sister Damien, better known as Doglips I discovered months later, was one of those embittered nuns in her fifties who regrets the enclosed life they've chosen by taking it out on those in their charge. She surely had a twin at my former convent in St Arnaud! She ranted and raved at the drop of a pencil. Humour and pleasure were not permitted in her classroom. She was far from charitable, unlike her namesake Saint Damien, who – I'd learnt in fourth grade – spent years caring for the physical, mental and spiritual needs of those who were banished to a leper colony. It wasn't a good introduction to my new school. Instead of reading us a chapter from a classic story at the end of the day, we sang a dirgy hymn while Doglips ploughed away at the piano like a combine harvester. It must have taken quite an effort to control her temper when student-teacher novices were in the classroom. One of them, Sister Jeanne, gave such a brilliant poetry lesson, I almost applauded. I wanted her to replace Sister Damien. During her lesson, I asked her if the poet had also written the music. She found me at recess and asked me how I knew the poem was also a song. I told her the customers at the pub sang it, and I accompanied them.

'You mix with the customers?' she asked me.

I shrugged. 'They barge in when I'm practising, Sister, so I play whatever they want to sing.'

Someone had said she was French, so I decided to try out the French I'd started learning the previous year in St Arnaud. *'Merci beaucoup pour la leçon, ma soeur.'*

'De rien, Molly,' she said with a beautiful smile.

She must have memorised all forty of our names within her first day in the classroom. Her voice sounded so musical. We all had a crush on her. I was about to ask her if she'd be teaching me French next year when she said that I must be the girl who'd boarded in a bush convent. How on earth did she know that?

'Yes, Sister,' I nodded. 'St Arnaud.'

She smiled. 'Pronounced in such a way that no Frenchman would recognise it!'

I had no idea what she was talking about.

'The town is named after a Frenchman. Jacques Leroy de Saint Arnaud.'

No one ever told me that. She pronounced St Arnaud more like *santarno.*

'Sister Anastasia spoke about you when we met last Christmas.'

It occurred to me then that nuns must have had nothing better to do than gossip when they moved around to different convents within the diocese for their holidays. What else could they do? Hardly an exciting holiday, surely, from four brick walls to four more in another location. The nun she mentioned, Sister

Anastasia, taught me for my first three years in St Arnaud. I adored her. As the baby of the convent, she looked after me like a mother hen. Perhaps she knew I'd been abandoned. That I went to friends and relatives for the holidays instead of home. I can't remember Anastasia ever losing her temper in the classroom. She had a sense of humour and could manage even the naughtiest boy without raising her voice. I was upset when I returned in my fourth year to learn that she'd been transferred to another convent.

Sister Jeanne spoke to me again. 'She said that Sister Berchmans won't have anyone to replace you on the organ because you played by ear. Apparently, no one else can manage pedalling and playing and reading at the same time.'

I don't blame them, but why don't they use their ears instead of their eyes? It's much easier. Sister Berchmans, my elderly piano teacher, snuffled and puffed her way through the rosary every evening in the chapel while I thought of ways to relieve the boredom. We had competitions to see how many decades we could fit into one of Berchman's Hail Marys. Bored with that, we resorted to playing jacks with our rosary beads, a challenge when two or more sets became tangled. At the end, we plodded along at snail pace with a hymn, Berchmans wobbling and wheezing away on the old harmonium. When her arthritic fingers got beyond her, she chose me to replace her. I teetered on the edge of the bench when I first started playing, my feet barely able to reach the pedals to pump them. After I got the hang of it, I decided it was worth enduring the agonisingly slow Hail Marys to have complete control of the music at the end. I upped the tempo from tortoise to hare and pulled out all the stops.

Within a few months of moving into the pub, accompanying hymns in the chapel at boarding school progressed to accompanying songs in the beery, smoke-filled piano room! It started when a regular burst in with a 'Struth, Molly. Let Mozart rest in peace and give us a proper tune.' I began playing whatever they sang, sometimes old Irish songs like *Galway Bay*, or *The Rose of Tralee* that I knew from school, or a few I remembered Mum singing before I was sent to boarding school. Now, it's pop tunes I pick up from the radio.

The women straggle up from the ladies' parlour into the piano room, where they can mix with the men. They're banned in the public bar. Tony gives the customers nicknames if they haven't already got one. One-armed one-eyed Nugget, a returned soldier, clamps his stump around a pot of beer, his good arm rolling a cigarette. With the gravelly sound of a working sawmill, he prefers war songs like *There'll Be Bluebirds Over* and *Lily Marlene*. Bluey, our redheaded boarder, is speckled with house-paint. Between his raucous coughing and dragging on a Capstan cigarette, he scarcely draws enough breath to sing, which is probably why Tony calls him 'Van Cough.' Mooney the Looney, with his poached-egg eyes and shaggy mane has got religious mania, the customers told us with a wink and a nudge. Dropping down on his knees, arms outstretched in supplication, a beer in one hand, cigarette in the other, he croons in Bing Crosby style his entire repertoire – *Hail Queen of Heaven* and *The Lourdes Hymn*. Dirgy hymns bore me silly, so I add a boogie-woogie bass for the *Aves*, bridging the interludes for his swigs and puffs with exaggerated cadenzas. When rock'n'roll becomes popular, I progress to a rock-bass line – *Quee-een of Hea-ven, the O-o-cean Star.*

We three girls look up to Tony and adopt his nicknames without question. Dad is the old man. Ella, with one functional lung, is Bung-lunged Cinders. She doesn't drink or smoke and sits sedately beside her mother, Winedot Wilma. Gyro Duck with red-crested hair, removes her teeth to quack and lisp her way through her only solo item *Three Little Fishies*. Tony says Fancy Nancy's husky-throated *Blue Moon* is a dead giveaway to a lifetime of unfiltered smoking and dedicated drinking. With a hand-rolled cigarette dangling from the corner of her cupid lips, she sings and dances with anyone available, including us girls. We like the customers. They're full of yarns, and you can always chat and argue with them. A bit of a change from the convent. They're part of our family. They talk to us much more than Mum and Dad ever have.

'This pub was named after an early Governor of Victoria when Ballarat was a gold-rush town,' Bazza the Barman told us. 'It's the only wooden-clad pub in Ballarat, and probably the oldest.'

With its tin-roofed veranda, saloon doors and semi-frosted windows, it could be a set for an American western. The Sir Henry Barkly might sound posh, but our customers are in a different class from Craig's Royal Hotel in the city centre. Only one block down Main Road towards Golden Point, an open drain flows between the mullock heap and alluvial tailings that ooze through the surrounding slums. Since moving in, we've been deluged several times from the slopes of the Ballarat East Gardens sweeping across the backyard into the hotel. The customers join us to bucket water from its bowels and gangways, the mustiness mingling with the stench of beer and cigarettes in the bar and parlour.

The regulars tap their muffled *boom diddledee ya daa boom booms* on the side door every evening, Dad furtively scanning the street for the law while the customers slink in with their lamp-lit shadows to the piano room. There, no outsider can hear the clinking glasses, the strident singing, the crescendoing conversations, the raucous laughs. Without after-hours custom, we'd have been deprived of the excitement of police raids. The bellow 'They're here!' creates a frenzy, everyone rushing around leaving half-smoked cigarettes and beer glasses on the tables. Even in the middle of summer, there's always something stewing and wheezing itself to death on the wood stove so regulars can become bona fide guests, the only requirement for serving alcohol after closing time.

'About as bona bloody fide as a dud fiver,' I once heard a policeman say, although a lone one happily accepts the £1 bribe Dad keeps in the bona fides' register.

Customers hide in the cellar or the wardrobes during a raid, the fitter ones scrambling over the side fence into the chook-house next door. Mum tears around, more agitated than ever, tossing glasses and ashtrays into the nearest cupboard, which is why the sheets and towels are dotted with burn marks, and reek of cigarettes and beer. Tony says it's why the rodents are all pisspots and easy to catch.

The phone runs hot every Saturday. '703 ACE,' Dad says furtively. 'Phelan to ACE,' is the typical response. 'Race Four. Caulfield. Half a quid each way Shenanigans.'

Word quickly spreads around the hotel network that the Flying Squad from Melbourne is on the way, the country constabulary along the highway having sometimes forewarned their Ballarat partners in crime. Only one Melbourne policeman's presence sets the pulses of Ballarat publicans to *tempo agitato* – Sergeant Orson Roberts, known throughout Ballarat hotels as Babyface. Maude, our favourite aunt, says he's a shyster Freemason – whatever that is – and there'd be more chance of the Pope becoming an atheist than him accepting a bribe.

On Saturdays, the races blare out of the radio like a swarm of blowflies, the punters' excitement sometimes diminished by

Babyface's determination to catch everyone red-handed. He and his men push past the customers Tony calls the *swaying palms*, who need the bar or a wall for support. No glass or ashtray is left unturned in their hunt for evidence of illegal gambling as they scurry around between the bars and the woodshed – the centre for the SP operation. It's as though we're playing a scene from The Keystone Cops. 'Come on fellers, join in,' Nancy teased them during a recent raid, ordering me to strike up *Babyface* on the piano, while the customers scooped to exaggerate the *Baaaay-by* until their voices rang throughout the hotel.

Dad refuses to give us pocket money, although there's a bowl of cash in the kitchen for the shopping which means I get away with taking a little extra for the weekly Girls' Crystal, and the picture theatre. I'm ashamed of my clothes, but when I ask for money to buy new ones, Dad tells me to wear my school uniform. When it comes to education, he's very generous, but if it's about pleasure or personal things like street clothing or recreation, we can't get a penny out of him. His miserliness stirs up our resentment, so we sisters form an alliance against him. We wonder why he hides money under the bed instead of banking it or giving any to us. Why he whinges rather than talks to us. Why he's always nagging about us not helping out enough. Sometimes Mum intervenes, but mostly she's in la-la land. When she suddenly disappeared for a week last year and arrived home with our baby sister Katy, and again this year with our little brother Patrick, we three sisters were curious. Here I am towards the end of Form 3, fifteen in November, and I've got no idea how babies manage to grow in Mum's stomach, although it could have something to do with *down there*. How they come out is another mystery. To us girls, an operation was the only possibility. From our convent education, any thoughts lower than the navel suggested sin, so it was never discussed. When Mum went on about storks and cabbages, I decided she didn't know either. Having babies was obviously something to be ashamed of, although this seemed a contradiction, with priests in the pulpit declaring that the Propagation of the Faith was not only about spreading Catholicism. Women should be doing their duty by having large families. I've given up asking. There's no point. I know the sacrament of marriage has got something to do with it.

I try to imagine having parents who love you and talk to you like Gabby's do. Do Mum and Dad really love each other like we see in Hollywood films? I've never seen them touch or kiss each other. Perhaps they don't understand what love is. Gabby's parents do. They're kind and always make me feel welcome. When her father walks in the door from work, he kisses her mother and starts chatting to the whole family. If ever I get married, my family will be just like theirs and my kind relatives. I'll never bring Gabby home here because I'm sure my parents would embarrass me. Then there's the pub itself. It's such a dive. Not the sort of place you'd want to bring anyone home to!

2

Juliette

Fourteen-year-old Juliette Rousseau inadvertently altered the course of her family's life by repeating a question a friend had put to her earlier in the day.

'Which country fought on our side during the war and has never had a war in its own country?' Madeleine asked her.

'This war? The one that's just finished?'

'Of course!'

Juliette named ten countries in succession, to which her friend gleefully replied 'No!' to all. They were dawdling along the pavement of Rue Gambetta, a Paris street in the 18th arrondissement that had survived the ravages of World War 2. Madeleine, having visited an exhibition at *Magasins du Printemps*, a large department store in the centre of Paris, finally told her the country was Australia.

That evening, on posing the same question to her family, Juliette's father immediately replied '*L'Australie.*'

Juliette was eager to go to the exhibition and asked him if he would take her. 'That's the one called *L'Australie dans la paix et dans la guerre*. I've seen it advertised and I'm not the slightest bit interested. Do you really think we need to be reminded of all those years of terror? The war has just finished! It's bad enough that I still walk down the street expecting to see the Wehrmacht wearing *Gott mit uns* on their belt buckles.'

'But papa, Madeleine says it's not just about the war. It's…'

'I not only risked *my* life when I was working with the résistance sabotaging railway engines. I put the rest of you at risk. I still…'

'Please, papa! We've been learning about the Southern Hemisphere. Madeleine says there's a really interesting section just about Australia itself. We can ignore everything else.'

Her father sighed and turned to her mother. 'And you, *chérie*. Are you interested in going?'

'Not really,' Sofia said with a shrug. 'But *Magasins du Printemps* has some new fabrics, and we've got nothing better to do tomorrow.' She turned to Juliette's brother. 'If you're not interested Paul, you could hold a place in the queue at that big market nearby.'

He agreed reluctantly, protesting about the cold and the length of the queues. Sofia reminded him that she'd spent half her life doing that during the Boche years.

'But it's nearly 1946 and we're still queuing for hours for food,' Paul grumbled.

'And will be for another few years according to the government,' Claude said to a collective groan.

When they arrived, the exhibition was packed. The photographs of a carefree, sunny lifestyle attracted them. Australia looked exciting with its coastline fringing the seas; its sandy beaches so close to the capital cities; the blue skies and mild winter climate; no greyness or overcrowding and no war-torn cities in need of repair. They noticed an advertisement offering assisted passages to people with specialist skills. When Juliette's father said he was an electrical engineer, an official said that it was an area where there was great demand in Australia. It was very likely that there would be a position in his field waiting for him if they were to emigrate. Juliette was surprised that her father was asking so many questions about the type of job it would be. She knew he hated his present one. Or was it more that he hated his boss who he believed to have been a collaborator with the Boche?

When her father consulted the family that night about the idea of emigrating, Juliette wondered how he knew so much about Australia. He reminded them that Australia had strong relationships with France during both world wars. Its people were known to be friendly and supportive. They could make a fresh start in this new country. Juliette was enthusiastic, but her mother and Paul were cautious about the idea.

'What about Paul's scholarship to the Sorbonne next year?' Sofia said. 'And don't forget! I'm the only one in the family who doesn't speak English.'

Claude had an answer for everything.

'I've been thinking about that,' he said. 'Universities in Australia start much earlier in the year. With Paul's results, he'll have no trouble getting into one, and if he's not happy, he can return and take up his scholarship here in September and live with your parents. As for you learning English, *chérie*, we'll all help you with that.'

Juliette and Paul learned English at school. Claude had spent some years in England in his youth, and his English was good. Having lived in Italy as a child, Sofia's only other language was Italian. By the end of the week, after much discussion, it was decided. They would go and try this new country with its sunshine and open spaces.

Juliette's family only had a few weeks to pack up and sell their apartment. On their arrival in Melbourne in early 1946, Claude accepted a senior position in Ballarat with the State Electricity Commission. Juliette and her mother were disappointed, having expected to live in Melbourne with Paul, who had been accepted at Melbourne University.

'Ballarat's hardly a city, papa. Only 45,000 people,' Juliette complained. 'It'd be *un commune* in France. Like Annecy or Narbonne.'

She soon learned that history had a different meaning in Australia. It was all relative really, the family agreed. After all, when Australia was settled in 1788, the French Revolution was just about to begin. Their new hometown of Ballarat, founded during a gold rush, wasn't even 100 years old. The piece of local history that most intrigued Juliette was that in 1871, when Ballarat was declared a city with a population of 47,000, there were 56 churches and 477 hotels. She calculated that this was one hotel for every 100 residents!

Juliette wondered why her parents chose St Martin's College for her final two years of schooling. Like most of their Parisian compatriots, they never had a formal adherence to religion. Their church attendance at Christmas and the odd festival was more of a social thing. A part of their culture. And after the millions killed during the war, with everyone claiming God on their side, Juliette knew they sometimes wondered whether they believed in a God at all. They told her the convent was highly recommended for its results by a neighbour. As a bonus, St Martin's was a few minutes' walk from their home.

The new term began in February, and Juliette soon settled into her routine. Every day following after-school sport, an elderly nun gave her extra tuition in English. She was distracted by the music that surrounded her – the chamber choir, the orchestra, the boarders practising their instruments. It seemed that her new school floated on music, as much a foundation of her school as the strong focus on religion. Was it that music had a higher power? That it honoured God as much as prayer? She regretted never learning an instrument, although with the long two-hour lunches at French lycées, she'd at least had an opportunity to join a top choir.

As a Catholic and pupil at St Martin's, Juliette was required to go to Mass every Sunday and Holy Days. She avidly absorbed all the Catholic rituals – Mass, Confession, Benediction, the Rosary, the hymns and processions. Her parents laughed about her fervour when it came to religion.

'You'll soon grow out of it, *mon coeur*. All that pomp and grandeur! It's a novelty,' Claude said after Juliette was inspired by her Confirmation. 'You're like a convert. Your mother had all that shoved down her throat as a child, didn't you, *chérie*?'

Sofia nodded. 'I grew out of it, I suppose.'

'It brings meaning to my life,' Juliette insisted, determined not to be put off.

She was happy and had adapted well to her new life. Like Paul, she was concerned when their father was forced to take out a bank loan to pay for his accommodation and fees at Melbourne University. With her school fees as well, it would take them forever to own a house like most Australians. Fortunately, her ingenious brother found a solution, hitch-hiking to Ballarat for the weekend to tell everyone the good news. Juliette was the only one home when he arrived. He hadn't been back to Ballarat for weeks, and she was thrilled to see him. They greeted each other in the French style. A hug, a kiss on both cheeks.

'I've got some good news,' Paul told her excitedly. 'I'll wait 'til maman and papa get home.'

Juliette had been about to cut him a slice of cake. 'That means you get none of this until you tell me. They mightn't be home for ages.'

'I've been offered a scholarship for the remainder of my course. Residential, fees, the lot!'

'That's fantastic, Paul.'

She threw her arms around him and hugged him. He couldn't stop grinning.

'I saw the Dean of the Faculty two weeks ago and asked for advice on how I could become more self-supporting, as I had financial problems. I explained how maman and papa were immigrants and had taken out a loan to pay for my accommodation and fees. I said it was a struggle for them, and...'

'Did you tell him you had a scholarship at the Sorbonne?'

'He knew that, but I told him I wanted to become a specialist and stay in Melbourne.'

'And isn't there a shortage of doctors?'

'That probably helped.'

'So how come he can just offer you a scholarship like that?'

'It had to go to a committee. He came back yesterday telling me that my results have been so outstanding they've offered me a full scholarship if I agree to take on tutoring.'

'Fantastic. Maman and papa will be thrilled. Well, maybe not maman. I've got a feeling she wants us all to return to Paris.'

He pulled a face. 'I suspected that. I'll talk to her after I tell her my news.'

Despite the neighbours going out of the way to help her, Sofia had been complaining that she was missing her parents and friends and wasn't coping with the perceived lack of culture. There were other day-to-day things that never really bothered Juliette or her father. After Paul relayed the details of his scholarship around the dinner table, Juliette noticed that her mother didn't appear to be very excited about it. Almost tearful.

'I'm sorry the *ragoût* is not up to its usual standard,' she complained. 'They've never even heard of garlic and aubergines here. And...'

'But it doesn't matter, maman,' Juliette interrupted. 'Whatever you cook is always great. With or without those other vegetables or spices. Anyway, papa says we're going to grow our own. We couldn't do that back in Paris.'

'They wouldn't know what a baguette or croissant is here. As for those tasteless loaves of bread without crusts!'

'I agree, maman! If you ate foam rubber, you wouldn't know the difference. It springs back into place after you prod it. I'm lucky. I found a great French baker right in Little Bourke Street. The flour here is not quite the same, but…'

Claude glared at his son. 'Well why didn't you bring us up a loaf?'

'I didn't have time. Anyway, I was hitch-hiking.'

Sofia had more to complain about. 'And what about the cheese?'

They'd all joked about the chalky, processed cheese. Was there much difference between the cheese and the cardboard packaging anyway?

Claude sighed. 'Cheese and baguettes would have to be the defining characteristics of French culture and diversity, I suppose. The persona of France. What an opportunity for an enterprising Frenchman here in Ballarat. But not me!'

Sofia threw her hands in the air. 'And where does one find poultry? *C'est rare comme le merle blanc*,' she said, using the French expression *rare as a white blackbird*.

'Sister Hilary says Australians say *rare as hens' teeth*, maman.'

'Well *rare as hens* will do. At least lamb and beef are cheap and always available,' Sofia admitted. 'And much superior to the mutton and horsemeat we ate back home.'

'There weren't too many chickens back home either, maman,' Paul reminded her. 'The Boche took them all.'

When the discussion turned towards cars, Juliette and Sofia began clearing up. That was when Sofia said she wanted to return to Paris. Juliette was horrified.

'But maman! I love it here. You like it too!'

They'd only recently talked about Ballarat's main street with its beautiful bluestone buildings only ten minutes' walk from their house. Her mother had wondered who, in such a small city, had the foresight to create a boulevard centred with bandstands and elegant statues, its fountain and lush gardens an oasis on a hot day. At weekends if they caught a tram to the lake, a brass band was usually playing in the bandstand. Cheery tram drivers waved to the musicians, dinging on the beat of a stirring march as they trundled past. Juliette was sure the boulevard was nearly as wide as the Avenue des Champs-Elysées. Sofia and Claude thought it closer to a third the size, the gardens along its centre perhaps giving one the illusion that it was much bigger, they told her. Not as grand as the Champs-Elysées, but more attractive. Juliette knew that her father liked his job and their adopted country, and desperately hoped her mother would come around to their way of thinking.

'You know, *chérie*, I'm saving every penny,' Sofia said suddenly, passing Juliette a dripping plate to wipe with the tea towel. 'I'd like us to be living back in Paris within a year.'

Juliette nearly dropped the plate. What about her new friends? The school she now felt at home in. She loved her new life in Ballarat. 'But maman, surely you don't mean that! We really like it here. I heard that one should always give a new place at least two years.' She noticed tears in her mother's eyes.

'I miss maman and papa. They're not getting any younger, you know. Then there's Camille and all my friends.'

'Well maybe we could start saving for *mémère* and *pépère* to come here. I nearly forgot to tell you maman. There's a girl in

Matriculation who's having trouble with French because she's been away with glandular fever for ages. Her parents want to pay me to help her, but I said I didn't have time and that I'd ask you. Will you do it?'

'Of course, but I couldn't take their money.'

'She said her parents insist on paying, otherwise they won't bother. They're quite well off.'

Her mother shrugged. 'Well, I'll do it then.'

Soon, through word of mouth and Juliette's school-friends, Sofia was privately coaching several students in French and Italian. Twelve months later, the family began to feel part of the community. Melbourne wasn't so far from Ballarat and the trains were frequent enough. After two years, everything was going well. They couldn't have had better friends and neighbours. Claude was promoted, Sofia was offered a job tutoring at the Grammar School, and Paul loved his student life in Melbourne.

The Saturday evening before the Christmas of 1947 was a double celebration, Juliette's outstanding Matriculation results having won her a scholarship to a university college, and Paul topping his year once again and winning an award. He arrived from Melbourne with two loaves of bread from the French baker, who had managed to get his hands on two bottles of Beaujolais and cheese from a friend in the Consulate.

'And who pays for this University College scholarship, *chérie*? The government?' Claude asked Juliette when they had completed the toasts.

'No papa. St Mary's Hall is run by Loreto nuns.'

'*Mon Dieu!* More nuns! I thought you'd be able to get away from them.

'No, papa. It... my scholarship was organised from St Martin's.' She knew she was about to shatter their equanimity, but it was time to break the news. 'I'll be a postulant, then a novice while I'm there.'

'A what?' and '*Quoi*?' the three of them said in unison.

'It's what you're called before you become a fully-fledged nun.'

Her family stared at her during a long silence. Was this some sort of joke?

Claude slapped his hands on the table. 'You're not serious!'

'I don't understand, Juliette,' Sofia said. 'What are you saying?'

'It's something I've been thinking about for a while. I want to do something for God. For society. I have a calling.' She shrugged and smiled. 'Life has been good to me. I want to teach and help others.'

Claude was angry. 'Well you can do all that without entering a nunnery, for God's sake!'

When they began voicing their objections, Juliette tried to calm them down. 'But maman, papa, I'll be staying here in Ballarat after my studies! I was going to become a missionary nun, but Reverend Mother talked me out of it. I could be sent away anywhere and might never see you again. I can commute to Melbourne while doing my degree.'

Sofia began to sob. Juliette threw her arms around her, but her mother pushed her away. 'Not now Juliette,' she said. 'You can't do this to us now when we're all so happy here in Australia.'

'It's just not happening, Juliette,' Claude said. He'd rarely been angry with her. 'We're not going to allow you to be smothered in an institution for the rest of your life. In this country, you're our responsibility until you turn twenty-one. You're not subject to the jurisdiction of the church, the nuns or anyone else if we say so. It's what *we* say. Not you.'

Eventually, after more tears and arguments, they compromised, Claude doing most of the talking. 'Let's not discuss it anymore, *mon coeur*. You're only seventeen. Twenty when you graduate. Do your degree, but not as a nun. You'll be able to make a more mature decision by then.'

Juliette settled into her new accommodation after Paul took her for a tour around the university. St Mary's Hall was very small in comparison to its male counterpart, Newman College, but she loved it. The large mansion was like a home away from home, and the Loreto nuns were kind and intelligent. She got to know many students, and within a few weeks, was tutoring in French. One of her students was besotted with her, as were two of Paul's friends. She socialised with them regularly. Had even kissed them, but scarcely felt her heart fluttering. Where were the butterflies in her stomach? Where was the passion, the rapture she was supposed to feel? Her friends suggested that everything would change when she met Mr Right. She conceded that while some might consider convent life harsh, she was attracted to a teaching life and to God. Or was it that she had no desire to marry? To put on an apron and wait on a husband, her only means of support. With marriage considered to be a woman's ultimate goal in life, she was destined to become a housewife. Defined by whom she married. Listed as having no occupation. A teaching life in a convent was surely the best option for a single woman, and it did have a touch of romance about it.

The subject of entering the convent was never mentioned at home again during her next three years of study, but after the Conferring of Degrees the following February, Juliette broke the news to her family that she'd be entering the convent. For a long moment, her parents were so shocked, they could say nothing. Sofia burst into uncontrollable sobbing.

Her father spoke first. 'You can't do this to us, Juliette,' he said calmly. 'Your mother has been saving every penny from her tutoring for a trip to Paris so you can see your grandparents. It was going to be a surprise for your twenty-first birthday. Your grand-parents are very excited about it.'

Juliette threw her arms around her mother. '*Merci maman*! I must have the best parents in the world. I'd love to see *mémère* and *pépère* but it's impossible. The postulant intake is next month.'

Her parents looked at her in disbelief. 'Just when I'm settled here, Juliette, you do this to us,' Sofia said in between sobs.

'But maman. It's been at the back of my mind for the last few years. You promised you'd let me choose after I finished my degree.' Tears were beginning to trickle down Juliette's face.

'We thought you'd grow out of it.'

The subject was not mentioned again until a few days later when Claude pulled out a letter he'd received from the convent. 'Can you explain this? Something about a dowry. A dowry?' he said angrily. 'Isn't that payment to the groom's family for the sale of your daughter? Where's the groom?'

'I'm sorry, papa. I know nothing about that.'

'Your mother has been crying herself to sleep since you told us. Just when we're settled here, Juliette, you abandon us. I don't think we'll ever forgive you.'

Juliette loved her parents and was mortified about upsetting them. They were all seated around the kitchen table the evening before she was to leave for the convent. 'I just want you to think about this again,' Claude pleaded. 'You've been seduced into a choice which you're too young and immature to make. Twenty-year-olds are vulnerable and defenceless. This is 1951. Nuns are dying out in France now. No one takes the church seriously there like they do in Australia. Church and state are separate. Here the church runs the country. Like in Ireland.'

'But papa, that's got nothing to do with it. I want to teach and carry out God's work in the convent. I want to…'

'Nuns can never leave convents,' her mother interrupted. 'Not like clerics. They come and go as they please. They can travel around the world. Here in Australia they own cars, even racehorses. They play tennis and golf and have a few weeks holiday every year. They can visit their families whenever they like. But you won't be able to, Juliette. You might as well be in jail! We'll be grieving for you as though you're dead.'

Many things were said in the heat of the moment, but Juliette kept calm, never raising her voice.

'You're so clever. So beautiful,' her mother said between sniffs and sobs. 'All your beauty and talent will be wasted! Camille said just before we left Paris that with your high cheekbones and huge brown eyes, you looked like Maria Jeanne Falconetti, the French film star. She portrayed *Jeanne d'Arc* in the film *La Passion de Jeanne d'Arc*. You didn't see it. She…'

'*Jeanne d'Arc?* How opportune is that? Jeanne is going to be my new name, maman!'

When the time came, Claude and Sofia said their goodbyes at the front door, having refused Juliette's invitation to walk to the convent with her. One month later, on their first visit to the convent, Sofia, shocked to see Juliette dressed in black stockings, skirt, blouse, vest and tulle fascinator, asked Juliette what being a postulant and novice was all about.

'St Martin's has its own teaching certificate. Those of us who are a little older, or with a degree, like me, remain postulants for eight months or so. We attend theology and philosophy classes. We pray for the ill, the holy souls in purgatory, and for the conversion of the world to Catholicism.'

'God forbid!' Claude exclaimed, switching to French. 'Millions of perpetrators during the war were Catholics. Millions of Jews and Christians prayed for the war to stop and millions of them were killed. It made no difference.'

'When that came up in Philosophy, Mother Phillip said it was prayer that stopped the war.'

Claude gave a typical Gallic shrug and rolled his eyes. 'Well. One can't argue with that logic.'

Juliette tried not to think of her doubts. How she wasn't sure about Reverend Mother Alphonsus, who had replaced Reverend Mother Paulinus when she'd died suddenly during the term. After recently approaching the nun in charge of the novices to discuss her doubts, Mother Phillip had responded by saying that the devil was tempting her. That her personal qualities of flexibility and focus gave her a missionary zeal to do God's work here on earth. If she ignored God's call, she'd never be happy.

She hoped the pained look in her parents' eyes would lessen over time when they visited every month, but if anything, it got worse. There was always pleading in their eyes. Tears, and covert arguments in French. Juliette told herself that at least her parents had not disowned her, like two of the novices, the wealthy parents of one having offered her a trip around the world instead. After six month's postulancy, more arguments and tears during their visits, Juliette eventually talked her parents into attending the 'wedding' where she would be 'married' to Jesus.

'And how do you think we'll feel while we're sitting there, Juliette? Proud? Like we were at your graduation?' Claude said when Juliette described the forthcoming ceremony to them. 'Happy that *notre belle fille* has been stolen from us? That you've been indoctrinated into marrying a man who died two thousand years ago? Proud that you'll be in a wedding dress and wearing a gold ring without a real live groom standing beside you? Nuptial Mass indeed! The whole thing sounds nauseating. Bizarre.'

Not to be deterred, Juliette smiled at her parents, when not yet twenty-one, she walked down the aisle in the cathedral, a flower girl on each side carrying a posy. She saw the tears in their eyes and glanced around the gathering. Which ones were tears of joy? Which ones of grief? In the school hall, nuns served morning tea to the short-lived brides and their relatives. The Rousseau family spoke French in quiet undertones. On a signal from one of the nuns, Juliette told them she had to leave, but would be back shortly.

The six brides had rehearsed this part of their special day. After their hair was chopped short by two nuns, they changed out of their wedding dresses into full nuns' robes, the only difference being that they would wear a white veil for two years before taking their final vows to wear the black one. Having renounced their names along with their bridal robes to indicate the break with their previous lives, they would no longer hear their first or family names. The assumption of a new name was the high point of the renunciation ritual. It marked the final stage of their exit from the world.

There was a concerted gasp when the former brides, radiant and glowing in their new attire, glided into the hall looking as though they were about to perform a medieval play or ritual. Instead, they joined their relatives, some of whom smiled with pride, a few who stared with looks of dread and incredulity.

'From now on,' Juliette told her parents and Paul, I'll be called Sister Jeanne, after *Jeanne d'Arc*. It's the same initial, maman. Perhaps, like her, I can be ahead of my time,' she laughed. 'They wanted me to be Sister Mary Joan, because Australians say Joan of Arc. On the list of nuns' names for the

Bishop, I wrote *Jeanne, pronounced zsharhhnn to rhyme with barn,* and he still got it wrong. He pronounced it with the hard English G, like in Jean.' She glanced at the Bishop. 'Do you think he knows *Jeanne d'Arc* is the patroness of soldiers and France?'

'*Mon Dieu*! Your hair!' her mother gasped. 'They've chopped it all off under that white veil, haven't they? Like the guards shaving Maria Jeanne Falconetti's exquisite tresses in the film. I cried during that scene.'

'It's so we won't be too uncomfortable under our veils, maman.'

'That's what they tell you. It's more about renouncing the symbol of femininity. Just like in the film. The punishment before the execution.'

'But maman, in the hot weather…'

'Did they put your hair on a silver platter, like John the Baptist's head? You've been sacrificed like your namesake! She was burnt to death at the stake by the church. About the same age as you, Juliette,' Sofia shuddered, her tears flowing again. 'You might just as well be marched to the scaffold.'

Paul nudged Sofia. 'Shh maman…'

'Camille will have grand-children, but I won't.'

'*Ne t'inquiétes pas trop, maman,*' Paul whispered. 'Don't worry too much, maman. One of these days, I'll give you grandchildren.'

She ignored him and glared at her daughter. 'I don't care what you call yourself. You'll always be Juliette to us!'

'*Maman!* Please. Not on my special day.' Juliette wrapped her arms around her mother, kissing her on both cheeks in the French style. 'You're still allowed monthly visits on Sunday afternoons. And on Christmas Day.' She embraced her father, unperturbed that Australians never kissed or touched in public. Especially between male and female.

'It's not *our* special day, Juliette,' her mother insisted. 'In fact, 1951 will always be the worst year of my life.' She paused a moment to look at her daughter. 'If you decide to leave, we'll always be here for you. Won't we, Claude?'

He nodded, trying to hold back his tears. 'But don't leave it too long *chérie*. The longer you do, the more difficult it will be to enter the real world again.'

They were silent. Someone near them was joking about it taking longer for a nun to get a divorce from Christ than it did for the real thing because the Pope had to give permission.

Claude widened his eyes and gave a pout of disdain. 'Permission to leave the convent! Permission from Italy? The Vatican? Permission to obtain a divorce from a dead man! Please tell me he's joking, Juliette!'

'No, papa. It's because…'

'Don't tell me. I don't want to know.'

3

The Priest

Religion was woven into Hilton Kelly's family life. The family that prays together stays together was the mantra of both the church and his mother. She sometimes insisted on her sons accompanying her to daily Mass. The family said Grace before and after every meal.

'We will pray for the conversion of the world,' Mrs Kelly said when the family knelt down in their modest Ballarat cottage to say the rosary every evening. She was manipulative and domineering. Hilton, her second son of three boys, was destined in the Irish tradition to become a priest. The family could ill-afford a college education for the three boys, and there was no way Hilton would be going to a godless government school or taking up an apprenticeship in a trade. Attending a junior seminary run by the Christian Brothers where board and education was free was the next best thing to becoming a priest.

Hilton wanted to complete his education, although he wasn't sure about becoming a Christian Brother. Did he really have a calling to God? Religion surrounded him at home and at school, so it was simply a matter of accepting or denying a life totally dedicated to God. Perhaps at the end of his education he could opt out, despite being warned that after he matriculated in 1947, he was bonded to become a Brother. Trained to teach in one of the Christian Brothers' Colleges.

The junior seminary on the outskirts of Melbourne was a life of austerity and loneliness. Then by a tragic quirk of fate at the beginning of his Matriculation Year, Hilton's father was killed in an industrial accident at work. Having been close to his father,

Hilton found it difficult to deal with the tragedy, aware that his mother scarcely showed a flicker of emotion. 'He has gone to a better life. I will see him again in heaven,' became another one of her mantras.

The compensation Mrs Kelly received following her husband's death meant that she could now afford to send Hilton to Corpus Christi at Werribee. 'A real seminary,' she said. 'Now that you've had all that spiritual training, you'll be the top student.'

In 1947, following his Matriculation exams, he found that he was becoming more and more reluctant to enter any religious order. He'd prepared exactly what he was going to say to his mother after Christmas, but when he arrived home, she was ill, suffering severe headaches and nausea. Dizziness and problems with her vision led to several seizures, which were diagnosed as a large brain tumour. The surgeon warned Hilton that his mother might not survive the operation. When he broached the subject about his uncertainty of becoming a priest, Mrs Kelly became very emotional. Her illness changed everything. Hilton promised her, and God, that if she survived, he would immediately enrol at Corpus Christi Seminary in Werribee to become a priest. When the tumour was found to be benign, Mrs Kelly triumphantly declared it a miracle.

'It's a sign from God,' she said. 'He has chosen you.'

The Catholic superstition and guilt ingrained in him since childhood made it difficult to break his promise to his mother or to God. Fortunately, he had a change of heart during the first few months of his six years in the seminary, making new friends and finding that he admired the intellect of the priests who ran the college, despite the rigidity and monastic lifestyle they fostered. He discovered that he had a craving for culture – the classics, art, music, the Latin language. He was annoyed that radios and newspapers were not allowed, but at least the front page of The Age was displayed daily in the common room. He found it hard to believe that back in 1877, only one family had lived in this magnificent Italianate mansion. Several wings had since been added now that it accommodated 130 students, but it was the valuable furnishings and paintings, the surrounds that impressed Hilton. From his bedroom upstairs, he could just make out the river meandering around the thousand-acre estate. Together with the lake, it provided opportunities for swimming and other aquatic events. He'd never been fond of football, liked cricket and tennis, but who wouldn't develop a passion for golf with the College's magnificent golf course? And when one tired of all that, there were the games rooms for hookey, table tennis and billiards. Smoking and alcohol were forbidden, although Hilton succumbed when wealthier students managed to sneak out and return with beer and cigarettes to share. They were never required to take vows of poverty and chastity. It was taken for granted that celibacy and the priesthood were inseparable.

After graduating at the end of 1953, he was given a temporary post in a small country parish where he remained for six months. The local priest had been involved in a car accident and would be laid up for weeks in hospital. Among the several albums of art in the presbytery's bookcase, one drew his attention. A well-thumbed art folio of prints of naked and semi-naked women. At the Junior seminary, women and girls were never mentioned. Hilton had never seen a naked girl or woman. Except for the nuns who did the domestic duties at Corpus Christi, women were regarded with suspicion. There was a culture of silence where sexuality was concerned. Seminarians were warned about girls trying to seduce them. 'Even convent girls and parishioners won't hesitate to lure you away from the priesthood,' his tutors said. Impure thoughts and any form of touching in certain parts of the body was sinful.

Halfway through 1954, Hilton was appointed to his first permanent parish in the small country town of Rose Hill. He'd been desperately hoping to become a curate in a larger parish like his hometown, Ballarat. While he came across as caring and charismatic, underneath this façade, resentment was breeding. Having accepted a celibate life, the development of his sexual desires had been halted as though he himself remained an adolescent. He felt he had missed out on his youth. At age twenty-five, he found himself envying the boys in the confessional. Not when they confessed to masturbating. After all, every time he opened the album he'd purloined from his first parish, he was doing the same thing. It was more that he was envious of them touching their girlfriends. It was about the forbidden. Prying into his penitents' sexual proclivities aroused him. He inhaled every detail. 'And where exactly did you touch her?' he'd ask them. Or 'Where did you let him touch you?' he asked the girls. 'Outside or inside your underwear?' Sometimes they were too embarrassed to tell him exactly *where* their boyfriends had touched them. Or was it more that they didn't have the vocabulary to explain? From what he'd picked up inside and outside the confessional, girls were more malleable. They could be talked into anything. If only confessionals didn't have barriers between the priest and the penitent, he could get closer to them. Ask them, 'Was it here that he put his hands?' Or 'Show me where he touched you.'

One Sunday morning the following year, an opportunity presented itself. Having just said Mass, he was sitting at the dining-room table in the presbytery reading the newspaper. He suddenly realised he couldn't hear Mrs Ryan's usual hustle and bustle in the kitchen. The kettle whistling. The smell of bacon and eggs wafting into the dining room. All was quiet. Next moment, Mrs Ryan's thirteen-year-old daughter walked in and placed his breakfast before him.

'Mum isn't well,' she told him.

'Well what a clever girl you are Mavis,' he said as he put his arm around her waist.

'Mum cooked it at home, Father,' she said politely. 'Then she had to go back to bed.'

'I bet you'll be a good cook just like her when you grow up,' he said as he turned around slightly, and eased her onto his lap. 'Your mother is very special, just like mine. And you must look after her when she's ill.'

'Yes, Father,' she said.

'Do you remember your father, Mavis?'

'No, Father. I was only two when he died.'

'Well it's sad that you've grown up without a father. They're very special,' he said as he drew her closer to him. 'They like to cuddle their daughters. Did you know that, Mavis?'

'No, Father.'

He began rubbing his hand along her thighs. 'Fathers like to touch their daughters in special places, Mavis,' he said. 'They like their daughters to please them.'

His right hand began creeping subtly up under her skirt, with his left hand on her lap holding her firmly in place on his legs. When his hand was between the top of her legs, stroking her, he felt her trying to edge away from him. Resisting him.

'This is what all fathers like to do with their daughters, Mavis,' he whispered. 'I can replace your father and we'll keep it our special secret. A secret between God and us. Do you understand?'

She shook her head. He relaxed for a moment, releasing his hold a little when he thought she was co-operating. She took the opportunity to suddenly jump up. 'Mum is very sick, Father. I have to look after her,' she said as she rushed out the door.

He was surprised more than angry. A priest stood on the highest rung of the Catholic community. A community that made priests invincible by accepting their dictums, though not necessarily always agreeing with them. Surely children should be more compliant and naïve than their parents. Why had his housekeeper's daughter been so uncooperative? Perhaps he'd rushed her a bit. Next time he'd move more slowly. Cultivate a close relationship with her, or whoever it might be. That evening, when he was wondering about his dinner arrangements, he answered the doorbell to an angry-looking woman who was definitely not one of his parishioners.

'You filthy pervert!' she screamed at him. 'I've heard of priests like you. I was going to give you some of my rabbit stew, but I'd rather poison it first! Mavis was too terrified to come here until I got the whole story out of her. Just as well her mother warned her about your sort. If in doubt, get out, she's always told Mavis. She told me what you did. You dirty child molester!' she yelled. 'I'm going to the police. And I'm going to phone your Bishop if they do nothing. I'll tell him what you've been up to. And if you're not out of this town by next Sunday, I'll be telling everyone about you! Including the newspapers.' She began walking towards the gate.

He stood staring after her, jaw dropped slightly. No one had ever spoken to him like that. No one ever spoke to priests like that. He couldn't believe it. And a woman! Well, some protestants hated Catholics, didn't they? *Roman* Catholics they liked to call them. He was about to close the door when she returned.

'And on top of all that, you pay Mrs Ryan a pittance and tell her you can't afford to pay her sick leave. She hasn't had a holiday for years! Well I hope you bloody-well starve to death because she won't be cooking for you again when I tell her what you've been up to.'

The following day, Hilton received a long-distance call. He was ordered to pack up his belongings and go straight to the Bishop's Palace in Ballarat.

4

Cecilia

Cecilia and Bernice were lying down on a patch of lawn behind the sport storage shed. Saturday free time for St Martin's boarders was playing tennis or basketball, chatting to friends, or finding a quiet, unsupervised spot to read a book. In the distance were the sounds from the tennis and basketball courts; balls bouncing and thudding; feet running and stamping; girls grunting as they stretched to reach the balls; the rhythmic thunk of balls on tennis racquets.

'If they could keep up a rally, their tempo per minute would be around forty,' Cecilia said.

Bernice frowned. 'You must have an inbuilt metronome!'

'It's the speed I play the Minute Waltz.'

Bernice frowned. 'Does the title mean you're meant to play it at sixty, or finish the whole thing in sixty seconds?'

'Neither. It takes about two minutes on average to play. Sister Angela said that Chopin's publisher called it the Miniature Waltz because it wasn't very long. Then it somehow became the Minute Waltz.'

'In that case the *mi* should be pronounced as *my* and the second syllable should sound like *newt*. As in *eye of newt.*'

'What?' Cecilia frowned. 'Oh. I see what you mean. Minute meaning tiny. I never thought of that.'

They were silent for a moment.

'I don't get it Celie,' Bernice said. 'How come you were already a brilliant pianist when you arrived here last year, and yet you come from an outback place no one's ever heard of? I thought all the top music teachers were in cities. Like Melbourne, or here in Ballarat.'

'For a start, I'm *not* brilliant,' Cecilia said, raising her eyes and sighing in exasperation. 'But my teacher was. She was a top teacher in Melbourne before her husband was transferred to a two-teacher school in Kingston. I just happened to be around when I heard her practising after my first day at school. I was just lucky. Serendipity, as Issy would call it.'

'No. It's more than that.' Bernice shrugged. 'Well, it's good teaching. And it's more than talent. It's about dedication. Like nuns dedicating themselves to God.'

Cecilia had a sudden flash of her first day at the tiny rural school, momentarily drifting back to her happy childhood. Plopping down on the edge of the veranda at the end of a long, hot day; legs dangling; her older sister Meg and friends digging tiny holes in the parched earth to prepare for their game of marbles under the meagre shade of the eucalypt. All she wanted was to go home and dive in the dam. Better still, the Creswick Lake, a few miles away where the family sometimes picnicked after Mass. The water was cooler and clearer there, catching the light on the surface to feel silky against her skin. How she loved swimming! The way sound thickened when her ears dipped beneath the surface. The waterfall trickling on her head before she dived down to the bottom in search of shiny pebbles. The pine forest quivering and shimmering in the water as they skimmed the pebbles across the lake. How was it possible that now, at the age of fifteen, she could recall that first day at school so vividly? Perhaps it was the music that had prompted her memory; the music merging with the watery images in her mind. Drawing her to its source like the Pied Piper luring the children to his mountain cave. She remembered sidling towards the open doorway of the classroom; squatting down cross-legged on the floor. Mrs Wilford, the wife of the new school principal, was playing the school piano with a straight back and beautifully rounded fingers. Fingers that were gliding and zigzagging over almost every note on the piano. It was after Mrs Wilford stopped suddenly to review a section that Cecilia's life took a different course.

Bernice suddenly interrupted her reflections. 'Penny for your thoughts, Celie!'

She blinked back to the present. 'I was thinking of your question about my home-town. It brought back memories of my first day at school and why I started learning the piano, then coming to board here. Mum and Dad wanted me to work on the farm with my sister Meg.'

'Because your two little brothers drowned?' Bernice said sympathetically.

Cecilia shook her head. 'No. We were all destined to work on the farm. That's how it is in the country. Nearly everyone leaves school when they turn fourteen. Mum and Dad would be quite happy for me to leave here. I nearly did after I arrived last year in Form 3, but Sister Jeanne talked me out of it.'

'Jeanne? How come?'

'I was crying my eyes out in bed one night because it was the third anniversary of Chris and Benny's deaths. We always look at photographs and talk about them at home. Anyway, someone found Jeanne so she took me down to the kitchen and gave me a cup of warm cocoa.' She shrugged. 'She asked me all about my family, my music, the farm and how I came to be a boarder here. I told her the whole story. How Mrs Wilkins had me accompanying everything. All the songs she taught us. She got me playing tone poems for art and writing classes to inspire the children. I think performing and sight-reading became as instinctive as breathing for me. But in sixth grade, on the day I was supposed to be playing for a special concert in a nearby town, my elation was short-lived.' She paused for long moment and sighed. 'It was a day I'll never forget.'

Her father had parked the truck twenty yards from the deep side of the dam. He noticed a lamb caught on the barbed-wire fence in the distance. He ran across to free it. The lamb was making such a fuss, he didn't hear the truck as it gathered speed and went into the dam. In his frenzy to free Chris and Benny, her father had nearly drowned. Even his muscular farming arms weren't strong enough to smash the window or open the door. How did it happen? Hadn't he put the brake on, or did one of the boys release it? He was always so fastidious with his children about the dangers of dams. He'd never forgive himself, no matter how much Cecilia and Meg and his wife insisted the accident was not his fault. He'd focussed on the lamb, he said. Ignored the safety of his two little boys.

'I know Dad will replay that scene in his mind every day for the rest of his life. The truck rolling silently into the dam. *Like a crocodile gliding into the river* I wrote when Perpetua gave us an essay topic entitled *A Sorrowful Day*.' She sighed. 'Meg and I have never swum in a dam or a river since. I didn't go near the piano for six months because Chris and Benny wouldn't be bursting into the front room to strut around on the beat with their tin drums and tambourines when I played *Rondo Alla Turca*, or *Marche Militaire*.'

'I can't imagine anything worse, Celie.'

'I was sure Mum would have two more boys just like Chris and Benny,' Cecilia said, blinking back her tears. 'But Meg said something went wrong with Mum after Benny was born and now she can't have any more children. Anyway, the reason I ended up here was because my piano teacher was leaving, and somehow, she and our local parish priest arranged for me to get a scholarship here 'til I've finished Matric.'

'A Good Samaritan! Like Jeanne.'

'Jeanne said she thought that most girls didn't really enjoy boarding, but they made good friends, and I'd be compensated by my music. She said I inspired others to take up the piano. I suppose I felt I had a sort of obligation to the school after that. I wanted to tell her I hated the place. All the religion and rules. It was such a shock coming here after nine years in a government school.'

'More of a shock for someone from Melbourne like me. Especially with a mad woman running the place.' Bernice sat up against the shed. 'I can't believe this dump after my old school. Sometimes I hate Mum for sending me here.'

'It was her old school, wasn't it?'

Bernice sighed. 'Yes. She said it got good results. But I think it was more that she was paranoid when a girl in my class contracted polio. There's none of it around in Ballarat, apparently.'

'Really? I didn't know that.'

'And I could learn golf because apparently some wealthy old chook left this school a mansion and golf course! Who wants to chase a bloody little white ball around anyway?' Bernice said derisively. 'On top of that, Mum raved about the fantastic orchestra and Katerina being a brilliant teacher and violinist. As if I'm going to become a musician, for God's sake!' She paused for a moment. 'Well, I think she really thought I was getting keen on boys too.'

'And were you?'

'Of course. Aren't you?'

'I suppose so, but if I'd known my friend Rita wasn't coming back, I probably wouldn't have returned this year. I was thinking about staying on the farm.'

'I'd rather be in this dump than on a farm.'

Cecilia shrugged, the same thought having recently occurred to her. She never minded feeding the baby lambs, but cleaning up during the sheep-shearing? Cooking for all those men? Doing that for the rest of her life? Then Bernice had arrived a few weeks after the Intermediate year began, and Cecilia was asked to show her around. She'd taken an instant liking to her, but Bernice had looked disdainfully around the convent, insisting she wouldn't be returning the following term, 'Even if it means getting myself expelled,' she'd confided to Cecilia.

That was it, Cecilia decided. What was the point in pursuing a friendship with someone who was going to be leaving? 'Funny isn't it?' she said. 'My parents want me to leave here, and yours want you to stay.'

'Mum more than Dad. But that weirdo wasn't in charge when Mum was here. For God's sake, it's 1954. The big year of the royal visit! When I arrived here in March, Dad asked the old cow when the school would be lining the streets to see the Queen and Duke in Ballarat. She bleated about it being inappropriate and demeaning for convent girls to be cheering and waving flags. Dad thinks she's crazy too. I told her my convent in Melbourne was making arrangements to see the Queen and Duke early last year and no one thought it improper.'

That was what Cecilia liked about Bernice. She said what she thought. Cecilia wanted to be assertive like that. She tended to agree with others to avoid conflict. To mull over a conversation or something outrageous that was said rather than speaking up at the time. Or just to give an honest opinion like Bernice when

Sister Isobel was discussing emotion and how they needed to put themselves in the writer's shoes. Writing in first person sounded convincing because one could put oneself at the scene. Famous writers like Charles Dickens and James Joyce sometimes wrote in the present tense. Fictitious or factual, it was plausible if it came from the heart, Isobel said. The class had compiled a list of emotions on the board. *Fear, anger, joy, sadness, surprise, shame, disdain, pity, indignation, envy, wonder, pride, love.* Cecilia looked at the list and wondered where emotions crossed over with the Seven Deadly Sins she'd never heard of until coming to St Martin's. Nor had she realised that religion was actually a school subject. Having gone to a government school for so long, she felt intimidated here when it concerned religion. Isobel asked the girls to give an example of an emotion without actually naming it. Cecilia noticed Bernice's disdainful expression. Her curled lips. Bernice had been keeping to herself. Silently stubborn in all classes, unless challenged. Conforming, but never contributing.

'Perhaps you could give us an example of how emotion can be used in writing, Bernice. Or how John Buchan or Charles Dickens portray emotions in their novels,' Sister Isobel said.

'They wrote what they wanted to write,' Bernice replied sullenly. 'Here at St Martinet's, there's an eleventh commandment: Thou shalt not emote. Emotions are stowed into your empty suitcase after you've unpacked, then flung into a storeroom until you take them home with you for the holidays!'

The class had gasped.

'Nevertheless, perhaps you can give us an example, Bernice,' the unflappable Isobel said in a bemused voice.

Bernice looked defiant. 'Well. If I wrote home that the food is pig swill, I know I'd have to rewrite my letter because they're all censored.'

The girls looked like they couldn't believe what they were hearing.

'We spend half our lives on our knees praying.'

'A slight exaggeration, Bernice,' Isobel said.

'And the only books around the place other than those in the syllabus are boring because they're all religious.'

Cecilia giggled at the girls' wide-open mouths and eyes, staring between their teacher and Bernice. It was almost a tennis match in slow-motion. It was about time someone said what most of them thought.

Bernice continued. 'The ones I'd like to read are locked away, and only for sixth formers. Even then, whole paragraphs have been blacked out. My parents can't even express their true feelings because they know that some nosy parker here with nothing better to do is going to be devouring their private mail. At my old school, we voted for the prefects, but here at St Martinet's, the nuns choose girls who are Holy Joes or stooges. So *there's* my example of frustration.'

Cecilia grinned, agreeing with everything Bernice had said.

'All the same, Bernice,' Isobel said, not perturbed at all, 'perhaps you could include some emotions in your next essay without naming them and without being overly negative.'

Cecilia wanted to express herself like Bernice. How clever of her to change Martin to martinet. Not that she knew what it meant until she'd whipped out her dictionary. Ironically, a nun had been unwittingly responsible for Bernice staying on and the two girls becoming close friends. Sister Katerina, head of music, was Reverend Mother's pride and joy. When she was getting desperate for more vocations, Mother Alphonsus liked to tell the girls at assembly how Sister Katerina had chosen to follow God's calling over a career as a violinist, despite having received a begging letter from Fritz Kreisler to take her on as his protégé. Not that they'd heard of him.

Katerina called Cecilia into her music room one afternoon towards the end of Term 1.

'I think Cecilia, that you've gone just about as far as you can go in piano here at St Martin's. Don't you?'

'Yes Sister,' she agreed.

'You said you weren't interested in taking up the violin. Do you still feel the same?'

Cecilia definitely felt the same, although her piano teacher, Sister Angela, had also been telling her that she needed an extension. It would surely be a struggle learning a new instrument while she was doing her Intermediate Certificate. And how would she cope with others in the orchestra, especially Bernice, who would be streets ahead of her?

'There's an alternative now,' Katerina told her. 'Mr Connelly, the cathedral organist, is offering a scholarship and we think you should audition.'

Cecilia argued that she'd heard a recording of a pipe organ but wasn't particularly impressed.

'Recordings are not quite the same, Cecilia. Why don't you go down to the cathedral for the demonstration next Saturday,' Katerina said. 'Maybe you could take the new girl, Bernice. She's not looking too happy.'

Bernice had jumped at the opportunity when Cecilia asked her if she'd like to accompany her to the cathedral. 'A break from prison without the guards around!' she whooped. 'Who knows what adventure awaits us! The cathedral is near the boys' college!'

'It's a one-off,' Cecilia said. 'I've already got a scholarship. I don't need another one. I'm auditioning to please Katerina and Angela!'

It was the first time either of them had had a close up of a pipe organ. Mr Connelly's fingers glided onto each note, drifting from one keyboard to another on the three-tiered organ console, as Bach chorales surged from his fingertips. Four students from three different schools were auditioning for the scholarship. They watched him like hawks. Following the music. His hands. Turning the pages. They gasped at his prowess. This was not self-aggrandising. It was all about their observations. Where, when and why he changed to another keyboard. What organ stops he was using, and why. The difference in their sounds, the timbre. His technique on the pedalboard. While he played, he elaborated on the pipe organ's history and how it could be traced back to the water organ in Ancient Greece in the 3rd century BC, in which the wind supply was created with water pressure. They learned that it was played for festive occasions and had nothing to do with churches for hundreds of years. After giving each of the candidates a lesson the following week, he would decide on the winner of the scholarship.

Cecilia was beginning to think she could enjoy learning from this wonderful organist. 'It's much more complicated than playing the piano,' she whispered to Bernice.

'You'd do it standing on your head Celie,' Bernice whispered back. 'You've got to go for it. We'll be able to come down here a few times a week for your practice and ...'

'We?'

Bernice rolled her eyes and grinned.

Mr Connelly wound up with Bach's Toccata and Fugue. The music cascaded from the pipes, the cathedral reverberating with musical passion to thrill and inspire the students. Cecilia couldn't imagine ever progressing onto something more grandiose than Bach's Chorales and other minor works by Handel and Mozart. Mr Connelly explained that one day they might be church organists and that although organists in Catholic churches never received stipends, they were paid quite well for weddings, 'which is often in a large parish like this. As long as you can find the groomsman,' he said, proceeding to relate some humorous wedding stories which he insisted happened to all organists, his best being about the priest who read out the wrong names of the future couple, and another who forgot to show up for the wedding because he was at the grand final. He finished with a light-hearted warning. 'Never let Aunt Florrie sing a solo because she'll always choose something atrocious and scooping and off-key like *This Is Your Lovely Daaaaay*. Just tell them soloists are banned unless they're professionals. In any case, some priests won't allow female soloists.'

Bernice raised her hand. 'Is that because women's voices might be too beguiling and could demean the solemnity of the occasion, Mr Connelly?'

Cecilia grinned. Only Bernice would ask that sort of question. Mr Connelly smiled and explained that some older priests still subscribed to the belief that women shouldn't take any vocal solo part in a church service. 'It's something to do with what St Paul said, I believe. If Dame Nellie Melba herself came back to life and was asked to sing for a wedding here, Father Brennan wouldn't permit it if he was doing the marrying,' he said.

'You'll win that scholarship, Cecilia,' Bernice said on their return to the convent. 'Why don't you have a go on the old harmonium in the chapel to get the feel of it?'

'I don't know. It'd mean I'd be staying on here.'

'Me too! Well, for a while. Depends.'

Cecilia stared at her. 'On what?'

'Whether we meet some boys,' Bernice said excitedly.

Cecilia grinned. 'And here I was thinking you came with me because you liked music.'

'Well, that too. I'll be your page-turner.'

'In any case, *if* I win, Katerina could choose anyone to accompany me to the cathedral.'

'I've been thinking about that.'

A week later, following her audition, a delighted Sister Katerina called Cecilia into her music room to inform her that she'd won the scholarship. Cecilia had raced excitedly into the corridor to tell the waiting Bernice, who threw her arms around her.

'Just a minute, Celie,' she said, knocking on the door to Katerina's music room.

Ten minutes later she emerged, telling Cecilia triumphantly that she'd be accompanying her to the cathedral for her lesson and practice sessions.

'How on earth did you manage that? She needs you for the chamber orchestra.'

Bernice sighed. 'I told Katerina I was dropping out of it.'

Cecilia gaped. 'But she's nice. Why…'

'Then she said my only alternative was to help supervise junior sport. So we compromised. If I play with the orchestra once a week, I can accompany you to the cathedral. She was quite happy about that.'

Now, here they were in Term 3, still hating boarding school, but enjoying their camaraderie.

'This place would have to be better without that old cow in charge,' Cecilia conceded.

'Weirdness hangs around that woman like a bad smell. For God's sake! Blazers with our sportswear!'

'It's to hide our gorgeous figures so we don't look provocative.'

'Last time the old bag was going on about temptation in assembly, I wanted to tell her that the only problem with temptation is that you might never get another chance.'

They both laughed.

'Sorry. It's not original. Dad said one of his clients said it.'

While she laid back in the warm sunshine, listening to the girls at sport, Cecilia couldn't help thinking about Bernice's family. How different they seemed to be from her own. Bernice had invited her to spend part of the school holidays with her family. Never having been to Melbourne before, she was really looking forward to it.

5

Molly

The best thing about Form 3 is the variety of teachers. Not being stuck for a whole year with a bad-tempered old witch who hates teaching and hates children. All the same, I've got two teachers I can't stand – Sister Gregory and Sister Rosario. I've already had a run-in with each of them. This morning, Rosario told me off for being late for Religion, the first – and what she considers the most important – period of the day. I was only five minutes late. I'm still wearing my blazer, having raced straight past my locker to scoot up the stairs two at a time. I'm sitting with my satchel scrunched between my legs, my felt hat flattened to an inch inside my desk. Period 2 today is English. Sister Perpetua glides into the Form 3 classroom, eyes watery and red, her veil of authority silencing the class. After setting down a pile of exercise books on the desk, she bursts into a spasm of coughs and sneezes. I feel sorry for her, but I wish she'd stayed in bed so we could have had a free period. She looks as wrung out as the handkerchief she extricates from the pocket deep down in the depths of her habit.

'Laryngitis,' she croaks, after her usual greeting, pointing to the white coif wrapped around her neck and head.

When she picks up the chalk and writes *A Memorable Experience* on the blackboard, I know what's coming. An essay! I hate having to write an essay in just one period. I like time to think about it.

Perpetua looks up from a pile of exercise books she's correcting in between her coughs and snivels. 'If your essay is fiction, your descriptions should be convincing enough to make me believe it's fact,' she croaks again, her voice barely audible. 'You're nearly in Intermediate. You're old enough to begin writing more like adults now. Use some of the interesting words from your class lists, and at least four original metaphors or similes.'

A few girls have already started. Next to me, Bernadette is writing about her Confirmation. Well she would, wouldn't she, being a bit of a Holy Joe. My best friend Gabby will be describing her trip to Sydney, and how they drove across The Bridge in their new car. Mary Halloran will write a brilliant fiction story. Apparently, she's got a large bedroom all to herself with books up to the ceiling. I'd rather write about a real event as my imagination hasn't caught up with me yet. During my primary school years as a boarder in St Arnaud, I craved for a real book in my hands. The sort of book that our teachers read sparingly at the end of the day. I was desperate to open the squeaky gate in *The Secret Garden* with poor little unloved Mary. To climb the Swiss Alps with Heidi. It was comforting to know that others had been abandoned like me, but I wanted to turn the pages myself. Read my favourite parts over and over. The only bookcase in the convent was full of the lives of the saints. It's the same at St Martin's College. When I started here last year in Form 2, the only book I owned other than our textbooks and Victorian School Reader, was *Alice in Wonderland*, which I almost know off by heart. At least now in Form 3 we have our own novels for the English syllabus, and as a day-scholar, I can visit the public library whenever I like. The only problem is the librarians. They're not there to help anyone, especially children.

I think of my *Memorable Experience* on the day we moved into the hotel. The day my life of irreverence and disorder began. The problem is that it's ongoing. In any case, it would shock my teacher. She'd know immediately that my essay wasn't fiction.

Then it would get back to Mother Alphonsus, who'd think I was in moral danger. 'You are unfit to mix with anyone from St. Martin's College,' I can hear her saying.

My mind flashes back to St Arnaud. Nothing outstanding there. I can hardly write about the convent. They're all the same, especially if you're a boarder. The tedium of religion and regimentation with Mass every morning, chapel every evening. Disgusting food. Kind nuns. Nasty ones. Good friends.

Now I'm really starting to panic. I glance around the classroom for inspiration – the record player; yesterday's French conjugations on the board; the piano; the prints on the wall. I stare idly at Rembrandt's *Woman With a Water Jug*, thinking that with her long dark gown, her starched white headdress and yoke, she looks little different from a nun. Then I notice a reflection in its glass of the view through the window – the tip of the distant cathedral spire. The penny drops! The magnificent music! Cecilia! I'd write about Cecilia playing the organ at the cathedral for a special High Mass last week for Ballarat Catholic schools to celebrate a hundred years since the first Mass was said at the Ballarat diggings in 1854. Perpetua will think I've gone all pious like Bernadette until she realises my essay is not about religion.

Before we left for the cathedral, Reverend Mother Alphonsus warned us that St Martin's girls were to cast their eyes towards the altar at all times, her pathetic way of telling us not to ogle the boys. Gabby was going on about our prison-grey and navy-blue uniform. 'Those pleats on our tunics are designed to make us look as dowdy and bustless as possible, so who'd want to be ogling us?' she said. I agreed, which is why, in my mind, I've drawn up a classy, knee-length fitted uniform in charcoal grey and orchid pink. Smarter than the posh Loreto Abbey uniform with their cute little bowler hats!

I began writing: *After a cold September wind blustering against us during our walk from school, it was a relief to enter the cathedral. Girls from the three convents genuflected and glided gracefully into the pews, while the college boys, perhaps a little distracted by the girls, lumbered and stumbled into their allotted area, some of them looking about as elegant as an elephant trying to do a tap dance. The only bright patch amongst the funereal colours in the nave, was the Loreto Abbey girls in their smart royal blue uniforms and bowler hats.*

Beyond the communion rail in the sanctuary was a sea of colour and light. Altar boys in their red and white robes; priests holding ceremonial candles; celebrants wearing lacy white amices and colourful chasubles; the bishop on his throne, dressed up to the nines in his golden cape and mitre, holding his crosier like a shepherd with a crook. On the altar, candles flickered between the lilies and gladioli in huge brass vases. Ornate gold vessels glinted and reflected a patchwork of colours from the stained-glass windows.

The organ's muted tones wafted around like incense, I wrote. *It was mysterious and soothing, with a mellow mixture of soft flutes and a reedy instrument like an oboe. I swivelled my neck around like an owl to look up at Cecilia, but the balustrade blocked my view. All I could see was the music stand at the top of the organ console, and the choir on the risers. The rose window rippled reds and golds across the angled organ pipes as though they were on fire.*

It was just as well my French teacher was sitting behind me. She didn't mind me turning around. If it had been Rosario…

I know now that what I called an organ at boarding school is properly called a harmonium, I wrote. *Compared to the pipe organ, it sounds like a wheezy old squeezebox.* Katerina, that is *Sister* Katerina – we only say *Sister* to their faces – said during Music Appreciation that the pipe organ is majestic and celestial, fit for royalty and our creator; that its sound transported one straight to heaven. Mozart called it the King of Instruments. I began changing her quotations around to suit my essay. *Imagine being deaf and not hearing the sound of the King of Instruments. A sound that transports one straight to heaven*, I wrote, which set me wondering why God would create anyone who couldn't hear any music at all.

Katerina plays us recordings of instrumental and choral works by all the great composers, yet in her compulsory choir before school, we sing tuneless Credos and Glorias written by an Australian priest whose music is about as boring as standing around waiting for trees to drop all their leaves in autumn. It's the same for the chamber choir when they sing at Mass. Apparently Mother Alphonsus selects the repertoire. She censors everything, moveable or immoveable. She must be about as tone deaf as a statue. The tight coif around her face can't help, what with the ruffling and bulging of all her chins, desperate to escape the constriction. She wouldn't have noticed the celebrant singing the first line of the Credo and Gloria totally out of tune, made more glaring by the chord from the organ for the choir to pick up. *As usual, the celebrant was whooshing notes all over the place like a deflating balloon*, I wrote. *The first time I hear one of them singing in tune, I'm going to stand up on the pew and cheer as though I'm at a football match.* I'd prefer to have said that he sounded more like one of the drunks at the pub when I'm accompanying the sing-alongs.

Words and phrases are tumbling onto my pages as I merge Katerina's musical descriptions with flowery lyrics about rivers and seas from a library book I pull out of the satchel clamped between my legs. Others are using dictionaries and thesauruses, so what's the difference?

Cecilia was playing a solo over the sound of the choir clunking down the spiral staircase for Holy Communion. It was as though she was painting a picture of a river swirling around, eddies curling, softly meandering, its pebbles of notes more precious than any jewels. It was probably Mozart.

Simple, yet mystical, with a sense of peace and tranquility. I was transfixed. My ears were brimming with sounds that warmed the cold cathedral. Enveloping me. It was not the confining boxy noise from a record player. As the last school to leave the cathedral, we had an opportunity to hear Cecilia's pièce de résistance. If she'd played it during the Mass, she would have upstaged everyone. The music cascaded from the pipes in a waterfall of sound, the cathedral reverberating with musical incense and spirituality. Images in my Bible History of trumpeting angels and God hurling thunderbolt spears around the sky must have seeped into my subconscious. *It was triumphant*, I wrote. *Loud and majestic! It was as though a troupe of trumpeters was up in the gallery playing a fanfare, chords of light and sound spearing down from above. I can imagine hearing this sort of music played for celebrations like weddings, or when souls arrive at Heaven's pearly gates.*

The following week, Perpetua, now well over her laryngitis, tells us that one must be circumspect and quite enterprising when writing a scene that includes instruments and sound. She looks at me. 'I can't recall anyone ever doing that. You chose a serious subject but managed to embellish it with humour and original similes, Molly. Well done!'

I'm thrilled. I'd never been praised for my writing before. Perhaps I'm starting to get the hang of it. She asks me to read my essay to the class. They laugh about the celebrant singing out of tune, the boys stumbling because they were gawking at girls. They probably recognise *funereal* and *reverberate* from our weekly word list on the board. 'A word a day keeps banality at bay,' Perpetua says occasionally. I don't have a clue what *circumspect* means, but it's my moment of glory. And here I was thinking Perpetua would be driven crazy by my rushed handwriting and pile of cross-outs. That my conclusion was pathetic, and I'd overdone it with the lyrics from the poetry book. I float all the way home on a cloud of confidence and pride. I only tell Veronica and Brigid about it because Dad's always too busy and Mum wouldn't be interested. Well, she might be, depending on her mood.

The following day after lunch, someone says Cecilia was looking for me. I'm surprised because she's an Intermediate boarder and I'm a lowly Form 3 day-scholar. She wouldn't have a clue who I am. Everyone knows Cecilia because she's the most brilliant pianist in the school. Assemblies are boring if she doesn't get to play. I also envy her looks. She's tall with olive skin and long fair hair, always beautifully braided, and here's me, nearly two inches shorter with bobbed, dark hair showing up my white Irish complexion that sizzles and freckles in the summer sun.

'I heard that you wrote a really good essay about me playing the organ at the cathedral for the High Mass. I'm really flattered,' she says, sounding as though she means it.

I'm the one who's flattered. My marks have always been mediocre for English. I fluked it with the organ story. 'I don't think I did you justice because I've never seen a pipe organ close up,' I reply.

'Would you like to?'

Of course I wanted to! She gives me her practice times and I'm there in a flash. The outlook from the gallery is spectacular, but I'm only interested in the organ. Cecilia is so involved she doesn't realise I'm standing nearby, mouth open, staring at her. Wondering how she can read the music when the music stand is a mile from the lowest keyboard. Just as well her friend Bernice is there to turn the pages. The two of them are in their sports clothes, which seems strange. Mother Alphonsus says that bare legs must never be displayed in public, which means we wear thick grey stockings, summer and winter.

I'm in awe when I see Cecilia's hands gliding like feathers from one keyboard to another. If only I'd seen all this before I wrote about it! The harmonium I played in St Arnaud had a single keyboard and a dozen stops. All I had to do with my feet was pump two pedals up and down to keep up the air supply. Now, instead of bellows, Cecilia's feet are dancing over a pedalboard. Playing beautiful deep notes I've never heard from our classroom record-player; changing the stops in between the phrases; reading music and playing different keyboards simultaneously with her hands and feet! She's a contortionist! It's as though she's part of this complicated-looking instrument in front of her. The sound is breathtaking. I can't place the composer. When I inch forward to look at the music, Cecilia tells me it's Mendelssohn's *Wedding March* which she's practising for her cousin's wedding. How does she do all those things at once and carry on a conversation with me?

'If you're wondering why we're not in uniform, Molly, it's because we've come straight from basketball,' Bernice says as she turns from the organ to face me. 'Katerina had to convince the old cow that Cecilia would lose half her practice time if we had to go back and change into our uniforms after sport. There was nearly a stand-up fight between them. Eventually, Alphonsus agreed, after she set up a string of conditions.'

Cecilia stops playing and turns around to face me. 'Tunics are too long and bulky for playing the organ anyway!'

Bernice is flicking through an album of organ music. 'Like playing tennis in your full school uniform, I imagine. Our sports skirts are long enough anyway! Shorts would be better,' she says. 'Especially in the summer.'

Cecilia agrees. 'Wouldn't Al love that! I just don't get why she hates bare legs!'

Bernice rolls her eyes. 'It's what's in between them that worries her.'

I've got no idea what she means, and by the look on her face, neither does Cecilia.

Bernice is smirking. 'Celie, do you remember me telling you I saw *An American in Paris*, and how that French guy performed *Stairway to Paradise*?'

Cecilia nods. 'I'd like to see that film!'

'St Kevin's boys call girls' legs the *Stairway to Paradise*.'

Cecilia stares at Bernice for a moment, then a look of understanding spreads over her face.

I don't get what they're grinning about, but I know the song. Whenever I play *Stairway to Paradise*, I picture Georges Guétary lighting up each stair as he sings and dances to the top of the staircase and down again.

'She makes us hide our *vulgar protrusions* with those,' Bernice says indicating their blazers thrown over the balustrade. 'We have to wear them here over our sportswear. *You must walk down to the cathedral via the back street, girls, never Sturt Street, and you must never enter the cathedral via the main door in that bloody regalia.*'

She says it in perfect imitation of Mother Alphonsus with spread, pursed lips of condemnation, over-articulating every syllable. The *vulgar protrusions* and *bloody regalia* has me in fits. Bernice would make a great actress.

Cecilia invites me to play, but I think of the little harmonium I played at boarding school. I'm overwhelmed, and refuse. Cecilia is brilliant, yet unassuming, which is why I admire her so much. When they begin packing up, I thank her and tell her I'd do anything to have her talent.

'Someone told me you play anything by ear. I can't do that,' she says.

I wonder how she knows until I remember Gabby getting me to play the piano one wet lunchtime for a singalong. Someone must have told her. 'I can accompany pop songs. Nothing like what you play.'

'Just as well the old bag wasn't hanging around when you played pop music. It's a sacrilege at St Martinet's,' Bernice says.

St Martinet's? Cecilia must have noticed a puzzled look on my face. 'A martinet is a strict disciplinarian like a drill sergeant,' she explains.

I love it. It suits our school régime! Nicknames are usually reserved for the nuns. *Kat* for Katerina. *Pet* for Perpetua. *Issy* for Isobel. Others are not so polite, like *Goosey* for Sister Gertrude, a plump, fleshy nun with a funny walk, or *The Walrus*, for our maths teacher. *Al* is one of the more polite names for Mother Alphonsus.

I'm ready to go when Bernice asks me to play a pop tune on the organ.

Cecilia doesn't look too keen. 'One of the old biddies praying her knees off down below might report it,' she tells me apologetically. 'I have to watch my step because I'm on a scholarship.'

'You could jazz up *In the Chapel in the Moonlight* to sound like a hymn,' Bernice insists. 'Just throw in an *Amen* at the end and old chooks below won't know the difference.'

Cecilia still looks doubtful, so I tell them I have to go. It's heading towards closing time at the pub anyway, and some of the customers might be waiting for a singalong. I begin walking towards one of the spiral staircases.

'Not that one, Molly,' Cecilia calls out. 'No one uses it. Not even the choirs. It's always locked at the bottom anyway. Use the one you came up on.'

I'm about to go downstairs when I remember something. 'When I was coming up here, I looked across to that other staircase and there was a cassock disappearing up it.'

'*Sacre bleu!*' Bernice says slowly with a fake shudder. 'I told you I've heard creaky noises coming from that direction a few times Celie.' She looks at me. 'Quasimodo! Or Count Dracula. Or *peut être... Le fântome de l'opéra*. Are you sure it wasn't a cloak?'

Our French teacher occasionally discusses French literature or composers and artists, so I know what she's talking about.

'*Le fântome de la galérie* you mean!' Cecilia whispers. 'Or one of Al's stooges.'

Bernice is already racing over to the stairwell. 'If I don't come back, send out a search party for me,' she calls out as she disappears downstairs. 'Nope,' she says when she returns a minute later. 'The door at the bottom is locked as usual. No one there but I heard a creaky noise.' She shrugs. 'It's so dark, it's hard to see. Perhaps there's a secret door somewhere.'

Cecilia and Bernice look at each other, make big moons of their eyes, and chant 'Spooo-keeey!' in scary unison.

I love those two girls.

'Molly,' Cecilia calls out when I'm halfway down the stairs, 'come back whenever you like!'

I will.

6

Jeanne

The adage *Idle hands are the devil's workshop* was particularly apt in the convent, and like others, Juliette, now Sister Jeanne, accepted her novice years without complaining. The order of the day was completely structured until lights out at 10 pm. Rising at 6am every day to the call of *Benedicamus Domino*; responding impassively with *Deo gratias*; teaching in any classroom until a position became available, despite not having completed her teaching certificate; supervising boarders; a few kitchen duties; saying daily *divine office*. Free time was for lesson preparation and correction of homework. Silence and prayer ruled the remainder of the day, except for unavoidable communication. It was what she'd expected. It all came under the vow of obedience. The other two vows, chastity and poverty, were irrelevant as they concerned the outside world. All her possessions, her worldly goods and chattels, were left with her parents.

Wearing the veil was a visible statement of difference. Of separation from the world. Sometimes Jeanne looked at the brick wall, her view from the staff room, and wondered why she decided to seal herself up like a pharaoh in a tomb. There was so much life teeming beyond the convent. Their family's favourite picnic spot in the Botanical Gardens by the lake with its conservatories, the fountain, and the maze based on the original at Hampton Court. The Eureka Stockade with its interesting gold rush history. The Ballarat Observatory. If the family didn't fancy a walk around the lake, they could cross to the other side on a paddle-steamer or hire a rowing boat. There was always the zoo, and the lake's natural fauna – the black swans. For a moment, Jeanne's eyes were teary when she remembered her mother looking up at the Flight From Pompeii in the Statuary Pavilion. 'We could almost be in Italy,' she'd said. Lately Jeanne found herself envying the nuns going off to parish primary schools every morning. Their chauffeur, Sister Bertrand, measured distances by how many decades of the rosary her passengers could finish before reaching their destination, but at least they got a glimpse of the outside world each day. One of the nuns told Jeanne they *needed* to pray because Bertrand drove a car as though the devil was chasing her.

Was the lack of exercise, the deprivation of fresh air and sunshine responsible for those aches and pains the elderly nuns complained of? If only she could bring a little of the outside in. Then there was the food. The best chef in the world couldn't make her mother's *boeuf bourguignon* or *cassoulet*. Convent food was to be endured. All part of the sacrifice. The permanent penance. At least her mother was allowed to donate gateaux or pastries to the nuns during their monthly visits. But of all things Jeanne really missed were her parents' loving embraces. Their goodnight kisses. Her mother's perfume lingering on the pillow.

For much of 1952, Jeanne had been thrown in the deep end, having taken over teaching French from the elderly Sister Winifred in the senior school. As a result, her teaching certificate, all but a formality considering her time in the classroom, was delayed until term one of 1953. Her final prac teaching round was with Sister Damien, an embittered nun in her fifties who only embraced the term *Criticism Lessons* – for that was what they were called – in a destructive sense. Renowned for storming down the aisles and whacking the desk with a ruler to frighten her Form 2 students not paying attention, the latest rumour going around the convent was that Damien had slapped a boarder over the face, the sharp, heavy smacks jerking the poor girl's head from side to side. Her crime had been to whisper to her friend. The poor girl had not long lost her mother. Jeanne was horrified. Sister Damien's objective seemed to be to drain all confidence out of her students and teachers in training. She instructed Jeanne to teach a poem for her first lesson.

Determined that this nun would not get the better of her, Jeanne decided to show her how the girls could enjoy lessons. Their minds would not be a blank mangle of dread and anxiety. Their responses would be more spontaneous if they were not living in fear of this nun's vicious temper. Other novices and young nuns gave her enough advice to fill an exercise book.

'Create a strategy to deal with her or you'll have a nervous breakdown.'

'Understand that she's the one with the problem, not you.'

'No matter how well it goes, everything she writes in her report will be negative.'

'She'll be jealous if you win them over.'

'Have the girls eating out of your hand. Check that they don't already know the poem because she'll rip you to shreds if you give them anything they already know or that's inappropriate. They'll know most of the poems suitable for their age as the best ones are in the School Readers - Kipling, Rosetti, Robert Browning, *The Brook*, *The Pied Piper*.'

Poetry for thirteen and fourteen-year-olds! A French poem would have been easier. Something different was what she needed. Sister Brigid might have some Irish poems.

'I've got a book of beautiful Irish poetry, but except for the one by William Allingham about the wee folk, sure they're all rather mournful or romantic, I'm afraid,' Sister Brigid said in her lilting accent. 'All about lovers. Or the clergy. The church. The rest are all dirges, to be sure. Dying. Death. The ones about the famine are fine but they're more for seniors. Alas, my dear! All the poems with beautiful descriptions of the landscape are far too romantic for these young girls, to be sure.'

Jeanne flicked through the book. Sister Brigid was right. They were all inappropriate for Form 2.

Sister Brigid scanned a book of Irish songs. 'The girls will know most of these, to be sure, my dear. Some of them were written originally as poems.' She paused at one page. 'Ah! Here's one they won't know. It's full of imagery, and beautiful lyrics,' she said, handing the book to Jeanne. 'But you must use only the first verse.'

Jeanne began reading it. Yes. Plenty of teaching points here. Iambic tetrameter. Landscapes. Metaphor. The length was perfect. It was ideal for discussion and memorisation. This would easily fill a fifty-minute period.

Dear Mary this London's a beautiful sight
Where the people are workin' by day and by night
They don't sow potatoes nor barley nor wheat
But there's gangs of them diggin' for gold in the street
At least when I asked them that's what I was told
So I took up my hand at this diggin' for gold
But for all that I found there I might as well be
Where the Mountains of Mourne sweep down to the sea

'It's perfect Sister, but how can you be sure the girls won't know it?'

'Because the lyrics of the other verses are too vulgar for the likes of nuns and convent girls, to be sure,' Sister Brigid said. 'In any case, the first verse is long enough for your lesson. And the final line is beautiful, my dear. Despite it not being the ending, it gives you the sense of an ending.'

Juliette glanced at the second verse and giggled.

I believe that when writing a wish you expressed
As to know how the fine ladies in London were dressed,
Well if you'll believe me, when asked to a ball,
They don't wear no top to their dresses at all.
Oh I've seen them meself and you could not in truth,
Say if they were bound for a ball or a bath.
Don't be starting such fashions, now, Mary, mo chroí,
Where the mountains of Mourne sweep down to the sea.

'You see what I mean about the last line, Sister. Beautiful! The melody is beautiful too, but indeed 'tis more likely to be sung in a pub,' Sister Brigid said smiling. 'It was written by Percy French at the end of the nineteenth century, but the same melody was used by Thomas Moore for another poem in the eighteenth century.' Despite her crackly old voice, she sang it with nostalgia in a lilting tonality. Jeanne thought it one of the most beautiful melodies she'd ever heard. 'Show the girls a map of Ireland and explain that *The Mountains of Mourne* are in County Down,' Sister Brigid said wistfully, indicating the area on a map on the album cover. 'I lived near there as a child.'

Jeanne copied the first verse and left Sister Brigid with a '*Merci beaucoup, ma soeur.*'

The Form 2 classroom was a desert. No pictures. A map of the world. A map of Australia. Ancient desks with inkwells. The classroom, together with the girls' drab uniform of grey and navy-blue, befitted the vacuous stares in their eyes. Jeanne was determined to brighten the room. She smiled at the girls and recited the poem in her most exuberant manner. When she read it the second time, she asked them to close their eyes. It would help their concentration; help them get a picture. Was it a conversation? No. *Dear Mary* indicated that it was a letter. Who do you think Mary was and where was she living? What is the rhyming scheme? What form is the poem in? Can they suggest a title? What images does the poem create? Juliette knew she'd catch them there. Men digging for gold in London streets, someone said. Like in Ballarat a hundred years ago? Perhaps, they said. Like in Dick Whittington's time. But that was a seventeenth century fable. Were London's streets really paved with gold? They weren't sure about that until someone realised that *diggin' for gold* was a metaphor.

One of the girls raised her hand. 'Is it anonymous, Sister?'

Jeanne suddenly realised she'd forgotten to write the poet's name on the board.

'I'm sorry Barbara. I forgot about that. Percy French wrote it at the end of the nineteenth century,' she said, writing his name on the blackboard.

Another hand went up.

'Yes, Molly?'

'Did he write the music too, Sister?'

The music? So this girl knew it was a song? 'No, Molly. The music was written by Thomas Moore a century before that.'

The bell sounded for recess. 'Could we just read it through together using an Irish voice like Sister Brigid,' another girl pleaded.

'Perhaps you could ask her to sing it,' Jeanne suggested.

'Pleeeease, Sister,' they begged.

'Well,' she smiled. 'Your Irish accent would have to sound better than my French one.'

It was following this lesson that Juliette knew teaching would be her life. No matter what subject she was asked to teach, she felt she would cope. As expected, Sister Damien's report was negative, the main complaint being that she'd forgotten to mention the name of the poet! And was it really a poem, or was it a song? The class became much too excited at the end of the lesson, to the point that they were out of control.

'But Sister,' Jeanne said, undaunted. 'Did you see the girls' faces? They were so enthusiastic. They would have willingly given up their recess to say the poem several more times.'

Sister Damien contemptuously stared her down, turned her back and walked away.

7

Molly

On special feast days like St Patrick's Day, or All Saints Day, we attend Mass in the school chapel, where, on a much larger scale than my former convent in St Arnaud, individual prayer stalls for the nuns line the walls between the aisles and the pews. Everyone knows the Latin Mass backwards so I can't help wondering if all that mindless repetition bores them to death as much as it does me. Monotony always sends me drifting through the looking glass.

Chess piece Alice characters merge with the nuns swishing and rattling in to take their places in the stalls. Among the forty or so are my teachers. Nuns might all look similar in their black and white garb, but they're about as different from each other as the animals in the Ballarat Zoo. Sister Wilfred, the moustachioed walrus maths teacher is the football player swaggering onto the oval, red-faced from her strangling coif from which protrudes a wisp of grey hair. Her starched white bib is loose, flapping around like a cockatoo's wings. Clouds of chalk dust coat her sleeves and veil. My White Rabbit geography teacher flaps and bustles around, her nose twitching above her buck teeth. She elbows the Mad Hatter art teacher in the ribs while burrowing around for her pocket watch under her bib. Obsessed with punctuality, she mutters '*Oh dear, oh dear, I shall be too late*!' Sister Gregory, the ferocious Bandersnatch with her snapping jaws, snarls at my English teacher who is rearranging her rosary beads and wimple, occasionally tightening her cincture to show off her tiny waist, her only remaining vestige of vanity, I suppose. Rosario is grumping away as usual. With her bulbous face and googly eyes, she's either Tweedledum, or Tweedledee. Her twin is probably persecuting some poor girl in another convent. She has a habit of getting at an itchy ear by pulling back the starched coif constricting her face. It's so razor-sharp she's going to behead herself one day. Queen '*Off with her head*' Alphonsus is yodelling an Ave when Sister Gerard calls out '*Tis the voice of the sluggard.*' The remaining chess piece nuns are waiting for proceedings to start. Or preferably to finish. The grand jury of the remaining Alice characters sit in the pews. Finally, there's me. Alice in a blue gown and white pinafore, the presiding judge. Seated in the throne reserved for the Bishop, I superciliously sweep my eyes around the courtroom to declare disdainfully 'Silence. Rule forty-two. All persons more than sixty stone to leave the court immediately.' And after Alphonsus's protestations, 'Stuff and *nunsense*,' I say as she exits.

At assemblies, I sometimes see Alphonsus waltzing into the pub during the swill like the Salvos; threading her way through the drinkers, their discarded cigarette packets and butts burning on the linoleum; handing out *War Cry*; rattling a collection tin despite the cursing and blasphemy. Alphonsus tells us to cross ourselves if we ever hear anyone swearing or blaspheming. She'd be crossing herself nonstop if she tried to squeeze her way down the passage past the customers to the piano room. What would she say to the lapsed Catholics who, she says, are 'worse than atheists,' one of whom told us about bad Popes. An eleven-year-old Pope. A female Pope. Popes who had children. Not that I believed him for a moment! 'Popes are infallible,' I declared.

The first time I was sent to Alphonsus was during Form 3 – my second year at St Martin's. The girls were standing around chatting and drawing on the blackboard, waiting for the bell to sound for afternoon classes in the main classroom. We'd been learning about the germination of seeds, so my puerile contribution was to draw eyes and a smile on the two large kidney-shaped cotyledons Sister Dominique had meticulously prepared amongst other botanical illustrations on the board. I added long eyelashes and curls to one so it looked as though the seeds, in mirror image, were flirting with each other. Everyone was shrieking with laughter. When the bell sounded, I went to grab the eraser, but the girls wouldn't give it to me, all swearing they wouldn't say a word. I was flattered by their attention, but dubious about the whole thing when Sister Gregory rattled in for History. Halfway through the Battle of Hastings, she noticed some girls ogling the blackboard. Grinning at the defaced cotyledons. Her eyes darted around the classroom, determined to find the culprit. The Bandersnatch ready to pounce.

'It was Molly Harrington, Sister,' said a crawler who had promised not to say a word about my pathetic artwork. Gregory would have looked more at home with an axe in her hands as she escorted me to a study dominated by Reverend Mother Alphonsus, seated behind a large desk that nearly swallowed her up. She gave me a forced Cheshire cat smile.

'Are you going to follow in your aunt's footsteps and become a nun?' she bleated after The Bandersnatch relayed my crime and left the scene.

With an uncle a priest and an aunt a nun, Alphonsus must think I'm odds-on for a vocation to the nunnery. 'Yes, Mother,' I said to humour her. 'I'm still considering which order to join. My aunt's Good Shepherd Order or the Mercy Order.'

She hasn't caught on yet that most of us are desperate to get away from her clutches. I suspect I'm not the only one who placates her by pretending they're entering the convent. *Always speak the truth,* the Queen said to Alice. In certain situations, you can't tell the truth, can you? What would Alice have said when asked about which order she should join? *Disorder or datorder?* More likely *Stuff and nunsense!* While Alphonsus prattled on, insisting that every other religious order was second-rate to the Mercy Order, I saw her playing croquet, the nuns bent over on all fours to make the arches; long skirts billowing around like sails in the wind, obstructing the balls every time she drove her golf-stick mallet.

Alphonsus looked like she was going to break into song and dance when she thought she'd convinced me that the Mercy Order was the best order of nuns in the world. After her ramblings subsided, she dismissed me without mentioning the blackboard incident. Sister Dominique, Dom as we usually call her, came into the classroom to give her lesson just after I returned. When the Bandersnatch showed her my crime, Dom was trying her best not to laugh.

Fortunately, most of my teachers aren't like Gregory. My favourite nun, Sister Jeanne, is quite young. Occasionally I try to picture her in ordinary streetwear. I know she's got a whoosh of dark curls, because when we were doing *ma famille* in conversation, she showed us photos of her family and relatives when they were living in France.

Jeanne is a combination of all the wonderful nuns in *The Bells of Saint Mary's*. There are never any nasty nuns in Hollywood films. What a waste for such beauty and brilliance to be confined to convent walls! On the other hand, we're lucky to have her. She's so enthusiastic! So inspiring. She uses actions to indicate the sense of the word when we're having trouble, and she's full of suggestions for how to remember the vocabulary. My German teacher is very serious, calm and patient, and a good teacher, but she hasn't got Jeanne's personality. She's tall and has such a regal manner that I think of her more as a lady-in-waiting in Queen Elizabeth's Court.

We memorise poems because Jeanne says the vocabulary is useful in many contexts. She flicks through a book of the French countryside with images of the bridge and water lilies in Monet's Garden. '*Le pont et les nénuphars*,' we repeat while making the shape of the bridge and water lilies with our hands. She turns to a page where instead of a *host of golden daffodils,* there's a host of shimmering purple flowers no one can identify.

'In France,' Sister Jeanne says, 'crocuses – *les colchiques* – are the fragrant autumn flowers in the meadows. *Les fleurs dans les près* at the end of summer. *La fin de l'été.*

'There's a beautiful song about *l'automne* which became very popular throughout France during the war. Most French children and adults know all verses *par coeur*,' she says, placing her hand over her heart. She hurriedly writes the lyrics – *les paroles* – of the first verse and refrain on the board.

Colchiques dans les près
Fleurissent, fleurissent
Colchiques dans les près
C'est la fin de l'été
La feuille d'automne
Emportée par le vent
En rondes monotones
Tombe en tourbillonnant

We know that *la feuille* is the leaf, *le vent* the wind, and *porter* means to carry. 'So *emportée* is self-explanatory as is *rondes*,' she explains. We guess *tourbillonnant* relates to turbulence, although she says whirling is a better translation. *Fleurissent* includes *fleur*, so we assume it means flowering or blooming. Gabby asks her if it's a song, why doesn't she sing it?

Jeanne shrugs. 'It's easier to discern *les paroles* if I recite rather than sing.'

'But we've never heard a proper French song, Sister,' Gabby insists. 'Only, *Au clair de la lune.*'

The class pleads in a chorus of 'Pleeeease, Sister.'

'Shhhh! *Alors. La chanson.* You must try to translate *les paroles* of the other verses. *Les autres couplets.*'

She sings *L'automne*, enunciating each syllable for clarity and for our comprehension. I can almost smell the perfume of the crocuses. Her voice is angelic, bell-like, spiralling right up for the refrain. Floating on a wave to be gently lowered and washed onto shore. I picture the autumn leaves, swirling around to spread a velvet-soft carpet on the earth. We're spellbound for several heartbeats at the end, scarcely breathing. She smiles, and we immediately burst into applause. If we didn't all have a crush on her before she sang, we do now. We want to sing all three verses.

'If you learn it by heart. *D'apprendre par coeur,*' she says, indicating her heart, 'I'll invite Sister Katerina to hear you sing it. We'll do actions as well to help with comprehension and memorisation.'

Jeanne has a light in her eyes. In her smile. When I look around the classroom, everyone seems to be as inspired as me. Every night I sing *l'automne* in my mind as I drift off to sleep. It's the most beautiful song I've ever heard. The haunting melody follows me everywhere, swirling and whirling around in my head. Weaving its way through my dreams. It drifts with the crocuses and autumn leaves onto the piano keys. My fingers. I want to accompany on the classroom piano when we sing it for Sister Katerina, but I haven't got the nerve to ask.

I like to think that my father's only sister, Aunt Bernadine, the nun Alphonsus referred to, is a great teacher like Sister Jeanne.

She certainly makes a fuss of us all when we visit her at the Good Shepherd Convent. My Uncle Michael, Dad's only brother, is a priest. He was so kind to me in St Arnaud that I wish he were my father. Sometimes Dad frightens me. He gets into awful moods, pushing and pinching me as he walks past. Sometimes he lashes out, telling me I'm not helping out around the place enough. When Tony gets into trouble, Dad flogs him.

I adore Tony because he's mischievous and amusing. At the penny arcade by the lake, he showed us how to use machines without putting coins in. When the circus comes to town, he lifts up a flap so we can sneak under the tent and watch the show for nothing. He does paper rounds and collects manure in his billycart to sell to the Chinese market gardener so he can buy a bicycle. His outdoor bungalow is close to the outside toilet which means that while he's making crystal sets and other gadgets, he can keep his eye on the customers passing by. 'Your money or your life,' he declares as he brandishes his cadet rifle. Or 'Stand and deliver.' All he needs is a horse. Just as well the old man doesn't know what he's up to. He makes a fortune from Lager Len and Billy the Quid who, when they aren't guests at Lizzie's Lockup, are about as regular as the trams rattling down Main Road. With Dad being such a Scrooge, I was desperate to make money like Tony, so when Billy the Quid – alias Billy *Not* the Full Quid – arranged to meet me in the woodshed for ten shillings, I snatched the note after he grabbed my leg, and ran off to share it with Tony, who'd been hiding behind the woodpile with his cadet rifle. 'Just in case,' he said, although neither of us appreciated why.

I must have picked up a few clues from Tony. We girls had been introduced to calisthenics through a cousin when we moved into the pub. Suddenly, halfway through 1954, we had to raise money for our costumes. We knew Dad wouldn't be paying. He hated us learning dancing, even though it cost next to nothing. The only reason we were learning was because Mum, having been a dancer, got her way with Dad for once.

I decided that if Tony could charge customers to go to the toilet, I could charge them as they entered the piano room. They're more generous on Saturday afternoons. Joined by a cousin, we began entertaining them with our song and dance routines, costumes and all. I'm usually on the piano. We raffle imaginary bottles of whisky, won by imaginary relatives. I steal a bottle from the bar to pretend it's the one we're raffling. Dad would kill us if he knew. Bridget, being the youngest, is more pious than the rest of us. She was going to ask the priest in confession if what we were doing with the raffles was a sin. Tony told her she was behaving like an old nun who had nothing to confess but farts. 'We're doing the customers a favour like the Salvos,' he finally convinced her. 'Saving all those pisspots from getting too plastered. If you start blabbing to a priest, it'll get back to the old man and he'll flay us alive. Priests sometimes get talking. They tell tales. Everyone knows the confessional's about as seal-proof as a dunny door.'

'What do you mean?' I asked him.

'When the woodshed was burnt down at boarding school and no one owned up, we were all bundled off to confession. The nuns knew immediately which boys were responsible because their penance was to weed the garden. Boys don't do jobs like that unless they're asked. They were thrashed. They'd been smoking.'

Tony's full of stories about his old boarding school. He hated it! He loves his independent life at the pub. A life that allows him to do odd jobs so he can make a fortune. I was desperate to make money like Tony because I needed new clothes. Our family has an account at Myers where I can buy whatever clothes I need for school. It's the same for my textbooks and music. If it's to do with education, I can buy anything. But as the oldest girl, I needed ordinary clothes. Street clothes! I'm so ashamed of my old-fashioned dresses that I decided I wouldn't go to a Friday night film at the convent again until I had some new ones. When I tell Dad I've grown out of my clothes and need new ones, he seems to take delight in refusing me. No amount of begging or pleading makes the slightest difference. 'When you do a bit more work around the place, I'll consider it,' is his favourite response or 'wear your school uniform!' To add to this, I have a passion for fashionable clothes. Not that there's much of a range in Ballarat, but there was a beautiful dress in Myers I was desperate to wear to *Great Expectations* at the convent one Friday evening. I knew this particular dress would show up a few others in my class whose clothes I always envied. I was almost tempted to put it on our Myers account, hoping Dad wouldn't notice. I also needed new shoes.

There was only one way to solve my problem. One evening during the swill, I crept into Mum and Dad's bedroom, one of the rooms we girls never clean. If the police bothered to search it for evidence of illegal gambling, they'd think it had already been ransacked. Mum is disorganised and to make matters worse, she's a hoarder. As she never leaves the hotel, I'm sure Dad brings her home all the junk from St Vincent de Paul that's been rejected. A mound of underwear, unironed shirts and dresses cascade over the dressing table. The wardrobe is choking, its overflow smothering the bed. Underneath it, the rug sheds fur like a mangy dog, warped furrows half-concealing tins stuffed with rolls of bank notes.

Despite telling myself that Dad would never leave the bar at peak hour, I was still nervous. He'd thrash me if he found me fossicking around under the bed. I knew there were tins of money there because Veronica had discovered the hoard months ago.

I crawled right under the bed. I opened the first tin and counted about £360 in rolls of £5 and £1 notes. I'd never seen so much money in my life! My eyes must have been as big as saucers as I stared at it. There were random amounts in each tin, adding up to thousands. £10 out of each of a few tins would never be noticed. Necessity rules, I told myself. The oldest girl in the family must have decent clothes to start with before handing them down to her sisters.

I felt little guilt because I loathed my father and knew I could confess my crime. The priests don't have a clue who you are at St Alban's because it's such a large parish. Nearly as big as the cathedral parish. I reasoned that I'd done enough work around the place since we moved in to deserve much more than the amount I'd stolen. Dad would never know. He never notices what I wear, but if he does, I'll tell him my tall friend Gabby – who isn't tall – has outgrown all her clothes and is passing them on to me. I'm a good liar. Neither Mum or Dad would have a clue as they've never met Gabby and I'll never be inviting her to the pub!

8

The Priest

The elaborate iron gates of the Bishop's Palace in Sturt Street were wide open. As a child when he walked past, he remembered them as being rather ominous. Always closed. Unwelcoming. He and his brothers had peeked through the bars, trying to envisage what lay beyond, but it was tantalisingly hidden by the trees in the foreground. Later, he'd learned that the eleven-acre property was the most valuable private residence in Ballarat. Now, as he drove along the white-gravelled driveway, he noticed two gardeners in the distance tending manicured lawns and shrubs; magnificent trees and statues scattered around the lawns; a landscaped roundabout encircling a marble fountain set into a pool, and finally, the imposing two-storey bluestone building known as the Bishop's Palace.

An elderly housekeeper opened the door within a minute of him ringing the doorbell. 'Ah! Father Kelly?' she said with a smile.

'Yes,' he said politely. 'To see the Bishop.'

'Well. Not today, Father. On Thursday afternoons His Lordship plays golf. You will be seeing his private secretary, Monsignor Stinson.'

He'd met Bishop O'Collins briefly at his ordination and was relieved that he wouldn't be seeing him now. All the same, he was apprehensive. Nervous. The housekeeper led him down the wide parquetry passageway, its ceiling surely fifteen or sixteen feet high. The chandeliers and furnishings in the huge room on the right-hand side suggested that it was a reception hall, its walls lined with an impressive art collection, the fireplace almost large enough to accommodate the grand piano that was in a corner to its right. On the opposite side, he noticed a library and grand staircase. Somewhere there would have to be a chapel. He'd only seen such opulence in mansions or manor homes in British films. Well, he'd learnt through his History studies that humility and constraint were not quite virtues of the religious hierarchy. But all this for one man? Perhaps his secretary also lived here. Just as the housekeeper opened a door into a room towards the end of the passageway, he got a quick glimpse through the full-length conservatory windows of a swimming pool, surrounded by a magnificent garden. The stone wall beyond ensured complete privacy, but from upstairs, the outlook would surely have a superb panoramic outlook of Lake Wendouree and the surrounding botanical gardens. Next year they'd have a bird's-eye view of the rowers practising for the Olympic Games.

'Monsignor Stinson will be with you shortly,' the housekeeper said.

It was a large study with a view to a tennis court, and a colourful display of flowers and shrubs lining a gravelled avenue that, like his former seminary, probably led to sanctuaries for prayer and contemplation. On the wall behind a large desk hung a Catholic calendar, looking much more decorative than usual with pictures of saints and feast days. Not a mention of Anzac Day coming up the following week. He looked at it more closely, realising that this particular calendar was Italian. *Aprile* 1955, it said. No wonder Anzac Day didn't get a mention.

An official-looking priest entered the study. 'Ah. Father Kelly,' he said with indifference rather than cordiality. 'I'm Monsignor Stinson. Neville will do. Please sit down.' He gestured towards a chair. 'This won't take long. I just need your version of events in your parish to record here in the diary. The woman who phoned last Monday was so irate I could hardly understand a word of what she was saying, except that if you weren't removed, she was going to the police and the press. I gather it was something to do with her daughter.'

Following the phone call from the Palace ordering him straight to Ballarat, Hilton had three days to prepare what he was going to say. 'The woman who reported me got it all wrong and second-hand. She's renowned for being an anti-Catholic bigot. She lives next door to my housekeeper, Mrs Ryan. When Mrs Ryan was ill last Sunday, she sent my breakfast up with her daughter, Mavis. I was comforting her because she was sad that her father had died. That bigot of a busybody got it into her head that I was molesting Mavis. I'm very upset about her malicious lies, and…'

Monsignor Stinson sighed. 'Well, you should try not to take it personally. It seems that your parishioners do not have a bad word to say about you. We all know that children tend to misreport incidents, and there is no doubt that gossip and rumours are carried by haters, spread by fools, and accepted by idiots. All the same, there's no way we could leave you in that parish because that woman is up to no good.' He looked down at his diary and began tapping his fingers.

Hilton felt like a naughty boy at school awaiting his punishment. Surely there couldn't be many places that were more remote than Rose Hill. Where would they send him? He was almost trembling now.

'You've packed all your personal belongings?'

'I have,' he said.

Monsignor Stinson looked up from his desk. 'I believe your family lives here in Ballarat.'

Hilton felt his stomach tightening. What was coming? Surely this incident wouldn't be reported to his mother! Not that she wouldn't be onside! 'Yes. My mother, and my two brothers and their families.'

'It seems you're in luck. It's a simple matter of swapping positions with Father Nolan here at St Alban's who likes the idea of having his own parish. I believe he has family around that area too. Father Bob Bourke is now your PP.'

Hilton nearly jumped out of his chair in excitement, thrilled to be sent to his hometown. As a curate instead of a Parish Priest, he would have less responsibility. Among many advantages of living in a city, he would have anonymity and more time to himself. Golf and tennis with his old friends. A drink of beer after the game. He could join a decent cricket club. Drive down to Melbourne without the whole town wondering where he'd gone. There was a choice of picture theatres. It was bad luck that a non-Catholic had been involved in his indiscretion, but worth it all to be back in his hometown with his family again.

'You may report immediately to Father Bourke after visiting your family. His Lordship has asked me to remind you to try and avoid putting yourself in such a situation again. Especially one that is likely to involve outsiders.'

'Certainly. Thank you very much, Neville.'

When he met up with his mother, it was easy to spin a few lies about why he'd been relocated.

'That's the best news ever,' she said excitedly. 'St Alban's is a very large parish. You're very lucky to be promoted at your age. It couldn't have come at a better time with your twenty-sixth birthday coming up next week. Twenty-six on the twenty-fifth! We'll have a family get-together to celebrate.'

The public holiday for his birthday was always a family joke. He didn't bother explaining that his new position at St Alban's was scarcely a promotion, but all the same, he was looking forward to seeing his two brothers. He'd never envy them, tied down with their wives and families. Both had heavy mortgages, large families, and second jobs. They'd have a lot to talk about, with the split developing in the Labor Party. It was going to be full steam ahead on Catholicism versus communism from now on.

He was impressed with his new parish, the large Australian colonial-style presbytery set back from the bluestone church. Father Bourke, the parish priest, told him he could use the front parlour as his office. Full-length windows gave views of the front gardens and the side entrance of the church.

'The starboard side,' as O'Doherty calls it. 'Same view from the window in your bedroom next door.' Bob Bourke steered Hilton into a study adjoining a bedroom and bathroom on the other side of the long hallway. 'My domain,' he said with a sweep of his hand. 'It includes the veranda area around the other side with my private entrance.' He gave Hilton a set of keys. 'The bedroom right down the end next to the dining-room is O'Doherty's. The other six are for visiting priests.'

'O'Doherty?'

'Bloody useless! He should be at the knackery. He comes and goes when he pleases. I've had a stack of complaints about the penance he's been giving. Last week he told one of our oldest parishioners to run around the college oval ten times and to follow it with five decades of push-ups.'

The two priests laughed.

'So I've relegated him to only helping out with communion. You wouldn't believe what happens if you let him say Mass.

Head Office has no idea what he's like. We could do with another priest.'

Bourke 'call me Bob' showed Hilton around the impressive building while explaining the routine. The housekeeper, Mrs Rawlings, cooks breakfast, prepares lunch, and returns to cook their evening meal at 5pm. On Sundays or special feast days, they must arrange for friends, relatives, or parishioners to invite them out. The parish men were rostered to do the gardening.

Hilton moved his belongings from his Humber into the bedroom. His list of shared duties was answering the phone, pastoral care at the public and Catholic hospitals, the parish school, confession, Mass, weddings, funerals, baptisms, Benediction and novenas. Ballarat was full of Catholics!

He met Father O'Doherty that evening during dinner, after which Bob Bourke hurried off, telling the two priests he didn't want to be disturbed.

'Cunning devil,' O'Doherty said to Hilton. 'Likes them young does our PP.'

'What do you mean?' Hilton already had his suspicions about his superior.

'Huh. Thinks I don't know what he gets up to.' O'Doherty leant over to speak confidentially. 'Got the housekeeper's keys to his comfy flat one day when he wasn't there.' He rolled his eyes. 'Says he's educating them for the priesthood. I searched his bookcase, and guess what?'

'I can't imagine.'

'Imagine?' asked Father O'Doherty after a long pause. 'Imagine if the whole world was converted to Catholicism. Would it be a perfect world?'

Bob Bourke had warned Hilton about O'Doherty's non sequiturs. 'Well. I…'

'Yes. Communism. That's what'll overtake the world. And praying won't help! The army would need to run things. Not the clergy. And I should know. I was an army chaplain. They get everything wrong, those Presidents and Prime Ministers. And the Pope during the last war. He liked the krauts, you know. Supported them.' He began rambling about the red peril and all the wrongs of the world.

Hilton interrupted him. 'You mentioned Father Bourke.'

'He should give poor Mrs Rawlings a rise. She's a widow. They're either widows or single. They slave away on a pittance for the good of their soul.'

A week later, Father Bourke left to attend a conference at the Bishop's Palace. After the housekeeper had gone home, Hilton grabbed the keys. No surprise there when he saw the pornographic photos in an album in his bookcase, carefully hidden away behind a set of religious textbooks. He suspected that his superior was visited by young boys. The locked cupboard was probably full of booze.

That evening after O'Doherty had left the dining-room, Hilton spoke to his superior. 'The young lads who come here, Bob. Their parents don't mind?'

'Well, my boy,' Bob Bourke said with a sly grin. 'They're altar boys. I bring them here to help with their education. They're interested in becoming priests and need help with their schoolwork. Their parents encourage it.'

Hilton looked at this ugly little man with beady beetle eyes. His jug-handle ears. His Adam's apple see-sawing between his dog collar and stringy neck as though trying to decide where to settle. It certainly wasn't his looks that charmed the boys. All he had to do was show them some pornography, lay on the grog and cigarettes, and Bob's your uncle. Or more likely, Bob's *their* uncle. Nice and convenient in his self-contained flat with its own entrance. Hilton wouldn't mind a similar set-up. Perhaps he'd say nothing yet about being rostered twice as much on the confessional as his superior. He'd bide his time. Wait for an opportunity.

The little box was *his* penance except when the penitents' sexual proclivities aroused him. It was the only time he devoured every detail. His eyes always took a while to adjust to the gloom. It was like being shut up in a coffin. No ventilation except for the curtain above the priests' half-door. He drew it back. Just a sliver at the bottom. They never realised he could see them. They waited in the pews, heads bowed down. Light streamed in as they entered the confessional. Just a fleeting glimpse as the door opened. The grille was no visual barrier. From his booth and with time, he learnt to recognise voices. Make out profiles. Sometimes they hid their faces, hands in votive prayer. Like this one. The girl he saw from the presbytery parlour on Saturday mornings. Bouncing along the footpath and for some reason, always swinging a rod. Fluffy dark hair in a bob. Elfin almost. Fourteen or fifteen years of age. Just blooming.

'I've been stealing, Father,' she told him reluctantly.

'From whom?' he asked.

'From my father,' she said, embarrassed, head bowed low.

He put his head closer to the grille and asked her why.

'Because… because he's got plenty of money and never gives us any,' she said, hesitating.

Ah! Typical. Girls could justify anything. Vulnerable too. Probably despised her father. And at the age of placing her trust in a priest without question. He gave her no counselling. 'Three Hail Marys to be said before the statue of the Blessed Virgin Mary,' he said.

He slid the wooden screen back across the grille, turned towards the centre and pulled back the curtain an inch. He watched her walk up to the statue to kneel near the altar rail. Wedges of colour from the stained-glass window lit up one side of her face like a rainbow. A little thin, he thought. But innocent and beautiful in her pale summer dress. An idea began fermenting in his mind.

9

Molly

I got quite a shock one afternoon when Mum joined in with the customers in the piano room. I was playing *Chesapeake Bay*, an item the seniors from my calisthenics club were learning. Instead of emptying the ashtrays and wiping down the tables, Mum started singing. Imitating the churning of the paddle steamers, the banjos, the silvery moon. Sashaying up to Nancy while she sang *'Come on Nancy put your best dress on, Come on Nancy 'fore the steamboat's gone.'* She became the lead star in a musical comedy, her voice trying to say something that went beyond the lyrics of the song. I was embarrassed at first but must admit she performed it better than any calisthenics senior. The customers were mesmerised. It wasn't just her voice. It was her movements; her facial expressions; the way she drifted into another world, oblivious of anyone around her. I was transported back to the neat little cottage we lived in before I went to boarding school. Mum never read to us, but then, there were no books in the house. She floated around performing song and dance numbers, as if for some distant audience rather than for us. With eyes sparkling to match each facial expression, she'd sing *I Got Rhythm* while she tap-danced, twirling an old walking stick between her hands and over her shoulders. Bouncing and tapping it on the floor. *Sweet Georgia Brown* was a mixture of high kicks and soft shoe. *The Wedding of the Painted Doll* had her imitating all the nursery characters in the song, and *Ship Ahoy* turned her into a sailor with folded arms and ship-style steps.

Back then, Mum sometimes accompanied herself in a vamping style on the old piano. Most of the lyrics meant nothing to me. I couldn't imitate her beautiful voice, but the melodies burrowed into my brain. There was nothing else to do. I played simple tunes like *Blue Moon* and *Little Brown Jug*. At three and four years of age, I couldn't stretch an octave, so I added notes with my left hand that seemed to suit the melody.

The only other time Mum comes to life is when my aunt drops into the hotel to help out with the cleaning. We all adore Maude. She's kind, with a wonderful sense of humour. She seems to accept that Mum is disorganised and needs a lot of help. On Saturday afternoons when the two of them sit down in the kitchen to have a shandy, Mum becomes quite animated. It's as though Maude waves a magic wand, somehow rousing Mum from her reverie or whatever it is that's going on in her mind most of the time. We discuss the customers. Our relatives. The past. Boarding school stories. The teachers we despise. Those we admire. The latest songs and dances we're learning in calisthenics. Mum knows most of them. When we rave about the latest musicals, Mum rattles off a few songs from *Rose Marie* and *Rio Rita* from stage shows she was involved in when she lived in Melbourne before she married.

During one of these afternoons, we three girls were whinging about being sent away to St Arnaud when Tony happened to walk in. 'What about me! I was sent to Villa Maria with the Sisters of No Mercy at the age of four,' he said glaring at Mum. 'I told you about Sister Theophane but you did nothing. One of these days I'm going back there to put a dead snake and a hundred spiders in her bed.'

Tony often tells us stories about his old boarding-school, a former mansion donated to the nuns by a wealthy widow. Its golf course is used by priests, nuns, and senior students from St Martin's.

'Mick and me were only about seven or eight when Theophane stripped us of our pyjama pants and made us lie across a refectory table in front of other nuns. Then she beat us black and blue with a golf stick. All we did was giggle when we heard her piddling into her chamber pot during the night.'

Mum was upset, but Maude was horrified.

She stared at Mum open-mouthed. 'Why didn't you do something about it, Elsie?'

'Because the old man would have backed the nuns,' Tony retorted before Mum had a chance to speak.

Maude went on about it for a while. She tends to disparage the religious, but never when Dad's around. I suppose with Dad's only brother, Uncle Michael, being a priest, she wouldn't feel inclined to. She often comes out with inexplicable sayings like 'Priests are velvet-mouthed hypocrites. In the pulpit they preach water, and in private they drink wine.' I'm sure her vague religious prejudices come from Irish superstitions rather than faith or instruction, although I imagine she'd want the last rites on her deathbed.

'Priests don't even know how to boil an egg, or to keep a stove alight let alone chop the wood for it, although opening a bottle of beer or wine never seems to trouble them!' When Uncle Michael dropped in unexpectedly and announced that he was staying the night, Mum went into her usual flurry, racing off to clear out the spare bedroom, piled high with junk. 'What would priests know about families when they're waited on hand and foot like the Queen of Sheba?' Maude said derisively. 'They smell of hypocrisy. They're all about making us feel guilty while they do what they like. They expect women to do the bloody lot and to keep having babies until they drop.'

Mum works day and night in the pub. Her cooking is first class, but she leaves a terrible mess in her wake. No matter how much we girls clean up after her, everything is in chaos again within a day or two because she puts everything back in the wrong place, to the point of mixing the groceries with the crockery. Coping with her constant clutter is difficult after the pristine conditions and neatness at boarding school. We daren't complain because Dad says he'll send us back there if we do, which is when Tony always tells us, 'Don't worry. I'll dynamite the place before he does that!'

Without Maude, I'd never have known anything about our family. Every Sunday night, she puts on a special spread in her neat little cottage for all her nieces. I think she likes spending time with us because she doesn't have any children of her own. She answers our questions about the family, but like Mum, she's evasive when I ask her why we were all sent off to boarding school.

Mum and Maude were young children when their parents died within a year of each other. Their sixteen-year-old sister wasn't fussy about sending everyone off to school or church, which might explain why none of them are as educated or as religious as my father's side of the family. Dad's only sister, Aunt Bernadine, is a nun and a teacher.

'No one came to check up on us,' Maude said. 'But our tiny cottage rocked with music every night. The ten of us danced and sang around the piano. The boys played the spoons and kazoos. Or the jew's harp and the harmonica.'

'But what about the dancing. Who taught Mum to dance?'

'Elsie took up ballroom dancing when she was first working in Melbourne. It's how she met your father. She danced and sang in the chorus line at the Tivoli for a while. When your grandfather learned that, he called your mother a tart. She doesn't talk about her past because he made her feel ashamed of it. He's more Catholic than the Pope himself. He gave your mother an inferiority complex.'

According to Maude's husband Harry, Mum was more outgoing before she married. 'She was a stunner,' he said. 'Your dad adored her. It's his bloody old man that ruined everything. The old misery guts always put your poor mother down. They had to live with the old bastard after they were married.'

Maude seems to know as much about Dad's side of the family as her own. 'When your father became a clerk in the Ballarat Railways, he had to pay for your uncle Michael to study for the priesthood in Werribee. It's why he had to delay getting married and why he makes every pound a prisoner.'

I suppose having a family to support and send to Catholic schools made Dad shrewd with his money, although we'll always think of him as a scrooge. Maude says that since his youth, Dad supplemented his salary by playing poker. He's clever at maths, and a first-rate bookie. Gambling is in his blood. Before emigrating from Ireland, my grandfather was studying to be a priest but left the seminary because he got too keen on the races.

'Your great grandfather kicked him out of home and gave him his fare to Australia. In Ireland, leaving the seminary is as shameful as leaving the priesthood,' Maude said. 'It's the same here. Church always comes before family.'

It probably costs a fortune to keep us all at school, but I wish the old man would stop whinging about us not doing enough to help out around the place. He hasn't got an ounce of warmth or sympathy in him. Sometimes when I look at Dad's hard eyes, I see myself as a five-year-old again when he drove me to boarding-school without a word of explanation. He's the opposite to his brother, Uncle Michael, who we all adore. He sometimes called into the convent in St Arnaud to take us out at weekends.

Mum is very warm and loving with the babies, but sometimes with the four of us older ones, it's as though we're not part of her life. When I was in the Ballarat East Gardens behind the pub playing hide and seek with Veronica and Brigid, I fell onto a tap that didn't have a handle. The pointed shaft pierced me just above the area no one mentions. I was in agony, and bleeding everywhere, but Mum was unsympathetic. Perhaps she was too shocked to help me.

Aunt Bernadine would get quite a shock if she heard Maude going on about nuns and priests. We visited her at the Good Shepherd Convent Orphanage in Abbotsford usually around Christmas. After being served a sumptuous afternoon tea in the parlour, we'd all walk around the beautiful grounds. I can remember flashes of the Yarra shimmering between the huge trees and garden beds around the perimeter. I knew there were hundreds of orphans there, but I never saw them wandering around the paths like us. On one occasion, when Aunt Bernadine directed me to a toilet, I turned in the wrong direction, bumping into a few girls about my own age who were playing in a courtyard. After they got chatting to me, I told them how lucky they were to have such a beautiful garden to play in. 'It's like a secret garden,' I said.

'You're the one who's lucky,' one girl replied. 'We always play here. The only time we've been in the garden was for a photo with the Bishop. You wouldn't like living here. This place is a house of horrors.'

I think that was when I realised how lucky I was. Not as lucky as my friends who all went away on holidays with their families, but better off than orphans. We never go anywhere as a family, not even to Mass. The only exception is our obligatory trip to

Melbourne to see Aunt Bernadine. Mum has to be pushed into it.

'It's a nightmare, anyway, with Mum and the babies and you girls spewing over each other all the way to Melbourne,' Tony said, relieved that he doesn't have to go, Dad having decided eight was one too many to squash into the Morris.

In 1954, Aunt Bernardine became principal of the local Catholic Primary School adjoining the Good Shepherd Convent in Albert Park. High-walled and prison grey, my aunt's convent in Beaconsfield Parade is right opposite the beach, occupying the whole block. We staggered out of the car in the height of summer feeling like death warmed up because we'd all been carsick. We inhaled the bracing, salty scent of the sea, and gazed wistfully at the beach, only to be whisked indoors to sit politely for hours in a parlour that smelt of incense, floor-wax and candles, and an occasional whiff of cabbage. While Aunt Bernardine asked enough questions to fill ten exam papers, my mind kept drifting to the sparkling sea beyond the high wall. During one visit, someone opened the parlour door. I caught a glimpse of two burly policemen forcing two teenage girls along the corridor. It was my chance to get my own back by interrogating my aunt.

'Why are the police bringing those girls here?' I asked her.

'They're girls who never had our advantages, Molly' she said.

'But why do they come here?'

'Because they have nowhere else to live,' she said evasively.

'Are they orphans? Like the girls at the Abbotsford Convent?'

'Well, no. Not exactly.'

'Do they go to your school next door?'

'No,' she smiled. 'They do God's work in the convent. I teach the orphans and locals.'

God's work? Does that mean they pray all day? This year, 1955, when all the family minus Tony visited Aunt Bernadine again, we sat on benches in the rose garden. In the distance, several nuns were ferrying large baskets to a barred gate. Having lived for so long in a convent, I know that some nuns cook, clean, or do the laundry, even the gardens. These nuns were going in and out of a large building that seemed to be separate from the main part of the convent. They weren't dressed like Aunt Bernardine. They were wearing brown habits with black veils, their faces red from exertion. My aunt wears a cream-coloured habit, white bib and coif, and rosary beads suspended from the cincture. A large silver heart-shaped locket hangs from a blue cord just below her bib. God knows how they keep their habits clean!

'They never had our advantages, Molly. They are carrying out God's work by doing the laundry for hotels and institutions around Melbourne,' Aunt Bernardine said when I asked her about them.

While the adults were chatting, we three sisters went walkabout. Around the back of the rose garden, we noticed another building, its windows frosted and barred. It was surely a jail! Was it for the girls we saw the police dragging along the corridor? But why? What had they done wrong? Another building adjacent to the jail must have housed the nuns in brown. A convent within a convent! At least I had a chance to see the beach when we arrived in Melbourne, but I knew that these poor girls and nuns were never given a sliver of the beautiful world outside. A world within a breath of them. Hordes of swimmers cooling off on a hot day; waves murmuring and drenching the sand; excited, squealing children with buckets and spades collecting shells to adorn their sandcastles; seagulls squawking, swooping and beating their wings. Nuns like Aunt Bernadine volunteered to intern themselves for the rest of their lives, but apparently those poor girls and the nuns in brown had no choice.

Maude knew all about the girls. 'They're the ones the police bring in from the streets or the courts,' she said. 'They're incarcerated for life. All the Good Shepherd Convents in Victoria are orphanages and reform schools!'

'But what did they do wrong?'

'According to the police and the nuns, they're in moral danger.'

I didn't have a clue what that meant, and Maude didn't explain except to say that they didn't have families. 'But surely they can leave eventually!' I said.

'Some escape, but others become frightened of the outside world. It's all about exploitation and cheap labour. The poor things are so brainwashed they slave away in laundries forever. They don't get a penny and they think they're saving their souls. We've got two of those Catholic shitholes right here in Ballarat. One for boys and one for girls. They're all over the country. Just ask anyone who's been there, and they'll tell you they were beaten and treated like shite. When they turn thirteen, the girls are forced to slave away in their laundries from dawn to dusk. Why else do you think parents threaten to send their children to a Catholic orphanage when they misbehave? They're flogged and starved for misdemeanours. If anyone tries to run away, they're locked in cupboards or put in solitary confinement. Little Orphan Annie and Oliver Twist are spoilt brats in comparison to anyone living in a Catholic orphanage!'

We three sisters made a vow after that last visit. No way would we finish up hiding from the world behind high walls, either as first or second-class nuns.

10

Cecilia

At the beginning of the last term in Form 4, Cecilia walked quickly with Bernice down the narrow street behind the convent grounds towards the cathedral, passing a few houses and the back of the presbytery. Instead of turning right to make their way to the cathedral as per Mother Alphonsus's instructions, they walked for two more blocks, turning right to cross Sturt Street. They headed back towards St Bernard's College impressive iron gates to the circular drive, continuing along the fence line until they were close enough to watch the boys finishing a game of cricket. No teachers were in sight.

'Funny, isn't it?' Bernice said. 'In the winter when it's freezing cold, they wear shorts, but when the weather's warmer, they wear long pants and pullovers. I think they look hunkier in their whites, don't you?'

'Maybe long pants make them look older.'

Three boys sauntered across the oval and began chatting to them. After a few minutes, Cecilia nudged Bernice, who told the boys they'd better be going. Bernice was already smitten with one of them, Tom, a day-scholar. Two days later they repeated their little escapade.

'If you want to hear Cecilia practising, we're in the organ gallery between five and six o'clock on Mondays, Wednesdays, and Fridays,' Bernice told Tom. 'I'm always there too.'

The following day when they were called to Reverend Mother's office, they knew what to expect.

'Bernadette Gannon for sure,' Cecilia whispered while they waited in the corridor. 'I saw her when we crossed at the lights.'

'Bloody little sneak. She's jealous. No wonder no one can stand her. Just ignore Alphonsus if she starts making threats Celie. She's all bluff. Leave her to me. I can manage her.'

They moved away from Al's office.

'I haven't had a chance to tell you,' Cecilia continued whispering, 'but just after I was flooding everywhere yesterday and raced off to get some pads, I bumped into Molly. I asked her what she was doing in this part of the convent and she said Al wanted to see her about her dancing. The old cow doesn't approve of it, apparently.'

'Why not? There are Dégas ballerinas all around the place.'

'Maybe she thinks ballet is more cultured than the sort of dancing Molly does.'

'You mean calisthenics?'

'Yes. She apparently carried on about her taking one or two days off school to compete in the competitions. Something about mixing with protestants as well. Molly should have just said she was sick. She's too honest.'

Bernice raised her eyes to the ceiling and sighed. 'Some of my friends at my old school in Melbourne did calisthenics and the nuns didn't mind. In any case, Molly's a day-scholar. What she does outside this place has got nothing to do with the old busybody. She sits around all day thinking up things to bitch about.'

Cecilia put a finger to her lips. 'Shh. A few around here have ears like bats. Anyway, to get back to Al. She told Molly off about the vulgar costumes they wore. *Doing high kicks and exposing the sacred parts of your body to boys in the audience*, she actually said.'

'You mean the *Stairway to Paradise*?'

They looked at each other and giggled.

'Was Molly upset?'

Bernice shook her head. 'I don't think so. She thinks Al is mad as we do.'

Mother Alphonsus suddenly called out, ordering the girls inside. She was sitting at a huge mahogany desk, her hands steepled piously on the starched white bib mantling her bosom, her namesake, Saint Alphonsus, looking down benevolently from the wall above. The two girls stood side by side before the desk. When she began to berate them for publicly parading themselves in their sportswear, Bernice interrupted.

'But Mother, my cousin had just finished playing cricket and I was desperate to know if they'd trounced Ballarat Grammar.'

Cecilia grinned inwardly. Bernice was so clever. So ingenious.

'You were warned not to deviate from your regular route. What about your bare legs? We here at St Martin's are responsible for your safety and your welfare. Right now, Cecilia, I'm ready to cancel your organ scholarship. Your school scholarship can be rescinded at the convent's whim. What would your parents think then? You are both very privileged to be at this school.'

'Yes Mother,' they sighed in unison. Privilege, like modesty and behaviour in public, was always done to death in assemblies.

'Percentage-wise, this school has one of the best results in the state. Better than St Bernard's and the non-Catholic schools, and way ahead of that other convent by the lake whose examination results are not worth mentioning. Every teaching nun here in the convent has a degree and if they don't when they enter, they commute to Melbourne University or another recognised educational institution.'

The two girls exchanged glances. How many times had they heard this before?

'You Cecilia, have been chosen from many who covet your God-given talent and who'd do anything to have private lessons on a first-class organ from Mr Connelly.'

'Yes Mother,' Cecilia agreed.

Alphonsus looked at Bernice. 'And how do you propose using your talent after you've matriculated Bernice?'

'Well, Mother. I've been thinking that after I finish my degree, I'd like to come back here and teach.'

Having urged the girls to become nuns rather than going out into the wicked world, Reverend Mother Alphonsus now smiled up at Bernice, her whole disposition changing. 'You'll be entering the convent, Bernice? You have a vocation to serve God?'

Bernice nodded. 'Yes Mother,' she said with passion. 'It was the cathedral that did it. Cecilia was playing that beautiful *Ave Verum* and I was looking down at the altar from the gallery. I... I can't quite explain it, Mother. Suddenly I was spiritually inspired. It was an awakening.' She paused for dramatic effect. 'My epiphany!'

Alphonsus beamed. 'This is magnificent news Bernice. I'm sure you'll make a wonderful nun.'

'Thank you, Mother.'

Alphonsus looked pointedly at Cecilia. 'And you, Cecilia? Do you, like Bernice, also have a vocation to enter the convent?'

Cecilia had no doubt that Mother Alphonsus expected her to at least become a musician or to teach music. She couldn't think of anything worse than returning as a nun to teach and accompany all those boring hymns on an old harmonium. In any case, she was too interested in boys. 'Well. I...'

Bernice kicked her, interrupting. 'She does Mother. She just hasn't yet decided which order she should join. I'm trying to talk her into coming here.'

Cecilia smiled at Bernice's ingenuity, Alphonsus mistaking it for zealousness and smiling up at her expectantly.

'Yes, Mother. It's true.' She'd learned a lot from Bernice in a short time, but would she ever sound as convincing as her friend? She'd string the old cow along for a while. 'I've been thinking about joining the Loreto nuns, Mother. An organ student from Loreto said that their school has a magnificent chapel and pipe organ.' She'd like to have added that she heard all the girls loved the place. The building and its surrounds, the regime, the principal. Even the food sounded better. The girls had more sport than religion and were allowed to go out at the weekend.

Mother Alphonsus was shocked. 'But you wouldn't join *that* order Cecilia! It would be an act of disloyalty after all we've done for you! We may not have such a chapel or pipe organ, but we are your benefactors.'

'Yes Mother. I hadn't thought of that.'

Mother Alphonsus moved into lecture mode again. 'You must remember girls, that nuns live in a superior state to the world outside. They are set apart from everyone else and therefore able to follow an easier path to reach the highest place in heaven. Ordinary mortals will find it more difficult to attain paradise. On judgement day, God will be more demanding of those living in the secular world.'

'Yes Mother,' Cecilia enthused. How many times had they heard this at assemblies?

'Very well,' Reverend Mother said after a two-minute pause, during which she stared up at Saint Alphonsus as though awaiting divine intervention. 'I will overlook your indiscretion this time in view of the fact that you were thinking of your cousin, Bernice.' She looked at Cecilia. 'However, if you ever digress from your regular route again, it will be the end of any scholarships.'

'Yes Mother,' Cecilia said earnestly.

'I hope you've learned your lesson.'

'Bernice is a wonderful assistant, Mother. She never misses a beat. Without her it'd take me twice as long to set up the organ and music,' Cecilia gushed, concerned that Alphonsus might replace Bernice with someone else.

The phone rang and Mother Alphonsus waved them away. Buoyed by their victory, Cecilia and Bernice nudged each other all the way down the dark corridor, opened a door at the end, and exploded into laughter as they stepped outside into a bright sunshine that reflected their mood.

'You were brilliant, Celie. You got to her! You sounded so genuine. Loreto indeed!'

Cecilia was thrilled. Finally, she felt like she was keeping up with Bernice.

'It's true about the chapel and organ at Loreto. That girl who has her lesson before me told me about it. She boards there. Apparently, it's one of the best school organs in Australia. The school sounds pretty posh.'

'It is. It's a branch of that swanky Mandeville Hall in Toorak. I'll show it to you in January.'

Never having been to Melbourne, Cecilia was looking forward to spending a week with Bernice, but when she arrived at the Dobson's Art Deco home in Kew, she felt a little out of her depth. Surrounded by hedges, the stone paths from the garage to the front door curved around velvety lawns, flower beds, and a gurgling fountain amidst a pool filled with goldfish and water lilies. A few exotic trees were of the type she'd only seen in House and Garden magazines in dentist waiting rooms. There were upstairs and downstairs bathrooms, and every room was tastefully furnished. The ultra-modern kitchen had every electrical appliance imaginable. She thought of her simple wooden farmhouse in Kingston, relieved that she wouldn't be reciprocating. Bernice had declined her offer, declaring that she was a city girl through and through. Besides, there was her boyfriend Tom to consider now.

Bernice's family took her around all the sights – the Museum, the Gallery, Brighton beach, St Kilda, Luna Park. She was enthralled with the two musicals they saw in town – *Kiss Me Kate* and *Guys and Dolls*. The two girls entertained the family with their school music – Cecilia accompanying Bernice's violin pieces and playing a few piano solos. Bernice's father arrived home one afternoon with the piano score of *Kiss Me Kate*. 'A present for you, Cecilia' he said. 'On the condition that we have a few sing-songs around the piano before you leave us. It's our favourite Shakespearean musical. Well, more like our favourite musical.' Cecilia stared at him, not understanding. '*Kiss Me Kate* is based on *The Taming of the Shrew*. It's in the bookcase if you want to borrow it.'

Bernice's Ballarat boyfriend, Tom, was staying nearby with relatives, having arrived the day before Cecilia was returning home. The three of them decided to see *Niagara* in town and were almost ready to leave when Bernice asked her if she minded her older brother Daniel joining them.

'He rarely goes anywhere with me,' she said, rolling her eyes. 'I think you're the attraction Celie. Do you mind?'

Cecilia didn't mind at all, having watched Danny out of the corner of her eye since she'd arrived.

'He's a bit shy,' Bernice said. 'He's never been out with a girl before.'

'We're both in the same boat then.'

She hardly spoke a word to him on the tram into the city or during the thriller, although she nearly grabbed his arm a few times during moments of suspense.

'How come the convent allows boarders to go out with boys?' Danny asked her, when they were sitting together in the tram on the way home.

Cecilia laughed. 'That'll be the day. Bernice just happened to meet Tom on our way to the cathedral where I'm learning the organ. We're not usually allowed out at all, but Alphonsus had to make an exception for us. Bernice helps with setting up the organ and turning the pages, and sometimes Tom joins us in the gallery. They just sit together and talk.'

'I really enjoyed your playing yesterday. I wish I could watch you in the gallery. Like Tom.'

She smiled. 'Not much chance of that.'

'So that's the only time Tom and Bernice ever see each other?'

'Yes. But she's working on something else. I guess if you were desperate you could sneak off for an hour or two at the weekend. As long as no one sees you.'

'When are you returning to Ballarat?'

'I'm going home to my family tomorrow until the beginning of the term.'

She thought he looked disappointed and was pleased.

'Do you like boarding school?'

'I'd prefer it to working on a farm for the rest of my life.'

'But do you like it?'

'No. I hate it. We've got some good teachers and some shockers, like any school, I suppose. I think we have the best music teachers in Victoria, including Mr Connelly, my organ teacher.' She paused for a few moments. 'I think everyone hates boarding. Well, maybe it's better at posh schools. The food's shocking, and you've heard what a freak Alphonsus is.'

They were silent for a while, watching passengers alight and board the tram, Danny pointing out places of interest along the way. The Melbourne Cricket Ground. The Yarra River. 'This is the tram stop for Xavier College,' he said.

'But you're at St Kevin's, aren't you? Isn't that further away?'

He nodded. 'One year to go. I can't wait.'

They passed Kew Junction until they reached the cemetery, where they got off.

'Can I write to you after you return to school?' Danny suddenly said as they walked towards his home. She was thrilled. It would be difficult. She'd never written a letter to a boy.

'They read all our letters, you know.'

'Bernice told me. I can't believe they do that.'

'Tom has a young sister at the convent who could pass your letters onto me. And vice-versa! It's how Bernice sends Tom messages.'

He grinned. 'Ah! The undercover emissary.'

'I won't have much to write about, although I suppose Al's latest pronouncements are always a bit of a laugh.'

Within a month of returning to school in 1955 as a Form 5 senior, Cecilia had something other than Alphonsus's latest proclamations to tell Danny in her letter. Mr Connelly was going to allow her to play for a wedding, but the best story was related to a funeral. Her practice time had been changed to an earlier free period when the cathedral was going to be unavailable one afternoon. Looking down from the balustrade, Cecilia noticed a sacristan stepping back from the altar to check her floral artistry. Lilies and votive candles were everywhere – the main altar, the side altar and every statue imaginable. A coffin covered in wreaths was before the main altar, a sign that there would be a Requiem Mass some time that day. The two girls were preparing the organ and music when they heard an army of footsteps lumbering in from the main entrance.

Bernice raced back to the balustrade. 'Celie,' she said. 'Come here. A chance to ogle the St Bernard's seniors. Look! A few good sorts down there!'

The boys, accompanied by four Brothers, were walking up the centre aisle towards the front of the church. Cecilia stared down at them, not the slightest bit interested. She only had eyes for Danny now, and he was miles away in Melbourne.

'Finally! An audience, Celie, after all your hard slog. Tom said one of the Brothers carked it. That'll be him in the coffin. Brother Henry! *Requiescant in pace.*'

'I'll drown them out when they start saying the rosary!'

'That gives me an idea. Don't do any warm-ups, Celie.' Bernice began setting up full diapason stops, coupling the Swell to Great with Great to Pedal. 'We'll scare the pants off them with the *Toccata and Fugue!*'

'No. I only know the first page from memory. And I've never played it flat out.'

Bernice ignored her. 'Here it is, Celie,' she said, placing the music on the stand.

'Well. I suppose Mr. Connelly's not around to hear me.'

'Quick, Celie. Before they start the rosary!'

In the console mirror, she noticed about ninety boys spread along the front rows. They were kneeling now, staring at the coffin. A few with rosary beads in their hands. Danny had wanted to hear her play. *If only you'd been there*, she told him in her letter.

The Toccata always sent shivery chills down her spine. Trying to master the sudden changes of stops and keyboards was quite a challenge, which was why she'd vowed to memorise it by the end of term. She liked to think of its three opening flourishes as bursts of thunder and lightning, the ensuing pause as the quiet before the storm, and the low, growling rumble of the pedal note under the slow, rolling chord, as a beast emerging from the bowels of the earth. Mr Connelly described the arpeggio as 'building up like a huge, billowing wave that comes crashing to shore.' It did exactly that, she thought as she glanced at the mirror again, the wave pummelling every boy and teacher to swivel around and look up at the gallery. Almost in fear. She held the chord at *fff* for as long as she dared. Surely its vibrations would crumble the cathedral's very foundations or at least awaken Brother Henry, *requiescant in pace.*

It was during the *prestissimo* triplets that her peripheral vision picked up Bernice at the balustrade giving the royal wave and grinning at her captive audience. A minute later, she was puckering her lips in the style of Marilyn Monroe; blowing kisses on the first beat of every bar and flinging her hands towards the boys. Cecilia was furious. She stopped playing halfway through the second page, which seemed as good a place as any to finish. So far, she'd only had to pedal the bass D and wasn't at all confident with any further footwork.

'Finally, you've been noticed Celie,' Bernice said as she grabbed Cecilia's hand and held it up. 'Just turn around and acknowledge your audience with a bow and smile like a proper virtuoso. Stand up otherwise they won't see you.'

Cecilia did so but wasn't happy about it. 'I can't believe you'd deliberately get us into trouble. I saw what you did. Al won't allow us here again. I'm on a scholarship. It's all very well for you.'

'It's okay Celie. I was just throwing kisses to Tom. Did you see those Brothers? They were grinning their heads off. They loved it. One almost applauded when you stopped. Bit of a change for the poor buggers. They must get bored out of their brains.'

'It doesn't matter. There's always someone. It'll get back to Alphonsus.'

'I'll bet you ten quid it won't. Boys don't dob like girls. Crawlers get bullied. Even the Brothers loathe them. And no old biddies were down there praying their knees off. I nearly fell over the balustrade looking.'

'Well. That's a relief!'

Bernice fossicked around in Cecilia's music. 'While we've got it on this setting, how about you stir them up with the Trumpet Voluntary so that Brother Henry gets a rapturous send-off. They'll sing your praises forever and ever Amen.'

Cecilia grinned, sighed and rolled her eyes as she launched into the triumphant fanfare of the voluntary. They would always be the best of friends, but sometimes she wondered if Bernice had chosen to remain at the convent because of Tom, rather than her. On the other hand, if it hadn't been for Bernice, she'd never have met Danny, Bernice's brother. She'd loved her week in Melbourne and would stay there forever if she could. Was she finally becoming a city mouse?

11

Molly

I can see why Alphonsus doesn't like us mixing with non-Catholics. A girl from my calisthenics club said that when Catholics have communion, we think we're eating Christ's body, so we're no better than the cannibals in New Guinea. They say other nasty things about Catholics which I ignore, but when someone said our church was based on fear of God, rather than love, I knew she was right. Love of God was never mentioned after my First Communion Day. It was all about fear and punishment from then on. Our bedtime prayer in the junior dormitory led by Sister Benjamin told us *I must die. I know not when, nor where, nor how, but if I die in Mortal Sin, I am lost forever.* On the wall was a large image of burnt black devils with pitchforks amid orange, yellowy-red flames shovelling sinners into the fiery pits of hell. I couldn't help thinking of Sister Benjamin as one of those devils. One night when I was coughing my heart out, she emerged from her cell to tell me that if I didn't stop, she'd beat me and put me outside. Terrified, I smothered myself deep down under the blankets to stifle my coughing for the rest of the night, surfacing and gasping for air like an underwater swimmer. It's a wonder I didn't suffocate. In Grade 3 and 4, fear ruled Benjamin's classroom. She gave the strap to those who couldn't parrot back the catechism exactly word for word. It was the same for mental arithmetic, for which during my two years with her, I missed the answer twice.

Reverend Mother Alphonsus is responsible for all the Mercy nuns in the Ballarat diocese. She does nothing about cruel nuns like Sister Benjamin, who are in all her schools. She's so obsessed with modesty and chastity she probably doesn't bother about anything else. At the beginning of Intermediate this year, we got the 'convent girls lying on the sacred parts of their bodies, sunbaking and splaying legs provocatively like lizards lazing in the summer sun,' lecture. If we must go swimming, 'someone should be waiting to wrap you up in a towel when you emerge from the water.'

'She'd need a tent,' Gabby whispered to me. 'She's jealous of us.'

Having seen Danny Kaye in *The Secret Life of Walter Mitty*, I feel better about daydreaming now. I picture Al at the beach in black neck-to-knees, starched white coif and bib encircling her face. Lolling around in the sand like a beached whale. Al likes to go on about how one should get up from the table feeling hungry, much to the boarders' disgust. They're always starving. I'm convinced Al became a nun so she could hide her blubber under all those robes.

'God did not intend bodies for displays given by the likes of Hollywood hussies who bare themselves to expose their darkened souls,' she pontificated during one assembly. 'The sacred parts of girls' bodies have become objects of beauty rather than function.' With magician-like sleight of hand, she produced a boarder's writing-pad featuring a glossy Marilyn, her scarlet waist-deep neckline moulded to her skin.

'What thoughts must be in Our Blessed Lady's mind when she looks down on this wanton with a face straight from Satan's paintbox? A hussy whose apparel clings like a slithering snake ready to burst out of its skin,' she said in an aggrieved tone.

A few wanting-to-please girls proffered their responses about immodesty and vulgarity until a senior thrashed her hand among the sycophants.

'Our Lady *could* be thinking that Marilyn needs a darker shade of lipstick and more eye-shadow, Mother,' she volunteered with an innocent smirk.

Al is never sure what to say when someone gets the better of her. During the stifled sniggers, she extended her mountainous bosom to its maximum as she breathed in, compressed her lips in grim determination, and severed the offending part of Marilyn's anatomy from the neck down. There was a collective gasp around the hall. Gabby and I sometimes play 'hangnun' during Al's diatribes, but we pricked up our ears when she mentioned 'non-Catholic pharmacies selling lewd and disgusting commodities for girls.' Our only purchases at pharmacies were Kotex sanitary pads. Did she want us to go back to wearing rags like they did in the olden days? Gabby's mother said Al must have been referring to the latest thing called tampons, which could be inserted inside our bodies to absorb blood. We wondered how you'd go about confessing to using them.

Perhaps, inadvertently, the hotel customers baiting me about the church make me think differently about religion. Have I developed my own conscience? Am I allowed to have my own conscience or is the church our conscience? Perhaps hotel life, so contrary to my school life, has given me another view of the world. At school when we pray for the conversion of the world to Catholicism because of the evils of communism, I remain silent. I don't want the world to become Catholic or communist. There are so many rules in the church which must be obeyed without question. Do most of the girls in my class blindly accept everything we are told about the church, or do some of them think like me, but say nothing. Why should we go to hell for eating meat on Fridays? Not that it bothers me because I love fish and chips. It's just strange that it's in the same category as murder. I once asked Rosario if she thought God was unfair for sending Catholics to hell if they missed Mass on Sundays or ate meat on Fridays whereas Protestants had no such rule. She nearly sent me to Alphonsus. I never asked her any more questions after that.

I was pleased that I wasn't the only one who queried religion. When I dropped into the cathedral gallery one Friday after school, Cecilia asked me if I happened to notice that a memorial photograph of Arthur Calwell's son on the wall above the piano in the assembly hall had been removed.

I shook my head. 'I was probably too wrapped up in the Chopin you were playing.'

'Someone said there's been a split in the Labor Party. Have you heard that?'

I nodded, wondering what on earth it had to do with the photograph. 'Our parish priest at St Alban's said that Catholics shouldn't vote for the Labor Party in the next election because they support communists.'

'I told you Celie,' Bernice interrupted. 'It's the Catholics versus the commos. Calwell's staying put in the Labor Party which is why the old cow removed his son's photograph. What a bigoted old witch. A few of the nuns here would have taught that poor boy.'

Cecilia looked upset. 'I can't believe she'd do something like that over religion. At home we've got a photograph on the piano of my two little brothers who drowned. I always think of them before I start playing. It's the same at assemblies. I'd look up at that photo and think of that poor little boy, and how sad his parents must be.'

'I asked my brother about that photograph once because the boy was wearing the Villa Maria uniform,' I said. 'Tony knew him from when he was boarding there. He said he died of leukemia.'

'So sad,' Bernice said. 'But worse is how religion twists people.'

Sometimes I drop into my own parish church on a Friday afternoon because unlike the cathedral, it's right on my way home. It might seem a contradiction after everything I've been saying about religion, but this year, my Intermediate year, St Alban's has become a sort of a refuge. I don't rattle off prayers. I'm delaying my return to the pub on the busiest day of the week. The calm before the storm. Time to myself before returning to the raucous voices; the clink of glasses; the cigarette smoke; the smell of beer. It's as noisy as a circus sometimes! I love the peace and serenity of a silent church; the candles and perfumed flowers; the statues that will never come to life and ask me to do more jobs. Today there is a lingering fragrance of incense from Benediction. It takes me back to the parish church in St. Arnaud; the fragrance from the aromatic burning of incense from the altar boys as they processed along the aisle, swinging the thurible; the priest in his long golden cape holding a gold crucifix on high as he entered the sanctuary; flowers and candles in candelabras all over the huge marble altar; altar boys tinkling the sanctus bells as though something magical was about to happen. As a child, I lived in hope that one day, when the priest turned around to expose the host encased in the gold-spiked monstrance, he'd perform a magic trick like Merlin the Magician. His luxurious gold cloak and mysterious hand movements certainly suggested some sort of wizardry. I don't go to Benediction anymore because it's not compulsory.

It's the last day of Term 2. I'm not in my Walter Mitty or Alice mode as I sit in a pew near the side entrance of St Alban's.

I'm making resolutions for a change. I'll see a film or two with Gabby. I'm going to practise the piano every day so that I get an Honour instead of a Credit. I'll go to the library where I can study in peace and quiet. I've decided to become a language teacher. There's a shortage of teachers, so if I study hard during the next two years, I might get a scholarship, which means I can live in a university college. I can't think of anything better than going to Melbourne to get away from the pub and my parents.

I'm sitting here in the church thinking about all this, when I have a weird feeling that someone is watching me. My spine seems to be vibrating. Shimmying. I must have goose bumps. I look up at the statue of St Joseph near the side entrance. No! He hasn't come to life, and no one's hiding behind him. The only sound is two old ladies in the front pew murmuring the rosary. Beyond them, the sacristy door is slightly ajar. I look across the church to the two confessionals on the other side. The purple curtains in the centre. One of them is rustling. My skin tingles. The hairs on the back of my neck must be standing on end. Why would anyone want to hide in a place that's smaller than a telephone box? I look again and heave a sigh of relief. The curtain appears to be moving, but I realise it's a trick of the light. The last rays of the late afternoon sun are slanting and flickering through a stained-glass window. I've got the jitters. I must be subconsciously thinking of the scary film I saw last week. *Gaslight*. The flame of the gas lamp flickering and creeping down the walls like moving shadows, its mantle gradually glowing white. I realise I'm panicking over nothing and stand up to leave. For some reason after I genuflect, I turn around to look behind me. I'm sure there's a shadowy figure in the darkness of the alcove behind the baptismal font, but there's no way I'm hanging around to check it out.

12

Jeanne

French, the International language, was taught from Form 1 to Form 6 at St Martin's College. Jeanne, during her second year as a novice in 1953, had taken over from the elderly Sister Winifred in the senior school. The following year, she decided that students did better with comprehension and conversation based on the recall of lyrics from poems. There was something about rhythm and rhyme that prompted the memory. One of the big changes she made was full French immersion for Form 5 and Form 6. 'Just like it was for me with English when I arrived here in Form 5,' Jeanne told her students. 'A lot of guesswork!' Occasionally she relented.

They asked about Paris and *la guerre*. How did it affect her family? What did they call the Germans? Did she ever see Hitler and his soldiers? Rather than give them a direct translation if they didn't understand, she acted the word like a game of charades, giving them hints by changing her facial expression.

They asked her to sing something that was popular during the war. She sang the first verse of *Lily Marlène*. 'Some of you might know the English version, but it's unlikely to be exactly the same,' she warned them. 'The overall sentiment is similar, because it's a love song, but a translation must accommodate rhyme, rhythm, and context. She sang it slowly the second time so they could write down every phrase. The song was once *un poème*, written by a German, she told them.

'It became an international hit when another German turned it into a song during the Second World War. The Germans banned it, thinking it wasn't militaristic enough,' she said demonstrating a marching stance with Hitler salute, moustache and all. The girls laughed. She knew that humour in the classroom – rarely used in the convent – opened shuttered minds. The key that allowed teachers to reach out to the unmotivated.

She played recordings of Charles Trenet songs her mother brought for her on visiting days. 'He was one of France's most famous singers and songwriters and wrote *Douce France* to sweeten the sufferings of the French people during the war.'

The girls loved imitating his crooning style, particularly with his internationally popular song, *La mer*. They told her he was a little like Frank Sinatra. 'Except that Trenet wrote everything he sang,' she reminded them. When appropriate, she played games, and taught songs and poems with actions as an aid to memory. One afternoon, there was a letter for her on the desk which she read before her lesson. *Dear Sister Jeanne. We think you are the best teacher we've ever had. You make learning a foreign language fun.* It was written in French, and signed, *Your appreciative students.*

She smiled. 'Thank you, girls. I'll rewrite your message on the board and underline your grammatical errors. Don't be offended.'

Jeanne's students were so motivated that the school took out the top prizes in *dictée* and poetry in the Victorian *Alliance Française* competitions in 1954. Their results in the state public examinations in French improved so dramatically that the convent was awarded a special commendation from the French Embassy. Jeanne wasn't bothered that Mother Alphonsus didn't congratulate her. Praise was reserved for the school in general, never the individual. Praise led to conceit, self-adulation, egotism.

Deeply committed to her students and her teaching career, Jeanne felt humbled by these young girls, eager to learn and please her. At times she wondered if she was closer to the girls than to her colleagues. No one else was in the staffroom when Sister Dominique smilingly held out her hand to congratulate Jeanne on her outstanding results in the *Alliance Française* competition.

'Virtually no unruly students here to speak of, so perhaps that makes our job easier,' Jeanne replied modestly.

'To a certain extent,' Dominique said. 'The difference is, you enthuse them. I heard about it on the grapevine, although the convent will take credit when the Bishop hands out the prizes on Speech Night. You're the youngest to achieve results like this, Jeanne.'

'But you get good results in science! And you're not much older than me.'

'Ancient. Twenty-seven next July. And you?'

'Twenty-three next Wednesday,' Jeanne said.

'Then it'll be a double celebration on Sunday what with your outstanding results and commendation. You'll be telling your parents, won't you?'

Jeanne nodded. 'Yes. I suppose I'll be committing one of the seven deadly sins.'

Dominique frowned.

'Pride, of course!' Jeanne laughed.

'Alphonsus might think so, but you're really just sharing the good news.'

'Maman is making a *croquembouche* for my birthday. She's learnt how to make choux pastry.'

Dominique frowned.

'You'll see on Sunday,' Jeanne said grinning.

When Jeanne was serving the *croquembouche* to the nuns on Sunday evening, Dominique asked casually if they were for special occasions.

'The little custard pastry balls are called profiteroles, and are served at restaurants for a dessert, but the whole cake, the *croquembouche*, was invented by a French pastry chef in the eighteenth century. They're normally reserved for weddings or special celebrations like baptisms or Holy Communion,' Jeanne said, not daring to mention the word *birthday*.

Age is not mentioned amongst the nuns. Birthdays are never acknowledged or celebrated, although when a parent brought a special cake on visiting day, the nuns suspected a birthday was imminent. One of them said the *croquembouche* ran rings around 'those fruit cakes encased in concrete.'

On the evening of Jeanne's twenty-third birthday the following Wednesday, Jeanne was supervising senior homework when Dominique entered the classroom. 'Could I have a word please Sister?' she said seriously. Together they walked to the corridor. Dominique quickly glanced around, pressed Jeanne close, and kissed her on each cheek in the French style, mimicking the Rousseau family in the convent parlour on visiting day. She handed Jeanne a card, and with a whispered '*Joyeux anniversaire*,' she disappeared into the darkness in a flash, as if in an apparition. Jeanne was momentarily taken aback. When she opened the card at her desk, she saw that Dominique had drawn a *croquembouche* decorated with smiling lips of red profiteroles, the topmost one adorned with a tiny *tricolore*. The caramel toffee threads were in the shape of a nun's veil, dark strands of hair blowing in the wind. The message underneath said *Joyeux anniversaire et félicitations*, and a note in English. 'The two chocolate almonds are your beautiful brown eyes, the pale sugared ones for your sweetness and charm.'

Other than cards the previous Sunday from her relatives, Dom's was the only other birthday card she'd received. Being hand-made and from a colleague, Jeanne felt it was special. Her eyes moistened. She blinked and gulped as she read the card over and over. Yes. That's what had been bothering her. Emotions. She'd been protecting herself against them. Closing them down. Well, most of them, depending on the situation. Fear. Anger. Pride. Wonder. Indignation. Love. They were put on hold at the convent. Frozen into a glacier, some melting a little on visiting day. Others never put aside. Like shame and guilt. There was love of God, wasn't there? Or was it more about vengeance and punishment. About guilt and shame rather than love. She swept her thoughts aside. Nuns were not supposed to think like this. It was bordering on doubt.

'We have a connection, *ma soeur*,' Dom said when Jeanne thanked her the following day.

'In what way?'

'French.'

'Really, or should I say *vraiment*?'

'Think about it.' Dominique smiled. 'I told you my birthday's in July.'

'Ah. Your birthday's on July 14th. Bastille Day.'

'*Exactement*. It's why I chose a French saint when I entered the convent.' She shrugged. 'My parents knew nothing about the French Revolution or Bastille Day when I was baptised. 'How many Australians do? I learnt about it in French, then History.'

Despite the rule about friendships, Jeanne knew she had a connection with this nun. Other nuns had special friends although it was against the rules. Now was her chance to ask Dominique a few questions. 'What happened to your predecessor, Sister Agatha? She taught me science in Forms 5 and 6.'

'She left! Agatha's the only reason I'm teaching science here now, otherwise I'd probably be in a country convent.' She looked at Jeanne as if deciding whether she could trust her. 'But in answer to your question, she ran off with one of the priests from the cathedral. Agatha's birth-name is Paula. Mum smuggles her letters into my pockets when she visits. She's happily married now with two children.'

Jeanne had heard similar stories and although it had never shocked her, she knew it brought shame and disgrace on the convent. It was interesting too that Dom admitted to receiving smuggled letters. Perhaps one day that could come in handy. Presently, she only asked her family for anything related to teaching. Only the previous week, Jeanne's brother Paul and sister-in-law, Andrea, had arrived unexpectedly on visiting day from Melbourne. Having recently visited Paris for a medical convention, their car was loaded down with presents. Paul handed Jeanne a poetry anthology and some recordings of French songs.

'Early Christmas gifts,' he said. 'Just in case we don't get a chance to come up again before Christmas.'

Sofia asked him if he was able to get the book she'd wanted.

Paul pulled a wry face. '*Oui maman!* With great difficulty. It's in the car.'

Jeanne wanted to know the title.

'It's called *L'histoire d'O*,' Paul said, looking at his mother and grinning. He switched to French. 'Not for nuns. A very hot book in France at the moment. If a copy made its way here…'

'It would spontaneously combust' Claude said, making nearby visitors turn around at their resounding laughter.

Paul grinned. 'As only an electrical engineer would know.'

'It sounds like you've already read it,' Sofia said.

'*Bien sûr, maman!* Both Andrea and me! We had to have something to read on that long plane trip back. I still find it hard to believe that it was written by a woman. Did you know it was awarded the French literature prize '*Prix des Deux Magots*?'

Sofia nodded, turning to Jeanne. 'Let me know if you'd ever like to read it, *chérie!*'

Jeanne smiled. 'By the sound of it, I don't think so, maman.'

'I believe it's beautiful writing. Very poetic. Pure fantasy, of course. Camille recommended it, but she says there's too much emphasis on women being expected to please the male.'

Paul and Andrea began talking to Claude about their trip, but Sofia turned back to her daughter. 'You might find this hard to believe, *chérie*, but I blame myself sometimes that you entered the convent.'

Jeanne's eyes widened. 'Maman! What are you talking about?'

'I should have given you more *romans permissifs et érotiques* like the one we've been talking about. Perhaps you wouldn't be in this parlour right now if I'd done so.' She shrugged, looking a little embarrassed. 'I know I explained the facts of life to you and gave you a book on the subject. But I never discussed... Well. Women's pleasure!'

'But maman, one didn't really speak about that sort of thing, surely! And as far as I know, nothing's changed.'

'Well, no. At the time, I suppose I probably decided that the book I gave you would do, but now I know that anything like that is mostly from a man's perspective. How girls should please men. Men's gratification. Rarely from a woman's point of view. Women are expected to be child-bearers and housekeepers for their husbands.' She paused for a long moment. 'As well as that, society assumes all women are born maternal and want to bear children. We forget that some, like you, may not have that instinct.'

Jeanne wasn't sure how to respond to this.

'If you ever change your mind, *chérie*, I've got a few books you could borrow. They're quite an education. Even at my age!'

Ironically, it was a book by another French author that turned Jeanne's life around, Mother Alphonsus having inadvertently brought this about by her interminable rules. As a former day-scholar at St Martin's, Jeanne had little to do with boarders and the restrictions imposed on them until Mother Phillip told her to supervise the unpacking of luggage in the Form 5 dormitory when the girls returned after the Christmas holidays.

'But why, Mother?' she asked, surprised.

'They bring back books! Just remind the girls to label them before placing them on the trolley. They know the rules!'

'Books? They're not allowed to keep them, Mother?'

'Mother Alphonsus will check them for suitability and most will be returned. A few girls bring back rubbish which will be confiscated. Don't worry too much if you miss anything, Sister. I'll be going through the lockers while they're in class.'

Searching through their personal belongings? Were the boarders aware of that? Would she like anyone going through her things? Not that she had anything to hide. She greeted the girls as they straggled in with their luggage in ones and twos. They placed their clothing in their lockers, excited to see each other again and comparing their books before stacking them on the trolley. Jeanne introduced herself to a new girl, explaining the rule about the books.

'Well I won't be doing that, Sister,' she said. 'I refuse to be treated like a child.'

'I can't argue about the convent's rules, Yvonne,' Jeanne said. 'But Mother Phillip will be searching the lockers.'

Yvonne looked horrified. 'But that's invading my privacy! In any case, I think my book is inappropriate for nuns. I... I borrowed it from my mother. Could you mind it for me please Sister? Until the end of term?'

'Very well, Yvonne. You must remind me.'

The girl reluctantly handed the book to Jeanne, who slipped it into one of the deep pockets of her habit.

Later in the staffroom, she looked at it – *The Second Sex*. From the date on it, the translation was very recent. She remembered her mother talking about *Le deuxième sexe* to her father years ago and how she wanted to order it. Hadn't there been a scandal relating to Simone de Beauvoir, its author? She read the synopsis on the dustcover. *De Beauvoir passionately articulates her central argument that women have been objectified and defined only in relation to men in a massive critical analysis of misogyny over several millenia.*

Women being objectified? Wouldn't Reverend Mother Alphonsus agree with those sentiments? Perhaps the Vatican banned the book, preferring to hide the power the church wielded over women. What would Sister Aquinas think of the quote about her namesake? *Woman is an occasional and incomplete being, a misbegotten male. Were it not for procreation, another man would be always of more help to a man than a woman.* She flicked open another page on which there were several quotes she could scarcely believe. Saint Alphonsus said *A woman could only achieve sanctity if she became male.* And Saint John the Apostle. *Amongst all the savage beasts, none is found as harmful as woman.* What did they think of their own mothers and sisters? *A misbegotten male?* Where was the logic in that? Was Aquinas saying that God made a mistake in creating woman? Further on, De Beauvoir said that *Christianity and its clergy served to subordinate women.* How many nuns taking on names of male saints were aware of their namesakes' attitude to women? Just as well she'd chosen a female saint's name. A woman who'd saved France from

English rule; who had led thousands of men to war. But after all that, she was murdered by the clergy.

Jeanne wondered why it had taken her so long to realise that the world revolved around men. Australian women may have been given the vote fifty years ago, but how long would it be before they really caught up with men? In marriage, the women promised to love, honour and obey and must accept the male's surname at marriage. As *Mrs Claude Rousseau*, her mother was not supposed to have ambitions beyond the domestic. Jeanne remembered *maman* sounding off about the practice of parents having to pay for their daughters' weddings; how females received a tiny portion or none of their inheritance because they were expected to marry. At university, Jeanne and her friends agreed that women were disadvantaged from the moment they left school. They couldn't apply for a bank loan. They were paid two-thirds of a male salary and were unlikely to hold senior positions in government schools or the public service, being forced to resign upon marriage. Women could easily get a job in a bank, but how many became bank tellers or managers? Perhaps there was a subconscious reason for her becoming a nun, after all. Like the Abbesses in Mediaeval times setting up Priories to be independent of men. Was there an underlying reason for her not wanting to marry? Perhaps she didn't want to be ruled by men! Her parents had a beautiful caring and sharing relationship. No one ruled *their* marriage.

'One of the hardest things about teaching is trying not to have a pet,' Dominique said to Jeanne one afternoon in the staff room during their shared free period.

'I suppose so. Who are you thinking of?' Jeanne said.

'Cecilia. She's got a lot of potential. But she'll probably make music her career rather than science.'

'Molly's my favourite. And my top student. She's such a natural. As soon as I gave the girls a new poem for the *Alliance Française*, she knew all twelve verses by heart in a flash. And without a trace of an accent. She's got an incredible ear.'

'She's not quite so good at science. Probably not interested.'

'To change the subject totally, have you ever heard of a book called *The Second Sex*?'

Dom shook her head.

'I confiscated it from Yvonne when I was on dorm duty. It's full of moral ambiguities,' Jeanne said. 'And men making too many decisions in life.'

Dominique guffawed. 'Don't you mean making all the decisions in life? Did you know that 85% of saints are men and 75% of them were priests? Not much of a chance for us, is there?'

'I've never really thought about it before.'

Dominique grinned. 'You're excused for reading the book because you're checking it out, aren't you? Saving Alphonsus the trouble.'

Jeanne couldn't believe what she was hearing. Had she found someone to confide in at last?

'And now that we've been given a torch each so we don't fall over and break a leg on the way to the bathroom in the middle of the night like poor old Benjy,' continued Dominique, 'you can always read in bed. Just scrounge a few extra torch batteries from your family like I do. Can I have the book when you've finished? Then I'll lend you some of mine you might find even more interesting.'

The two nuns looked at each other conspiratorially and grinned. Something seemed to pass between them. It was as if they had an unspoken pact. Jeanne felt a warmth for Dom that she knew she could not suppress. A bond that seemed to be undeniable.

13

The Priest

It was now August – four months after he'd moved back to his hometown to become a curate at St Alban's. Surely it wasn't too soon to broach the subject of having his own study. Mrs Rawlings had shut the door into the dining-room to clatter away in the kitchen with the breakfast dishes, and Father O'Doherty was on his way to Melbourne despite his doctor telling him he shouldn't be driving. Father Bourke had just finished reading the Ballarat Courier.

'I can't get over the number of spare bedrooms in this presbytery, Bob. Bit of a waste,' Hilton said, recalling one of his brothers going on about how he wouldn't mind a house half the size of the presbytery for his large family.

'If you reckon this is big, think of the Bishop's Palace. Anyway, the parish is growing. We'll have another priest soon. Maybe two after O'Doherty's gone to the knackery.'

Hilton decided it was now or never. 'I wonder what you think of a simple alteration to convert the bedroom next to mine into an adjoining study, Bob?'

'And your own private entrance off the veranda? Like mine on the other side? Of course, mine was built into the original design. I only needed an internal connecting door for my two rooms.'

Plus your own bathroom. Almost a separate flat, Hilton wanted to say. Instead, he tried to look as though the idea of having an external entrance had never occurred to him. 'An external door?' he said enthusiastically. 'That would be very convenient. With the sacristy and the side entrance of the church being on the right-hand side of my bedroom, I think it makes much more sense. Save me having to go through the kitchen and back porch every time.'

'There's always the front door,' Father Bourke said.

Hilton had a feeling he was teasing him. 'Well, yes. Of course. Although the front entrance is very public. With all those spare rooms, I was thinking I could have my own study for visitors and to spread my belongings.'

'And your wings?' the parish priest asked a little lecherously. 'Well, the money shouldn't be a problem, especially if you raise it yourself!'

Hilton stared at him. Surely he was joking! 'You mean telling the parishioners what it's for?'

'Not quite,' he grinned. 'It could come under charity. Sometimes they need to be reminded that the box with the little white envelopes in the vestibule is not an ornament. It's not exactly a law of the church to give a tithe like the protestants do, but they need to be reminded that their pennies on the Sunday plate scarcely cover the church expenditure like the electricity bill, or the flowers and candles etcetera. Some churches have resorted to shaming parishioners into giving more money by reading out a weekly list of names and amounts from the pulpit of those who *have* donated. It shames others into donating.' He laughed. 'We could make it a mortal sin if they don't pay up.'

Hilton felt disillusioned now. It would take forever rather than a few weeks. He'd never seen the church accounts, but he knew St Alban's was a mixture of poor and well-off parishioners. 'I suppose I could get someone to organise a raffle for charity,' he said lamely.

'Nothing like that! Relate your sermon to the scriptures. I use the one from Matthew 25: 35. *I was hungry and you gave me something to eat. I was thirsty, and you gave me something to drink. I was a stranger and you took me into your home.* You must know others that are still fresh in your mind from the seminary.'

There was one that sprang to mind immediately. Philippians 2:3-4. *Do not be interested only in your own life, but care about the lives of others too.* Better still, there was one he'd read recently in the newspaper from Billy Graham. *God has given us two hands, one to receive with and the other to give with.* He could modify it in some way so that it would look original.

'Of course, it's up to you whether you want to use the hellfire and brimstone approach, or friendly persuasion.' Bob gave a broad grin. 'Don't look like that. I'm joking. There's plenty of money in the coffers, so you can start right now if you like. No one queries anything we do. But it still wouldn't hurt you to do the sermon on charity.'

Hilton was overjoyed. 'Really? You mean it?'

'Why not? Follow me.'

He steered Hilton into the large bedroom opposite the sacristy. 'It'll be easy to convert this into a study and to have a connecting door into your bedroom. All it needs is a few bricks knocked out alongside this window for a new outside door. See what the architect says. Brian Cleary's the one the church uses. A good Catholic!'

Hilton couldn't believe it was this easy to convince his parish priest.

'And who might your visitors be?' Bourke asked him as they left the bedroom.

'Well,' Father Kelly stumbled. 'I... I know a few people in Ballarat. My family's here, of course.'

'You're lucky, aren't you? You'll always have somewhere to go if a parishioner doesn't invite you on Sunday. What takes your fancy?' He nudged his curate. 'What age do you like? They'll go for you with your mane of dark hair, and that suntan from all your golf and tennis.'

Hilton felt himself reddening and suddenly realised that Bourke knew all about his 'indiscretion' at his previous parish, just as he knew about Bourke and other priests in the diocese. The word soon got around.

'Vocational counselling works for most of us,' Bourke said with a lecherous wink. 'Easy with boys, of course. And if you're buying grog, for God's sake don't buy it in Ballarat. And dress in civvies when you do.'

Boys? Of course, it was easy with boys! Altar boys! Choir boys! But he was interested in girls. Adolescents. Occasionally, he'd seen one or two convent girls call into the church after school to 'pay a visit,' particularly on a Friday. He noticed the sacristan, Mrs McKinnon, carrying a large bucket of flowers into the sacristy, and vaguely wondered why she didn't return in the morning to do the flowers. He'd only just begun to realise how much one sacristan had to do in a large church. All unpaid work for the honour and glory of God. They arranged the liturgical books, the vestments, the candles, and everything required for special celebrations. Cruets, ciboria, chalices, linens, oils. Then there was the supply of fresh hosts, wine, hand towels and the incense and coals for the thurible used in Benediction. Just setting up the altar for daily Mass must take at least half an hour and longer on Sundays, depending on whose feast day it was. Then they cleared everything away after Mass while the priests socialised with their flock, who invited them home for the Sunday roast.

'You have an enormous job, Mrs McKinnon' Hilton told her one Friday afternoon. 'It's wonderful that you give so much of your time to the church.'

'Thank you, Father. I enjoy it.'

'I didn't realise that after Friday morning Mass, you had to return in the afternoon. Why don't you do the flowers tomorrow morning before Mass?'

'The flowers for the week are delivered on Friday, Father. If left 'til Saturday, I'd need to get here at 5.30 in the morning to prepare for Mass and the weddings.'

'So after setting up for Mass on Friday mornings, you return later to remove the old flowers and arrange the fresh flowers for the week?'

'Yes Father,' she said. 'Shortly after the florist delivers them. Otherwise they'll wilt.'

'You deserve a medal,' he said magnanimously as she moved off to attend to the side altar. An idea was beginning to emerge in his mind. He wouldn't tell her until he thought it through. She could train someone else to do the Friday flowers. He'd arrange it. He wouldn't give her a choice. Sacristans could be quite proprietorial.

As if in accordance with his thoughts, he noticed a young girl enter the church by the side door. Wasn't she the one who had confessed to stealing? The one he'd seen the previous Friday. He stared at her as she genuflected. Surely she was the image of the girl in the folio! The Guerin portrait had come to life. From where he was standing, he knew she could not see him staring at her. In any case, she seemed to be in another world. Sitting rather than kneeling. Eyes half-closed. Relaxing rather than praying. Well, it was Friday. The end of the school week. He made his way to the presbytery parlour. As soon as he saw her leaving from the side door about fifteen minutes later, he left via the front door, and began walking casually across the lawn.

'Hello,' he said, as though they were meeting accidentally. 'I see you're from St Martin's. I'm wondering if Sister Stanislaus is still there.'

The girl thought for a moment. 'I've heard her name, Father. Perhaps she teaches in the Primary School. Or one of the parish schools.'

'Will you tell her that Father Kelly says hello if you ever come across her?'

'Yes, Father,' she said politely. 'Although we rarely see the Primary School teachers.'

'And what's your name?' he said.

'Molly, Father. Molly Harrington.'

'Molly,' he said. 'I could be wrong, but sometimes I see someone passing by on Saturdays with a metal rod in her hands who looks a little like you.'

Molly brightened. 'It was probably me, Father. I would have been on my way to calisthenics. Unless it was Brigid or Veronica, my sisters. We go at different times because we're all in different groups.'

'What on earth is calisthenics?'

'It's a bit of everything,' she said, seemingly flattered by his interest. 'It's dance and exercise to music. Sometimes with rods or clubs. Marching. Plastiques. Folk Dancing. Song and actions or song and dance.' She frowned. 'Oh,' she said enthusiastically. 'There's the Gym Spec which stands for gymnastic spectacular where we do all sorts of acrobatic things.'

He feigned enthusiasm. 'Sounds like fun.' He wondered how she managed to steal money without her father knowing. 'And your family? They're all parishioners here?'

'Yes, Father,' Molly said warily.

'And where does your father work?'

'He's the licensee for The Barkly, Father.'

Ah. The run-down Sir Henry Barkly Hotel two blocks away. Her father probably made a fortune from illegal gambling. Starting Price or SP betting they called it, didn't they? He'd stash it all away somewhere because they can't bank their winnings. He wouldn't miss the few quid his daughter stole.

'Well. Nice to meet you Molly.'

He continued on into the church. Yes. She was perfect. But he wouldn't rush things this time.

14

Molly

In the middle of English in Intermediate, a nun I've never seen before whispered something to Sister Isobel, then beckoned me to follow her. 'You must address the Bishop as *My Lord* if he speaks to you,' she said. 'And never turn your back on him!'

A Bishop? Turn my back on him? Oh my God! Did that mean I had to walk backwards? And why did the Bishop want to see me? As a day-scholar, I wasn't familiar with this part of the convent. I couldn't quite believe what I was seeing when the nun opened the parlour door. My father, my three-year-old sister Katy, and my mother, her face partly obscured by my baby brother, were all seated on velvet-covered chairs. Brigid and Veronica were standing near them. Alphonsus and a flap of nuns were smiling obsequiously at Uncle Michael and his friend Bishop O'Collins, the Bishop of Ballarat. To my great disappointment, he wore a crimson biretta and cassock, rather than the resplendent jewelled mitre and gold cope he wore at my confirmation.

Nuns were running everywhere like ants on a hot brick path. Taking the Bishop's hand and kissing his ornate ruby ring, the sign of his ecclesiastical authority. Bowing and backing away from him as though he were the Pope himself. I knew that nuns always acted in a reverential manner in the presence of priests, but this was the royal court. They were positively fawning. It's a wonder I hadn't been told to curtsy.

Reverend Mother Alphonsus and other nuns waddled around the clerics, pandering and subordinating themselves to the needs of their male superiors. Smiling nuns were delivering polished silver teapots and matching trays laden with delicate sandwiches, butterfly cream cakes, an ornate crimson and gold tea set, and milk jugs with bead-weighted crocheted doilies. None of it for us lowly students, of course. We convulsed when Katy, after feasting her eyes on the exotic spread with an unwavering stare, was offered a cream cake by the Bishop and replied, 'Thank you, your Majesty.'

Alphonsus had undergone a personality change. Smiling, congenial, speaking to us three girls as though we were the royal princesses. She purred over my sisters' scholastic progress, and my foreign language prowess in such terms that I was confused more than amazed. Flattery and praise would have to be about as rare as her riding a bicycle, so I stood there looking stupid.

'A puking pretentious Hollywood performance if ever there was one,' I whispered to Brigid after I sidled backwards towards them. Puking was the 'in' word with my class that year.

Mum sat silently, probably relieved that she had baby Patrick to distract her from the proceedings. She smiled nervously, looking like she wanted the world to swallow her up. She wore the floral frock I'd brought home 'on apro' from Myers. It fitted her perfectly. I stared at her and suddenly realised how beautiful she was. She could have been a film star except she was too thin. Almost as frail as Sister Angela, my elderly piano teacher. I wondered how Dad managed to get her to the convent. Mum would have been so anxious about coming here she'd have been vomiting all morning. I don't understand why she does that.

'Katy sings like an angel,' Uncle Michael boasted to the nuns and the Bishop.

How did he know that? Was Mum teaching her while we were at school? It wouldn't be nursery rhymes.

Mother Alphonsus extended her *I know what you're up to* lips into a gracious Bishop-pleasing smile. 'Perhaps she should sing for us now,' she gushed.

I wondered if she knew Mum had been a dancer at the Tivoli. She seems to know everything else that's going on in Ballarat. And what did she think of Dad being a publican when she exhorted us all to take the Pioneer Pledge of total abstinence from 'Lucifer's liquor?' I didn't need anyone telling me that. The drunks and the smell are enough to put me off alcohol until eternity.

Katy's clear confident voice rang through the parlour as she began dramatising *She Wears Red Feathers*, a popular song the customers sometimes asked me to play. Uncle Michael interrupted, ordering Katy to start again with me accompanying. I was reluctant. This sort of music belonged in the hotel, not a convent parlour.

I sat down at the piano and hammered out the tom-tom rhythm of the bass fifths. Katy was in her illusory grass skirt, arms waving and hips swaying in imitation of ocean waves and the trees in the breeze to *She Wears Red Feathers And A Huley Huley Skirt*. She indicated the coconuts up in the tree – *She lives on just cokey-nuts*. Clamping her hands together, she imitated the fish swishing around, *And fish by the sea*. Her smile was Marilyn Monroe seductive as she gestured towards her hair and eyes. '*With a rose in her hair, and a gleam in her eye*,' she finished with her hands over her heart and a saucy swing of her hips '*and love in her heart for me, boom boom boom boom boom boom*.'

I have to admit that she sang it very well, but I was *so* embarrassed. The Bishop and Uncle Michael applauded rapturously. My father seemed to have enjoyed the performance. Mum wore a pained but proud face. Unsure if the nuns would approve. They tapped their hands together politely, appearing to have appreciated it, but glancing warily at Alphonsus who attempted a seraphic smile and deferential applause to ingratiate herself with the Bishop. I know *her* views on song and dance. When she discovered we sisters were learning calisthenics, she called me to her office to bleat about jezebels performing depraved popular songs and dances, immediately sending me into Walter Mitty mode. Al leapt onto the stage to become the can-can soloist; performing high kicks and cartwheels; showing off her frilly white pantaloons over her black stockings; pirouetting around like the hippos in *Fantasia* and flouncing onto centre stage to finish with the splits. Her white bib doesn't budge an inch until she tears it off in a flourish at the end to toss it at the cheering audience. I must have inadvertently smiled at the time because she accused me of being impudent and told me to wipe the smile off my face.

A week after the 'hula' incident, a deluge kept us inside the classroom for lunch. We were sitting around as bored as statues when Gabby reminded everyone that I could play anything they wanted. Not just exam pieces. They circled around the piano while I played pop tunes and rags. They sang at the tops of their voices. *Rock Around The Clock, Melodie d'amour, The Great Pretender, Skokkian.* All the melodies I'd heard from the customers or on the radio. When someone began singing *Unchained Melody,* I changed to a more suitable key because she'd pitched it too high. A few fifth form boarders on their way back from lunch were standing at the door looking like they wanted to join in.

Cecilia wandered over to the piano. 'Molly, how on earth do you play their requests and modulate so smoothly in the middle of a song?'

I shrugged. 'I've been doing it forever.'

During my next piano lesson, there was a tap on the door. It was Cecilia.

'Ah, yes Cecilia,' Sister Angela said. 'I haven't mentioned it to Molly yet'

Angela turned to me. 'Cecilia asked me if I had any suitable duets for the two of you.'

Cecilia looked apologetic. 'I'm sorry, Molly. I didn't get a chance to ask you.'

'It doesn't matter,' my piano teacher said. 'I've got something here which I think you'll both really like.'

I was surprised to say the least. Cecilia is conservatorium standard and already licensed to teach piano, whereas I'm only doing Sixth Grade piano for my Intermediate exams. My teacher Sister Angela knows I always do the bare minimum. I began making excuses. 'But there's Mary Bourke, and Geraldine Donovan. They're much better than me.'

Cecilia agreed that they were very good. 'I tried playing *March Militaire* with them, but they... we didn't always keep together. It should work with you.'

'But I'm not in your class when it comes to playing the piano because I'm a hopeless sight-reader. There's no way...'

'It would be very good for you Molly,' Sister Angela interrupted. 'Haven't I always said you'll never do really well in your exams until your sight-reading improves. You need to read a new piece every day.'

'I can help you,' Cecilia said.

I kept making excuses. 'But Sister, what's the point in playing duets?'

'You could perform them,' Sister Angela replied. 'And playing with someone else is a very good exercise in musicianship.'

She began fossicking around on her bookshelves, muttering something about my ears being more of an asset than my eyes.

That was when Cecilia asked me how it was that I could play by ear. It was something I'd never really thought about until I was expected to learn classical music that was too difficult and precise to play by ear. 'I think I was too young to read when I started playing,' I said lamely. 'I just tried to copy what Mum sang.'

Angela turned around to Cecilia with an album in her hands. 'The only way it can be explained is that no one taught Molly when she was a toddler, so the names of the notes were unnecessary, in the way that colours are irrelevant to artists as they're creating. It's a spatial sort of thing. To do with hearing and interpreting the intervals. Melodies filter into her mind and she remembers them.' She looked at me. 'But it doesn't work so well with classical music, does it Molly?'

'No, Sister.'

She opened the album. 'Have you danced to any of these Molly?'

I flicked through the album and indicated a few folk dances I recognised. Amongst Sister Angela's many gems of advice about duet playing, we learned that the two great composers, Brahms and Dvorak, were the best of friends so it was appropriate that their music should be performed together. 'You'll love playing these dances. They're full of syncopation and strong contrasts in dynamics and tempo,' Angela told us. 'I can't think of any other composers that have such sudden mood and mode changes from minor to major and major to minor.'

I found two Brahms and two Dvorak dances I'd danced to. Sister Angela decided they weren't too difficult, and we should alternate between *primo* and *secondo*. She's got a totally different attitude about dancing to Alphonsus, because she asked me to demonstrate the dance movements of one of them. Before I knew it, she was lah-lah-lahhing the melody, Cecilia was sight-reading the *secondo*, and I was whirling and stamping and pivoting in a space that was hardly big enough for two dancing mice.

'You'll have to use a classroom for your practice, of course' Sister Angela said after complementing me on my dancing. All these music rooms are taken during lunchtime.'

I decided to go along with it all because I like Cecilia. As for the music, I'll have to put in hours of practice. Cecilia seems to get it right when she reads the music the first time.

15

Jeanne

Jeanne handed *The Second Sex* to Dominique during their shared free period. 'Sorry for taking so long, but you know how it is.'

Dom began flicking through the book. 'This was published two years ago. 1953.'

'The original was published in France long before that because I remember maman talking about it!'

Dom began reading aloud. '*De Beauvoir was banned by the Vatican partly because of the book's explicit passages on the functions of the female body and descriptions of lesbian sex. She also links the subordinate role of mothers, wives and prostitutes in one single, sweeping passage.* You'd have to wonder what she thinks of nuns!'

Jeanne stared at her. 'I thought you were going to mention lesbian sex!'

Dominique shrugged. 'I heard about it vaguely at uni. Does she go into more detail anywhere?'

'Well. I'm not sure if…'

'Don't worry, I'm just curious about how she describes it.'

Jeanne caught Dominique's eyes for a few moments, flicked through the book and began to read. '*The lesbian is characterised simply by her refusal of the male and her preference for feminine flesh; but every adolescent female fears penetration and masculine domination, and she feels a certain repulsion for the man's body; on the contrary the feminine body is for her. Lesbians mostly fall into two categories: masculine lesbians who try to act like men, and feminine ones who are afraid of men.*'

They heard the rattle of beads and a door opening. Jeanne placed an exercise book on top of the de Beauvoir, and

Dominique resumed correcting her work. Sister Isobel breezed in to collect a book, greeted them, and rattled out again.

'Why do some writers put everyone into pigeonholes?' Dominique sighed. 'All the same, I'm annoyed that so much was hidden from us. I wish I'd known at sixteen what I know now.' She took some sheets of paper to the duplicator. 'If it hadn't been for Paula leaving me all her literature when she left, I'd have thought I was a freak. Now I know I'm just different. My eighth year here, counting my novice years at university, and your fourth, and we know nothing about the world. Talk about ignorant!'

'Well. That's probably most of us here. Is Paula ...'

'Your ex-science teacher. Sister Agatha, who married an ex-priest. Anyway, you'd be surprised at what's hidden from women. Not just nuns. My sister Genevieve said that there she was breeding away like a rabbit until someone told her the Vatican castrated little boys so they could retain their angelic voices for their choirs. No females allowed because St Paul's directive was *Let women be silent nor use authority over man. For Adam was first formed, then Eve.* Genevieve says there's a recording of the last tenor castrato, who only died around 1922.'

Jeanne rolled her eyes. 'I remember a book at uni that mentioned something about eunuchs. Is that the same thing?'

Dominique sighed. 'Apparently the Vatican mutilated little boys in the genital area before puberty. You wouldn't want to know how. When they sang they sounded like women, only better, they believed.' She laughed. 'Well, males have to be better, don't they? Anyway, the poor offered their small sons up to the church as it was quite lucrative, and it pleased God. It was enough for Genevieve. There's no way she'll be having any more children now. The Vatican wasn't going to tell *her* what to do with her body when they'd emasculated little boys.'

'Makes me wonder how many more things we're ignorant of.'

'Between Paula and Genevieve, I'm learning. Paula told me in one of her letters via Mum that her ex-priest husband says women have to ignore the clergy on issues like birth control. Mum had one baby after another. Mum and Dad had to scrimp and save to send me here. I was desperate to do science. There were no scholarships so they couldn't afford to send me to university. I had to commute to Melbourne from here for my degree. It was hard work fitting it around our extra duties and prayers and everything else. But if it hadn't been for the convent, I wouldn't have a science degree and teaching certificate.'

'So it was really to do with being educated that you entered?'

Dominique made a gesture of ignorance with her face and hands. 'Well, partly. Others in my class were boy mad. I preferred girls' company so I told myself God must have wanted me to become a nun. Then before Paula absconded, she told me to help myself to all her science books and others that might interest me. What a revelation!'

'How on earth did she get them?'

'She used to accompany the girls on the bus to Villa Maria. She played golf as well. He, Father Morris at the time, played golf there regularly. That was how they met. He gave her books on the sly when they got to know each other.'

Jeanne grinned. 'He fell for her and wanted to educate her.'

'Or to tempt her. One day during the girls' golf lesson, Paula got into his Studebaker and they drove off into the sunset. She left some very informative books behind for me.'

Jeanne grinned. 'I'm trying to imagine the two of them sitting up in the car, and the look on Alphonsus's face when she's given the bad news.'

Dominique was flicking through the de Beauvoir. 'This confirms everything,' she said indicating a paragraph. 'It's one of the reasons why I never confess my private feelings. Priests have been indoctrinated for centuries to despise women.'

Jeanne glanced at the paragraph. *The temptations of the earth, sex and the devil are incarnated in women. All the church fathers emphasise the fact that she led Adam to sin. That woman is the devil's gateway. It is her fault that God's son had to die. She should always dress in mourning and rags. All Christian literature endeavours to exacerbate man's disgust for woman.... Des Laurens, the French doctor, dared to ask how 'this divine animal full of reason and judgement that is called man, can be attracted by these obscene parts of the woman ... All venereal diseases are caused by women.*

'I was horrified when I read that.'

'It's disgusting. But it says it all. I've got one of Paula's books for you!' Dominique opened her drawer and pulled out a book. 'This was the first one to get me going. It's a bestseller by Tereska Torres, a French woman. It's called *Women's Barracks*. It's a true story she wrote about living in the London barracks during the war.' Dominique slipped off the brown paper to show the dustcover with several girls dressed in provocative lingerie in a barracks' bedroom. 'Al would have a fit if she saw that, let alone read it, although it's harmless. It's mostly about relationships between men and women, but sometimes between women. This paragraph is about when they're in the barracks bedroom. It might give you an idea.' She handed the book to Jeanne.

Ursula felt herself very small, tiny against Claude, and at last she felt warm. She placed her cheek on Claude's breast. Her heart beat violently, but she didn't feel afraid. She didn't understand what was happening to her. Claude was not a man; then what was she doing to her? What strange movements! What could they mean? Claude unbuttoned the jacket of her pajamas, and enclosed one of Ursula's little breasts in her hand, and then gently, very gently, her hand began to caress all of Ursula's body…

Jeanne wasn't sure what to say although she knew her face must be scarlet. She had feelings of guilt and pleasure simultaneously, not daring to look directly at her new friend.

Dominique put the book away, pulled out another and flicked open a page. 'Here's another one you won't find in the bookcase,' she said. 'I suppose one could say it's trashy and clichéd, but it's still an education for the ignorant and naïve. *Appointment in Paris* it's called. The French are ahead of the rest of the world when it comes to sensuality, aren't they?' She handed the book to Jeanne, indicating a paragraph.

Her hand curled and uncurled against Marcelle's bare breast. Marcelle drew her closer. Marcelle's hand began that tender exploratory creeping down Havoc's spine. The shuddering began — Havoc's and this time Marcelle's, too. It was a curious sort of desperate rhythm that the two women played together like musicians toward some crashing finale. It was all a great rhythmic tenderness. There was no shock, no brutality. There was no part of her body that Marcelle did not explore and come to know
…

Jeanne continued to blush, aroused by what she was reading. How must it feel to have a woman touching you like that? To touch all parts of your body. And to be able to reciprocate. 'I wouldn't have believed anyone could write like this about women if you hadn't shown me,' she said calmly, trying not to show any emotion.

'And here's me thinking that being French you'd know it all.'

'When I was a student here in Forms 5 and 6, I think I knew more about the facts of life than my school friends. But maman never mentioned that women could love each other physically.'

'So you didn't meet the love of your life when you were studying in Melbourne? No one came near me.' Dominique pulled a face. 'They tend not to when you're a novice or a nun.'

'I... I felt nothing much when I kissed boys. But after reading de Beauvoir and what you've just shown me, I think...' Jeanne was too embarrassed to continue.

'You think differently, perhaps?'

Jeanne nodded. 'Do you think Alphonsus knows about... about lesbians?'

'Who knows? I think she's more into telling the girls about the dangers of the opposite sex. Leading the boys on. Terrible things happen to girls when they dress and behave provocatively. It's always the girl's fault. We know that.'

Jeanne sighed. 'Why do I have the feeling that Alphonsus is as biassed as those saints in de Beauvoir's book?'

16

Molly

I'm having a really bad day today. I was spooked after my last visit to St Alban's, so I haven't been back for weeks except for Mass and confession. I should have walked on the other side of the street when I was on my way home from calisthenics this morning. Just as I was passing the side gate of the presbytery, Father Kelly was standing there. I don't like getting to know priests. They might figure out who you are in confession.

'Hello Molly,' he said.

'Hello Father,' I replied, racking my brains as I tried to think which nun he'd asked me about when he last spoke to me.

'I haven't seen you visiting the church lately.'

'No, Father. I've been busy helping at home.'

'Very good, but of course you should always make time to drop in for a visit.'

'Yes, Father.' I could hardly tell him the main reason I sometimes called into the church.

'When you visit the church, Molly, do you always *ask* God for something?'

I wondered what he was getting at. Probably that I should *thank* God for all the good things in my life instead of sitting there, wishing my parents were like Gabby's or Maude and Harry.

'Well, of course, most people *want* something from God. They *ask* his help. Perhaps, Molly, you could actually *do* something for God rather than ask.'

Wasn't I already doing enough things I was required to do for God?

'And of course, you would be rewarded.'

I frowned. 'Rewarded, Father?'

'By doing extra things for God, rather than those you are required to do, you can receive spiritual benefits.'

He was probably talking about being rewarded in heaven, but right now, I'd prefer to be rewarded here on earth.

'I'm talking about indulgences. A plenary indulgence.'

Plenary indulgence? We were asked to define it once for an exam for Rosario. *A plenary indulgence is a remission of the entire temporal punishment of sin given to one who is in the state of grace, and who fulfils certain conditions specified by the church.* I'd never thought about it much until during a yearly retreat – when classes are cancelled for three days of prayers and sermons, a sixth former asked the Redemptorist why the Pope had allowed the clergy to sell indulgences. The priest waffled around for a while, saying that it involved only a handful of priests. 'History says that it was widespread, which is one of the reasons why Martin Luther abandoned the church,' Hannah insisted. 'Yet we're taught that Martin Luther was evil. Can you explain that, Father?' He couldn't. 'I know from a relative, that when the Reformation is in the Matriculation Modern History syllabus, Catholic schools in Melbourne drop the subject,' Hannah continued. 'They don't want anyone knowing that the church was corrupt,' to which the priest muttered something about anti-Catholic bias at the university. Hannah queried everything. I'd like to be like that, but I haven't got the courage or the intellect. I heard Hannah was threatened with expulsion if she ever argued with Sister Gregory again about The Reformation.

I wasn't prepared to argue with Father Kelly about how anyone would know what God could possibly have in mind for your soul. I told him I had to go and began edging away.

'I'll meet you at the side door of the church next Friday after school, Molly. I have an idea how you and another girl can help God and the church for a short time every week. The time you normally drop in. I'll know more details by next Friday.'

I was annoyed and about to tell him I was busy, when the housekeeper called out from the front door that he was wanted on the phone.

He smiled. 'I must go, Molly. See you next Friday.'

I didn't have a chance to tell him I couldn't come, so I suppose I'll have to show up. I can't imagine what he's got in mind, but I'll think up some excuse. That incident was nothing in comparison to what was waiting for me when I arrived home. I walked into the kitchen and knew my father was in one of his moods.

'What's this film you went to see last Saturday?' he snarled.

'You mean *The Seven Year Itch*?'

'Didn't Mother Alphonsus warn you not to go to it?'

'Yes, but she's always doing that. Day scholars don't take any notice of her because…'

Whack! He slapped me over the face.

'She said she warned you all not to attend it. She said it was banned in Ireland.'

'I never heard that. It was for General Exhibition at the matinee session anyway.'

He'd never have heard of the film until Alphonsus mentioned it. He wouldn't know Marilyn Monroe from Elizabeth Taylor.

'You disobeyed her.'

Whack! This time it was from my calisthenics rod which he snatched from my hand and smashed it twice against my legs. I was terrified, sure that he was going to kill me. I hid behind

Mum who murmured meekly, 'Leave her, Kevin. Don't hit her.' Why doesn't she scream at him?

He wedged his way into the corner behind her, and grabbed me by the shoulders, shaking me. 'Don't you ever disobey her again. She said that dancing interferes with your schoolwork. You'll have to give it up.'

I knew that was coming. He's threatened us with it before because he knows it's something we enjoy. 'That's not true. I won prizes in French and German again this year.'

He didn't know what to say to that. I hid behind Mum again. 'Everyone at school knows Alphonsus is a weirdo,' I gasped. 'My friends say their parents laugh about her.'

'Look out if I hear another complaint about you,' he snarled as he stormed out of the kitchen.

Just as well we wear stockings because the rod left terrible marks on my leg. If this is a prelude to my next two years in Forms 5 and 6, I think I'll leave school after I've completed my Intermediate Certificate at the end of this term. I can't cope with him anymore. Or Alphonsus. The old bag had warned us about *The Seven Year Itch* with 'that scantily clad strumpet, Marilyn Monroe,' but Gabby decided we'd go, just to spite her. We're day-scholars after all! We swooned over the music, deciding that Rachmaninov, who we'd never heard of before, was as romantic as Chopin. The following week, we were speculating with our classmates about why Alphonsus objected to the film.

'Probably because Marilyn stood over the sidewalk grille with her dress billowing up around her,' I volunteered.

'Or maybe for saying she kept her undies in the freezer in the hot weather?' Gabby said. 'She's got a thing about underwear. Remember that boarder's frilly undies she held up in assembly?'

One of the girls imitated her. 'No girl from St Martin's should wear underwear like this. *Gorgeous Gussies*, I believe they're called. Named after an American tennis player who is now more renowned for her underwear than her overarm.'

Someone must have reported our conversation, which is why Al phoned Dad. Gabby's mother stormed up to the convent to tell the old cow that what day-scholars did out of school hours was none of her business. That everyone in the Mothers Club agreed there was no point in having school balls if the college boys couldn't be invited. I envied Gabby for having parents who supported her. Parents who could speak their mind about the ridiculous things that went on in the school, unlike my father who believes that the religious are never wrong.

One of my aunts says Dad is proud of me because of my piano playing. I can't see that he cares for any of us, although he probably doesn't hate us as much as we hate him. If he loves us, he's got a strange way of showing it. It's more about control. He takes out all his anger and frustration on us. I'm thinking about giving up my idea of becoming a teacher and getting a job in a bank in Melbourne. I could stay with one of my aunts and study part-time! Anything to get away from here. Dad might appear to be concerned about us because he expects us all to go to university. I suppose he works hard to keep us at school. I was surprised at his reaction when I told Mum that Billy the Quid wanted to meet me in the woodshed. The next minute Dad was screaming at him. Threatening to knock his block off and ban him from the hotel if he ever went near any of us again. When I came tearing into the pub one day and said that a man had just exposed himself to me in the gardens, Dad tore out of the bar, looking like he was ready to kill him. Perhaps you could say he's being protective, but it's not quite the same as being loving, is it? His interest in us is purely proprietorial.

17

The Priest

Mrs McKinnon was preparing the Friday flowers in the sacristy. Hilton smiled at her. 'I've got an idea to help lighten your load so that you won't need to return on Fridays, Mrs McKinnon.'

She smiled back at him uncertainly.

'I know someone you can train,' he began. He changed his mind. That might look suspicious. 'In fact, two girls living nearby are willing to do the flowers.' He was being presumptuous, but confident his plan would work. 'You'll need to train them, of course, but they can take over after that. Just the flowers. If you're concerned, I'll pop in to check up on them.' He wouldn't give her a chance to refuse.

She looked annoyed. 'I quite like preparing the flowers, Father. It's my favourite duty. Maybe they could just help me out with other duties.'

'No Mrs McKinnon. You work too hard, and it's the sort of job young people can do. I wouldn't trust them with anything else. Good training for them! After all, you've got quite a distance to come, and twice a day is ridiculous.'

'Yes Father,' she said resignedly. 'Will we start next week?'

'I'll let you know, Mrs McKinnon.'

Ah! Perfect. All he needed to do now was convince Molly and another girl to do the flowers. He decided to ask the rather dopey-looking girl who was sometimes on her knees up near the main altar with her mother.

'Hello Mrs Sullivan,' he said as they were leaving the church one afternoon. 'We're looking for a girl to share doing the flowers with another girl for less than an hour on Fridays. Starting around September. I notice you're here sometimes, so I wondered if your daughter could help out.'

'Fridays would be perfect, Father,' Mrs Sullivan said. 'Maureen loves flower-arranging and doesn't work on Friday afternoons.'

Maureen nodded, smiling up at him, as though he had done her a favour.

Molly looked sullen when he asked her the following Friday. 'I have to mind my baby brother, Father. Fridays are very busy at the hotel.'

'With two of you doing the flowers, you'll be finished in no time. If you can't do it occasionally, I'm sure Maureen will manage alone.'

He could tell by her face that he wasn't getting anywhere. 'Tell you what, Molly. My objective in this parish is to get parishioners to do more of God's work. It's already happening with the garden and building and general tidying-up around the place.'

She looked at him doubtfully.

'Our sacristan works many hours a week, especially on a Friday when she returns to the church to do the flowers. Come into the sacristy so I can show you what she does.' He gave her his best Rock Hudson smile.

'I… I have to go home,' she said. 'There are some other girls who…'

'Yes. I've already asked them,' he lied. 'They have all sorts of commitments. You sometimes call into the church on Fridays.' She didn't look happy. He'd try one more thing. 'Tell you what, Molly. How about I ask your parents if they can spare you?'

Molly looked horrified. 'I'll… I'll try it out with the other girl. I mightn't be able to help out every Friday.'

He'd certainly said the right thing there. He got the impression in the confessional that she despised her father. Perhaps she didn't want them to meet because she was worried that he might run her down. Or that he might say that Molly could do the flowers for as long as she was required. 'Good girl, Molly. You'll be helping God, and poor Mrs McKinnon who works so hard every day. You can meet her and Maureen after school next Friday.'

'Yes, Father,' she said unenthusiastically.

How to get Molly to the presbytery eventually? It was all very well for Bourke and his altar boys. Every Catholic mother wanted one of her sons to be a priest, but he could hardly use recruiting as an excuse for a girl to visit the presbytery.

'How did you go with your little protégé?' Bob asked him when they were having a beer later in the front parlour. 'I saw you chatting to her.'

'I've getting her and another girl to do the flowers on Fridays after Mrs McKinnon trains them.'

'Well, that's a start!' he said with a knowing smirk. 'I've got some more good news for you.'

Hilton raised his eyebrows.

Bob Bourke walked over to the calendar and studied it. 'Yes. Nearly three weeks since those sermons you gave on sacrifice and charity. Looks like you convinced your congregation better than I convinced mine.'

'What do you mean?' Hilton said.

'The money's pouring in. Just about paid for the alteration already. I'll have to hire you out.'

Hilton searched his superior's face. Was he joking? He had a tendency to do that. Perhaps it was sarcasm. 'Is that true?' he said.

'Definitely.' Father Bourke nudged him. 'You're a bit of a con-man, aren't you? I heard you got around them with friendly persuasion. Well, I suppose it all depends on the delivery. Which reminds me while we're on the subject of sermons. I'll have to get you to do the same for a subject I do my best to avoid. It always causes a few problems. I was up at the palace this morning. The boss gave us outlines from the Melbourne archdiocese over Archbishop Mannix's signature on the subject of birth control. Mannix says we must preach about it at least once a year, and if we haven't done so already, we'd better get cracking. He says it should be subtly dealt with under the subject of the dignity, sanctity, and obligations of marriage, which means that contraception should inevitably be addressed. It encourages adultery and fornication. He says it can be introduced by way of Our Lady's or Christ's feast-days. Like his baptism or the transfiguration. Even Christmas.'

'Christmas?'

'St Nicholas – Santa Claus – and his love for children.' Father Bourke grinned. 'Mannix thinks that too many Catholics are straying from the path. Marrying for fun rather than having children. Anyway, it's now September and I haven't mentioned birth control for a year or two, so we'd better get cracking I suppose.'

Hilton nodded. 'The only feast-day I can think of is All Saints Day. We could discuss the humility and restraint of the saints. It'd be more appropriate than Christmas and St Nicholas.' He stood up and walked over to the Catholic Calendar. 'There's also the Feast of Christ the King coming up in November.'

'Another good one, Hilton. We could suggest that this feast offers us the opportunity to acknowledge our faith. We could emphasise that rejecting or questioning any of the church's rules is tantamount to rejecting Christ. We'll focus on the church's authority. Anyone practising birth control denies their faith, and consequently repudiates the authority of Christ himself.' Bourke handed him a copy of the Archbishop's guidelines.

Hilton knew from the confessional that penitents wrestled with the problem of contraception. The previous year in his Rose Hill parish, he'd had to inform a mother of four that it made no difference if her doctor said another pregnancy would kill her. Heart condition or not, the rule was that sterilisation was not permitted. Her problem could only be solved by abstinence. Then there was his older brother, with whom he'd recently had an argument on the subject.

'Here you all are, a bunch of single men with no bloody idea about bringing up families, telling us how to run our married lives,' John had said angrily. 'We're committing a mortal sin if we don't send our children to Catholic schools, then we have to scrimp and slave away to pay the school fees. How would you like to be me, with six children under ten, wondering how you're going to pay the next bill? Desperately hoping your wife is not going to get pregnant again! And don't talk to me about the rhythm method! It's unreliable.'

'I didn't make the rules,' Hilton had told him. 'Few of my parishioners query it. Except those with health problems.'

'And from what I've heard, they're still not given permission. Some obviously ignore the ruling, and others turn to booze or women when their wives are fearful of having more children. It's like me telling you how to cook when I've never cooked in my life. That's the illogic of it all.'

A few days after Father Bourke had brought up the subject, Hilton perused the sermon guidelines. They were to use carefully crafted language, so that children would be blissfully unaware of what the sermon was about, but terminology that perhaps adolescents might understand. The congregation must be told that artificial birth control is the prevention of conception by the use of mechanical, chemical, and other similar means. It is evil because it perverts a natural faculty.

Hilton decided to begin his sermon by discussing the feast of Christ the King; Christ and his authority; the Wedding Feast of Cana. Then he'd move onto the privilege and purpose of marriage, which was to have children. He would tell them that God brought Adam and Eve together to increase and multiply. Somehow, he would have to link this all to modern marriage. *Mechanical, chemical and other similar means,* Mannix's directive had said. It was something priests would never have to worry about. All he wanted was to cultivate a relationship with a young girl. Someone he could look at. Touch. Feel his body against hers. It would be a girl who needed someone to confide in. One who despised her father. A girl like Molly.

By popping in and out of the church while Mrs McKinnon was training the two girls, he would gradually gain Molly's trust. He'd be careful. Take his time. Six years at the Junior Seminary and another six years at Corpus Christi and all he learned about sex in an all-male environment was to be wary of the opposite sex, that sex was for procreation, and that sex before marriage and any form of contraception was forbidden. In his self-righteous hypocritical world, he warned penitents against using sheaths or *coitus interruptus.* Masturbation was a sin, he told them when they confessed it, but he could hardly give a heavy penance considering his own misdemeanours, for which he had little guilt.

Hadn't he unwittingly rendered his adolescence null and void to please his mother? Fellow seminarians joked that it was their mothers who had vocations to the priesthood. That when it came to sex, all priests knew about it was what they learned in the confessional. He felt justified in rekindling the part of his life denied him in his youth. Entitled to be compensated after the baggage that had encumbered his upbringing. Leaving the priesthood was not an option. He could never admit to wasting all those years in the seminary and he didn't want to be pitied as a failure. What else could he do, and how would he face his mother? How could he relinquish all the power and status he'd earned as a priest? He was revered by the community. Accorded a kind of deference available to few other professions. Rumours of colleagues' transgressions in the Ballarat diocese helped to assuage any guilt about his own behaviour.

He was excited about his new study. It was now September, and apparently it would be ready in October or early November. The door beside the window was an exact replica of Father Bourke's external door on the other side. He'd be moving in as soon as the internal door between his bedroom and study was fitted, and the furniture in place.

'And how are you going with the little flower girl?' Bob Bourke said conspiratorially to Hilton. 'How do you plan to entice her here?'

He felt quite comfortable with his superior now. 'Actually,' Hilton said with a sardonic smile. 'I'm going to coach her when I find out what her least favourite subject is.'

Father Bourke grinned. 'Ah. Education is the key to everything.' He sighed. 'Well, we spend our time helping the community, so we sometimes need our little diversions. We become priests to guide the misguided and then we struggle with lust. But watch out. Too many complaints and you'll be moved on again.'

'I will. This time it'll be a lay down misère.'

The parish priest opened another bottle of beer. 'They all love it, although some of them pretend they don't.' He clinked glasses with his curate. 'I think you and I can absolve each other from our sins tonight.'

In early November with the study completed, and the desk and oak bookcase having been delivered from Myers, Father Bourke knocked on the new external door. 'To celebrate the transfiguration,' he said, presenting Hilton with a bottle of whisky and two crystal glasses. 'Six months after you moved in and you've got yourself a new study.' They clinked glasses. 'May the holy spirit be with you. Let us pray.'

They laughed, and while Hilton was wondering if he intended *pray* to be a *double entendre*, Father Bourke placed a book in the new bookcase. 'For your perusal when you're in the mood,' he said. 'Keep it behind your more respectable books or lock it up. In other words, keep it away from snoops.'

'Thanks Bob. I appreciate everything you've done!'

'Just be careful. You wouldn't want to be sent to the back of Bourke next time. Ha ha. No pun intended.'

It took him a few seconds to get the second *double entendre*. He nodded and grinned.

'And Hilton. A word of advice. Make it casual the first time. Bring her to the kitchen. Not here.'

He nodded, happy to have his own study at last. As for his external door, the shrubbery between the sacristy and veranda surrounding the presbytery would tend to hide passers-by. He thought of Molly, and how it wouldn't be long before she'd be in this very room with him. He pulled out Father Bourke's gift, the *Kama Sutra,* with its images of couples in the most varied and obscene positions imaginable. Alongside it, he opened the purloined album from his former parish. Of all Pierre-Narcisse Guerin's Portraits of Young Girls, there was one that obsessed him. With her tousled hair and rosy cheeks, she looked like a gamine-faced pixie. Just like Molly. Her hands were half-crossed over her breasts. The only original painting he'd ever seen of a full-sized nude was the infamous Chloe at Young and Jackson's pub. The work of yet another Frenchman.

'And how did your sermon on birth control go, Hilton?' Bob Bourke asked him two weeks later.

'Not so well,' he replied.

'Ditto,' his superior said. 'It never does.'

Despite Hilton putting his whole heart and soul into it, it hadn't taken him long to see that the congregation was far from inspired. Most of the faces were blank or annoyed. No one commented on his sermon after Mass. It was not the sort of topic one discussed in public. Questions about birth control were reserved for the confessional. Why is it a sin for Catholics to practise birth control, but not protestants? God didn't mention contraception in the ten commandments, so who invented the rule for Catholics? There were certainly church rules that at times, didn't seem logical, but did it really matter?

18

Jeanne

Like other nuns, Jeanne always looked forward to their thirty minutes in the community room before evening prayers. The topics usually merged into each other. Examination results; the curriculum; a few girls deemed to be difficult. Family news – someone was always being baptised, married, or buried. This evening was more relaxed because it was the 1955 August/September holidays. The room was buzzing with the nuns' chatter. Jeanne was sitting beside Dominique, flicking through a wallet of family photographs. 'I think we've got more than a connection, Dom,' she said softly.

'Definitely,' Dom replied, indicating a photo as though asking a question about it. 'We'll have to make discreet plans.' She sighed. 'I do my best thinking in a hot bath. Which reminds me. I've decided to stick to showering. I can put up with a lukewarm shower, but not a lukewarm bath. It was my one luxury, especially when I'm rostered last and can take my time.'

'Mine was cold last week too. Raf and Felicity have their baths before me. Perhaps they're using too much hot water.'

'I'll have a word with them.'

Immediately after evening prayers, there was a rule of absolute silence in the bathrooms for both boarders and nuns. Shower and bath-times were strictly rotated and regulated by using mechanical timers set for four minutes for showers, and fifteen minutes for baths, including the time it took to run the bath. That evening, following her discussion with Dom in the community room, Jeanne was lying back luxuriating in the hot water, thoughts of schoolwork far from her mind. Her life had changed now, and all because of a book she'd confiscated from a boarder. Why had the church and society deprived women knowledge of their own sexuality? And what about her faith? Her future. She twiddled her wedding ring. How long had she been wearing it? Getting on to four years now. Was this ring weighing her down just as much as a married woman? Had she become a nun because like Dominique, she was subconsciously attracted to women?

She suddenly realised that in her pensive mood, she hadn't set the timer. When she released the plug, the noisy gurgling almost drowned out the quiet knock. She was about to call out 'Sorry, not quite ready,' when she changed her mind. Dominique opened the door, and gasped as she looked at Jeanne's dripping-wet nakedness. They stared at each other, Jeanne knowing instinctively that this encounter presaged a change in their relationship, the two of them having come to the conclusion that women could enjoy loving each other as much as ordinary couples. Dominique leaned forward, kissed Jeanne on the lips and quickly exited the bathroom. Jeanne touched her lips. Dominique's kiss lingered on them like a butterfly hovering around a rose. Every part of her was tingling. Perhaps they could do this again, although it wasn't very private. Anyone could walk in.

Years of suppressed sexuality brought the realisation that there was something more to life. They were individuals, each with their own personalities despite a regime that would have them all behaving exactly the same. What was the matter with her? Here she was, steeped in religion with all its societal expectations, and she was in love with a woman. Jeanne adored this clever young nun and couldn't wait to see her again. Parts of her that had been cold and dark for so long were suddenly springing into life. They stole moments together like thieves.

Smiling at each other. Eyes twinkling. Touching each other like a gentle breeze. A quick kiss when no one was around. Now they were consummate confederates, justifying their thoughts, their passion for each other. The sixth commandment concerned relationships between male and female. They would not confess their love.

Jeanne decided that her mother's reaction was more of excitement than shock when she asked to borrow *L'histoire d'O*. 'Are you losing your vocation, *chérie?*' maman might well have said, when she handed over the book, having switched the dustcover with the famous French classic, *Les Trois Mousquetaires*. Jeanne read the synopsis by torchlight in bed. '*The Story of O relates the progressive wilful debasement of a young and beautiful Parisian woman who wants nothing more than to be a slave to her lover ... the deliberate erotic stimulation of The Story of O portrays explicit scenes of bondage and violent penetration in spare elegant prose.*' This wasn't what she wanted to read about. She moved on to the next few chapters. It was certainly elegant prose, but the book appeared to be erotic and repellent at the same time. How could a woman write about such debasement of their own sex? Surely it was a male using a pen-name as Paul had suggested!

In later chapters, Jeanne learned that O was happy to have sex with men and women. The chapters dealing with explicit sexual relations between the women excited and aroused her. She almost stopped breathing as she read one passage over and over.

'*For more than an hour, Jacqueline moaned to O's caresses, and finally her breasts aroused, her arms thrown back behind her head while her hands circled the wooden bars of the headboard on O's Italian-style bed, she began to cry out when O, parting the lobes hemmed with pale hair, slowly began to bite the crest of flesh at the point between her thighs where the dainty, supple lips joined. O felt her rigid and burning beneath her tongue, and wrested cry after cry from her lips, with no respite, until she suddenly relaxed and she lay there moist with pleasure.'*

Jeanne felt things happening within her body while she was reading. A tingling *down there*. She wanted to be Jacqueline, and Dom to be O. Or would she prefer it the other way around? She caressed herself *down there*. Why had she never done this before? Of course, it would be much better with Dom's clever fingers. She thought of specific paragraphs in the book and began to feel an overwhelming pleasurable wave that started in her pelvis and spread throughout her body. She was moist with pleasure, like Jacqueline in the novel. How could she have lived to the age of twenty-four without having had this overwhelming experience before? She felt a certain shame, however, when she thought that she'd like to be in Jacqueline or O's place. In that bed! More-so when she thought of Dominique's hand touching her in the most private parts of her body.

A week into Term 3, Jeanne had her first opportunity to speak to Dom alone.

'The language in the book is beautiful,' she said. 'But *érotique*.'

'Will you be able to read it to me somewhere?' Dom whispered.

Jeanne shook her head. 'The French is quite difficult because it's very poetic. You wouldn't understand it. Besides, where could we…'

'We could appear to be reading our Office in the garden if no one else is around. 'I love the sound of the French language, whether or not I understand it all. I also adore your accent when you speak English or French, *mon amour*.

Jeanne grinned. 'You'll get the gist of it I suppose. My translation won't be quite as poetic.'

And so their relationship began with nothing more than the odd kiss, and reading. Reading in the garden, the cloister, the staff room. It was difficult to be in the same room without wrapping themselves around each other. Jeanne wrote poetic messages of love in French, placing them inside Dominique's notebook in a drawer of her desk. *Love is the touch of softest silk.* Dom reciprocated with a French dictionary by her side. It was safer to write in French. *Love is honey on a pair of heavenly lips.* As the months went on, the messages became more sensual and provocative. *Love is your fingertips exploring my body and soul.* Jeanne giggled at Dom's grammatical errors as they read them out to each other during their shared free period.

All Jeanne could think about was how they could fulfil their relationship. Consummate their love. They tried to maintain normal composure, hoping no one could see the flush that was more than the discomfort of the tight headdress around their faces. The smouldering under their heavy robes.

After some months, they found that their embraces were not satisfying their sexual needs. Their love and desire could never be completely fulfilled because of the risk of discovery. Until Jeanne realised that an opportunity was right there in front of them. Staring at them in the face. She couldn't wait to tell Dominique.

19

Molly

Mrs McKinnon, the sacristan for St Alban's Church, is trying to teach me flower arranging. She must realise I'm hopeless, although I must admit, I'm not making much of an effort. One of the heavy brass vases tipped over on the altar and spilt water everywhere, so she got cranky with me. Apparently, I made it top heavy with too many flowers. The other girl, Maureen, has a real flair for floral arranging, although I get the impression that Mrs McKinnon will never be happy with either of us. She supervises us polishing vases and filling them with water, cutting the flowers to the right length, placing them on the altar or pedestals, then arranging them 'so that they are pleasing to the eye, and pleasing to God,' she says. Every time we pass in front of the altar, even when I'm staggering around with a huge brass vase of flowers that's heavier than me, we have to genuflect and bow our heads. She's holier than a nun. The type who'd welcome the stigmata on her hands! I bet she makes perpetual novenas to Our Lady to store in her heavenly bank, so she'll be on the top floor of paradise with all the saints. If they're anything like her, they must be bored out of their brains.

Veronica and Brigid suggested doing the flowers so badly Mrs McKinnon would give me the sack. Two weeks later, she told us what she wanted done, then left a few minutes later. We'd just got going when Father Kelly walked into the sacristy and looked around. He told Maureen to finish up on her own, so I happily picked up my satchel and walked outside. Father Kelly followed me out and asked me to come with him to the presbytery. A path behind some shrubs led to a back porch into the kitchen. He told me to sit down at the large wooden table.

'You deserve a drink after all your hard work,' he said.

I was surprised because I'd hardly done anything. The kitchen was spotless and ten times larger than our tiny hotel kitchen. The door into the dining room was ajar. I saw a huge polished sideboard and table with about twelve matching chairs. Pretty posh! There were pictures of the Pope and Bishops and saints hanging from a rail on clean white walls. A statue, probably St Alban, was in the corner. Father Kelly took out a bottle of soda water from the fridge, mixed it with lemon cordial, and handed me a drink. He asked me about my schoolwork. What were my favourite subjects? English, French, German and Music I told him. What was my least favourite subject? Mathematics.

'Is your teacher a bit fierce?' he asked me with a grin.

I shrugged. 'Sometimes, Father. She gets a bit cranky when we don't understand something. I just don't like maths. Especially algebra.'

'Maths was my best subject. Have you got your maths textbook there?'

He flicked through the book and asked me about my homework. I indicated my algebra and geometry due the following week.

'How long will it take you?' he said.

'About two hours, Father.'

'Tell you what, Molly. I bet we can knock this off within half an hour.'

I was surprised that he had time to help me. Some of my classmates' parents help with homework. Dad has never helped us, and we'd never think of asking him. Father Kelly is as kind as Uncle Michael, Dad's only brother, also a priest. Father Kelly showed me a great method of solving my dreaded algebra problems and made me promise not to tell anyone that he was helping me. Why would I? Now my weekend is free. He's saved me hours of work. It makes up for doing the flowers.

I thanked him and was standing up to leave when Father O'Doherty plodded in from the hallway. He's tall like Father Kelly although much older and bald as a bandicoot. Maybe blind as one too, with the lens on his spectacles as thick as the bottom of milk bottles. When he asked me why I was in the presbytery, Father Kelly explained that I did the flowers every Friday.

'So what are you doing here?'

'Well. Father offered me a drink,' I said a little hesitantly. 'After...'

'Ahh. The Offertory. Did he offer you bread and wine? Watch out for what they offer you,' he said in a mysterious voice.

I don't think Father Kelly likes him. He ushered me outside. 'I'll see you next Friday. Mrs McKinnon had to catch a train to Melbourne today. Her father is ill, so she'll be there for a week or two. The other sacristan can't return on Friday afternoons. Maureen should be okay by herself and I'll be able to help you with your maths again.'

I wasn't expecting that. I'm not sure about making a habit of it, but there was no way I could object. I thought of two sixth formers I heard swooning over Father Kelly at school. Wouldn't they be envious?

Speaking of school, I'm having awful trouble with the Brahms. I thought the *primo* would be easier because I know the melody, but I think both parts are difficult. I know I should read a new piece every day, but I always end up spending more time playing popular music. It's not that I like it any more than classical. The trouble is I'm lazy about reading any music other than what's required for my music exams, and now I've been forced into it.

During our last practice, Cecilia wanted to know why I went to boarding school when I was so young. I told her it was because Mum was too ill to mind us. I said the same to Gabby. I hate lying to friends. The last time I was talking to my sisters about why we were all sent away for so long, Brigid said she overheard a conversation between Mum and Maude which made her think that Mum wasn't always living with Dad. But where was she living? We decided that she must have put in an appearance for a short time when we returned home for Christmas. Obviously, everything changed when we all moved into The Barkly.

Cecilia asked me how come I played by ear.

'Mum was always singing, so I copied what she sang. I played all her tunes at home and at boarding school.'

'Then you learned properly?'

I shrugged, because I never thought I learned properly, even though I did piano exams. 'I still copied. My piano teacher at boarding school had a rule that she wouldn't teach anyone until they turned six, but I was allowed to tag along with my two older friends. There must have been as many pianos around the place as statues, like here. So I copied anything I heard. All the tunes I heard the girls practising as well as hymns and classroom melodies. And the theme music from films.'

'You must have impressed them.'

'I didn't think so. I thought I was hopeless because I was cheating. A copy-cat! I couldn't understand the squiggles that the others were reading. My teacher must have decided that my ears would eventually catch up with my eyes when she took me on. She watched our fingers because she was as deaf as a statue. She never took me aside to teach me how to read music, and by the time I worked it out, it was too late. It's why I'm such a bad sight-reader now.' I wanted to change the subject. 'Do boarders here have to go to Mass every morning and say the rosary every evening like we did in St Arnaud?'

Cecilia nodded. 'Probably the same in all convents. We have to be at death's door before we can sleep in.'

Cecilia likes to know all about hotel life. I tend to gloss over the more unsavoury side of things. I'd never tell her about my parents, although I told her Mum was a dancer. I can't believe how patient Cecilia is with me. In fact, she smiles when she's helping me, and I can tell it's genuine. She says things like 'Molly. Think of the chords and arpeggios based on these notes, then you'll get it,' or 'See this phrase here? It's just a variation of that motif on the previous page.' Then she plays the bass and treble together to demonstrate, explaining the notes within the chords that I'm trying to get right. She must realise I'm behind in music theory as well. I fully expected her to give up on me and was half-hoping she would. Then I began memorising the music, practising as soon as I got home so that I didn't forget everything. After a few weeks, the Brahms started to come together. I was a little more motivated. Finally, we managed to get through the whole piece. We were revising it when Sister Jeanne crept into the Form 4 classroom to prepare the blackboard before the first bell rang for afternoon classes.

'You play as though you're dancing,' Jeanne said when we'd finished. 'I know nothing much about the piano, but you two certainly listen very well to each other. Your entries, your endings and rallentandos are perfectly synchronised as if only one were playing.'

Cecilia and I grinned at each other. It was our first compliment. Jeanne must know that it's Cecilia who's holding the whole thing together.

'It's commendable to see a boarder and day-scholar doing something together too.' She smiled. *'C'est rare comme le merle blanc.'*

I had to think for a moment, then I got it. Last week, someone asked her what the French equivalent of *rare as hens' teeth* was. *'Oui, ma soeur,'* I said smiling. *'Je suis d'accord.'*

Cecilia frowned. 'I got that you agreed, Molly, but nothing else.'

I was pleased to be able to tell Cecilia, older than me and a fifth former. 'The French say *as rare as a white blackbird.* Not *hens' teeth.'*

'I like that,' Cecilia said, after Jeanne repeated it for her in French. 'I'll try using it from now on.'

Sister Jeanne walked over to the piano and looked at the music as we began packing up. 'Yes. I thought it was Brahms. They'll all be tapping their toes when you play that. What else are you playing for the concert when the grand piano arrives?'

Cecilia and I stared at her, then at each other. I had no idea what she was talking about, and by the look on her face, neither did Cecilia.

'Uh oh,' Jeanne said. 'I've put my foot in it now. Didn't Sister Katerina or Sister Angela mention the grand piano to you?'

Cecilia and I exchanged glances and shook our heads.

'A wealthy parent donated it. I'm not sure when it's arriving. It's a concert grand. I obviously wasn't around when we were told not to mention it to anyone. I'm sorry about that.' She grinned. 'You'll have to look surprised when you're told about it.'

'You needn't worry, Sister. It'll be Cecilia playing solos, not me. I'm...'

'No, Molly,' Jeanne replied. 'They were talking about the two of you playing duets for a concert.'

Cecilia was jumping up and down with excitement. A concert grand piano. All I could think was how I'd quite happily play for a singalong for a hundred, but never for a formal concert. I was half-hoping the piano would fall off the ship on its way from Germany when Jeanne said it wouldn't be arriving until next year. What a relief!

'Apparently it's a special concert as a thank-you to the parents who donated it. But please don't forget to look surprised when you're told about it.'

Celie and I laughed our heads off about a nun asking us to keep a secret from other nuns.

20

Jeanne

Jeanne's blossoming relationship with Dominique changed everything. Not that they had much time in private, with only one concurrent free period a week in the staff room. A quick glance in the corridor. The chapel. The community room. They had little time to confide in each other. To discuss the insurmountable impracticalities of convent life. Whinge about their grievances, like trying to manage their habits and rosary beads in the toilet. Worse during the curse. All those things that they hadn't really thought about when they first entered the convent. Alphonsus was another story. Her suspicious nature. Censoring the prescribed books for the English syllabus which sent Isobel up the wall. Banning St Bernard's boys from the school ball and insisting on the girls wearing frumpy old frocks. And what of her paranoia about excursions? Dom, who trained the girls' basketball teams, was furious when Alphonsus refused permission for the girls' invitation to play against Loreto Abbey – 'that convent come finishing school!' When Sister Margaret wanted to take her students to the local art gallery, they had to compromise by arranging a time not opened to the general public. The 1955 Catholic Life Exhibition in Melbourne was about the only excursion the secondary school and most of the nuns attended. Alphonsus declared that talking was forbidden on the bus. The rosary and litany must be said on both journeys. Jeanne remembered the girls' sullen, barely audible responses. They were angry, but with one strict nun aboard each bus, they were limited to whispering.

Jeanne and Dom agreed it was therefore ironic that it was Mother Alphonsus who gave the two of them an opportunity for their relationship to flourish. Sister Alfredo, the elderly school projectionist for the 16mm films was getting beyond it, ignoring the sound getting out of sync with the picture and forgetting to check the focus. She'd once shown Jeanne how to change reels, so when things were going from bad to worse one Friday evening, Jeanne hurried to the back of the hall to see if she could help. She was getting nowhere until Dominique joined her. Between the two of them, they managed to get the film back on track. The girls applauded. Alphonsus nominated Jeanne and Dominique to be the projectionists. So that there would be no disasters during the next film – *A Tale of Two Cities* – they practised over and over during the week the film was to be shown.

'I know this film backwards now,' Dom said.

Jeanne looked at her, raising her eyebrows. 'You'll need to for what I've got in mind for Friday night.'

Like most of the other nuns, they removed their rosary beads from their cinctures on the evening the film was to be shown. Beads were as distracting as crinkly-wrapped sweets and jaffas during a moment of suspense in a picture theatre. It was bad enough having to put up with the elderly Sister Gertrude, who rattled and wheezed her way through every film like an old steam train.

With the December heatwave having hit Ballarat by film night, Jeanne decided she and Dom should discard the tight underclothes that encumbered their bodies. Who would notice? They had the added advantage of the projector being right at the back of the hall, the girls and nuns much closer to the screen.

'After all, the missionary nuns in those hot African countries wear cool white habits. Don't they know that Australia can get nearly as hot?' she whispered to Dom when their plans were evolving. 'Who'd have thought when we entered the convent that getting dressed would be so awkward and time-consuming? Not to mention trying to keep our yokes and coifs clean while we're eating!'

'Priests and Brothers have it easy. I've heard they wear civvies sometimes.'

'I think our clothing has evolved from the belief that nuns' lives should be a permanent penance. The design has scarcely changed since the Middle Ages. Anyway, it'll suit us tonight, won't it?'

They exchanged glances, grinning. Their white bib or guimpe, starched more stiffly than a shirt collar, was designed to hide any hint of a figure. Tonight, it would be an advantage, as would also be the bodice of the long black habit with its hooks and eyes fastened down the front to just below the waist.

Everything was meticulously planned. They slackened their cinctures for comfort and convenience, both frantic to explore, to touch every inch of each other's available flesh. After threading the first reel, Dominique maintained a relaxed face as her fingers slid under Jeanne's guimpe to the bodice exterior of the thick black habit. She moulded each breast with her hand. 'They are a perfect shape. I'm honoured to be your first lover,' she whispered, unfastening every hook and eye under the guimpe. After the hard serge material of the habit rubbing against her nipples, now stiff and erect, Dominique's fingers felt soft and gentle. No one heard their gasps or sharp intakes of breath above the noise of the projector as the scene unfolded. In the busy Paris street, a cask of red wine tumbled out of a cart, shattering like a walnut shell onto the cobblestones outside the wineshop. The noise of the crowd crescendoed as men and women knelt down to scoop the wine into their mouths. Their laughter resounded in the street, while children frolicked and danced around. Wine stained their faces, mixing with the mud. Someone scrawled BLOOD upon a wall.

'I wish you could scoop them into your mouth like they're doing with the wine,' Jeanne whispered. She felt quite shameless. 'And kiss them like you kiss my lips.'

Desire was now saturating her body. It was not just their passion for each other that seemed to intensify their emotions. Was it the secrecy? The forbidden fruit that set their collective blood to boiling point? Were they the only nuns who dared cross the boundary of sanctified chastity to passionate sexuality? A conflicting array of emotions shivered through her, the guilt making her feel more aroused. Rebellious.

'Your turn to change the next reel, *chérie*,' Dominique said. 'In twenty minutes.'

'I'm relying more on the cue dots and scraping sound at the end.'

Jeanne's hand was gently caressing Dominique's nipples when they heard a rattling of beads coming down the aisle. They were both breathing heavily, their eyes unfocussed, staring at the screen. The rattle continued straight on past them, their heartbeats synchronised with the throbbing of the drum as the soldiers led the marquis' murderer to his execution.

'I'll never curse the guimpe again,' Dominique whispered. 'What a perfect camouflage for wayward hands! It covers a multitude of sins. You're a wanton for dreaming this up, Jeanne. A wanton!'

Not wanting to leave the moment, Jeanne stood up quickly to change the next reel. She could hardly concentrate. Every part of her was primed and aching, a delicious tingle lingering between her legs. Her body seemed to be taking over from her mind, shaking with unknown sensations spreading through the centre of her being. There was no feeling of shame now. They whispered to each other, justifying their behaviour by reasoning that when they had renounced the outside world for a life of obedience and chastity, they weren't mature enough to fully understand what it was they were renouncing.

Having seen the film before, they were almost swooning in anticipation of what was coming. Their next arousal would be during a scene that guaranteed a symphony of sounds. Madame Defarge, armed with an axe and pistol, lifts her skirt and thrusts a knife into a pouch. She joins her husband and patriots to storm the Bastille with the thundering of drums, the muskets, the shrieking, the fire and the smoke. A perfect cover for their gasps and moans. No need for them to lift a skirt. Now their camouflage was black. Black on black. Having undone the seams of the deep pockets in their robes to render them bottomless, they were now wide enough for their hands to slip through each other's pockets; to caress their most intimate parts; to explore, to probe, to put into practice what they'd learnt from their covert literature. Their reference points.

Along the Paris streets, the death carts are rumbling towards the guillotine. The guard of horsemen ride abreast of the tumbrils. They point with their swords to a man in the third one. Sydney Carton. The noise of the crowd baying for blood swells as the tumbrils empty the condemned at the place of execution. 'To the guillotine all aristocrats,' they are screaming. The two nuns, fused by the scent of desire heard none of it, despite trying to restrain their passion and maintain their composure. No one could see the flush on their cheeks now as they attempted to quell the noise of each other's climax. If ever there was an exercise in restraint, Jeanne decided, surely this was it. Was it all about the forbidden? The secrecy? They began rewinding the last reel as the audience filed out.

'At uni, when I was socialising with my friends, or sometimes Paul's, I picked up that women could get quite aroused. Basically though, *their* pleasure wasn't important. Girls were vessels for boys' exploration. It was more that we were born to gratify the opposite sex rather than need it ourselves. Men initiated it. It was all about the primacy of... of...'

'Dare I say it?' Dom whispered. 'The primacy of the penis.'

Jeanne grinned. 'Well that's one way of putting it, and it's how I understood it to be when I learned the facts of life.' Everyone had left the hall, but she was still whispering. 'I can't believe what happened to me tonight, Dom. It was an explosion. A volcanic eruption. And I felt it happening to you.'

Dom nodded. 'Yes. I felt it too. It juddered right through my body. It was much more than being aroused. It must be like what happens to men. It didn't mention anything like that in all those books we've been reading, did it?

'Not even in *L'histoire d'O*. In fact, except for the scene with the two women, it was all about men's possession and physical power over women. *Their* pleasure. Nothing about them pleasing Jacqueline.'

Dom frowned. 'That's why I still think it was written by a male. Women wouldn't want to be *that* subservient to men, surely!' She paused. 'But to get back to tonight. What happened to us was very special. Magical!'

'Perhaps because you accidentally discovered something down there. A little button that sent me into a frenzy. A million times more sensitive than when you touch my nipples.' She sighed. 'Like a jolt of electricity. I need you to find it again. And soon!'

Dom stopped loading the equipment onto the trolley and stared at Jeanne. 'All this time I thought that men had to put their you-know-whats into you-know-where to arouse women.' She paused. 'At uni, there were four times as many boys doing science. When the word *penis* came up in biology, I can remember the smug looks on some of the boys' faces. It was as though they were smarter than girls because they had one.' She shrugged. 'Well, maybe I imagined it. Maybe I was self-conscious because I didn't have any sex education. It was all a lot of guesswork until I did biology.'

'Perhaps I picked up a little more because I had a social life in Melbourne.'

Dom laughed. 'No gallivanting around for us novices. We either went straight back to Ballarat or stayed at a Melbourne convent overnight.'

'Life will never be the same from now on,' Jeanne said as they wheeled the trolley back to the storeroom. She sighed. 'Do you realise that the next film night won't be 'til about March next year?

'What? 1956? We can't possibly wait that long, *mon amour*. My very soul is on fire.'

'I want to lie down beside you like Jacqueline and her lover in *The Story of O*.'

'There's a place where we can put into practice what we've learnt from our literature.'

Jeanne was horrified. 'Our squeaky beds?'

'Not in your life. Think of a place that won't be used during the holidays, *mon ange*.'

Jeanne pondered for a moment, then grinned. 'You mean the girls' infirmary?'

Dom nodded, her eyes twinkling. 'As long as no one else has the same idea.'

21

Molly

I was in the sacristy when Father Kelly walked in and said he'd see me the following week. I was about to agree when I realised I had a perfect excuse for not showing up. 'I'm sorry, Father,' I said. 'We're having extra practices for the calisthenics competitions straight after school on Fridays for the next three weeks, so I won't be able to come. After that it's school holidays and I'm staying with my cousins in Melbourne.'

He looked exasperated. I was hoping he'd tell Mrs McKinnon to forget the whole thing when she started carrying on about having to retrain us after the holidays.

'By then we'll be heading towards Christmas. They'll need a lot of help then,' she said.

Father Kelly didn't look at all happy. I don't understand why he wants us to do the flowers when it seems to me that Mrs McKinnon would prefer to do them herself.

I hate Dad more than ever now. He said that our 1955 calisthenics concert would be our last 'so make the most of it. In any case, Mother Alphonsus said it interferes with your studies.' Having been a dancer, Mum argued on our side, but she didn't get anywhere either. I had a hate session on him with Brigid and Veronica.

When I told Tony I was thinking of leaving school after my exams and running off to Melbourne to find a job, he convinced me to stay on. 'You're doing very well,' he said. 'Much better than me. Wait until you've at least got your

Leaving Certificate. Stick it out for another year. You'll have more chance of getting a better job.'

Then he admitted he wasn't returning to school to do Matriculation. 'What? Stick around with the old man for another year?' he said. 'No way. I hate school, anyway. I've got a job in a bank in Melbourne. Don't breathe a word to anyone, but I'm leaving next week.'

I was upset because I knew I'd miss him, although I understood why he was desperate to leave. 'It's not just the old man I have to put up with,' I told him. 'It's Al. She likes to run the day scholars' lives as well as the boarders. She's so small-minded, we have boyless balls. Unless you bring your brother!'

He laughed. 'I've got a good excuse for not going. I won't be around! In any case, I'd be terrified of all those girls.'

'I'm not going, anyway.'

'I was just about to suggest swapping with Tim,' he said grinning. 'He'd love to take you.'

'Tim? Your mate Tim? The one you're always getting into trouble with at school? I've only ever seen him with you at the picture theatre or the lake. You've never even introduced me to him.'

'He's got a crush on you. That bloody old witch at your school wouldn't know Arthur from Martha, would she? He'll take you to the ball.'

I was flattered to think that someone had a crush on me, but I had to laugh. 'If you bring your brother, you must be accompanied by your parents.'

He shrugged. 'Well. That kills it, doesn't it?'

'Perhaps you're right about school though. One more year and that's it. I'm going to work hard so I can get really good marks. I'm not the slightest bit interested in going out with boys until I leave Ballarat. I won't have time, and there's no way I'd ever introduce anyone to Mum and Dad. Boy or girl!'

I'm really upset that Tony is leaving. On top of that, Maude and Harry are moving to Melbourne because of Harry's job. Mum has come apart, Maude being her favourite sister. Worst of all, we have to get out of the hotel before Christmas.

It was progress that forced us from the hotel. The Ballarat Brewery closed the Barkly and other small hotels without compensating the publicans which explains why the old man has been off his head for so long. Taking it out on us! It was Maude who told us what was going on. She said our hotel was condemned. I don't understand why the City Council condemned the rat-infested slums near our hotel, yet allowed families to continue living in them. Whenever we walk down Main Road past the slums, we automatically cross to the other side to avoid the brown sludge and alluvial tailings from the mullock heap that ooze onto the footpath. It smells like garbage and it looks like sewerage. We shudder whenever we pass Gwen's place. A hotel regular, she left her baby sleeping in a drawer on the floor. When she arrived home one afternoon, a rat was gnawing at the palate of her baby's mouth.

We sisters were optimistic about moving, but soon changed our mind. No way will I bring anyone home to the dump we're living in now. It's not that I want to live in a posh house so much as wanting it to be liveable and tidy; for my parents to be kind and welcoming. Every room except our bedroom is filled with junk because Mum and Dad are hoarders. They're not house-proud like my aunts and uncles or my friends' parents. At school when we're learning a Keats poem beginning with *A thing of beauty is a joy forever*, I immediately think of Dad. He's always been so busy making money, he's never had time to appreciate beautiful things. Instead of making an effort to do up the place, he mopes around all day, his bitterness spiralling into misery. It casts a blanket of gloom over all of us. There's no money under the bed now, although I sneak around the place when he's out, determined to find out where he's hidden it. We can't even go to the picture theatre. A twinge of nostalgia stirs inside me sometimes. I hear the babble of voices. Someone bursting through the door with a cigarette and beery grin. Gyro Duck asking me to play *Irene Goodnight* or some other boozy waltz.

22

Cecilia

Every year in Term 3, Sister Raphael taught ballroom dancing after school for all Intermediate to Matriculation students for the end of year ball. The girls, partnered according to their size, practised the foxtrot, the Pride of Erin, the progressive barn dance, the waltz. Never jive or rock and roll. Once again, as in their Intermediate year, Cecilia and Bernice, being tall, would be 'boys'. Al's only concession was that girls could dance with their brothers on the night of the ball.

'A pukeworthy event,' Cecilia and Bernice had agreed the previous year, telling their parents not to bother attending.

This year, 1955, having picked up a few clues from sixth formers, they were determined to get the better of Alphonsus. Danny would arrive with Cecilia's parents, and Tom with Bernice's. Mother Alphonsus' attitude encouraged the girls to rebel. To scheme and connive. For some, there was more planning and preparation for the ball than for their final exams. Every year Alphonsus examined the ball-gowns to determine if they conformed to her dress code. The day-scholars in the know brought along their mothers and grandmothers' frumpiest dresses. More for a laugh rather than conformity or obedience. Others told her that the dressmaker wouldn't have it ready until the day of the ball. Some were so disgusted with Alphonsus's rules that they wouldn't bother showing up on the night. It wasn't so easy for boarders. They either brought back their dresses and shoes at the beginning of the final term or had them posted later. If Alphonsus didn't approve of the dress, Sister Mercy would help with alterations.

Cecilia had chosen a shot taffeta, its blue warp and pink weft giving a purple iridescent appearance. She left it up to her mother to find a suitable pattern to conform with Reverend Mother's instructions. All dresses were to have sleeves and must be calf or full-length, the necklines no lower than the collarbone. Pastel colours were preferable to bright flashy colours, particularly red. The girls were mystified about this until someone said she'd heard that old fuddy-duddies believed that red brought out the animal passions in the opposite sex. The standard joke was that soon she'd be banning patent leather shoes in case they reflected your underwear! When Cecilia's dress arrived during Term 3, she wasn't happy with the puffy sleeves that in combination with the high neckline, made it look childish. Not at all suitable for someone who'd soon be turning seventeen.

Bernice's dress in shocking pink taffeta appeared to conform with the requirements, but on her instructions, the dressmaker had attached a removable frill on the bottom of the skirt, removable sleeves, and a yoke which would convert to a scooped neckline. She stared at Cecilia's dress. 'We'll have to do something about that. Your mother really took Al's instructions seriously, didn't she? All you need is an apron and headband and with your long neck, you'll look like Alice stretched tall. We've got to get rid of those sleeves for a start.'

In the sewing room, they set about removing the sleeves and tried to rehem the armholes. The dress ended up looking such a mess that Cecilia was almost in tears. She'd wanted to look like a smart Melbourne girl for Danny, and now her dress was not only unfashionable. It was unwearable. They approached Moira, a creative sixth former who they'd heard wanted to be a dress designer. She said the armholes wouldn't be a problem.

'I assume the old cow has already okayed it,' Moira said.

Cecilia nodded.

Moira then shocked her by hacking a wide V shape into the neckline, front and back.

'Leave it with me,' she said. 'If a lower neckline is good enough for the Queen and the Mona Lisa and all those other prints around the place, it's good enough for us.' She started giggling. 'Do you remember the story of Hannah Murphy's ballgown?'

Cecilia nodded. 'Vaguely!'

'She made her own dress, but Al didn't approve of it. You must have been in the chapel at the time, Cecilia. Surely!'

'I know she desecrated a statue.'

'You've never told me about that, Celie!'

'I was half asleep at the time. All I heard was a crash.' She turned to Moira. 'Bernice won't know the story. She came here the year after me.'

'Al decided Hannah's dress was immodest, so she got Sister Mercy to put a huge frill in another material all the way around the top of it. It covered the top half of her arms and part of the bodice. It looked so hideous that Hannah decided she was going to be ill on the evening of the ball. She removed the frill, crept into the chapel that night and put it around the bust of Our Lady's statue so that it was there for Mass the next morning. She had nothing to lose because she'd finished all her Matric exams.'

'I wish I'd been there,' Bernice said.

'The blue frill toned in with the statue. No one noticed it 'til Mass got going. I suppose everyone's bleary-eyed at 6.30 in the morning. But if you happened to notice the BVM's bust above the frill, you couldn't help seeing two pink shiny melons poking out.'

'No!' Bernice said in astonishment.

'She nicked two breakfast bowls from the servery and painted them in the art room.'

'I love this girl,' Bernice said. 'Don't tell me they had to stop the Mass!'

'Not quite. But you can imagine the uproar. The priest had no idea what was going on. When a nun tried to do something about it, the false bust came crashing to the floor.'

'That's when I realised something was going on,' Cecilia said.

'Oh my God,' Bernice couldn't stop laughing. 'Imagine writing home about that!'

Moira was grinning again. 'But the pièce de résistance was the pedestal. Hannah painted *Our Lady of Perpetual Immodesty* around the top of it.

After the three of them stopped laughing, Cecilia asked what had happened to Hannah.

'Her name has never been mentioned again, but I heard that when she went to the university, she won several awards. Apparently, she was nearly expelled earlier in the year for arguing with Gregory about Martin Luther and corruption in the church. Telling her she'd got the syllabus all wrong.'

'Well that figures,' Bernice said. 'Dad says the church is always trying to hide corruption.'

'Hannah left a memento above her bed. Some of us know it off by heart.'

The Pupil's Prayer.
I wandered lonely as a cloud
That floats on high o'er vale and dells
When all at once I saw a host
A host of flabby pink Big Als
Beside the lake beneath the trees
Fluttering and dancing in the breeze
Wearing nought but ring and frown

Satan's slime scattered all around
Penguin suit abandoned near
Such a wanton she is I fear
Tis my last day in this dreadful dump
So farewell, you fossilised, feckless old frump.'

The three girls were nearly doubled over laughing.

'I'd like to think that Alphonsus got a copy of it, but I don't know,' Moira said.

'I'd like a copy,' Cecilia said. She turned to Bernice. 'Molly loathes Al. She'd love it, wouldn't she?'

'I'll write it out for you but be careful who you show it to.'

Three weeks later, Cecilia was standing near her locker when Moira returned with her ball-gown, its neckline and armholes now decorated with exquisite little beads.

'I had them for my own dress, but changed my mind,' Moira said.

Cecilia was thrilled with it. Now she was really looking forward to the ball. Couldn't wait to see Danny! 'It's beautiful, Moira. Thank you so much. All the work you've put into sewing on those beads!'

'What with our exams, that's why it's taken so long. I've shortened the hem, too!'

She showed Cecilia her own dress that she'd made during the holidays.

'The old bag didn't notice the tacking on the daggy bolero camouflaging the top. I'll wear it into the hall, but when I start dancing, it'll gradually separate from my gown – with a little bit of help – and go straight into my boyfriend's suit-coat pocket and voilà! A miracle!'

The dress design fell into Reverend Mother's category of 'suggestive and revealing, worn only by brazen lumps of girls.' In fact, the bodice was set quite modestly above the bustline, with two bejewelled shoulder straps. 'The old battle-axe thinks my boyfriend's my brother,' Moira said, rolling her eyes. 'Jacinta and I did a brother swap years ago. What have I got to lose when I'll be out of this dump forever in a few days' time?'

Cecilia thought Moira had made her day and couldn't wait to tell Bernice.

On the evening of the ball, Cecilia caught her breath when she saw Danny in a suit for the first time. Her parents enjoyed being involved in the deception, agreeing that the imbalance between the sexes was bizarre. Cecilia couldn't believe how well Danny could dance. They were fox-trotting to *Top Hat, White Tie and Tails*. 'Do they teach dancing at your school too?' she asked him.

'Yep. Same as yours. Forms 4, 5 and 6. Only we have a social twice a year with the Sacré Coeur girls.'

Cecilia sighed. 'Alphonsus prefers to think that boys don't exist.'

'We also have to partner them for the deb ball.'

'The Sacré Coeur girls?'

He nodded. 'St Kevin's sister school.'

She tried to imagine Danny dancing with another girl, but no matter how much she put it to the back of her mind, she felt a surge of jealousy drifting through her body. 'And how do you get partners?' she asked him, trying to sound as casual as she could.

'The Brothers line us all up like sheep at the Royal Show. A row of girls, and a row of boys. Then we're sorted in order of size. It's a bit of a circus. And a laugh and a bet about who's going to end up with whom.'

She hesitated. 'And did you... did you have a good partner? Was she a good dancer?'

'She was alright, but I kept wishing she was you.'

Cecilia smiled up at him. 'I wish I'd been there,' was all she could think to say. She'd be stuck at the convent doing Matriculation next year while he was at university, where he'd have his choice of girls. Hopefully he'd be so busy he wouldn't have time for a social life. She felt herself blushing when he told her that he thought she looked better than anyone else in the hall.

'The belle of the ball,' he said, grinning, a little embarrassed.

It was the first compliment she'd ever had from a boy. 'One of the girls in my class said she didn't know I had a brother, and would I do a swap with her next year for our last ball?'

They both laughed. 'Which one is the old dragon anyway?'

Cecilia pointed out Alphonsus. 'Once everyone begins to mingle, the nuns won't remember one family from another, and whose brother is whose,' she told Danny. 'Apparently that's how it's been every year since Alphonsus has been principal.'

The radiogram was playing foxtrots: *Mississippi Mud*. *Chatanooga Choo Choo*. Not quite suitable for rock'n'rolling, but some girls attempted it. 'They're exulting in having got the better of Alphonsus,' Cecilia told Danny. 'Just like us.' A few nuns were horrified at the legs and petticoats swirling around, but with parents everywhere, they could do nothing about it. Molly had said she knew how to rock'n'roll, so Cecilia was keen to watch her dancing. Being in Intermediate, it would have been Molly's first ball at St Martin's, but where on earth was she? She'd been attending all the practices.

Families of both day-scholars and boarders were leaving by the hall door exit that opened out onto St Elizabeth's Garden. Boarders could accompany their parents to the front gate, where Sister Gregory stood on guard. Danny grabbed Cecilia's arm so they could squeeze unseen between the grotto and the garden's high corner hedge.

'Are you coming to our house after Christmas?' he whispered to her.

'If Bernice invites me,' she said breathlessly.

'I'm inviting you! For two weeks this time.'

Cecilia felt herself blushing again. 'I'd like that,' she said.

That was when he kissed her. Her first proper kiss. Long, and passionate. They kissed again and again. She felt his hands on the V of her bare skin on the back of her dress and shivered. If there was one fantastic moment she'd remember about St Martin's in 1955, it would be kissing Danny behind the grotto in St Elizabeth's Garden.

23

Molly

Early in November, Mrs McKinnon said we'd be doing the flowers on our own. She was catching the 5 o'clock train to Melbourne to help her father who hadn't been well. Apparently, the substitute sacristan can't come on Friday afternoons. I'd been working for about fifteen minutes when Father Kelly walked in and asked Maureen if she could manage by herself, to which she happily agreed. He called me aside and told me discreetly to pick up my satchel and follow him. This time, we went up the side steps of the veranda and straight into a study smelling of new furniture.

'Too many interruptions in the kitchen,' he said. 'Anyone can pop in, and you can never be sure if the housekeeper's going to arrive early. She wouldn't be too happy to see us sitting at her kitchen table. This room is quiet and much more suitable.'

We were sitting side by side in comfortable chairs at a huge desk. I wish I had a desk. On the other hand, it wouldn't fit into our bedroom.

'I want you to get a good mark for your Intermediate maths exam Molly, so we're going to work hard today,' he told me.

I was pleased. I'd been having trouble with algebra again, having missed a few lessons because of the calisthenics competitions. After almost an hour, I was really beginning to get the hang of it. Father Kelly was so kind and patient with me. He looks a little like Edmond Purdom in *The Student Prince*. When he jumped up from the desk, I imagined him bursting into song. He strode across to a posh-looking cabinet, from where I heard the sound of a soda siphon. The next moment we were drinking lemon squashes.

I can't believe a priest is waiting on me! Helping me with my homework because I do the flowers. Why doesn't my father treat me like this? All he does is snarl at us. I feel so relaxed when I'm with Father Kelly. He puts his arm around my shoulders and says 'Well done, Molly' while he gives me a hug. He reminds me that the presbytery, like the church, is God's house, and what goes on in this room is between the two of us. 'Like the seal of confession,' he says. I can't see that it is, but as if I'd tell anyone! That would be admitting I'm getting help.

The following Friday, Mrs McKinnon turned up and told us that she wasn't too happy with the flowers. She began whinging about the hydrangeas being cut too short for the gladioli, and a host of other things. That woman will never be happy. Maureen looked like she was about to cry.

'It's my fault, Mrs McKinnon,' I told her. 'Maureen's much better with flowers than I am. I cut them, not Maureen.'

It was true, because it was the one thing I had time to do before I went to the presbytery. I must admit I did them in a bit of a hurry. Father Kelly seemed to be more annoyed with Mrs McKinnon than with us. He told her the flowers looked fine, whereas she was insisting that we'd need more time with her. Two weeks later, we were on our own because Mrs McKinnon had to go to Melbourne again. Once again, Father Kelly took me to the presbytery, telling Maureen he thought she'd be better off doing the flowers on her own, and that I should be studying for my exams.

I worked on equations with Father Kelly for half an hour. He said I was going to do very well in my maths exam and gave me a lemon squash. I shouldn't be fussy, but I wish he'd use lemonade instead of soda water. It was quite bitter. He must have noticed me wincing, so he gave me a chocolate. Bitter and sweet together! It reminded me of the shandies the ladies drank at the pub. Beer mixed with lemonade! Maude gave me a sip of hers once and I thought it was revolting. Fancy spoiling lemonade like that!

'Do you have any questions that you don't understand about religion,' Father Kelly suddenly asked me.

I had many of course, but during Religion this week, Rosario said it was a sin to hate anyone but the devil, so I asked him if it was true.

'Well, I suppose it depends,' he said, putting his arm around me as I stood up to leave. 'But who do you hate, Molly?'

'I… I'd rather not say, Father.'

'Someone at home?'

I nodded. I was thinking of the fourth commandment, *Honour thy father and mother.* How can I do that? If you had to honour your father, wouldn't he have to do the same? It's different with my mother. I'm not sure about her feelings. She loves my baby brother and sister. She's always kissing and cuddling them. I think with us not being together during our childhood, we're still strangers to her. I wasn't looking for sympathy, but perhaps Father Kelly noticed that my eyes were brimming with tears.

He put an arm around my shoulder and drew me to him. His other arm was around my waist, but after a while he brought it up higher, moving it slowly across my chest, under my blazer. I don't think he realised where he was touching me. I pulled away a little, but at the same time I felt very relaxed. He pulled me closer, breathing heavily. Then he kissed me gently on the lips just like Gene Kelly and Debbie Reynolds in *Singin' In The Rain*. It's the first time anyone has ever kissed me. I liked it but I was embarrassed. After all, he's a priest.

When the phone rang in another room, he stepped into the passage saying he'd be back in a few minutes. Meanwhile, he told me to make myself at home on the couch, and to have a look at the two volumes of art on the coffee table. Art is not one of my subjects, but with beautiful prints of great artists all around my school, I've learned to appreciate it without understanding it. I began leafing through the pages of the first book and was astonished that so many beautiful paintings and sculptures existed in the Vatican. The second book was called *Classic Renaissance and Baroque Art.* The first image was a Rembrandt called *The Jewish Bride.* The man was touching a woman's breast. There are Rembrandts at school, but not like this. I gasped as I turned the pages. There were several more Renaissance images of men touching and kissing women's bare breasts. I've always thought it was kissing that aroused couples. Did kissing lead to this? Now I was aroused. I felt rebellious. I knew I was blushing, but at the same time I was drawn to the images. Excited. Alphonsus wouldn't have approved of these pictures. Was that why I kept turning the pages? If Father Kelly approved, they must be okay. It was art, wasn't it? I looked up to see him near the cabinet, smiling at me. I was embarrassed. Next moment, he handed me a tiny velvet-lined jewellery box. Inside was a cameo of an angel encircled with marcasite. I don't wear brooches, but I politely thanked him. He picked up my drink and gave it to me to finish.

'This brooch has been blessed by the Pope,' he said. 'It's a reward for your hard work in the church and here in my study, Molly. You deserve it. It has a tricky safety catch,' he said, taking the brooch from the box, and sliding his hand down the top of my tunic.

I was terribly embarrassed. I told him we weren't allowed to wear jewellery.

He insisted that it was alright. 'Look at my hands. They've been consecrated by God. They are God's vessels.'

His hands were outstretched as though he was saying the *Pater noster* during Mass. His hands were not gnarled from age or rough from hard work. His hands have never built a house or flogged anyone. These hands were gentle, delicate, sensitive. They have blessed congregations. Served communion. Baptised babies.

'It won't be seen if I pin it here,' he said undoing my shirt buttons and sliding a hand between my shirt and singlet.

As he pinned the cameo on my shirt, his hands began moving around my breasts. I knew I was blushing, but at the same time, I felt a sort of tingle. Why was this part of my body so sensitive? Wasn't it supposed to be kissing that aroused people? Now the tingling seemed to extend all over my body. What was the matter with me? I was embarrassed and confused. Why was a priest doing this to me? My body seemed to be moving ahead of my brain. I couldn't control it.

My head was whirling around, and I began to breathe heavily, almost gasping. Strange sensations were erupting in my body. He was making a sort of guttural, moaning sound. Then he put his arms around me and pulled me close to him. I tried to pull away, but he held me even closer as though he was protecting me. I think he loves me. But aren't priests only supposed to love God? I think I love him, but perhaps I just have a crush on him. I know he loves me more than my parents do. They never touch me. I like being touched.

He took my hands in his, bringing them down below the waist of his cassock. 'We'll treasure our time together Molly and keep it as our special secret. I am God's representative on earth, and he has sent me to help you.'

I didn't believe him.

'You must never tell anyone I'm helping you. In fact, your school uniform's a bit obvious, so it would be much better if you went home and changed before doing the flowers. But don't forget to bring your maths books.'

I nodded. 'Yes, Father.'

'This is between God and us. And if you're feeling pleasure when we're together, it's natural. And never forget! Once you enter this room, Molly, it's like the seal of confession.'

There's no way I'd ever tell anyone about Father Kelly. Maybe my best friend Gabby, but I'm not sure. I'm not even sure I want to come back to this room again with Father Kelly. I know I'm going to do well in my exams now.

'Molly,' he said, just as I was leaving. 'I think you need a little more work on geometry. I'm busy most afternoons with pastoral care at the hospitals, and teaching at the college, but I'm free on Wednesdays from about 4pm until 5.30pm. I'd like you to come straight to the presbytery and knock on my door.'

'Wednesdays, Father?'

'Wednesday would be perfect, Molly.'

'I'm sorry, Father,' I told him. 'On Wednesdays in Term 3, we have compulsory ballroom dancing from 4 'til 5 o'clock. It's for Forms 4, 5 and 6 for the school ball in December.'

He looked very disappointed. I'm pleased I didn't have to lie to him.

24

The Priest

The Friday after Molly's last visit to the presbytery was the last one in November. Hilton walked into the church expecting to see Maureen and Molly, Mrs McKinnon having told him that the girls should be able to work by themselves until the Christmas period when they would need her assistance with the more complicated floral arrangements.

'Molly's got a dental appointment today, Father,' Maureen said, when she noticed him looking around. 'After that, she's got a rehearsal for her end-of-year calisthenics concert. She can't help out at all after that because she's got a job at Coles until Christmas Eve.'

He was angry. Just when he thought he had her in the palm of his hands. Molly hadn't mentioned that she wouldn't be around! Her exams would be finished, so he'd have to think of another excuse to bring her to the presbytery. After Christmas, he'd be holidaying in Lorne for three weeks, which meant he wouldn't see her again until the start of the new school term in February. He heaved a sigh of relief when Mrs McKinnon told him she'd be away in Melbourne then. Mrs McArdle would stand in for her, and the girls would be capable of doing the floral arrangements themselves after that.

He walked into the church on the last Friday in January. Maureen was positioning vases of flowers on the pedestals, and Molly was trimming gladioli in the sacristy.

'You're very capable of doing the flowers by yourself today,' he told Maureen. 'Molly might as well go home.'

He opened the external sacristy door, and discreetly asked Molly to follow him to the presbytery. She was reluctant.

'I can't come here again Father because my calisthenics practices have changed to after school on Fridays.'

He'd get around that problem somehow. Offer to coach her on Wednesdays now that they wouldn't be practising ballroom dancing. Meanwhile, he'd make the most of the next hour or so. The heatwave had cooked his study, but he wouldn't open the window onto the veranda. The housekeeper might walk past. The fan was humming on its lowest setting, the votive candles illuminating the statuette of the Virgin Mary. He pulled the heavy curtain across the window. Darkness would help shroud what he had in mind.

'Are things any better at home, Molly?' he asked as he poured her a large cool drink.

Her eyes welled up with tears.

'I'm here to comfort and help you always Molly. You know that. It's all part of my duties,' he said, putting a comforting arm around her and pulling her towards him. She seemed to be totally unaware of how his body was reacting. The swelling in his groin. 'So you're pleased to get away from home for a while, Molly,' he said, leading her to the couch.

'Yes, Father,' she said.

He asked her about the holidays. She told him she spent some of them working at Coles, some in Melbourne with her cousins.

'And today during the heat wave?'

'I've been swimming at the baths with my sisters, Father.'

He pictured her in bathers. Today she was wearing a blouse and skirt. She moaned with pleasure after he began caressing her breasts, but no amount of coaxing or flattery would press her into removing her blouse. Overcome with lust and desire for the forbidden, his hand crept inside the elasticised waist of her gathered skirt. She pulled away.

'Your... your hand,' she stammered. 'I don't think...'

He brushed it off as though it was an accident. 'I'm sorry,' he said. 'Your skin is like silk. My hand slipped. In any case Molly, God approves of what we're doing because I'm a priest.'

He picked up her glass, handing it to her. 'Have you had a drink since you've been to the baths, Molly?'

'No, Father.'

'Then you must finish this. During this hot weather you should be drinking more liquid. You look hot. Perhaps you got a little sunburnt today.'

He waited until she'd finished it, then sat down beside her on the couch. What did she know about Venice, he asked her. She told him haltingly that she'd heard of St Mark's Cathedral. The canals. The Murano glass. He showed her his album of Venetian art, featuring Canaletto and Tiepolo. The next album, *Famous Classic Nudes*, included Goya's *The Nude Maja*, Cezanne's *Seven Bathers*, Ruben's *Leda and the Swan*. He thought she looked aroused by these images.

'Beautiful, isn't she? But no more beautiful than you, Molly,' he said indicating Titian's *Venus of Urbino*. 'There is no doubt that when God created the world, he put all his effort into making girls look beautiful, didn't he Molly?'

Her eyes were glassy now, her posture beginning to slump. A few more minutes and he knew she'd be more pliable. The combination of alcohol and phenobarbital would take effect.

'What interesting things did you do in Melbourne, Molly?' he asked, subtly unbuttoning her blouse.

'We... we went to the beach. And Luna... Luna Park. Sssorry, Father. I feel a bit drowsy. I'm so tired. I don't feel very well. I'd better go home.'

'I think the heat has affected you Molly. You've obviously got a lot on your mind with your problems at home. You need to relax.'

She was breathing deeply when he carried her into his bedroom and laid her down on his bed. He stared down at her. She had become Guerin's *Portrait of A Young Girl.* All he wanted was to look at her naked body so that he'd have a picture of her like this every time he saw her. She didn't stir when he removed her clothing. As his eyes meandered over her prostrate body, he gasped with pleasure. A growl began in his throat as his fingers tore at the buttons on his cassock. He was losing control. All he wanted was to look at her, he told himself again. But after years of suppressed sexuality, he felt the heat stirring in him. The beast within him growing stronger. She was as limp as a rag doll, but could wake if he was astride her or in any of the positions he salivated over in the Kama Sutra. He slowly pulled her body towards the bottom of his bed, her legs relaxed. Pliable. In a sexual frenzy, and with the thought of his naked flesh against hers, he realised that he wouldn't be satisfied by touching her. Stroking her. He must complete the act, but he'd be gentle. She wouldn't know what had happened. *Coitus interruptus* would free them of any consequences. With little effort, he slid the hips of the unconscious but beautiful Molly to meet his.

25

Molly

I'm lying in bed, nearly keeling over every time I stand up. Groping my way to the toilet. Vomiting into a bucket. I woke up on Saturday morning with a terrible headache, still in my clothes and unable to eat anything. My mind is in a fog about what happened after I went to the presbytery. Mum said Father Kelly drove me home after I fainted in the church while doing the flowers. It seems that priests tell lies too, like me telling him my calisthenics classes were after school on Fridays this year. He told Mum I must have had sunstroke, so she believes him, of course.

Three days later it's Monday, February 2, 1956. *The year of the Games of the XVI Olympiad, to be opened by Prince Philip*, as they're often saying on the radio. Just as well I'm feeling a lot better because school starts tomorrow. I'd hate to be away for my first day in Form 5. While I'm getting all my school stuff together, I think of Father Kelly. The canals. Gondolas. Nudes. He insisted on me having a drink. Did he put a Bex powder in it? Maybe two of them! It was quite bitter. Perhaps it upset me. Mum takes Bex powders when she's worried or upset about something, which is often lately because she's miserable without Maude. She gave me a Bex once when I had a bad headache with period pain. It tasted bitter, but it seemed to ease the pain and made me feel quite relaxed, the way I felt when I was with Father Kelly. Except that last time I was limp and floppy. I remember him fumbling with my clothing, but I couldn't do anything about it. I didn't feel like doing anything about it. I was lying on a couch like one of the nudes in his album. Floating down the Grand Canal in a gondola. Someone carrying me.

I'll manage maths without any help from Father Kelly this year. Sit at the back of St Alban's for Mass so he doesn't see me. Do my homework at the library to get away from home. Practise the piano regularly so that I get an Honour for my exam. I'm missing calisthenics, but at least Alphonsus will have less to whinge about now. The old cow began the school year by making ridiculous proclamations she'd have dreamt up during the holidays.

'If any day-scholars post or collect letters for boarders, you will be in serious trouble,' she bleated. 'If anyone has any information about this, it is your duty to report it immediately to me. Your name will not be disclosed.'

Cecilia and I rolled our eyes at each other. During our first duet practice this year, she gave me a letter to post to her boyfriend, Bernice's brother.

I think it was around the middle of March when I started getting headaches and dizziness. Then the nausea and vomiting began, similar to what I had the weekend before school returned. I've been home from school for two weeks now, hardly eating, and thinner than ever. When Mum took me to see Doctor Doyle, I felt so ill, I could hardly answer his questions.

'Look,' he said. 'I'm not asking you to explain Einstein's Theory of Relativity. I just want you to tell me if you're only vomiting in the morning.'

'No, Doctor. Any time!' I said, at which point I had to rush into the toilet off his surgery to vomit.

When I returned, I was feeling a little better, but I still had a throbbing headache. He looked exasperated when Mum suggested that maybe it was appendicitis. I don't think doctors like anyone diagnosing illnesses.

'Mrs Harrington,' Dr Doyle said politely. 'It could be any number of things. Appendicitis, constipation, irritable bowel syndrome. A hormonal imbalance. Or maybe an ongoing bladder or urine infection. I need to give Molly a thorough examination, so I will call you when I need you,' he said as he opened the door to the waiting room.

He helped me onto the examination table. 'Tell me where it hurts when I apply pressure to different parts of your abdomen,' he said.

His prodding and poking didn't hurt, but it made it me feel more nauseous.

'Is your vomiting and nausea worse in the mornings?' he asked me.

'Yes.'

'Are you sleeping well, Molly?

I shook my head. He told me to step onto the scales.

'For your height, Molly, average at around five foot four, you are very underweight. When was your last period?'

I stared at him. Why on earth was he asking me such a personal question?

'I don't know,' I replied. I couldn't think clearly.

He looked exasperated. 'We are almost two months into the school term. You must know if you've had one since you've been back at school.'

'I think my last one was during the holidays.'

'Possibly you're not menstruating because you're underweight,' he said. 'But I'd like to pinpoint exactly when you had your last period.'

'In January, I think. When I was in Melbourne.'

Then I remembered something. The day after I last returned from the presbytery, I noticed a few spots of blood on my underwear and assumed my period had come early. It was obviously a false alarm.

'Do you have a boyfriend?' Dr Doyle suddenly asked me.

'A boyfriend?'

First of all, he was asking personal questions about periods, and now it was boyfriends.

I frowned. 'I don't understand.'

'Perhaps there's someone you've been keeping company with this year. Or maybe last year. Someone other than your school-friends.'

I had no idea what he was getting at. 'I don't understand,' I said.

He sighed, pursing his lips. Impatient with me.

'Have you been seeing someone, Molly?' he asked me. 'A boyfriend, perhaps?'

I must have looked like an idiot. Mouth and eyes wide open in surprise.

'Let's try a different tack. For a start. You must know that you could be pregnant. I can't tell at this stage. I'm guessing.'

'I don't… I don't know what you mean,' I said.

'Pregnant,' he repeated. 'You must be aware that when you fool around with your boyfriend you have a very good chance of getting pregnant.'

The word pregnant was not in my vocabulary. And a boyfriend? 'Fool around?'

'You could be having a baby.'

'A baby? But that's impossible. I'm not married.'

He laughed. 'Unless you're having a virgin birth, it's the sort of thing that happens when you go all the way with your boyfriend. Does he know?'

'I don't have a boyfriend,' I told him. 'Just... just someone who... who...' I wanted to say that a priest had been kind to me, but I felt I couldn't tell him that. I burst into tears. I'd been feeling so wretched for two weeks, and now my Doctor was asking me stupid questions.

'Look,' he said, losing patience. 'I don't really care if you have one or several boyfriends. I just need you to tell me if you've been playing around. It could have happened about two months ago. Think who you were with then. You need to be aware of your options. You're a minor and your boyfriend could be charged. Just think who you were with back then.'

I didn't know what to say.

'So,' Dr Doyle continued. 'One option is to marry the father, although you're a bit young for that. Who is he? We may need to inform the police.'

'Father?' I gasped. 'The father? The police?'

I didn't want to show my ignorance, but I thought women had babies *after* they were married. That somehow God must have had something to do with it, although Gabby once told me she was sure it had something to do with *down there*.

'Yes,' Doctor Doyle interrupted my reflections. 'I might have to report it.'

'But I don't have a boyfriend. I don't know any boys. The... father?'

'Yes. The father,' the doctor sighed. 'One of the customers in your father's pub, perhaps?' He looked at my card. 'Ah! You're not living there now.' He paused for a moment. 'Have you been alone with someone you know well? A male. Whatever you tell me won't leave this room. Although you're a minor, of course.'

The only male I've been with about two months ago was Father Kelly. Did he do something to me when I fainted? I mumbled something about 'Father.'

'Father?' he said. 'Your father? You've been with your father?'

He had a weird look on his face. 'My father? He... he's been upset. We can't talk to him. How can I tell him I'm...' I burst into tears.

'What has he been doing Molly?'

'He mopes around the house. Acting weirdly. Hardly speaking.'

'But what does he do after you go to bed?'

I shrugged. 'Goes to bed like the rest of us I suppose.'

'Molly,' he said gently. 'I only want to help you now. You mentioned your father.'

I stared at him. Puzzled. It's very difficult trying to carry on a proper conversation when you're feeling nauseous. 'I thought *you* did.'

'You mentioned him earlier.'

'No. Not him.'

'Who then?'

I hid my face in my hands and sobbed. 'Father... Father Kelly. At Saint... Saint... I shouldn't have gone to the presbytery. I think he did something to me.'

He sat there staring at me, as though he couldn't believe what I was saying.

'Molly,' he said kindly. 'This is not your fault. You mustn't blame yourself.'

'But I don't understand how...'

'It doesn't matter. You just need to understand your options. He'd be years older than you. You're a minor. Did he entice you to the presbytery?'

'Yes,' I said.

'Did you agree to him having intercourse with you?'

I've read that word before in *The Courier*, but I've never been sure what it meant. Perhaps a man doing something to a woman. *Down there.* 'I can't remember anything after the lemon drink he gave me.'

'He must have given you alcohol. Perhaps you passed out and that was when he assaulted you.' He began tapping his pen on his desk. 'There's a place in Melbourne where girls in your condition are looked after. It will be quite some time before you start showing, so return to school and try to act like everything is normal for the moment. Concentrate on your classes. No one in Ballarat needs to know. Only your parents. You should leave Ballarat after the May holidays.'

He wrote something on his letterhead pad, placed it in an envelope, and handed it at me. 'This might help explain your absences or inability to do your homework. Or anything else you're having trouble with. Show it to your teachers when you return to school.'

Act like everything is normal. How can I do that?

'I've said that you're suffering from a low-grade ongoing gastric disorder which is not contagious,' Doctor Doyle said. 'It's the truth. I'm not sure why you've got headaches and why you're vomiting during the day. It's usually only in the mornings that this sort of thing happens. It'll go soon, I'm sure. You can have aspros or a Bex for your headaches, but you must try and eat more. You need a healthy diet for yourself and the baby. You'll be able to get back on with your life after the baby is born. There are many women who want to adopt these babies, so you won't need to worry about anything.'

He called Mum back into the surgery. She had such a look of horror on her face when he told her that I was pregnant, I don't think she took in any other details of what Doctor Doyle was saying.

'Just act like everything is normal,' he reminded me again as I was leaving. Difficult enough at home. Even more difficult at school. When I returned, I stared at the note stuck on my desk. *Don't forget!!! Brahms and Dvorak in the Hall at 12.55 pm on the concert grand.* Why did I agree to play duets with Cecilia? *Just act like everything is normal.* How on earth is that possible? We were about eight weeks into Term 1, and I'd have to tell her that I couldn't play in the concert the following term. I've been feeling so wretched. Avoiding Gabby and other friends. During French, Sister Jeanne wanted to take me to the infirmary. I handed her the doctor's letter, excused myself, and raced off to the toilet. Despite a headache that was grinding into my temples, I returned, determined to stay at school. At lunchtime, I threw up in the toilet, then began looking for somewhere to hide until I felt better.

26

Cecilia

Cecilia gulped down her lunch in the refectory. The grand piano! It was all she could think about. The first concert grand she'd ever seen. It had arrived two weeks ago. Now that it was tuned, they'd been given permission to practise their duets on it. She raced to the hall, raised the piano fallboard, and propped up the lid with full stick. Now to test the range and dynamics. Her silvery arpeggios rose and cascaded in the air, echoing around the empty hall to sparkle like a string of pearls. She gasped. What a sound! Next, a Bach fugue. The difference! So much more resonant. So sharp. Each voice separate and distinct when it entered. So clear. No fuzzing or distortion of sounds. How she loved the mathematical contortions of Bach! How could she ever play an upright again? Now for the dynamics. Beethoven's *Apassionata* should do it. So tempestuous! The fury of the *fortissimo* must surely be reverberating throughout the convent. As for the *pianissimo*, it's just a suggestion of touch. A caress of the keys. Then there was that extra magic pedal, the *sostenuto*. Useful for modern composers like Debussy to sustain a pedal point or chord so one can play on top of it without muddying the sound, Sister Angela had said. Like having three hands or an organ pedal!

She looked at the clock. Twenty minutes left. No time to try out the *sostenuto* now. Molly was very late. With the concert coming up in June, the five-day Easter break and May holidays in between, there was only time for a few more practices. Molly had been away and missed several. But hadn't she seen her back at school yesterday? Her friend Gabby said she was at school today but had disappeared at lunchtime. Where on earth was she? Molly knew their practice was in the hall today. Perhaps she'd gone home. She'd check out the music rooms. Molly was in the last one, sitting with her back to the piano, head in her hands.

Cecilia tried to hold back her anger. 'What's the matter, Molly? Why didn't you come to the hall? I've been waiting for you for ages.'

Molly slowly raised her head to look up at Cecilia. 'I… I'm not feeling very well,' she said. 'I couldn't make it to the hall to tell you.'

Cecilia had to admit that Molly didn't look great. 'Perhaps you should be home in bed, Molly.'

Molly bit her and lip lowered her head. 'I won't be here for the concert. I'm sorry.'

Now Cecilia was stricken with remorse. Oh my God! Did Molly have some terrible disease? No wonder she was looking so awful. A girl from the Primary School had died from cancer the previous year and a senior had recently contracted TB. 'I'm the one who should be saying sorry. I shouldn't have snapped at you. I'm so sorry. I was being selfish. It doesn't matter at all about the concert.'

'It does. There are girls who are much better than me.'

'No they're not. The difference is that you listen so that we can keep together. Your timing is never out. You feel where the next phrase is, and your touch and dynamics are first rate.' She sat down on the bench seat beside Molly. 'Is it… Is it very serious?'

Molly stared into space, breathing heavily, her shoulders heaving up and down.

'I'm sorry Molly. I didn't mean to pry. I wish I could help you.'

Suddenly Molly started sobbing uncontrollably. 'No one can ever help me,' she gasped. Cecilia put an arm around her. It was this gesture of kindness, of sympathy that made Molly blurt it all out. 'The doctor says... the doctor says I'm having a baby. And I don't understand why. I didn't want to...' She buried her head in her hands.

Cecilia was shocked. Bernice had talked about a girl from her school in Melbourne who'd left to have a baby. But a girl from St Martin's? Perhaps Molly was forced into it! She thought of the novel Bernice had hidden under the primary school veranda. *The Fountainhead*. She and Bernice had discussed paragraphs that puzzled them. *It was an act that could be performed in tenderness as a seal of love. Or in contempt as a symbol of humiliation and conquest. It could be the act of a lover or the act of a soldier violating an enemy woman. He did it as an act of scorn. Not as love, but as defilement. And this made her lie still and submit.*

'Do you love him Molly? Your boyfriend?'

Molly said nothing for a while. 'I think I did. But perhaps... perhaps I needed someone to love me. Or I just needed someone to *tell* me they loved me.'

'Molly,' Cecilia said after a minute. 'Did he force you? Did he force himself on you?' She wanted to ask her if it was *an act of tenderness. A seal of love.* Or was it *defilement?*'

Molly hung her head. 'He... I don't know how he...'

Cecilia apologised, embarrassed now. 'I'm sorry. I shouldn't have asked.' She paused for a moment. 'Your parents will help you...'

'No. It's... it's not like that at home.'

Molly continued to sob, her head down in her hands. 'He said he loved me. But he couldn't have.' She looked up through her tears at Cecilia. 'The thing is, I don't understand why I'm having a baby. I didn't do anything. I thought you had to be married.'

Cecilia couldn't understand how Molly had no idea that what she'd done would lead to pregnancy. And why was she so ill? 'Did you say you have to go away?'

Molly nodded.

'Where to?'

'Melbourne,' she murmured. 'After the May holidays. Around June or July, I think. I shouldn't have told you. The doctor said not to tell anyone. To act normal. But I can't. I haven't even told Gabby. So please don't tell anyone. I... I had to tell you, so you'd understand why I'm not playing for the concert.'

The two girls sat in silence until the warning bell rang in the distance. Cecilia decided to ignore it. Molly's welfare was more important. The jumbled sounds of Chopin and Beethoven and Mozart suddenly stopped. She heard the clunk of fallboards closing, of doors slamming and footsteps scuttling away.

'There's only one nun I would ever go to in this place when I need to talk about something,' Cecilia said finally. 'I always speak to her when I have problems. She was very kind to me in my first few weeks here when I was crying in bed one night. She's very understanding.'

Molly looked at Cecilia, sniffing and wiping her nose. 'Sister Jeanne?'

Cecilia nodded. 'She might be able to give you some good advice. She's got relatives who are doctors in Melbourne. I know for a fact that if you ask her not to mention anything to Alphonsus or anyone else, she'll keep her promise. It's why the boarders trust her. I really think you should talk to her.'

The only movement in the practice room now was the quivering of Molly's shoulders. The only sound, an occasional sob from a shudder. 'Shall we go?' Cecilia said. She put her arm around Molly. 'Perhaps Jeanne has a free period now. We'll go to the staff room. She'll probably know a place where you can talk in private.'

'*Qu'est-ce qu'il y a?*' Jeanne said with her bright smile when she opened the door. All seniors were required to converse with her in French both inside and outside the classroom.

'*C'est* Molly,' Cecilia hesitated. *Je crois que… qu'elle préférait te parler en… en privé.*'

'*Merci*, Cecilia.'

27

Jeanne

In a small study near the staff room, Jeanne looked at the once bright-eyed girl she'd been teaching since Form 3. The girl who had won first prize in the 1955 *Alliance Française* poetry competition, and likely to do the same again in Form 5. The girl she'd seen happily practising duets with Cecilia.

Now she picked up instantly that something was very wrong with Molly. Something much more serious than the doctor's explanation had led her to believe. Molly said she'd speak to her if she promised not to mention it to anyone else. Jeanne felt she couldn't do that. What if it was some terrible disease that could affect her work? Something serious that could be passed onto others! Molly must have noticed her hesitation because she suddenly stood up and said she had to go. Jeanne changed her mind. She'd get around Molly somehow.

'It's okay Molly. This will remain between you and me. I promise.'

Jeanne was shocked when Molly told her she was pregnant. 'And how did your parents take the news, Molly?' she said casually after a long pause.

Molly looked evasive. 'I've got to go to a place in Melbourne after the May holidays. June or July. I'm not sure.'

Jeanne imagined that an out-of-wedlock pregnancy would be about the worst thing that could happen to a young girl in a Catholic family. Worse than a death. 'Have you told the father of your baby Molly?'

Molly shook her head. 'I can't. He… I don't understand how I can be having a baby, Sister!' she blurted out. 'I thought you had to be married.'

Jeanne wondered how many young girls became pregnant through sheer ignorance. 'Perhaps he could marry you, Molly.'

Molly shook her head. 'He can't marry me.'

'Is he already married Molly?'

Molly's eyes widened. She shook her head. 'No Sister.'

'What's his occupation Molly?'

Molly stared at Jeanne, then lowered her eyes. 'He… he's a priest,' she said in a flat voice.

Jeanne gasped. '*Mon Dieu*! In which parish?'

'Mine, Sister. St Alban's.'

Jeanne was outraged. She asked Molly for more details. How often did you see him? When and why did you start going to the presbytery? After Molly's responses, she was so angry she had to force herself to keep calm. The priest had used his ecclesiastical power to seduce her. Deliberately tricked this poor girl into visiting the presbytery so he could violate her. A girl so ignorant of the facts of life she hardly seemed to understand pregnancy and what was going on in her body. 'Do you know how many months pregnant you are, Molly?'

Molly looked vague. Confused. 'I… I'm not sure, Sister. The doctor asked me that. I don't really know. I don't know anything about having babies and that sort of thing because no one ever told me.' She looked embarrassed, tears watering her eyes again. 'I never let him touch me down there, so I don't understand.'

Jeanne was puzzled. Why would Molly lie to her? She'd always seemed so open and honest. She took Molly's hands in hers. In France, parents didn't make such a secret of it. Certainly, every girl knew what having periods meant, and what it meant *not* to have periods. It was different in Australia. For girls, and indeed women, sex was more about shame. As for this poor girl, she didn't even seem to get the connection between making love or pregnancy and periods. 'Why did you visit him again when you'd decided you weren't going to return, Molly?'

Molly frowned. 'I'd started doing the flowers with Maureen, but Father Kelly insisted on me going to the presbytery. I became dizzy when I was there. I fainted.'

'Have you ever fainted before Molly?'

Molly hesitated. 'Twice in church when I was fasting so I could receive Holy Communion.'

Jeanne understood that. She'd witnessed a few girls fainting during Mass. Often in the heat of summer she herself had been desperate for a sip of water before Mass, but missing communion was not an option for nuns. Having a period and wearing all those heavy clothes in summer never helped either. Man-made rules. What would men know about girls who were menstruating? Or pregnant women, for that matter. It wasn't easy for women. They never made the rules. She shouldn't be thinking like this. De Beauvoir had turned her into a cynic. 'And you were well when you arrived?'

Molly nodded. 'Yes, Sister. Earlier I'd been swimming with my sisters. He gave me a drink, but when I started to feel funny, he said I was probably sunburnt, but I wasn't.'

'And you were on a couch?'

Molly's face contorted. 'Excuse me Sister, I have to go to the toilet,' she said, suddenly racing off.

Finally, Jeanne thought she got it. The drink. It had to be something in the drink. Surely it would have tasted strange! It would have relaxed her, but enough for Molly to succumb to his advances. 'Are you alright Molly?' she asked when Molly returned ten minutes later, her face white and scarcely looking any better.

Molly nodded. 'Did the drink taste like a regular lemon squash Molly?'

Molly thought about it. 'Not as sweet, Sister.'

'Was it bitter?'

She shrugged. 'Yes. I prefer lemon drinks with lemonade.'

'Do you think it had alcohol in it?'

Molly's eyes widened. 'No, Sister. I hate alcohol. I once had a sip of beer at the hotel and wondered why anyone would want to drink it. I hate the smell of it too.'

'Did he give you a drink on other occasions Molly?'

'Yes, Sister.'

'And did you feel a little different afterwards?'

She shrugged. 'I always felt better with him because he talked to me. I felt relaxed. He was always nice to me. I could talk to him when I was upset about... about things. Except for the last time. I couldn't concentrate. I shouldn't have...'

'Molly. The reality is, no matter what happened, none of this is your fault, and I hope your doctor made that clear. You were molested. You're a victim. He should be reported to the authorities.'

Molly looked horrified.

'Without any names being mentioned! I promise I won't do anything until we both discuss this again. I need to think about how we can go about it without implicating you or your family.'

She walked with Molly back to her locker and sent a girl to find Brigid and Veronica to accompany her home. There were aspects of Molly's pregnancy and illness that she wanted to discuss with Paul and Andrea.

With Mother Alphonsus waddling around the parlour on visiting day, smiling and greeting everyone, Jeanne decided it would be safer to speak in French. Paul, an obstetrician, told Jeanne that there were many young girls in Molly's situation, most of them likely to end up at his hospital, the Royal Women's. Jeanne was more interested in how Molly could be violated without her being aware of it.

'So he gave her a drink?' Paul asked her. 'Vodka or gin is easily disguised in a soft drink.'

Andrea, Paul's wife, and also a doctor, insisted it would take more than that to knock Molly out totally. 'Phenobarbital would do it. In combination with alcohol it would knock her senseless.'

'Molly said he gave her a lemon squash,' Jeanne said.

'Huh! That's it then,' Andrea said. 'Did she say she was drowsy?'

'Yes, and the drink was bitter. Unfortunately, she can't remember everything. One thing I can tell you is that Molly is very honest. If she tells me she didn't... didn't make love to the priest, then I believe her.'

'Does it make much difference at this stage? She can't do anything.'

'It does Paul and you know it.' Andrea was adamant. 'We both know this sort of thing has happened before. It should be reported.'

Paul gave a typical Gallic shrug. 'Yes. And nothing's ever done about it. You might as well tell the bones in the cemetery. The police act on rape sometimes, but when it concerns the clergy, they're all about protecting them as much as they protect themselves. I told you about Mike and Rob reporting something similar to the police and nothing was done. Mike said it was about altar boys and Rob said the priest he reported violated boys and girls. They eventually removed him to another parish. Most children are too frightened to report it, and parents don't always believe their children.'

'All the same, it should be reported,' Andrea said. 'Even if they do nothing about it, we have a moral and legal duty to report anything like that. The poor girl must be terribly confused and depressed. I wish I could talk to her.' She turned to Jeanne. 'Could you ask her if she felt drowsy or dizzy or out of it that night Jeanne? And for how long?'

Jeanne caught sight of Molly the following day after lunch and called her aside. Why did the poor girl look so ill? Morning sickness wasn't supposed to last all day. Surely! Just as she thought, Molly answered yes to all the side effects of the phenobarbital and alcohol which was why she'd remained in bed the whole weekend. She vaguely remembered Father Kelly driving her home. He'd told her parents that she'd fainted while doing the flowers.

'What did your father say when your mother told him you were pregnant Molly?'

Molly looked down, saying nothing. Then her whole body started shuddering as she broke into uncontrollable sobs. 'He... he...'

'Did he slap you Molly?'

'He said I was a slut and wanted to know who I'd been with.'

'But didn't you tell him about the priest? You said the doctor told your mother. Surely...'

Molly shook her head. 'I didn't get a chance.'

Jeanne decided not to press her any further. Dom agreed that it should be reported to Alphonsus, but without mentioning Molly's name.

'I have an instinctive feeling that nothing will be gained from my efforts,' Jeanne said, after making an appointment to see her superior.

Dom was just as sceptical. 'Paula says clerical whitewashing has been going on for centuries. One of the reasons her husband left the priesthood was because the cover-ups ate away at his conscience. I can't imagine Alphonsus believing that priests can do wrong.'

'I'm going to have to stretch the truth so she can't identify Molly.'

'Play your cards one at a time.'

'I suspect everyone does that with her, *chérie*.' Jeanne sighed. 'Did I ever tell you that I would have joined the Loreto Order if Alphonsus had been around for long enough to show her true colours after Mother Paulinus died?'

Dom put on a hurt look. 'Which means we'd never have met each other.'

'Of course!' Jeanne gave her a quick kiss on the lips. 'We'll be forever thankful to Al for that.'

When Jeanne entered Alphonsus's office, she decided that whatever her own distance from the real world was, her superior in her mid-sixties must be light years away. The girls tended to seek out the younger more outgoing nuns when they had problems. Who would ever confide in this formidable woman seated behind her desk? *Formidable.* A word that had a different meaning and pronunciation in the French language.

'I asked to see you Mother, because something rather serious regarding one of our girls has come to my attention.'

Mother Alphonsus nodded wisely.

'But before I give you the details, Mother,' Jeanne continued, 'I've made a vow to the girl that her name won't be mentioned. She's adamant about repressing it to avoid a scandal, although she'd like the person concerned to be reported.'

'If it's that serious, Sister, how can I resolve anything if names aren't mentioned?'

'Perhaps by reporting the perpetrator to the authorities to ensure that it won't happen again, Mother. One of our girls has been molested.' She wouldn't mention the pregnancy.

Mother Alphonsus looked shocked. 'Obviously the girl is a day-scholar, so it's really out of our jurisdiction. Is it... is it her boyfriend?'

'No, Mother.'

'Not... not incest, surely!'

'No, Mother. However, the molester is known to the community.'

'And the girl could not avoid this... this person?'

'One could say that she was violated through no fault of hers. He's much older than her.'

Mother Alphonsus considered this for a moment. 'Why didn't she run away from him? Without a name, the police can do nothing anyway. Surely it's up to the parents to do something about it.'

'They don't believe that this man molested their daughter so it's up to us to report it, Mother.' Another lie to confess. Or was it a lie? Molly hadn't wanted to discuss her parents.

'And we can be sure that this girl is telling the truth, Sister?'

'The poor girl was drugged and passed out, Mother. When she came to, she realised by the state of her clothing, that she had been... been interfered with.'

'Dear God in heaven,' Alphonsus muttered, blessing herself.

'She's one of the most honest girls in the school, Mother. In any case, why would a girl fabricate a story like this? It's too serious. Her whole life will be diminished by the loss of her innocence.'

Mother Alphonsus began fingering her rosary beads as though the Virgin Mary might help her make a decision. 'I think it's your duty Sister, to give me the girl's name before I proceed any further.'

'I'm sorry Mother. I can't do that. I made a solemn promise to God and the girl not to mention her name.' Lies were sliding from her tongue like syrup now.

Mother Alphonsus sighed. 'As we know, Sister, it's usually the girl's fault for behaving provocatively. I suppose I could send an anonymous letter to the police. That way we can avoid a scandal for the school.' She picked up a note pad and fountain pen. 'You'd better give me this man's name and address.'

'He's a priest, Mother.'

Mother Alphonsus stared at Jeanne, put down her pen, and leant back against her chair. 'Mother of God! What are you saying?' She pursed her lips. Steepled and spread her fingers. Tapped her thumbs together. A minute passed before she spoke again, her voice an insurmountable wall of unquestionable authority. 'This could not have happened. If it did, the girl must have encouraged it.'

'No Mother. He enticed her to the presbytery when no one else was around on the pretext of getting her to help him with something. It was a hot day, and he offered her a soft drink which must have contained alcohol and a pill to knock her out.'

'Imagine the scandal this would cause, Sister. Protestants would have a field day. No. This cannot be reported,' Mother Alphonsus said dismissively.

Jeanne gritted her teeth. She would keep her emotions under control. Hide her frustration. Her anger. She had always admired her superior for advocating higher education amongst the girls and teachers. Many would say that she showed concern for the girls' welfare. The school ran smoothly and was well organised. Admittedly, Alphonsus was narrow-minded, paranoid at times, although most girls tended to ignore that part of her persona. She was forever telling them that their welfare was her priority. She was hardly protecting her students now. She was applying a different set of standards to a man because he happened to be a priest. Molly was an innocent victim. The victim of a male-run organisation that Jeanne was beginning to discover had little respect for girls and women. She wanted to quote de Beauvoir. *Her wings are cut then she is blamed for not knowing how to fly.*

'We're taught that a priest can never be wrong, Mother. But it's plausible that some can slip through the net, giving them a free pass to do anything they like. Children do as they're told. Some are desperate to please the powerful, because they've learnt that the church is infallible. This poor girl obeyed the priest and look where it got her! Surely a child's welfare takes precedence over a church scandal, Mother.' Her politeness was beginning to fray around the edges now.

Mother Alphonsus looked uncertain about how to respond to a junior nun giving her advice.

'The Bishop should certainly know about this, Mother,' Jeanne continued, although now she was beginning to think he'd react in exactly the same way. She recalled the anti-female quotes in de Beauvoir's book, particularly Thomas Aquinas. *Woman is an occasional and incomplete being, a misbegotten male. Were it not for procreation, another man would be always of more help to a man than a woman.*

Alphonsus looked at Jeanne for a long time before speaking. 'I don't think we'll bother the Bishop, Sister. It would reflect on the school. It might be better to leave sleeping dogs lie.'

A dog certainly, but hardly sleeping, Jeanne wanted to say. 'Isn't it important for the Bishop to know in case this priest has offended before, and might do so again, Mother?'

'Give me his name, Sister, and I'll think about it.'

As she wrote the priest's name, Jeanne suspected that the only follow-up to this conversation would be her own. The clergy would do nothing. Their hearts were embedded inside souls dedicated to themselves and the church. What was it she'd once heard *papa* say? *L'habit ne fait pas le moine. It's not the cowl that makes the monk.*

Her parents were right. She'd blissfully chosen to live in the shadow of the convent and the church. Embraced a religious life without thinking of the consequences. She stared at her superior, for a moment, trying to imagine her future. Would she become like this one day? Trapped within her body and mind? Confined by these walls and constrained by the narrow-minded expectations and decisions of those with little understanding of what goes on in the real world? Living in an institution whose rules and values she was finding herself imperceptibly despising rather than espousing?

She and Dominique would have to think of something else. There was more chance of Mother Alphonsus eating meat on Friday than of her reporting this atrocity to the proper authorities.

28

Cecilia

B ernice's boyfriend, Tom, was in the cathedral vestibule when the two girls arrived for Cecilia's practice. 'I've been coming here to Mass every Sunday for years and always wondered what was in there,' he said, opening a door into a small storeroom. 'It's full of Catholic newspapers and publications. The ones they put on display every Sunday morning.' He grinned at the two girls. 'We could peruse them while you're warming up, Celie.'

Cecilia rolled her eyes. 'Have a browse! Make hay while the sun shines.' Given a chance, she'd have done the same. If only Danny lived in Ballarat. On the other hand, she loved going to Melbourne to see him. Was counting the days 'til the May holidays. He'd promised to take her into town to see the beginning of the Olympic preparations.

'Don't bother coming upstairs 'til you hear me starting on the mile-long Wedding March,' she said to Bernice. I definitely need you for that.' It was one of the set pieces for her Matriculation Music exam. 'All sixteen pages of it,' Mr Connelly had said. 'Not just the done-to-death two pages of the opening theme.'

At this time of the year, sunlight poured in through the cathedral's stained-glass windows, rippling reds and golds across the angled pipes like flames, appearing to warm the gallery, still hot and stuffy in late March. Cecilia cooled off by tucking the sides of her skirt into her sports bloomers. Having a high instep, with the arch of her foot creating a natural heel, she felt she played better barelegged and barefooted. Not that she'd dare tell Mr Connelly who always insisted on her wearing her special shoes. The wooden pedals felt smooth and cool beneath her feet as she heeled and toed her way up and down the pedalboard. After her scales, she warmed up with the Trumpet Voluntary, which she knew from memory. 'The Voluntary is the most popular and triumphant exit piece requested by the bride, having trapped her man at last,' Mr Connelly had said, promising her that she could play it for the next wedding. Engrossed in her playing, Cecilia was unaware she was being observed until she heard the applause at the end. Turning around, she saw a tall, smiling priest of about fifty or so with greying hair. He must have crept up the staircase on the other side. The one that was always locked at the bottom.

'Beautiful playing from a beautiful girl,' he said as he began walking towards her with a slight sway.

She thought he resembled a sleek fox ready to pounce on a lamb. From the angle where he'd been standing, he'd have had a perfect view of her bare legs skittering up and down the pedalboard. She felt herself blushing as she tugged at the skirt she'd tucked into her sports bloomers. He sat down beside her, facing side-on to the altar side of the long bench seat.

She turned by her right shoulder to face him, embarrassed by his proximity. Her teacher, Mr Connelly, never sat that close to her. As she surreptitiously slid away towards the bass notes on her left, she noticed the pink piping around his cassock. Did that mean he was a Monsignor? How should I address him? Your Grace? Your Eminence? He sidled closer to her. She smelt his breath. She knew it was red wine because Bernice's parents had it with their Sunday roast.

'You must be Cecilia,' he said, turning towards her and putting his left hand on the small of her back. 'Named after your beautiful namesake, no doubt.

But oh, what art can teach,

What human voice can reach,
The sacred organ's praise?
Sequacious of the lyre
Bright Cecilia raised the wonder higher.'

He paused. 'Have you studied Dryden's *Song to St Cecilia?*'
She shook her head and he continued.

'When to her organ,
Vocal breath was given.
An angel in ecstasy appeared,
Mistaking earth for heaven.'

She noticed that he was slurring his words, *sacred* becoming *shacred*, and *ecstasy*, *eshtasy*. While reciting the poem, his right hand had been sliding up her bare leg under her sports skirt. She sidled away again, towards the end of the bench. What to do next? What to say to a priest who exuded arrogance and power?

'Now Cecilia. Don't be shy,' he said with a leering smile, slithering closer, his fingers sneaking up higher on her leg. 'What was that last piece you played?'

How did he know her name? Nervous now, she hesitated. 'It's… it's…' Still side on, she glanced towards the altar. Someone was walking along the transept. If they happened to look up, the high balustrade would block most of the view, hence the reason for the mirror above the console from which one watched for the cues from the bridal couple or priest. From the sanctuary or transept, it could be pupil and teacher, or someone turning the pages. She gasped as he gripped his left arm around her waist while grabbing her leg in a vice-like grip with his right hand. Now she was unable to move as his fingers began to slide under the elastic of her sports pants. It flashed through her mind that this might have been what happened to Molly. Did someone force himself on her just as this priest was doing now?

She gasped, struggling to pull away from him. He pressed his full weight against her, panting. Forcing her downwards with a tackle. Realising he was going to pin her down on the bench so that she couldn't move, she tried to claw his face. She could hardly scream in a cathedral. She suddenly flung an elbowed left arm onto the bass notes of the lowest manual, thankful that the Purcell finished on *fff* with full diapason stops, the Swell to Great coupled with Great to Pedal. Simultaneously, she ploughed both feet across the pedalboard, sustaining an uproar of such *sforzando* dissonance that hopefully someone might wonder what on earth was going on. The resulting cacophony alarmed the priest enough to release his grip. The organ stopped with a dying wheeze from the pipes while she raced downstairs and burst into the storeroom, white-faced and terrified.

'Celie! What happened. What's the matter?' Bernice said as she and Tom sprang apart.

She could hardly speak. 'He... he attacked me. He... he tried to... to...'

Bernice put her arms around Cecilia.

'Who did, Celie?'

'Quick, let's go,' she gasped. 'Oh God! My shoes!'

Bernice and Tom quickly put the storeroom back in order and stepped into the vestibule. He was already there. He stared at the three of them for a moment. 'Just a misunderstanding. Nothing to worry about,' he slurred, smiling as he exited through the cathedral's main doors.

'He attacked me. That priest attacked me.' She was trembling now. Sobbing.

'Do you mean the one that just left now?' Tom said in amazement.

Cecilia nodded.

'But that's Monsignor Ronaldo,' Tom said. 'No one would believe you if you said anything against him.'

Cecilia was trembling. 'I should have told you to stay with me, Bernice.'

In between sobs on their return to the convent, Cecilia explained to Bernice what had happened.

'We'll have to do something,' Bernice said. 'Tell someone about it. Without getting ourselves into trouble. And that priest. What a creep! I'm sure he knew Tom and I were in the storeroom. He knew you were alone!'

'This might sound crazy, Bernice, but I've got this weird feeling something similar happened to Molly. Like in that book. I can't explain it. It was just something she said to me. Have you seen her around?'

Bernice shook her head.

Cecilia was sitting in the senior classroom the following evening, gazing at her homework. Agitated and panicking. Staring into space. She would never return to the gallery again. What would Katerina say when she told her she was giving up the organ? It was one of her Matric subjects. She'd gone over and over the incident with Bernice, in the end, deciding that they'd report it to Jeanne. They needed to work on getting their story right first. Embellish it a little. For a start, Tom couldn't be mentioned. Sister Jeanne, on homework duty that night, was already giving Cecilia strange looks. At nine-thirty, the Matriculation students stood up to leave, Cecilia straggling behind everyone else.

'Can I speak to you for a moment, please Cecilia?' she heard Jeanne say from the desk.

Cecilia caught Bernice's eye, turned, and walked back towards Sister Jeanne.

'Are you alright, Cecilia?'

Cecilia looked at her teacher, bit her lip, and burst into tears. There was a knock on the half-open door, and Bernice re-entered the classroom, shutting the door behind her. Cecilia was too upset to tell Jeanne what had happened, so Bernice told her version of the story, the main variation being that the incident had occurred when she'd left the cathedral to go to the toilet block in the cathedral grounds.

Jeanne looked like she could scarcely believe what she was hearing. 'You poor girl, Cecilia. This is terrible. I can't believe what you're telling me!' She put her head down in her hands for a moment, stood up to place a comforting arm around Cecilia, and eased her onto the chair. 'I don't know what to say Cecilia. It's all so terrible.' There were tears in her eyes. 'After what Molly told me when you took her to see me, I can't believe what I'm hearing. We'll need to report this, of course.'

Cecilia and Bernice exchanged glances. 'We can't, Sister,' Bernice said. 'Mother Alphonsus warned us never to use the toilets alone in the cathedral grounds.'

Jeanne looked at Bernice. 'And when you said you left the gallery to go to the toilet, Bernice, you weren't meeting someone were you?'

Bernice's face gave her away. She was mortified.

'I'm not passing any judgement on you Bernice. I know it can be difficult for boarders. I picked up that the boy you were dancing with at the ball last December wasn't your brother.'

Bernice's face flushed scarlet.

'I'm just playing the devil's advocate here,' Jeanne said. '*L'avocat du diable.*'

They had no idea what she was talking about. English or French.

'By that, I mean that I'm not particularly concerned if you were meeting up with someone, but if this is ever to be reported, it would be like the Spanish Inquisition.'

Cecilia sighed with relief. She'd never heard of the Spanish Inquisition, but at least Jeanne sounded like she was onside.

'We wondered if the priest could be reported without mentioning our names,' Bernice said. 'I know I should have remained with Celie, but I can't say anything because I'd be expelled. Celie would lose her scholarships. We... we were warned when...'

'I understand the implications, girls. But there's more to it than that. With no witness, who do you think would be believed, a young girl or the Monsignor?'

'I know a priest can never be wrong,' Cecilia began to say. 'But...'

'You must look at it from Reverend Mother's point of view. She's responsible for the welfare of all the boarders, and that's why she stresses that in public, boarders can never be alone, even to visit a toilet in the cathedral grounds. They're open to the public, as she would have warned you.' The two girls nodded. 'Did the Monsignor see you with your friend, Bernice?'

'He saw the three of us together in the vestibule, Sister,' Bernice said.

Jeanne nodded. 'And there'd be other times when he's probably seen you entering and exiting from the presbytery side of the vestibule. He's got that over you.'

Bernice bit her lip.

'Obviously he must be reported,' Jeanne continued. 'Without mentioning your names. I need to think how to go about it.'

Cecilia felt her eyes filling up again. 'The problem is I don't know what to tell Sister Katerina. I'm not going back to the cathedral. That man's a creep, Sister. He knew my name. I've... I've got a feeling he's been watching me,' she said in between sobs. 'Perhaps when we walk past the presbytery, or maybe when... when...' Had he crept up the gallery stairs on the other side and spied on them? Listened in on their conversations? Molly had once seen a cassock disappearing up the stairs when she was on the other side of the vestibule. Bernice said she'd heard the stairs creaking. He might have heard them talking about boys. About things only girls discussed.

'It doesn't matter, Cecilia. You've got a lot on your plate with your music and this being your final year. Perhaps with the grand piano concert coming up, I could tell Sister Katerina that you're not coping and that you might need a break from the organ until after Easter.'

'But Sister, I don't ever want to ever go there again.'

'See how you feel after Easter, Cecilia. The Bishop and police could be informed about the Monsignor without disclosing any names or the circumstances. There may have been other complaints made against him. We don't want this happening to anyone else. He could molest any unaccompanied girl.'

Cecilia pursed her lips. 'But Mother Alphonsus will need to know, Sister.'

Jeanne sighed. 'Not necessarily. I have a contact. The important thing is that you and Bernice must report this to your parents over Easter.'

'That'll be the last thing I'll be doing,' Cecilia muttered to Bernice when they left the classroom. 'I'd be back working on the farm in a flash.' She felt that her life would change now. Did she really want to be a full-time musician anyway? Sitting at a keyboard for hours every day to stay at the top of her profession? Or teaching others to do the same? Recently she'd been pushing this thought to the back of her mind. This incident was prompting her to reconsider her career choices. What options were there? She should have listened to Sister Dominique who'd advised her to stick with physics and chemistry. She could easily have fitted them in. She'd gone for the easier option. Subjects requiring less work so she could achieve top marks. Too late now! 1956 was definitely not a good year. For her and for Molly.

29

Jeanne

Jeanne sat back in the warm sunlight and closed her eyes. The four walls were closing in on her. Crushing her. No longer was she drawn to traditional places of worship or structured prayers, preferring to seek her own revered space for meditation. Like this bench in St Elizabeth's Garden where she now sat with a mountain of Form 5 dictée to correct.

She made her decision. She'd leave the convent. The order of her life seemed to have reversed now. Teaching had become the central part of her vocation, religion the backdrop. Rarely did she think about her salvation, although the church remained a comforting if not perplexing part of her life. There was certainly a spiritual dimension, but the church no longer gave her solace. Her link to organised religion was surely fading, like the last whisper of summer. Why didn't she have these feelings earlier on in her life? Was it that she felt men held no real attraction for her? That the convent was a refuge? Was religion a creation for her needs? A cry for help? Now she couldn't wait to escape the constriction; the tedium; Reverend Mother's clutches and her blinkered opinions. She'd wanted to help the world through the church and teaching. Now with it diminished to teaching, perhaps she could be a voice for girls and women in another way. Dom was another complication. Hopefully, she would feel the same.

She stared at the few remaining roses clinging on to the warm autumn morning, reminded of *The Last Rose of Summer*. A girl with a voice from heaven had once sung it at a concert. Would there be roses in the Ballarat Gardens now? When was the

Begonia Festival? March? April? She'd already forgotten. The only information about what went on outside the convent was from her parents' monthly visits. One hour a month left barely enough time to discuss politics, friends and neighbours; Paul and Andrea's busy lives in Melbourne; the arrival of television and its impact on the community; her grandparents' forthcoming trip to Australia for which her family had happily contributed. Then there were the preparations going on in Melbourne for the Olympic Games. Her parents were excited about the rowing events on Lake Wendouree. She smiled, remembering the girls' faces lighting up after she suggested that 'If you're walking around the lake in Term 2 collecting autographs, you should practise your conversation with the French rowers.' The boarders had whined in jealousy. Anything to do with the Olympics was limited to their parents' correspondence.

She recalled the outings with her family to the Bois de Boulogne. *Papa's* parents had taken her there one day. It was the last time she saw them because they were killed shortly afterwards during the war. She found herself romanticising the past. Allowing nostalgia to drag up old memories from her heart. She recalled the zoo. The amusement park. The gardens. Papa said the Bois de Boulogne was more than twice the size of Lake Wendouree and its surrounds, but then there were many more people to accommodate. The *Parc de Bagatelle* had impressed her more than anything else. A perfect place for walking and relaxing. The château, the giant trees, the little bridges, the rocks, the caves, the ponds and waterfalls. Somewhere in her mind she saw the magnificent rose garden with its 10,000 rose bushes; her grandmother telling her to inhale the fragrance of a dark red rose that would linger in her memory forever.

The warm autumn sun was inducing her mind to flit around like a butterfly. She should be concentrating on the two girls. Her apprehension had been building up for some time, but the second attack was the final outrage. The match in the powder keg. If *she* knew of two recent incidents, how many more must there have been over the years? How many of them went unreported? Never in her life had she been so frustrated. She could make an anonymous report to the police and the Bishop via her parents, but without the names of the victims, was there a chance of justice being done? Dom might have a few ideas.

But Dominique was even more pessimistic. 'Ballarat has a higher Catholic population per capita than any other city in Australia. The Police Force here is full of Catholics, so you won't get much help there,' she said. 'They'll cover up crimes committed by the clergy and blame the children.'

'My name should be Sister Mary of Blinding Naïvety,' Jeanne said. 'I had no idea of what's been going on around me.'

'I imagine many on the outside don't either.'

'Well I can't cope with it anymore. *C'est la goutte qui fait déborder le vase.*'

'Ah! I'm guessing here,' Dominique said. 'The drop, perhaps like the last drop, that causes the vase to... to overflow? The last straw! Archimedes Principle!'

'*Exactement.* The last straw on the camel's back. Anyway, I've been thinking about it for a while Dom. I've decided I can do more for the world by leaping over the wall now rather than in a few years' time when I might be beyond it.'

Dominique stared at Jeanne and said nothing for a while. 'But you... you can't Jeanne. What about us? I thought that you... you loved me. That we love each other.'

Jeanne saw the tears in Dom's eyes. She bit her lip, trying to hold back her own. If someone had entered the staffroom, they'd have wondered what was going on. 'Of course I do, Dom,' she whispered. 'You know that! You know how I feel about you. I just can't stay here any longer. There are other things. Sometimes I wonder if I've got any faith at all. If I have, I want it to be my own faith in God. Not a religion ruled by a... *une hiérarchie misogyne.* You feel the same way as I do about it, so how can you...'

Dom was distraught. 'Are you worried they'll find out about us?'

Jeanne shrugged. 'Sometimes I think the secrecy embellishes our passion. But mostly I think we can do better than all this subterfuge and hypocrisy. Perhaps integrity comes into it somewhere too.' Having lost her spiritual vocation, she wasn't going to assume that Dom had lost hers. There was nothing she'd have liked more than for Dom to toss in her veil and join her. The joy she felt whenever they were together was tempered by knowing what it would mean to lose her.

Dom spoke in a quavering voice. 'When are you leaving?'

'The first visiting Sunday in May. You're the only one who knows. I'll be telling maman and papa during their next visit. I'm sorry Dom. Except for you, I just can't cope with being here any longer.'

Dom had tears in her eyes. 'I would have thought you'd stay at least 'til around exam time, Jeanne. What are the girls going to do without you? You're... you're leaving them in the lurch, aren't you?'

'I've thought about that too. You know that lovely new novice, Sister Rosemary?'

'The one finishing off her teacher training?'

'I was wondering why they'd arranged for her to spend so much time with me. Then I discovered on the grapevine that she's going to replace a lay teacher in a country convent. I gave her full marks for her lesson the other day. Her French is very good, and I was thrilled that she found a beautiful old French folk song and taught it to the girls. They loved her. They were eating out of her hand. I bet you anything they'll have her replacing me before she's finished her teacher training.'

Dom looked reproachfully at Jeanne. 'You've thought it all through, haven't you? I had no idea.'

'Neither did I until today. Well, I guess it's been building up. Surely you've thought about it!'

Dom stared at her. 'Of course I have, but I don't think I could leave Ballarat yet. Apart from Mum, I'm the only one in my family living here now. It was bad enough when Dad was ill in hospital for months and I couldn't see him. Then I couldn't even go to his funeral. You don't think of all these things when you enter the convent.'

'I've heard that after ten years it's much more difficult to adjust to the world outside. If you count the years since you began your degree, it must be...'

Dom sighed. 'Yes. Nine years coming up. But at least I've got an idea of what to expect in the outside world from my Melbourne brothers and sisters.'

'The real world.'

Dom began fidgeting with her rosary beads and looked at Jeanne. 'I'd been thinking about where on earth I could get a science job in Ballarat, then you came along and everything changed. You gave me a new life. I'll have to think about... about...'

'About tossing in your habit and morals to come and join me in Melbourne?'

Dominique's face lit up. 'I can think of nothing better. I'll have to talk Mum into moving to Melbourne, what with everyone else being down there.' She sighed. 'I haven't got a replacement like you. Not at this time of the year.'

'You'll need to write to all the Melbourne secondary schools so you can organise a job for next year like I'm doing now.'

Tears were streaming down Dom's face now. 'I'll miss you terribly, Jeanne.'

'*Moi aussi, ma chérie*.'

They took a risk and threw their arms around each other. Dom smiled through her tears. 'You'll be shuffled out the back door and called a Judas.'

Jeanne grinned. 'In that case, from whom will I be collecting my thirty pieces of silver?'

'Not a penny from here, *bien sûr*!'

'I'll be making appointments at schools in Melbourne as soon as I leave here.'

They began collecting books for their next classes. 'It won't matter about not having references when you explain the circumstances. Between your outstanding examination results and the Alliance Française, you shouldn't have any trouble getting a job, *mon amour*.'

'I hope not, but I'm going to have to get proof of everything. Meanwhile I'll organise my résumé, and anonymous letters to the Bishop and police about those priests.'

There were a million things to do before her parents' next visit. She'd have to hand-write a résumé and an explanation of why her principal must not be contacted for references under any circumstances, which was why she wouldn't be applying to convents. Without references, perhaps her outstanding results with the Alliance Française and the public examination results would see her through. It was too risky to use the staffroom typewriters. Anyone could walk in at any time and glance over her shoulder. Her mother would type up multiple copies for all the schools. Paul and Andrea would put her up for a while. As a single woman, she knew there was no way she could afford to rent, so her first preference would be for a boarding school offering a position of housemistress.

'By the way, *chérie*, I won't be shuffled out the back door as I won't be leaving in the traditional way,' Jeanne said with a mischievous grin. 'All that paperwork, not to mention RM's entreaties or the time it takes to obtain permission from The Vatican. I want my last few weeks here to be happy, so I certainly won't be leaving like a nefarious fugitive in the dead of night.'

Dom was lightening up a little now. 'Just as well. You wouldn't want to be treated like poor Sister Ann. That hideous garb she was wearing when she left! With her hair all cropped, she looked like she was about to be put in the stocks.'

'I'd like to see Alphonsus trying to intimidate me if I told her I was renouncing my vows. I spoke to Ann because I had a feeling she was leaving. She said her parents wanted nothing to do with her. Maman and papa will be bending over backwards to help me. I wouldn't mind betting that papa will put in for a transfer with us all living in Melbourne.'

'You should be able to catch up with Molly down there. Genevieve once told me that most unmarried mothers end up at the Royal Women's as outpatients and the Catholic girls stay in a place nearby.'

'That's what Paul said. I spoke to Molly yesterday. The poor girl looks like she's fading away.'

Dom shook her head slowly. 'I don't know why she comes to school. She can hardly concentrate.'

'I asked her to write to me, but she looked about as enthusiastic as a boarder about to eat a plate of tripe and cabbage. I'm wondering if she'll return after Easter.'

'Which reminds me, did you realise our next visiting day is Easter Sunday? The one after that isn't 'til the May holidays.'

Jeanne walked over to the calendar. 'You're right. I thought there was another one in between. I've got an awful lot to do before then.'

It was hard going, but she managed to finish her résumé and letters by Easter Saturday. They'd be using the hall and St Elizabeth's Garden for the first time on visiting day, the two front parlours having become too small to accommodate the growing numbers of parents and other relatives.

Easter Sunday was a perfect autumn day. Jeanne led her family from the front gate straight to the grotto near the tall hedge off the school hall, one end of which was set up for afternoon tea. She had decided they should begin with normal conversation before she told them the news, otherwise it could be difficult for her family, particularly her mother, to maintain their composure. As they passed one-year-old baby Matthew around from one to another, they discussed their jobs, friends, *mémère* and *pépère*, now great great-parents, the upcoming Olympic Games, and whether they would be supporting France or Australia. Both, they decided in the end, but Australia first. Jeanne was just about ready to change the subject to her 'abdication', as Dom liked to call it, when Paul's wife, Andrea, asked how Molly was going.

'Not very well at all,' Jeanne said, switching to French. 'I'm hoping you'll be able to see her, Paul, if she's at your hospital. She's quite ill much of the time.'

'Single pregnant girls are all treated like criminals,' Andrea said. 'Even by the hospital staff. Not to mention the maternity homes.'

'Those places don't exist in France,' Sofia said angrily. 'The girls stay at home and the parents cover it up. Or they go to an aunt in the country.'

'You've forgotten the abortions and shotgun weddings, maman,' Paul said.

'Yes. You're right. Plenty of those.'

Andrea looked around warily. 'I checked it out when we were in Paris for the conference. It's not such a crime there. Then everyone wonders why the maternal death rate from illegal abortions is so high in Australia. Sorry Jeanne. I didn't mean to be spouting one of my pet theories. Nothing will ever change until women start making the rules.'

Jeanne smiled to herself, thinking that was what she was doing. Making her own decisions. Not sitting around waiting for the Vatican to give her permission to leave the convent. She'd already written the letter she would be leaving on her pillow.

Dear Mother Alphonsus

I've had more than four wonderful years of teaching and friendship from colleagues and students, and I am very grateful for what I have learned in that short time. However, I have now lost my vocation because I am disillusioned. Furthermore, I would not be able to endure the waiting around for permission to leave, by you and an organisation that has had nothing to do with me or my reasons for entering the convent in the first place. Additionally, I do not wish to waste anyone's time should they feel obliged to talk me into changing my mind.

Yours in Jesus Christ

Juliette Rousseau.

She told her family that she had an announcement to make. As it would shock them, they should try not to look surprised, but rather, react as though they were discussing the weather or the Olympic Games.

'No one else here knows what I'm about to tell you except my friend Dominique,' Jeanne said with a smile. 'The next visiting day is during the May holidays. The only difference is that I'll be leaving with you, dressed in civilian clothing rather than my veil and habit. We'll take up a position near the front gate and I'll walk out dressed as Andrea.'

It was fortunate that they were in a semi-circle formation, facing Jeanne and the hedge, so that no one else could see the frozen smiles on their faces. Faces that, except for baby Matthew, tried to remain expressionless, but couldn't hide traces of incredulity. Raised eyebrows. Puzzled frowns. Open mouths. Her mother's astonishment began merging into absolute joy, with no hope of being confined.

Jeanne explained how their final visit should proceed. 'Andrea, you'll need to discreetly disappear out to the car after about half an hour.' She looked at Sofia. 'Maman, just bring the basket as usual with the tea-towel on top, but instead of the usual gateaux, fill it with my old high heels and stockings, and clothing and a wig that looks similar to Andrea's hair.'

Her mother could hardly contain herself. 'You'll need a handbag as well, *chérie*. And makeup. And spectacles like Andrea's.'

Jeanne nodded. They were speaking in French but lowered their voices to conspiratorial.

'But what if it's raining?' Claude said.

'Same thing, but we'll all be in the hall. When the corridor's clear, I'll take the basket as though I'm heading to the kitchen. I'll slip into the storeroom off the corridor. I'll change my clothes, hide my habit, and return with the empty basket, ready to leave immediately.'

'Very ingenious,' Paul said, 'but what if someone sees you coming out of the storeroom?'

'Dom will be nearby with her family. She'll knock on the door to give the all clear. I'll walk into the hall or garden from the corridor, looking like a visitor who's just left the toilet.'

'Ah. Dominique's the lookout,' Paul said grinning, while the rest of the Rousseaus were still looking stunned. '*La grande évasion*. The great escape from Stalag 17. Or should I say Stalag St Martin.'

Jeanne had no idea what he was talking about. 'What do you mean?'

'*Stalag 17*. It's a film about inmates trying to escape from a prisoner-of-war camp. They were always foiled by a snitch. Something you won't need to worry about. You've thought of everything. Your ingenuity is overwhelming.'

Jeanne shrugged. 'It'll be quite easy. All Andrea has to do is to wait in the car until we return.'

'Doesn't Mother Alphonsus sometimes position herself near the front gate to farewell everyone?' he said.

'We'll leave fifteen minutes earlier. I'll be Andrea, holding baby Matthew up to my face and walking right past anyone who happens to be around.'

Visiting hour was about to finish. 'I guess we'll see you on D-Day then,' Paul said.

Jeanne raised her eyebrows. 'D-Day?'

'Departure Day.'

'Oh. I almost forgot. I could have wrecked all my plans.' She turned to Sofia. 'Maman. I'm going to subtly slip my awards, my résumé and a few letters from my pocket into your handbag now. I'll need you to type everything and make multiple copies of the résumé and letters to the Bishop and police. Too risky using the staff typewriter! Can you do all that at the Grammar School before the May holidays, maman?'

Her mother nodded, still in a state of shock and elation.

Claude was frowning. 'Why can't we just pick you up and leave straight away as you are? No fussing around with dress-ups.'

'Because, papa, I entered as a civilian, and I'm going to leave as a civilian, just as others do. I want to leave unnoticed, so that no one will know how I did it. Someone else might want to leave the same way.' She was thinking of Dom. 'And if you're worried about them thinking I've been kidnapped, I'm leaving a letter to Mother Alphonsus on my pillow.'

'*Quel subterfuge*,' her father said, rolling his eyes. 'I can't wait.'

30

Cecilia

'Y ou certainly don't look the best right now, Cecilia,' Sister Katerina said sympathetically when Cecilia told her she needed a break from the organ. 'I think you've been working too hard. I'll speak to Mr Connelly. You'll be fine after Easter. The organ is one of your Matriculation subjects. It's too late to enrol you for piano.'

Two weeks to go until she'd be returning home for the five-day Easter break! How would she survive? A letter from her mother cheered her up. An aunt in Melbourne was having a twenty-first birthday party for her cousin on Easter Saturday. As the house would be chock-a-block with family and other relatives, would it be possible to stay at her friend Bernice's house? Because of loyalty to her own family, Cecilia had already refused Bernice and Danny's invitation to stay with them over Easter. She couldn't believe her luck. Now she'd be seeing her family *and* Danny before the May holidays!

On the Thursday before Easter, the two girls travelled down to Melbourne on the train with Bernice's boyfriend, Tom. Joined by Danny, the four of them attended a VFL match at the Glenferrie Oval on Saturday, a first for Cecilia. Thrilled by the atmosphere, she got into the spirit, screaming and barracking for Hawthorn, the team Danny's family supported. Later, at the party, she and Danny had a ball, the two of them picking up a few clues about rock'n'roll dancing. She wanted to stay in Melbourne forever. Thoughts of what happened in the organ gallery flashed through her mind every night as she drifted off to sleep. What would she say to her parents and Katerina about why she was giving up her organ scholarship? She loved the organ. She also missed playing duets with Molly. They'd chatted a lot during practice and had become good friends. Poor Molly. Where was she now? She'd gone looking for her a few times but couldn't find her anywhere. Jeanne told her Molly's school attendance was intermittent, and when she came to school, she didn't last long.

The Dobsons were having a special Easter Sunday roast dinner after Mass, to which Bernice's boyfriend, Tom, had been invited. As could be expected, the conversation revolved around the goings-on at their various schools during the term. Danny with a story about his friend who, when they were asked to write a list of original similes, had written that the confessional was about as seal-proof as a screen door on a submarine. He saved himself from being flogged by insisting it was satire, likening it to Swift suggesting in *A Modest Proposal* that the poverty in Ireland could be solved by selling poor children as food for the wealthy. 'Just let one of those Brothers lay their hands on any of you boys,' Mr Dobson said, 'and they'll wonder what's hit them!'

Bernice was impersonating Alphonsus, going on about 'the devil hiding behind every nook and cranny in the convent. The serpent under an innocent flower. The venomous viper inveigling his prey.' It was in perfect imitation of Alphonsus. The over-rounded vowels; the alliteration; the censure with the piety; clipping each point of punctuation. She launched into a diatribe on 'the thoughtlessness and inconsideration of girls whose parents have made enormous sacrifices to send their daughters to the best school in Victoria.' Her father said that such a dramatic homily on ingratitude was worthy of King Lear, and maybe she should consider a career in acting, at which her mother rolled her eyes and took a sip of her red wine.

Suddenly the sharp acidic aroma of the wine took Cecilia back to the scene in the organ gallery. What if she had to go back there again? She didn't even want to walk past the presbytery. She became aware that Bernice's father was speaking to her.

'And will you be doing an exam in organ this year Cecilia? Or piano?'

'I… I'm not sure, Mr Dobson,' she said, swallowing a lump in her throat. 'I think…' She paused, bit her lip, and burst into tears.

The whole table was staring at her, concern in their eyes.

'It's okay Mum,' Bernice looked at Tom and mouthed *tell them.* She put her arm around Cecilia, and they left the dining-room to go outside.

'I don't know what to do,' Cecilia sobbed. 'Jeanne thinks I'll be okay after Easter, but I know I won't be. I never want to go near the cathedral again. What will I tell Katerina and Mr Connelly? They've been so good to me. And I don't know how to tell Mum and Dad.'

'I think now that Tom's in there telling everyone what happened, you'll have to tell your parents as well.'

'But they'll take me away and I don't want to work on the farm. I'd rather put up with Alphonsus for another year.'

'Let's go inside, Celie. Mum and Dad might have a few ideas.'

When they returned to the table, Bernice's father was the first to speak. 'Tom has told us what happened, Cecilia. It's shocking. Something must be done. Another girl might be attacked and not be so lucky.'

'Lucky?' Mrs Dobson said, throwing her hands in the air. 'I'd be having nightmares about it for the rest of my life. You poor girl, Cecilia. I can't imagine what you've been going through.'

Mr Dobson looked at the two girls. 'Mother Matriarch wouldn't want the school to be tainted with that sort of scandal, so she won't report it for a start. The church would cover it up. *Who will rid me of this troublesome priest?* No one will. It'd end up being an expulsion for the two of you.'

They finished their main course in silence until Mr Dobson spoke again. 'If we do nothing, we're as bad as those who did nothing about Hitler.' He paused for a moment. 'Silence kills. An eighteenth-century writer once said *The only thing necessary for the triumph of evil is for good men to do nothing.* I'll be bloody-well doing something about it, one way or another. For all its worth.'

'It'll certainly be difficult for Cecilia to go back there.'

Robert Dobson looked at his wife, almost defiantly. 'Apart from having to make up excuses about giving up the organ, how can Cecilia possibly return? Or Bernice, for that matter.'

'But they're in their final year with two and a half terms to go. They can't just…'

'Yes they can, love. It's been done before. They're both seventeen now. Nearly at university. They don't need all that gobbledygook.' He looked at Bernice. 'I didn't say anything at the time, but I wanted to take you away from that place when you were going on about kowtowing to that statue they were carting around the country.'

'You mean Our Lady of Fatima?' Bernice said.

'That's the one. Those three little girls were starving and ate weird mushrooms that have been around the forest areas of Spain and Portugal forever. Especially around Fatima. Those mushrooms do freaky things to your mind! Miraculous indeed!'

Everyone at the table stared at him, eyes wide.

'Well, to get back to the point. I wanted to send you to McRob Girls' High then, but it's not too late for the two of you to go there now.'

Mrs Dobson dropped her jaw. 'You just can't roll up to a selective government school! In any case, we're not Cecilia's parents. How can you…'

'I'm a lawyer, my love. I think I know how to get around them and the school if there's a problem. Not that there will be with their academic record.' He looked at Cecilia again. 'When your parents arrive to pick you up on Tuesday Cecilia, I'll speak to them, if you like. After you've told them everything first, of course.'

Mrs Dobson was becoming a little more enthusiastic now. 'McRob has a wonderful music program, Cecilia. And outstanding music students like you can have their piano and organ lessons at the Conservatorium for free.'

'My niece is at McRob,' Mr Dobson explained to Cecilia. 'And my sister went to school there with the new principal. In fact, they were friends.' He turned to his wife. 'Trust me. A bit of bribery and corruption won't go astray there, love. I'll call her today.'

'But aren't you being a bit presumptuous? You haven't even asked the girls their opinion yet!'

He turned to them. 'I'm sorry. It's your decision of course. But I can tell you that you'll both be rapt in McRob after St Martin's. More time on sport and drama and debating instead of all that mythology and popery.'

Mrs Dobson glared at him, then turned to Cecilia. 'Perhaps as the one most affected by what happened Cecilia, you should give your opinion first.'

Cecilia wasn't sure what to say. 'First of all,' she said finally. 'It was my fault. I was the one who insisted I didn't need Bernice to help. If she'd been with me in the gallery from the start, it wouldn't have happened.'

'It definitely wasn't your fault, Cecilia,' Mrs Dobson said.

Cecilia blinked back tears. The Dobsons had become a second family to her. They were the kindest people in the world. 'As far as attending a government school goes, it wouldn't worry Mum and Dad. I attended one for nine years before I went to St Martin's. Anyway, they wanted me to leave school when I was fourteen.' She paused a moment. 'But they wouldn't be happy about you putting me up. It's kind of you to offer. They'd be a bit funny about charity. Unless they can repay you in some way, I'm...'

Mr Dobson was adamant. 'But Cecilia. It's only until the end of the year. You'll probably get a scholarship for the following year. It'll be a great preparation for living in Melbourne and going to the university. You'll love it. The girls at McRob aren't spoon-fed as much as they are at private schools. You'll learn how to think for yourselves. And it won't be charity. If you stay here, it's still cheaper for us to accommodate the two of you than paying tuition and boarding school fees in Ballarat.'

Cecilia nodded, relieved now. 'I'll tell them everything when they pick me up!'

Tom hadn't spoken for a while. 'I'm not sure about reporting Monsignor Ronaldo. I have a feeling that no one in our parish would believe a word said against him. He comes across as being caring and charismatic. My parents...'

'Ahh,' interrupted Mr Dobson. 'The charismatic chameleon with silken tongue. The diabolical entity under a godly veneer. I know the type.'

'Rob!' His wife gave him a warning glance.

'Hypocrites of the highest order,' he continued. 'They'll never learn that organised religion is no different from monolithic ideologies like fascism or communism. Any religion that prioritises institutional power over justice is fraudulent. Morality is basic and has nothing to do with the rules the church keeps inventing. They turn their followers into mindless robots instead of human beings. I…'

'Robert!' Mrs Dobson thumped the table. 'You promised that in front of the young ones you…'

'I'm sorry, my love,' he said, throwing his hands defensively in the air. 'Sorry, everyone, for getting carried away.'

'I don't mind, Dad,' Bernice said. 'I just wish I could have said all that to Alphonsus just before I left.'

They all laughed, relieving some of the tension. Cecilia and Bernice were upset at the prospect of not being able to say goodbye to their friends and favourite teachers.

Bernice grinned. 'I'd already worked out a way of meeting Tom at weekends. And I had an outrageous plan for our final ball.'

'You can send your friends' letters to my place,' Tom said, 'Felicity can still be your courier.'

Cecilia looked across the table to see Danny grinning at her. Yes. The Dobsons were a wonderful family. Especially Danny! She didn't mind going to a new school in Melbourne at all. In fact, she loved the idea!

31

Molly

Between Easter and the end of term, with my father snarling at me, 'the little tart', I drag myself off to school just to get away. I usually last for two or three lessons, and sometimes end up in the infirmary. Sister Jeanne checks up on me, but with nausea and a violent headache, I never feel like talking to her. She asks me how things are at home, but I can hardly tell her that my father pushed me so hard I fell over. That he accused me of seducing a priest, and when I tried to explain what happened, he didn't want to know about it. I've missed a lot of school, but I made an effort to go on the last day of term because I was sure Cecilia would be playing the grand piano at assembly. I haven't seen her for ages. There was no sign of her or Bernice anywhere. Sister Jeanne said goodbye to me. I'm sure she had tears in her eyes.

It was early July when Mum and I caught the train to Melbourne, Doctor Doyle having insisted that I wasn't well enough to go on my own. In any case, being a minor, Mum or Dad would be required to sign some documents. Dad had refused to drive us, which was probably just as well. Car sickness would be all I needed to add to my wretchedness. I can hardly put two thoughts together lately. I'm not sure how much sympathy Mum's got for me. It's hard to tell what she's thinking. I know she misses Maude terribly.

From Spencer Street Station, we took the tram along Flinders Street to the Exhibition Gardens. A ten-minute walk via the gardens was easier than catching another tram at Swanston

Street. I'd managed to stop myself from throwing up until we reached the gardens. We sat down on a bench for a while so I could recover. I've never really confided in Mum, but with no one around now, it was my last opportunity to speak to her.

'Mum, why does Dad say I seduced Father Kelly?'

She looked at me, but not into my eyes. 'That's what Doctor Doyle said!'

'No he didn't, Mum. He said it was the other way around. You don't listen half the time.'

'But you took yourself off to the presbytery. You didn't have to do that. You asked for it!'

'It wasn't like that. He was a priest. I felt I had to do as he asked.'

'But he didn't drag you in there!'

Mum is shackled to a religion obsessed with venerating the clergy, the Virgin Mary, and the saints. She has been bearing my pregnancy in harrowed silence. Enduring it, but never discussing it with me.

'I didn't even want to do the flowers. Then he offered to help me with my maths homework. Doctor Doyle told you Father Kelly gave me alcohol. I didn't know the drinks had alcohol in them! I passed out. Sister Jeanne told me it wasn't my fault.'

'You didn't tell the nuns, did you?' She looked horrified. 'It'll be all over Ballarat now. Our family will be ruined! You weren't supposed to tell anyone. I haven't even told Maude!'

'Sister Jeanne is my friend. She won't tell a soul, Mum. If there's anyone I trust, it's her. She's very kind. The nuns aren't all like Alphonsus. Jeanne doesn't blame me like you and Dad do. What you're both saying is not how it happened.'

'You must have known what that priest was up to. It's always the girl's fault.'

I wasn't getting anywhere. Mum's attitude about girls leading boys or men astray is exactly like Alphonsus'. Perhaps most people think that. All my life, I've naïvely believed that one had to be married to have children. That God must have had something to do with it. I'm beginning to realise that God doesn't always control what goes on in the world. I stood up and we headed towards Grattan Street. The large two-storey terraced building with arched balconies that Dr Doyle described is right opposite the Women's Hospital. It's not numbered or named, so it took us a while to decide that we were at the right address. The nun in the parlour, a life-size statue, was smiling and warmer than the nun who had shown us in. I had no idea what order of nuns they were. Images of Pope Pius XII and the Sacred Heart were hanging from the picture rail. A statuette of the Virgin Mary on the mantelpiece, complete with a star-studded halo, rosary beads entwined around her hands, gazed in ecstasy towards heaven.

'Just your daughter's full name and address, her date of birth, and sign at the bottom,' the nun said handing Mum a form.

Mum's face looked as blank as the pages in my exercise books at the beginning of the year. 'November 17th, 1939,' I whispered. Dates mean nothing to Mum. We three sisters are experts at concocting birthday and Christmas presents for anyone who asks.

'You'll need to hurry, Mrs Harrington. You were more than an hour late,' the nun said curtly.

By now, I could see that Mum was agitated and embarrassed, her face flushed. She was breathing quickly. It was bad enough for her on the train, but at least I was with her, despite me throwing up in the toilet. The thought of returning home alone must be sending her into a panic. With Dad not being here to manage things, Mum was forced to take the initiative for once.

'I'm sorry Sister. The train from Ballarat was delayed,' she said meekly.

'I'm afraid you'll have to say goodbye now, Mrs Harrington.'

The nun was determined to remain in the parlour. I'd been signed over, which I suppose means that my guardians will be making all the decisions from now on. Mum asked if I needed pocket money. Dad handed Mum £20 before we left, telling her it was a donation for the maternity home.

'All money must be handed over to me,' the nun said. 'So I can collect it now, Mrs Harrington.'

Mum opened her handbag, delved into it, looked at me, then the nun. 'I'm sorry, Sister. I must have left it behind,' she said.

There was no way Mum would hand over any money after being humiliated. She dug around in her handbag when the nun left to answer the doorbell and handed me two £10 notes. 'Hide it in your shoe. Whatever you do, don't give it to *them*,' she whispered. She had tears in her eyes. 'One thing I want you to do, Molly, when all this is over is what you always said you'd do. Become a teacher. Whatever you do, don't come back to Ballarat.'

I was pleased she said that, but my future is the last thing I'm thinking of right now. The nun returned, almost ordering Mum to leave. She didn't kiss me goodbye, but she had tears in her eyes. I was utterly bereft. Eleven years ago, my father had left me like this. No kisses. No fond farewells. He hadn't told me what was going on, and my future was just as uncertain now. Eleven years ago, the nun who greeted me at boarding school had been kind and compassionate. There was no warm welcome here. I was overwhelmed by a cloud of despondency and abandonment. I couldn't stop the tears streaming down my face. What was this place with no name? It wasn't a convent. Was it a girls' reformatory like Aunt Bernadine's Good

Shepherd Convent in Abbotsford or Albert Park? A place for wayward girls? Wayward pregnant girls!

The nun re-entered the parlour, ignoring my distress. 'Write your full name, date and age,' she said, handing me another document. 'And the name you'll be using while you're here. It must be a saint's name.'

I wrote Margaret Elizabeth Harrington. Age 16. Apparently, my birth certificate says Molly Elizabeth, but Mum chose Margaret at my baptism, because the priest decided Molly wasn't a saint's name.

'Here no one needs to know your proper name. No surnames necessary. Wait here until I return please,' the nun said rattling down the passageway until another door opened and closed behind her.

A few minutes later, the clock on the mantelpiece chimed 6 o'clock, in perfect synchrony with the deep clang of the Angelus bell further down the passage – the curfew that signalled the nuns' *knell of parting day*. Suddenly a single column of six nuns filed down the corridor. I was back at boarding school in St Arnaud. Robes swishing and flapping. Veils billowing. Rosary-beads rattling in rhythm with footsteps as they murmured *Angelus Domini nuntiavit Maria...* Didn't that only happen in convents? Why here? This wasn't a convent! What *was* this place? The first nun opened the double doors opposite the parlour to a chapel. They proceeded down the aisle, genuflected before the altar, and knelt down in the pews. One of them was the nun who had almost pushed Mum out the door. Her appointment with God had taken precedence over common courtesy to visitors.

Six o'clock! Why was it always a deadline? A bell at six o'clock. When did I last hear another bell at the same time? This year? No. Last year at the pub! For the last few months I've had trouble thinking about time. Trouble thinking about anything much at all. Except for that day. And I really didn't want to think about that.

The nun re-entered the parlour and pointed to my small suitcase. 'Cubicle five in the first dormitory upstairs is yours,' was all she said as she indicated the staircase.

Each cubicle was separated by crisp, white pull-back curtains, every white-quilted bed made with boarding-school precision. At the end of the dormitory was a statue of Our Lady of Lourdes. It reminded me of that day. Or was it night? The presbytery. The candle-lit shadows on the ceiling. I raced off to find the nearest toilet. I've had nausea and vomiting since the middle of March. And terrible headaches and nightmares. Doctor Doyle said that while morning sickness could last for a few weeks, it shouldn't last all day. What I had was possibly stress or depression.

I went downstairs to a room at the back of the building from where I heard voices. A few girls turned their heads and stared at me when I entered the room. Some were in the process of taking their places at two large tables, others were coming from a kitchen with plates of stew. A few were noisy, but most of them were quiet and subdued.

'Welcome to the Grattan Street baby factory,' a girl whispered.

'Pentridge for girls!' said another. 'Run by the compassionate Sisters of Saint Joseph.'

Someone asked me my name. When I replied that it was Molly, she asked if it was my real name, or my new name.

'It's... It's my name while I'm here,' I said.

'As long as it's a saint's name,' a girl with a huge stomach said.

'Think I'll change mine to Mary Magdalene. We're all sluts according to dunny breath.'

'Yep. Walking sins without a chance of redemption.'

Most of the girls – about thirty in all – were quiet during this exchange. Half of them looked like they were in shock, not smiling at the remarks. They'd probably heard it all before. A girl explained about cleaning and polishing the floors after daily Mass and breakfast; the washing up and laundry, some of which comes from outside; cooking and serving the boiled-up leftovers as soup for the tramps through a small cavity to the outside. Never at any stage were we allowed to leave the premises except for weekly check-ups across the road at the Royal Women's Hospital, usually with a supervisor.

'Hallvard intercepts all the incoming and outgoing mail,' one of the girls whispered. 'And we're not allowed to make or receive phone calls.'

Another girl told me her alias was Regina, 'Pronounced as in *eye*, to rhyme with…'

'Yes, we know.'

'*I only do it to annoy because I know it teases.*'

'You'd better stick to Gina for short, otherwise Hal might slap your face.'

'No she won't. She knows I'm not a minor and I just might slap her back. If you look in those boring *Lives of the Saints* over there, you'll find Saint Regina. She was a martyr. Just like me. Only I'm a living one. Like we all are. I looked up Hal's namesake too. He was a martyr as well. She probably thinks she's one for putting up with us.'

Someone explained that Hal was short for Halitosis or Hell for the head jailer from hell, Sister Hallvard. 'Take your pick,' she said rolling her eyes.

I asked where the downstairs toilet was and rushed off. 'I'm just warning you,' continued Gina when I returned. 'They'll want you to give up your baby to a nice Catholic couple. God makes us breed like rabbits, but the Holy Joes can do it all day and night, and nothing happens. Then they buy our babies from the nuns.'

'I thought the hospital got the money from the almoners,' a girl about my age said.

'The nuns get a share. They call it a donation, but who knows? We don't get a penny. Talking of which, if you've got any, don't hand it over.'

'A hospital almoner will see you about signing papers and everything,' Gina explained to me. 'And it's no use telling them you're going to keep your baby, even if your boyfriend says he'll marry you. The father's name isn't mentioned on the certificate because he's got no say. He doesn't exist.'

'Only when you committed the crime,' someone said.

'They'll tell you it's illegal to keep your baby,' Gina continued. 'You don't have any say in it. Everything here is about punishment. Your crime and your punishment. But I'll tell you something. They're not bloody-well getting mine.'

'You shouldn't be upsetting her when she's just arrived.'

'It's better if she's warned before she sees dunny breath. Gives her a chance to think about it all. You're not allowed out, by the way. Even if your boyfriend comes to the door, you're not allowed to see him.'

Boyfriend? Did these girls have boyfriends? As for keeping the baby, why on earth would anyone want to do that? Isn't this all about doing as you're told? Like those girls in the Good Shepherd Convents? I'll end up like them, won't I? Like Maude said. Carrying the stain of sin all your life.

32

Juliette

It was Sunday, May 18th, in the year of the Melbourne Olympic Games. D-Day, they all called it now. Departure Day. 'Nearly twelve years after the original D Day,' Jeanne's father had said.

Everything was going according to plan. The weather was quite mild for late autumn. The sun was shining, and there was no wind in the walled garden. The Rousseau family was gathered in the area closest to the gate. Jeanne was about to leave with the basket of clothing to transform her into a civilian, when Mother Alphonsus, smiling and congenial, waddled over for a chat. She greeted each of them and smiled at baby Matthew.

'I believe your parents will be arriving here soon. Won't that be lovely for you, Mrs Rousseau,' she said to Jeanne's mother.

Sofia looked surprised. Jeanne smiled. Her mother would have forgotten that the nuns usually shared all their news when they gossiped in the community room. Now Alphonsus began chatting and asking questions. Are they travelling by ship or by plane? By plane? Are they nervous about that? How long does that take from Paris? Are there many stop-offs? Will they be going to the Olympic Games? Will they be here for Christmas? Our hot weather will be such a shock for them over Christmas! Jeanne exchanged glances with Andrea. They were in a bit of a dilemma. Fifteen minutes to go before visiting time finished! How long would Alphonsus hang around? She seemed like she was never going to stop talking today.

Baby Matthew started grizzling. 'Excuse me,' Andrea said, handing him to Paul. 'I need to get him a rusk from the car. He's hungry.'

'And please excuse me too,' Jeanne said. 'I've got to take the gateaux to the kitchen and return the basket before you all leave.'

She managed to change in ten minutes, returned to the external hall door, and looked across to see Alphonsus still chatting to her parents. *Mon Dieu!* What on earth was her next move? She could hardly slip past them dressed as Andrea, who'd left by the front gate in full view of Alphonsus. But just as she was deciding what to do, another nun interrupted Alphonsus to call her away in another direction. *Merci, mon Dieu,* she said, almost crossing herself.

'I must tell you, maman,' Jeanne – now Juliette – said during their celebratory D-day dinner, 'that just after you all arrived at the convent today, Dom told me in perfect French, that *tu as ressemblé au chat qui a avalé le canari.* I would have said that you all looked like you'd won the lottery.'

'Until the big panic,' Paul said.

They could all laugh about it now, which led to speculation about what would have happened if Alphonsus hadn't been called away.

Having stayed with her parents in Ballarat for three weeks, Juliette was now living with Paul and Andrea in Parkville. It was now June. There was plenty to keep her busy. She'd looked up friends from her University days and decided to go in person to the Alliance Française in the hope that they would give her a letter confirming the St Martin's College award. Perhaps they'd know of a temporary position somewhere. Now that most of her credentials were in order, she called into a few schools to put her name down for relief teaching. A permanent position in a government school was out of the question because they didn't have boarding schools. With her experience, she would surely have no trouble finding a position as housemistress in a private girls' school.

A few days later, she was home chatting to Andrea. At a distance of seventy miles and specified monthly visits, it hadn't been easy for her to have a close relationship with her sister-in-law. Now she could be a friend to Andrea, and a proper Aunt to her nephew.

'Mum would be happy minding Matthew five days a week. She says it's the pinnacle of her nursing career,' Andrea told Juliette, who had asked about her medical practice in Carlton. 'It's quite a poor area. I scouted around for months until I found a partner who shared my own views. I also wanted a practice between here and Mum's place.'

Just what Andrea's views were, Juliette was not quite sure until she asked what made her decide to work with the under-privileged.

'My father was killed during the war so we weren't a normal family, I suppose. It was always a bit of a struggle for Mum, despite being a trained nurse. I decided I'd do the same, so I threw myself into schoolwork and was selected for University High School. I realised that I could go one step further than being a nurse. Then a part-scholarship and family assistance from Legacy saw me through med school.'

'You must have been the odd one out with all those wealthy males from top private schools. I remember some of them when I was doing my degree. Paul took me to a few parties.'

'Women are certainly in a minority in medicine, but someone put me on to the work of Victor Wallace. He was a medical practitioner and eugenicist who believed in the emancipation of women. Hard to believe, isn't it?' she said when she saw Juliette's look of surprise.

'Well, I suppose most men don't think of giving women a say.'

'He had weird views on selective breeding, but he was interested in birth-control clinics and maternal health, despite the opposition he got from the conservatives in the medical fraternity. He established a birth-control clinic with a Dr Mary Herring to help working-class mothers. Apparently, he witnessed suffering during the Depression, so he decided to throw himself into alleviating the hardships and crowded living conditions of the poor.'

'The Depression? But that was way before our time!'

'Yes, but their work is relevant for any generation. It's all very well for the wealthy with their populate or perish attitude, but hardly any of them give a thought for the poor. Anyway, I decided I'd try and do something similar. I've got a lot of sympathy for single mothers, and girls who've been abused, like that poor girl from your school.'

Juliette decided she wouldn't mention Cecilia for the moment. One of the girls had told her after Easter that she heard Cecilia and Bernice were living in Melbourne, although Alphonsus hadn't said a word about them to anyone.

'Molly should be down here soon. She was a bit vague about it when I asked her, but I'm sure it'll be June or July.'

'I think I know how we can find her.'

Andrea walked over to Matthew's bedroom to hear if he was awake. 'You might think because you were shut away in a convent for a few years that you've missed out on what's going on in the world, Juliette, but half the women I come across wouldn't have a clue either.'

Juliette smiled. 'In fact, I learnt quite a lot, so I don't regret my time there.' That was certainly true. She'd found herself at the convent. Better still, she'd found Dom. 'I'm glad I was around when Molly told me about that priest. Sometimes I wonder if she'd have told anyone if it hadn't been for another girl coming to see me with Molly in tow. Can you imagine what else has been ignored or covered up over the years?'

Andrea sighed. 'During my first few weeks in the practice, a pregnant 14-year-old girl presented at the surgery. After my examination and a lot of questions, it appeared she'd been impregnated by her father. The girl had no understanding of the implications. When I reported it to the police, they chose to believe the girl's father who blamed a boyfriend for his daughter's pregnancy. Since then, I've become a word-of-mouth advocate for sex education for the married and unmarried.'

Andrea told Juliette that a great deal of her work related to the needs of women who wanted reliable means of birth control to restrict the size of their families. They couldn't cope financially with the children they already had. 'It's the old story of *women must bear the consequences.* Believe it or not, most girls and women get pregnant because they're naïve. They're victims of double standards that condone the sexual adventures of their male partners. Some don't know how babies are born. Then when they find out they're pregnant, they have a backyard abortion. My partner and I have taken on the role of explaining different methods of contraception.'

'The sort the church doesn't approve of?'

Andrea laughed. 'Ironically, we cater for a number of married Catholic women whose regular doctors refuse to advise them on contraception. Except for the rhythm method which is unreliable. Ethically we see it as part of a service to give women some control over their lives.' She shrugged. 'Most of my conservative and judgmental male colleagues, Catholic or otherwise, refuse to give them any.'

They were silent for a moment before Juliette spoke again. 'Andrea, excuse my ignorance, but are you talking about an operation?'

'No. We fit and instruct women on the use of the diaphragm or cervical cap with a spermicide. It stops sperm from entering the uterus by covering the cervix.'

'So the church doesn't approve because it's not natural?'

Andrea shrugged. 'I suppose things will change when more women take up medicine. Most male doctors don't care. Too interested in lining their pockets than caring about social issues.'

'I happened to come across a book in the convent that made me wake up to how society treated girls and women. I might have lived in oblivion forever otherwise. But that's another story.'

'Some of my colleagues think I'm disadvantaging Paul and Matthew by working. I'm one of the few women who refused to abandon medicine for the traditional role of being a helpmate for a man.'

'I imagine Paul's on your side.'

'Of course! He doesn't see why his career should take priority over mine. Society doesn't see it that way though.'

'Anyway, I've been doing all the talking. What about you? How is everything going? Have you had any regrets about leaving?'

Regrets? Of course she had. She missed Dom terribly. It was something she could never talk about to her family. She'd be writing to Dom via Dom's mother before the next monthly visit. 'No,' she lied. 'I'm so busy running around Melbourne, I haven't given it a thought.'

'I know little about how convents operate. You'll have to tell me one of these days.'

Juliette nodded, wondering if she ever would. There was all that beautiful music, her colleagues, the girls. Perhaps if you loved teaching, it wouldn't matter where you worked. She would never admit to being a former nun unless someone asked her outright, so perhaps she did feel sensitive about locking herself away to dedicate her life to a dead man. That part was a mistake, but then, weren't there many women who dedicated themselves to the wrong man?

'You could write a book about it,' Andrea suggested. 'It'd have to be better than that boring *I Leap Over The Wall*. Twenty-eight years that woman stayed in the convent!'

Juliette was about to comment when the phone rang. She stood up and crossed the room to answer it. 'I think that's for me. Someone was going to call me about relief teaching. You'll be pleased to hear I'll be earning my keep from now on.'

33

Molly

One of the girls at the Home told me we would rarely have the same doctor at the Royal Women's Hospital. We're numbers, not names. We wait by the hundred in the corridors like a production line, and if you're an unmarried mother-to-be, it's as though you've been scraped from the bottom of hell.

At boarding school, we learnt to be modest, taking great pains to hide parts of our body, even from ourselves. At the Women's Hospital, modesty doesn't exist. Staff and students walk by as girls and women lie on couches in separate cubicles, legs raised in stirrups towards the light coming in from a long corridor. There's no such thing as privacy or dignity. The girls at the Home warned me that I'd be prodded and poked around. During my first examination, the doctor was acting as though he was onstage, and I was one of the props. When a group of medical students crowded in, he told me to lift my dress, which I'd clamped down between my legs. 'Come on now, girlie. You've lifted your dress for someone many times before,' he said, at which the students laughed. I wasn't going to have them gawking at my private parts. They soon cleared the cubicle when I said I felt nauseous. I raced off to the nearest toilet, but I didn't return. I went straight back to the Home and told Sister Leo on the door that I needed to lie down, which was true.

Like us, the nuns running the Maternity Home are not allowed to leave the building. An almoner or supervisor is usually around to take us across to Outpatients. During my second week, I had good reason not to go because of my splitting headaches. Groups of four or five girls leave for the hospital on any day of the week with a supervisor, so no one noticed that I didn't show up. No way would I be humiliated again, especially in front of students.

One morning during my fourth week at the Maternity Home – around the end of July – I was lying on my bed with a throbbing headache, when I was called down to the front parlour. I had a visitor.

'Doctor Rousseau is here to check up on you,' Hallvard said.

I panicked because I thought they'd caught up with me at last. And a woman doctor? I knew they existed, but I've never met one before. She began asking questions about how well I was eating, and what sort of exercise I was having. Hallvard told her I wasn't eating much, and that any exercise was related to domestic duties like cleaning, dusting, polishing and laundry.

The doctor frowned. 'I'm not talking about that sort of thing, Sister.' she said. 'I'm talking about pre-natal exercise and brisk walks in the fresh air and sunshine.'

Hallvard gave her a baleful look and shrugged. 'Once they're here, the girls only go outside to the hospital for their check-ups.'

Doctor Rousseau stared at her. 'We'll have to do something about that,' she said, turning to Molly. 'You don't look very well, Molly.'

'She often complains of being ill,' Hallvard said.

I had to excuse myself to go to the toilet to throw up, but as I walked out the door to race down the corridor, I heard Hallvard say 'Sometimes the guilt gets to them.'

When I returned, the doctor told Hallvard she was concerned about my physical and psychological welfare.

Hallvard seemed set to stay, but the doctor put her in her place. 'Thank you, Sister. As this is a private consultation, I must ask you to leave.'

Hallvard wasn't happy about it. I guess she thinks this place is her territory. She gives the orders around here, and no one should send her packing. Andrea closed the door after her and spoke softly, telling me she was certainly a doctor, although not from the Women's Hospital, 'but don't tell anyone here that. The nun on the door assumed I was from the hospital, so I didn't contradict her.'

'We're not allowed to have visitors, Doctor,' I told her.

'I'd prefer you to call me Andrea, so there's no confusion with my husband, Dr Paul Rousseau who's an obstetrician at the Women's. He's been looking for your details through someone in admin, but there's no record of you ever having visited the hospital. Sister Hallvard said you all had weekly visits to the hospital, so I'm not sure what's going on. I took a chance on finding you here.'

I was embarrassed, eventually admitting that I'd never returned to the hospital after my first examination. She was sympathetic when I explained why.

'You'll need to have a check-up, Molly,' she said kindly, 'but Paul might be able to organise it so that you'll have privacy next time. No more students. He'll try to see you, but he has to be around for difficult births and caesareans most of the time.'

I couldn't figure out why she was trying to help me until she told me Sister Jeanne was her sister-in-law. 'Jeanne told us what happened to you, Molly. We're very upset about it and we'll do anything to help you.'

I suppose that explained it, but the way I've been feeling most of the time, I don't get excited about anything much, so I just sat there, staring at her.

'Like me, Juliette, I mean Jeanne, wants to know if they're looking after you here, Molly.'

I nodded. I didn't feel like talking.

'You look like you're not eating enough, Molly. Is the food terrible?'

I shrugged. 'I don't feel like eating. I don't feel like doing anything.'

'You'll need to mention all your symptoms at the hospital. And by the circles under your eyes, you're not getting much sleep, are you?'

I shook my head. 'I have lots of headaches, but no aspros.'

She immediately delved into her handbag, handed me a small bottle of aspros, and said to take no more than four a day.

'Jeanne told me the circumstances of your pregnancy, Molly. I'm horrified to think of what you've been through. None of this is your fault. That monster took advantage of you by giving you soft drinks laced with alcohol and a barbiturate. Is there anything you can recall about the incident for when it's reported?'

I must have looked horrified because she added 'without dragging you or your family name into it, of course.'

I didn't want to think about it at all, let alone discuss it with someone I've only just met. It embarrasses me. I was so stupid to be talked into going to the presbytery with Father Kelly. That room. His study. The couch.

'Was there a door off his study into a bedroom?'

I suddenly got a flash of a bed. I nodded. 'I remember now. I tried to get up from a bed and vomited on the floor when I stood up. I was dizzy. My whole weekend was like that.'

'All the signs of a drug and alcohol overdose,' Andrea said. 'Did you have any burning, or irritation around your vagina the next day?'

I tried to remember. 'I think so.'

'Any spots of blood on your underwear?'

'Yes. I thought my period was starting.'

When Andrea said it would have been from the perforation of my hymen, she must have realised I had no idea what she was talking about.

'Now's not the time for a biology lesson. There's a book that I usually have copies of, but I've run out of them.' She sighed. 'They're hard to get. I've got some on order. Do you know if the girls here are given any information about pregnancy, and what to expect during labour, the birth, and afterwards?'

I shook my head. 'One of the girls said they don't tell you anything. If you haven't got a husband, you're a nobody.'

'Next time I visit, we'll go for a walk, and we can discuss a few things, if you're up to it.'

I told her we were only allowed leave to cross the road to Outpatients.

'We'll get around that. You need proper exercise, Molly. And you must have a check-up. If you go to Outpatients tomorrow, I'll get Paul to make sure it's written on your registration form that no students are to be present for your examinations.'

We went to Sister Hallvard's office.

'Sister,' Andrea said smiling politely. 'I'll be back in two days' time to take Molly for a walk around the block. The fresh air might do her good.'

'I'm afraid that's not possible,' Sister Hallvard said. 'The only time the girls leave here is for their check-ups.'

'But surely Sister, you and the adoptive parents want these young girls to have happy, healthy babies? Molly, and in fact all the girls, should be doing daily walking and pre-natal exercises. I know of other maternity homes that allow it.'

'Rules are rules. She's not allowed out. No one is,' Hallvard insisted.

'So she's a prisoner, Sister?'

Hallvard's face looked like it had been chiselled from the statue of St Joseph in the entry. 'It's about anonymity. The girls are safe here,' she said. 'We are responsible for them. We're here to care for them.'

'I'm pleased to hear that Sister,' Andrea said, 'because the treatment these girls get from society is a disgrace. From what I know, they might just as well be lepers and, in fact, would be better treated at Pentridge. At least they get fresh air and exercise there. I know from experience that some of these single girls are victims of ignorance and incest, Sister. And they're still bullied and shamed and made to feel guilty!'

Hallvard looked uneasy. Her eyes were flickering. Looking into the distance. As far as she's concerned, we're all Eves or Mary Magdalenes. *You made your own bed, you will have to lie in it*, is her motto.

'On top of that,' Andrea continued, 'they have no idea what's going to happen to them in the Labour Ward.' She smiled politely. 'If you like Sister, I know someone who would be very happy to give a talk to the girls.'

Hallvard said nothing.

'From my experience, Sister, I know that these girls should be healthy. Physically and mentally. I'm not sure what Molly's problem is yet, but I'm sure you agree it's quite serious. Fresh air, exercise and sunshine might lessen her vomiting. Walking might give her an appetite and help her sleep at night. I think we should give it a try.'

'I cannot change the rules,' the nun said coldly.

Andrea gave me a *We'll see about that* look on her face and said goodbye. I'm not up to walking anywhere, but I'd like to see Andrea get the better of Hallvard. At first, I thought this place might have been like boarding school, but it's more about atoning for our sins. We're locked inside and our days are regimented. These nuns are obsessed with shame and repentance, ensuring that our babies go to decent Catholic couples.

Sister Hallvard sometimes calls us sluts. I can guess what it means, but I can't look it up because there are no dictionaries. No reading matter other than the lives of the saints and religious journals. Not even a newspaper. Occasionally we knit or crochet, but most of the time we follow strict daily work routines to earn our keep. There's an old piano in the corner of the dining area but I'm never tempted to touch it. Why would I? Pianos are reminders of happier times. I'm ill much of the time so I don't feel like doing anything.

We heard the almoner and Hallvard arguing with Gina when she said she wasn't relinquishing her baby to the adoptive parents. Hallvard screamed that they were good, decent people who would look after the baby. Gina was immoral and shameless! The almoner insisted twenty-two-year old Gina had no means of looking after her baby, but Gina said she was keeping what belonged to her; what was part of her. Hallvard was banging her fist on the desk and shrieking that Gina would have to become a prostitute to support herself, and it would only be a matter of time before Child Welfare took her baby away. Gina later explained to me what a prostitute was. She told us that the almoner asked her to write everything she could give her child on a piece of paper. She wrote LOVE, but no money. On another piece she had to write what the adoptive parents would give the baby. She wrote MONEY, but not the love of a baby's real mother.

There's not one morning when I haven't raced off to vomit while eating, or cleaning or cooking. One young nun is sympathetic and kind to me. She tells me to sit down until I've recovered. Another one orders me back to work as soon as I return from the bathroom. They wouldn't want to ask me to do the flowers for the chapel. Just looking at the altar every day makes me think of *him*. I wouldn't be in this awful place now if I hadn't agreed to do the flowers, would I? I wouldn't be growing this thing inside me that makes me so ill. Months of sleeplessness and fatigue and vomiting is doing something to me. I don't want this baby, and this baby obviously doesn't want me. My stomach is always empty. I think it's filled with despair. None of the other girls are ill. They say I should have been over the vomiting months ago. Sometimes I want to curl up and die. Why do most of them want to keep their babies? How can they feel attached to something that causes so such misery? Why not let all those couples have their babies without any fuss?

There was a girl here who was five months pregnant, like me. Last week she lost her baby. I envied her. Why didn't it happen to me? I can't bear another few months of this. The girls were talking one evening about what they went through when they told their parents they were pregnant. One told of a girl who committed suicide by throwing herself off a bridge. Another had a story about a pregnant girl who killed herself by swallowing a bottle of her mother's sleeping pills. That must be the easiest way to die. No one knows what it's like to be as ill as I am. It's constant. Hallvard thinks I'm putting it on. Andrea knows I have trouble sleeping because she asked me about it when she noticed circles under my eyes. Next time she comes here, I'm going to ask her for some sleeping pills.

34

Juliette

From July, Juliette was inundated with requests for relief teaching, both in government and private schools. A few offered her a full-time position for the following year, but only one included accommodation.

Her interview had gone well at MLC – Methodist Ladies College, Doctor Wood having told her that one of their long-standing French teachers was retiring. A housemistress position would become available the following Easter, because a teacher was getting married. Doctor Wood's main concern had been that, as an ex-nun, Juliette wouldn't be prepared to accompany the boarders to the local Methodist church on Sundays, and that she wouldn't be happy about attending services in the chapel. She assured him she didn't mind. Having heard that the school had an excellent choral tradition, she was looking forward to hearing the chapel choir. Would even join it if she could. Their only disagreement had been her title. When she explained that she'd prefer the girls to call her Juliette, Doctor Wood said it was impossible. As soon as she decided whether she'd be called Miss or *Madamoiselle* Rousseau, the position was hers. Like many young French women, she hated the idea of the title *Madamoiselle,* indicating that one was a virgin, whether aged fifteen or fifty, and *Madame* meaning one was married. Of course, it was the same in English. One word covered all males, married or single. It wasn't relevant in the convent, but her world had changed now. There was only one way to resolve that problem. She'd do a doctorate. Preferably, something to do with women.

Having been told that the job was hers, Juliette decided the family would celebrate her good fortune. Andrea had put baby Matthew to bed, and Juliette was cooking coq au vin when Paul arrived home. She handed them both a glass of French champagne. 'A toast,' she said with a grin that couldn't be wider. 'I've got a full-time position at MLC next year, with accommodation to follow two months later.' After the hugs and congratulations, Juliette told them the oddest thing about the place was Doctor Wood being the principal.

'But what's so odd about that?' Andrea asked her.

'Doctor Alfred Wood. He's a male! Imagine that happening the other way around. Wesley College being run by a woman.'

They laughed. 'Well, when you put it like that, I guess it's odd,' Paul said. 'Why do I get a feeling that you're turning into a bit of an Emmeline Pankhurst? Are you making up for all those years in a nunnery?'

She looked at Andrea. 'Maybe I'm picking up a few clues from my sister-in-law!'

'Perhaps it's the other way around,' Andrea said.

'More importantly, how's Molly?' Juliette said. 'I assume you saw her today.'

'She's still vomiting. And dizzy. It seems strange at this stage of her pregnancy.'

'She was like that at school. Always looking ill and often racing off to the toilet.'

Paul frowned. 'It's August now. She should be well over morning sickness.'

'She vomits often,' Andrea said.

'Does she have headaches?'

'Yes. I gave her some aspros. She doesn't volunteer anything much. I discovered she went to the hospital once but didn't hand in her registration form.'

Paul frowned. 'I thought they all had to go to Outpatients.'

'They're supposed to, but Molly never returned because the doctor embarrassed her. Apparently, he put on an act for the students like he was Sir Lancelot Spratt in *Doctor in the House*. Except, from what I remember, Sir Lancelot humiliates his students rather than his patients. Anyway, to get to the point, can you arrange it so that Molly doesn't have any more students present when she's there?'

He nodded. 'I think so. Funny you should mention students. I had a bit of an altercation with a group of them today. I'd like to reduce the numbers to two or three at a time. A woman in labour complained that after ten of them checked the dilation of her cervix, she was left bleeding. I spoke to them about it later, and one cheeky sod suggested that maybe the woman's name was Mary, and perhaps she was a virgin.'

Andrea grimaced. 'I can't laugh at that, given how Molly was treated. No wonder everyone is treated so appallingly when doctors and interns make provocative references about women for male students to emulate. Not to mention their conservativism!'

'Speaking of which, I haven't told you about the lecture yet,' Paul said.

'You mean Don Moreton's?'

'First chance I've had to tell you about the bastard,' He turned to Juliette. 'Sorry Juliette, you'll have to get used to our occasional swearing and medical talk.'

'I'm all ears. I'm here to learn about the wicked world.'

'Well, here's a story about an ultra-conservative. His Featherstone Memorial Lecture will be in The Journal of course. He told us *to keep encouraging adoption on the basis that all unmarried pregnant women are the product of bad genes or bad blood, and their illegitimate children are full of original sin. The unmarried mother should be punished for stepping outside the rules of a decent society.* I quote verbatim.'

Andrea pulled a face in disgust. 'How illogical and bloody biassed! He's worse than Miss Barbary in *Bleak House.*'

Paul grinned. 'You'd have been proud of me, *chérie.* I reminded him that we were all born heathens with original sin until the pulpiteer chanted the magic spell, and if God gave unmarried mothers such bad genes, was it wise to advocate the adoption of their wicked children?'

Andrea and Juliette laughed. 'Pulpiteer?' Juliette said. 'Where'd you dig up that word? I love it!'

'Sounds like puppeteer,' Andrea said, grinning. 'Not much difference, I suppose.'

'Anyway. To continue. He glared at me. Probably wondered why a bloody foreigner had the gall to query him. I said I'd come across cases of girls involving incest, and a more recent one involving a priest raping a girl, now pregnant. Did he think these girls should also be punished for stepping outside the rules of a decent society?'

Andrea kissed him on his cheek. *'Je t'aime.* I'm so proud of you, *chéri.'*

'I don't think anyone's ever queried any of his sweeping statements before, so the bastard got a bit of a shock. He said incest is another story, but some girls throw themselves at priests. What can you say to that?'

Andrea rolled her eyes and pulled a face. 'It's as though girls contrive their own pregnancies! And with the culture of adoption he pushes, it makes the male invisible and exonerates them from any commitment.'

'Most of the audience was as conservative as the bloody clergy, which is why I wonder if there's any point in reporting Molly's case to anyone. The church has got more power than the police anyway. Look how they meddle in politics here!' He pulled a face. 'There'd be more chance of the Pope baring his backside from the window in Saint Peter's Square than admitting to what his priests get up to. They're without sin, remember!'

Yes, Juliette thought bitterly. They left the seminary conditioned by a naïve piety to believe that they were superior to their congregations, especially women. Unlike an actor who must prove his credibility, their omnipotence guaranteed them a captive, ready-made audience with the theatrics of Mass. How ironic that living in a convent had turned her into such a cynic.

'Priests deny their natural urges in their youth,' Andrea said. 'And whether or not they regret their vocation, they seem to be bent on inventing rules, with women always having to bear the consequences.'

'I started waking up to a few things like that in the convent.'

Paul shrugged. 'They're hypocrites! Fixated on sex and its consequences as the supreme sin.'

Juliette placed the coq au vin casserole on the table. 'Did you mention me to Molly, Andrea?'

'Yes. I told her how we were related. But not about… about your abdication.'

'I'd rather tell her myself anyway.'

Paul looked at Andrea. 'Did you check Molly's pulse, *chérie*?'

'No. Why?'

'Check it next time. If it's rapid, let me know.'

'Why?'

'I'm thinking it could be *hyperemesis gravidarum*. Women have died from it.'

'I've heard of it, of course, but I've never come across it.'

'Well, it's pretty rare, isn't it? When I was in London, they said Charlotte Bronte may have died from it.'

Juliette was serving dinner. 'Really? I thought she died of TB.'

Paul shrugged. 'There are lots of theories.'

'Anyway. Getting back to Molly,' Andrea said. 'You can't miss her, Paul. Beautiful elfin-like face like Audrey Hepburn. She's white as marble and skinny and doesn't look like she's pregnant. I'll try and get a photo of her.'

Paul sighed in exasperation. 'When would I have time to see her? I had nine hours in the Labour Ward today. I'm exhausted. God, it must be a dream to work in a private hospital!'

'The Queen Vic would do me!' Andrea looked at Juliette. 'It was founded, managed, and staffed by women. *By Women, For Women* is their slogan. Do you know why it was set up in 1896?'

Juliette shook her head.

'Because no one would employ female doctors. The only teaching hospital, the Royal Melbourne, wouldn't even accept female interns.' She shrugged. 'What's changed? Hospitals still favour men.'

'Maybe here, but not in France!' Paul said.

Juliette shrugged. 'Perhaps they realise since Marie Curie that women might have a brain.'

He pulled a face. 'You're right. It's more the hypocritic rather than the Hippocratic Oath, which is why I tell students that the poor should be treated no differently from the wealthy, and they should visit as many hospitals as possible to get another point of view.'

Andrea kissed him. '*Je t'aime.* I'm glad you do that, darling. It shows you care. Perhaps at least you could pass the word around about Molly's problem.'

He raised his hands resignedly. 'I'll do my best, *chérie.* I don't want you *and* Juliette on my back.'

'And while we're talking about the Women's, why do they use numbers rather than names at Outpatients?'

'Maybe because no one can pronounce the Greek and Italian surnames.' He shrugged. 'Who knows? I don't work in that area.'

'Wouldn't they tend to relax more if they were addressed by their names?'

He shrugged. 'Perhaps, but consultations and doctors are random so what's the point?'

'They should be asked their names. And given the option of having students and interns gawking at their genitals.'

'There are 16,000 admissions a year and everyone's running around like chooks most of the day, so I guess sympathy's not a high priority. Staff aren't trained to deal with feelings.'

'So they take out their frustration on single mothers. Why am I not surprised?' She looked at Juliette. 'You wouldn't believe how those same girls are treated at that house of misery across the road. Funny how it has no number or nameplate. It took me a while to find it.'

'Perhaps they don't want the place publicised,' Juliette said. She'd been listening quietly, fascinated by their hospital talk.

'*Bleak House* would suit. The nun in charge insists they care for those girls.'

'You mean like a crocodile cares for a chicken?' Paul said in French.

They swapped stories. Juliette's relief teaching. Andrea's packed out surgery, including one emergency. Paul's three caesareans, one stillborn. Juliette thought how wonderful it must be for a couple to love each other and to come home each day with something in common to discuss. One of these days, she and Dom would hopefully be able to do the same. They'd been corresponding via Dom's mother. Dom said that Alphonsus had never mentioned Juliette again, and she'd been right about the student teacher taking over her job. It had been fairly heavy-going for her, but Sister Winifred had come out of retirement to assist.

'One thing I don't understand,' Paul said. 'How can you spend nearly five years in a convent, and serve perfect coq au vin and crème caramel?'

'You've forgotten that maman was on holidays for most of the time before I came down here. I had intensive cooking classes every day for three weeks!'

'It was a beautiful meal, Juliette,' Andrea said. 'It'll be hard going back to boarding school meals at MLC next year.'

'I won't be on duty every day.'

'Have they got any idea of Molly's circumstances at Bleak House?' Paul asked Andrea.

'About the priest you mean?'

He nodded.

'Molly said her family didn't want anyone to know.'

Juliette nodded in agreement. 'That's what Molly told me.'

He looked at Andrea. 'By the way, did the commandant agree to you taking Molly out?'

Andrea shook her head. 'Not a chance. Not that Molly will be able to walk far in her condition. I'm still working on it. Mum's mantra for people like Sister Hallvard is to think of another way around the problem. I'm working on it.'

Paul folded his arms across his chest. 'Tell her you'll go straight to the police station to report her for kidnapping and cruelty. Better still, tell her I'll report her to the medical tribunal if she won't allow Molly out.'

Andrea's face suddenly brightened. 'You've just given me a brilliant idea. We can avoid a confrontation. Bring me home a few sheets of RWH letterhead paper, love.' She looked at Juliette. 'I'm hoping to take Molly for a short walk after lunch on Thursday. You could meet up with us!'

Juliette's face dropped. 'I'm booked at Camberwell Grammar for nearly three weeks.'

'Well. Never mind. Another time!'

'Meanwhile,' Paul said as he stood up to make the coffee. 'Tell Molly not to eat any greasy food, and to sip small amounts of water at a time. Frequently!'

'One doesn't need to be an obstetrician to know that, chéri,' Andrea said with a little bite in her voice. 'I've already told her that.'

35

Molly

It was busier than Bourke Street at Outpatients, women holding red numbered cards milling around everywhere. When I mentioned Dr Rousseau, a nurse wrote *No students during consultation* on my registration form, and reminded me to hand it to the doctor when my number was called.

After waiting for more than an hour and feeling wretched, I was directed to a cubicle. When a group of students began squeezing in after me, I indicated the memo on the registration form. The doctor apologised to them, muttering about why some people on this earth got special treatment. He wrenched a curtain across the doorway, obviously angry with me. How could students learn anything when they weren't allowed to observe patients? I told him my symptoms, as Andrea had advised me. He said it was all in my mind, and I must pull myself together for the sake of the baby and the adopting parents. He wasn't really interested in my health, although he told me not to eat greasy food and to drink plenty of water. He was more interested in the baby's heartbeat and its position in the uterus. I had a splitting headache so all I wanted was to get out of the place.

I'd just about decided that Andrea wouldn't be calling on me again when two days later, I was summoned to the parlour to see her. She wanted to take me for a walk, 'Even if we just walk up Grattan Street and sit on a bench for a short time,' she said, showing me a letter she was about to give Hallvard.

Dear Sister Hallvard

We, as a team of gynaecologists and obstetricians at the Royal Women's Hospital, recommend brisk walks, fresh air and sunshine for all our patients.

We are concerned about the general welfare of one of your residents, namely Margaret (Molly) Harrington. Her confinement is difficult and fraught with problems. Dr Rousseau or another colleague will be calling occasionally to accompany her on walks, which will be beneficial to her general health. I'm sure you agree that the prospective adopting parents would prefer a happy, healthy baby.

Below the *Yours sincerely,* there were four signatures, including Dr P F Rousseau, their qualifications listed alongside.

'She'll think I'm one of the specialists,' Andrea whispered as she knocked on Sister Hallvard's office door.

Hallvard pursed her lips while reading the letter. She was livid.

Andrea smiled and handed me a parcel. 'You should wear this whenever you go out,' she said. 'Like now.'

It was a beautiful blue paisley-design maternity dress, but I hardly had the energy to change into it. The fashionable empire-line style disguised my slight bulge. I thanked her and went upstairs to change.

'You look great,' Andrea said. 'That dress really suits you. Much better than those awful flour bags they put you in here.'

We sat on a bench at a nearby tram-stop because I didn't feel like walking. She checked my pulse. Apparently, my heart resting-rate at a hundred and ten beats per minute was way too high.

'Is your dizziness and nausea worse in the morning?' she asked me.

I nodded.

'Probably low blood pressure.'

I told her I wasn't sleeping well, and asked her about sleeping pills, but she said they could have an adverse effect on the baby. I wanted to tell her that the baby was having an adverse effect on me. I felt so wretched, I wondered why on earth she pulled out her camera and asked me if I minded her taking my photo.

Andrea called twice a week during the next two weeks. It took quite an effort for me to walk around the hospital block. Up Cardigan to Faraday Street, down Swanston Street, and back to Grattan. Occasionally I vomited in the gutter, which didn't seem to worry her at all. On one occasion, we walked down past the shops to her practice in Lygon Street where she checked my pulse and temperature. It's difficult to take in anything when she chats about what's going on in the world. No one can imagine what it's like to feel nauseous while trying to make conversation. Not that I think she doesn't understand. She's very kind.

On our last walk, Andrea pointed out St Jude's Anglican Church in the distance. 'Mum's parish', she said, 'where Paul and I were married.' I got a quick glimpse of a girl walking up the steps into the church and would have fallen over if Andrea hadn't grabbed me. She asked me if I was okay.

'That girl,' I managed to say. 'She looked like a friend from school.'

'It's McRob Girls High uniform. The conservatorium students use St Jude's to practise because it's close by and has quite a good organ.'

It was all a bit freakish for me. Two girls who are organists and who look alike! Before Andrea left, she described her husband Paul, and told me to watch out for him at Outpatients.

'He's usually busy in the Labour Ward, but he'll try and make time to see you,' she said.

When a doctor singled me out about two weeks later, I could see the resemblance between him and Sister Jeanne. Tall, with an olive complexion and dark eyes. He also had a similar French accent. As we walked along the corridor, he explained that he was Dr Rousseau number one. 'After all,' he said, smiling. 'I had the title first. I recognised you from the photograph Andrea took in Grattan Street.'

He probed my stomach with expert hands, waving away a group of students like a magician performing a magic trick, which was just as well because I was feeling like I could throw up at any moment. I managed a wan smile when he said he'd have been in trouble with his sister and Andrea if he hadn't found me soon. Somehow, he'd notify hospital admin, who'd phone Hallvard when he wasn't too busy in the Labour Ward so that I was allowed to go alone to Outpatients when it suited him.

I wasn't interested when he told me the baby seemed to be doing reasonably well despite me being underweight. Why would I be interested when I'm so ill, and the baby will be given away? I hate the baby twisting and turning inside me. I'm sure it sets off my vomiting and nausea, although Dr Rousseau disagrees. He's different from other doctors in that he seems to be more concerned about *my* health as well as the baby's. He said my blood pressure was too low, my pulse rate too high.

'The condition you have is called *hyperemesis gravidarum*. It's rare and I imagine that your vomiting and headaches don't exactly give you an appetite,' he said gently. 'The baby seems to be absorbing the nutrients, but at this stage I'm more concerned about you. Have any other doctors discussed your diet? You're more than six months pregnant and you look like you're wasting away.'

'One said to try not eating anything greasy.'

'Did they make any other suggestions?'

'One said I had a mental problem. And that one with the glasses we passed in the corridor said I should pull myself together and make myself eat. He said it was all in my mind and it was about time I started thinking of the baby rather than myself.'

'Hmm. Did he now? I've been thinking about your problem, Molly, and I'm wondering if you can eat a little a lot, rather than the other way around? In other words, nibbling throughout the day.'

I didn't feel like discussing food and suddenly rushed off to the nearest toilet. When I returned, I was surprised that he was still there. He told me to lie down and relax.

'I know that institutions don't cater for individuals, but I've written some suggestions for an alternative diet to give to the nun in charge of the kitchen. Is she approachable?'

'She's concerned when I hardly eat. But she knows I'll probably throw up again if I do.'

'I won't write a prescription for your nausea and vomiting as it might have adverse effects on the baby. Aspros for your headaches should be okay, but more importantly, you should have a bland diet that's nutritious. Stick to soft food that's low in fibre. Don't have spicy food like curries. Try to avoid raw food. If the food is fried or greasy, scrape or cut off the fatty bits. It probably means you can have most of the food but only in tiny portions throughout the day. Take your time when you eat and chew it well, even if it takes all day. And whatever you do, don't eat just before you lie down. Drink more liquid but slowly too, like the food. Water or weak tea is fine but sip it. I'm sure they'll work out something once you give them this letter explaining your condition and a list of food I've recommended. I'll arrange for Andrea to give you aspros and dry biscuits to nibble on.'

I thanked him and forced a smile.

'If it hadn't been for Andrea and my sister, perhaps I might never have understood how you and others in similar situations have suffered. They told me what happened in Ballarat, Molly,' he said gently. 'Did the doctor tell your mother what you told him?'

'Yes,' I said. 'But sometimes she doesn't take things in. She didn't talk about it. She cried.'

'And your father?'

'He was very angry with me. He's been strange since he learned the hotel was being closed down.'

'Has your mother been in contact with you?'

'No. Mum doesn't write letters.'

Even in boarding school Mum never wrote to us. I think she felt that the nuns would scrutinise her grammar and spelling mistakes. Dad wrote very good letters once a term, but they would have been more for the nuns than for us girls.

'Your family should be aware of how your confinement is progressing and how ill you are, Molly. Some parents visit their daughters in hospital after the birth.'

'Mine won't be.'

'If you don't mind,' he said. 'I'd like to write to them. I'm convinced they've got compassion for you somewhere in their hearts.'

I gave him my home address.

'Remember,' he reminded me when I stood up to leave. 'Never eat one main meal, Molly. Nibble throughout the day.' He grinned. 'Like a Tasmanian called Alexander I once learned about who said way back in the nineteenth century that it was how one should practise an instrument. A little a lot rather than a lot a little.'

He smiled and walked me back across the road to the Maternity Home. I was blinking back tears when he left me. It was the first time anyone at the hospital had been really kind to me. Then there was Andrea who had arranged it all and had been taking me for walks, thanks to Sister Jeanne. There is kindness in the world after all. All the same, I'm not changing my mind about the tablets. I'll sneak off from Outpatients to a nearby pharmacy for sleeping pills, or three bottles of aspros if I can't get them without a prescription. I've got the £20 Mum gave me to pay for them. I'll try out Doctor Rousseau's suggestions for two weeks, then I'll decide what to do.

36

Cecilia

Cecilia's long blonde braids hung down from her McRob High hat, a satchel slung over one shoulder, and clutching a folio in her hands. She was about to walk up the steps of St Jude's when a woman approached her.

'Excuse me,' she said. 'Are you Cecilia from St Martin's College Ballarat?'

Cecilia whipped her head around in surprise and stared at the woman. 'How on earth did you know?'

'It's a long story, but I found out your practice times from the vicar. Have you got a few minutes? I'm Andrea Rousseau, Sister Jeanne's sister-in-law.'

'Sister Jeanne!' Cecilia was excited. 'She spoke about you and her brother in French conversation. I can't believe it. Our favourite teacher. I miss her terribly. I wouldn't be here today if it hadn't been for her.' She noticed that Andrea looked taken aback. 'I was all prepared to leave shortly after I arrived at St Martin's in Form 3. If Sister Jeanne hadn't talked me out of it, I'd be working on the farm.' She shuddered. 'I'd rather not think about that.'

'So, my sister-in-law is not only the Good Samaritan, but the wise counsellor.' Andrea smiled. 'Have you got time to chat for a few minutes?'

Cecilia agreed, following Andrea around behind the church to a paved courtyard. They sat down on a bench under an old plane tree, bare now, its patchy outer bark flaking off to reveal inner bark in shades of grey, green, and yellow.

'I know this church well because I've always lived in this area. It's Mum's parish. Paul and I were married here. We posed under this very tree for our wedding photos. Only it was in the heat of summer, when this tree was a huge canopy of green.'

Cecilia wondered what Jeanne had thought of her brother marrying out of the church.

'Now. To get to why I'm here. I've been seeing Molly because…'

'Molly? You've seen Molly? Is she alright?'

'Well, who'd be alright if they were raped? By a priest, no less. And then as if that weren't enough, Molly gets pregnant and suffers from an awful illness.'

Cecilia stared at Andrea open-mouthed. 'A priest!'

Andrea pursed her lips. 'Unbelievable, isn't it?'

'I… I never knew the details. I had an idea that Molly was… forced into it. But a priest!'

'He tricked her into going to the presbytery then knocked her out with alcohol and barbiturates.'

Cecilia couldn't say anything. The priest. Perhaps it was the same one who'd attacked her! 'Which parish?' she blurted out. 'What was the priest's name?'

Andrea looked surprised by the depth of passion in Cecilia's voice. 'Father Kelly. From St Alban's.'

'Are you sure?'

'Definitely. Why?'

'A priest attacked me too.'

Andrea's eyes widened. 'Not the same one?'

'No. The cathedral. In the gallery. I was luckier than Molly. If you can call it luck.'

While Cecilia recounted what happened, she was biting her lip. Trying desperately to hold back her tears. Thinking of Molly rather than herself. She wiped her eyes with the back of her hands, releasing a small sob. 'And here I was feeling sorry for myself after I was attacked. Never again. And Molly still ill!'

Andrea put a comforting hand on her shoulder. 'You've got every right to feel sorry for yourself, Cecilia.'

'Poor Molly!'

'She says her illness started around the middle of March. About six weeks into her pregnancy!'

Cecilia nodded. 'Yes. She seemed okay at the beginning of the term. We were practising duets together for a concert.' She paused for a moment. 'She looked terrible the last time I saw her. I remember Mum talking about morning sickness, but Molly's seemed to be more than that.'

'She's got a rare pregnancy illness. She's barely managing the short walks around this area. It was because of her thinking she'd recognised you that I'm here now. I happened to mention to Juliette that Molly thought she saw someone who looked like a schoolfriend walking up the steps into St Jude's. Juliette said it was possibly you because one of the girls at St Martin's told her you were now living in Melbourne.'

Cecilia frowned. 'Juliette! Who's Juliette?'

'Sorry. A slip of the tongue. Juliette is Sister Jeanne's real name. Her birth-name.' She paused for a moment and grinned. 'You're going to have some scandal to relate now. Jeanne has left the convent and is living with us. Juliette, that is!'

Cecilia stared open-mouthed at her, until Andrea laughed. 'You should see yourself in a mirror! If your lips were covered in red lipstick, you'd look like one of those laughing clowns they have at fairs. Someone might come along and throw a ping pong ball in your mouth.'

Cecilia laughed. 'But it's such a shock.' She paused for a moment. 'The girls must be devastated.'

'Not the ones at MLC, where she'll be teaching next year. She's doing relief teaching now.'

'I'd love to see her!'

'She'd like to see you. She was wondering if you were living with your friend's family.'

'Yes. Bernice's family. In Kew.'

'I suppose Bernice also goes to McRob.'

'Yes. We've both been there since Easter.'

'If you don't mind me asking, Cecilia, how did you get into a selective school during your final year? It's most unusual!'

'Bernice's father pulled a few strings. His sister's also a friend of the principal. We had to do a few tests.' She grinned. 'We did exceptionally well in French!'

Andrea smiled. 'Well. Lucky you!'

'When do you think I'll be able to meet up with Molly?'

'My husband Paul's an obstetrician at the Women's Hospital. He's put her on a special diet which should begin working soon. On our last attempted walk, she felt so ill, we sat on a bench and she hardly said a word.'

'Can you phone me when she's feeling better? Perhaps we could meet up during one of your walks!' She pulled a notebook from her satchel, wrote down her full name and phone number, and handed it to Andrea.

'Seeing a friend would mean a lot to her because she hasn't got family support. You're at school during the times that mainly suit me. Juliette's taking over when Molly starts improving.'

'I can easily skip off from sport!'

They stood up and began walking towards the church steps. 'I don't want to stop you from practising, but I'm curious about you changing over to McRob with only two and a half terms to go. Was it difficult?'

'Difficult?' Cecilia rolled her eyes. 'It's The Promised Land after boarding in the most authoritarian and God-fearing school in the state. St Martinet's, we called it.'

'St Martinet,' Andrea smiled. 'Very clever.'

'There are so many extras at McRob. Sport and drama for a start. Bernice and I are involved in the production of *The Pirates of Penzance* with Melbourne Boys High School.' More than involved, she thought, grinning. Bernice had dropped Tom for The Pirate King.

'We never had excursions and competitions against other schools at St Martin's. I love everything about McRob. Even the tram rides to and from school because we get to know students from other schools.' Her greatest love, of course, was Bernice's brother Daniel, her live-in boyfriend. Things were really hotting up between the two of them.

'You're not involved in debating as well?'

Cecilia shook her head. 'Not enough time, even if I had the confidence. Can you tell Sister Jeanne that my French teacher knows about her reputation in the exams and the *Alliance Française* competitions? And that I miss her and all those French songs.'

'Juliette, you mean! Sister Jeanne no longer exists.'

Cecilia laughed. 'Sorry. Juliette. She's a brilliant teacher. St Martin's has good teachers and a few shockers. Like other schools, I suppose, although they're all good at McRob.' She rolled her eyes. 'Then there's Alphonsus. Boarding school is bad enough, but not with her in charge. On the other hand, she gave me a scholarship otherwise I'd be on the farm.'

Andrea grinned. 'She's quite charming to visitors. And from what I've heard, she's given you a good run with your music. Won't be long before you'll be a full-time student at the

Conservatorium.' She looked at her watch. 'Sorry, I guess we'd better be going.'

They both stood up and headed back towards the church. Cecilia was about to walk up the steps but stopped suddenly to face Andrea. 'The funny thing is, I've been thinking about doing something else. I don't want to make a career out of music. I'm not sure why I'm telling you this. I haven't mentioned it to anyone else.'

Andrea smiled shrewdly. 'Music can never be wasted. It's the backbone of the entertainment world, isn't it? So what else have you got in mind?'

'I'd like to help people. Not teaching or nursing. I couldn't stand putting up with bossy principals and matrons. Too much like boarding school. I really don't know what to do although someone at school was talking about social work or psychology.'

'There's a heavy emphasis on adoption placements now amongst social workers. Many of them are almoners. They spend their time between hospitals and maternity homes organising adoptions of single girls' babies to childless couples. They have to be quite forceful, but they're just doing their job,' I suppose. She shrugged. 'They used to be the official distributors of alms to the poor at public hospitals, hence almoners. That changed a little with maternity homes. Maybe there are other areas of social work. Perhaps you should speak to a teacher about it.'

Cecilia was doubtful. 'Maybe.'

'Of course, if you really want to help people, have you ever thought about doing medicine?'

'I can't. I haven't done enough science subjects. I should have continued with maths and science like Sister Dominique wanted me to.'

'In that case, you've got two alternatives,' Andrea said. 'You can repeat sixth form and concentrate on getting top marks in physics and chemistry, and maths of course. Or you could do music *and* science at University next year. After a couple of years if your results are good, you may be able to switch over to medicine.'

Cecilia listened, astounded as Andrea told her about her work and beliefs. There were not enough women in medicine, and they were the only ones who could fight to change the present system. Women's general health for a start, and education about birth control so they could control their own fertility. Most men refused to have anything to do with it which was why so many young girls became pregnant and had to suffer the consequences. Rarely the men. 'When I was a student, I asked a visiting specialist what sort of birth control advice he gave his patients back in England. His condescending reply was that the world would never be over-populated. Flood, famine and disease would see to that. He wasn't too happy when I said that was all very well for the wealthy because they didn't have to resort to backstreet abortions.'

Cecilia wasn't sure what to think or say about this. It was all new to her.

'If one thinks of young girls like Molly and the thousands of unwanted pregnancies around Australia,' Andrea continued, 'then something needs to be done. Girls like Molly who have been raped are not allowed to have an abortion.'

Cecilia looked at her disbelievingly. 'You mean the law doesn't allow it? I know the church doesn't allow abortion under any circumstances, but I'd have thought it was different for rape!'

'It's to do with always blaming the woman. And nothing will change as long as politicians and most doctors are male. They have a perfect solution while maternity homes farm out babies.

Med School is silent on these problems and God forbid any mention of contraception. Everyone seems to want the next generation to grow up the same way they did. In total ignorance of their bodies!'

'I've never really thought about it before.'

Andrea shrugged. 'Hardly anyone does. Girls should be educated about their bodies. And intelligent girls like you should think about doing medicine. Too many like you end up doing nursing because they're indoctrinated to believe that medicine's for men only.' She paused. 'I'm sorry. I might sound obsessed, but women need more of a voice. We have the vote, but it means nothing without social welfare. Or equal pay and better working conditions. You wouldn't believe the stories of some of my patients we're trying to help.' She pulled a notebook from her handbag and wrote her name and phone number in it. 'I'll let you know about Molly, but if there's anything you want to talk about, phone me any evening. You and Bernice might like to catch up with Juliette before you get too busy with exams.'

Cecilia struggled to gather her thoughts. Who at school would have handed out the sort of information that Andrea had just volunteered? At their last assembly, all they were told was that as soon as they got their exam results, they were to start applying for their intended course. On the other hand, McRob students were probably advised of their options at the beginning of the year when the two of them were still in Ballarat. 'You've really given me something to think about, Dr Rousseau. I think I need to talk to you. And Jeanne too!'

'Juliette,' Andrea reminded her, laughing. 'And call me Andrea. By the way Cecilia, did your parents report your attack to anyone?'

'They reported it to the Bishop and the police, but we haven't heard anything back yet.'

'Hmmm,' Andrea said skeptically. 'And you're not likely to.'

Cecilia remembered overhearing Bernice's father use an expression she'd never heard before when Mrs Dobson was talking about reporting the priest to the police and the Archbishop. 'There's no harm in trying, I suppose, love, but I've got a feeling you'll be pissing in the wind.'

Andrea and Cecilia said their goodbyes. As Cecilia walked up the steps into the church, all she could think of was seeing Molly and her former teacher again.

37

Molly

I'm seeing Doctor Rousseau regularly now between caesareans and difficult births. His time is limited, so a nurse phones the Home when he's available. It's September, and about ten days since I started my new diet. I'm feeling slightly better. Sorting it out can be difficult when you haven't got an appetite. Stews have fibrous vegetables like carrots and onions and beans, which means I have to pick at everything. Mashed or boiled potatoes are fine, so I have small helpings and save some later to have cold, which is disgusting. I'm not complaining. I'll do anything to stop my headaches and vomiting.

I feel heavy and awkward, like I'm carrying a watermelon in my stomach that's pressing on my bladder. I'm sure the baby is going to fall out when I'm walking around or when I'm on the toilet. Dr Rousseau says it's all quite normal. That my lungs and stomach will have a chance to stretch out soon, so that breathing and eating will be easier.

With only a slight headache and a little nausea, I enjoy my walk around the Exhibition Gardens with Andrea. She tells me that the following week, her partner will be taking three weeks' leave, so she'll be working full-time. Someone else will be walking with me. A few days later when I'm called to the front door, Andrea is introducing someone to Sister Leo. The woman seems familiar. I stare at her and notice a sort of moistness in her eyes. When she says 'Bonjour, Molly' I realise it's Sister Jeanne. I'm so astonished I can't speak. I'm all choked up and begin to cry. Andrea introduces Jeanne in French as Juliette. She throws her arms around my shoulders and kisses me on both cheeks in the style she once told us had been introduced during the French Revolution. Her floral shift and smart sandals show arms and legs that I've only ever seen covered in black. She looks beautiful with her Mediterranean complexion, and dark, wavy hair. Andrea apologises and says she has to race back to the surgery. I can't believe my former teacher is standing in front of me. Calling her Juliette will seem strange. She explains how she left the convent during the May holidays, and one of these days she'll tell me why.

'You're looking much better than the last time I saw you in Ballarat, Molly' she says. 'Would you like to go into town?'

I nod. I'm still in shock. It's after 4pm now, and so far, I'm fine, even with the tram bumping and grinding its way along the tracks. Juliette grasps my arm when we alight at the Town Hall and asks me if I'm okay. I tell her that I felt everyone in the tram was staring at me, probably because I'm not wearing a wedding ring.

'They're just jealous of your pretty face and the lovely lilt in your hair Molly,' she says. 'They could be thinking you're a little pale and thin at this stage of your pregnancy, so now that you're beginning to improve, you could try eating a little more each day. And remember what Paul told you. 'A little a lot. Which reminds me. Have a Sao,' she says, delving into her handbag.

While I stand there, subtly nibbling on one, Juliette begins twiddling her wedding ring, now on her right hand. Next moment, we're in a pharmacy where she purchases a jar of face cream.

'This should do it,' she says, smearing the cream on her finger. 'This ring was always too tight.'

After a minute or two, she manages to pull it off, then wiggles it onto my ring finger.

'It's a little loose,' she says, wiping off the excess cream, 'but firm enough as long as you never take it off. You'll be treated better at the hospital if they think you're married.'

I think it's too late for that, but when I protest, she says she doesn't want it back until after I've had the baby. We continue walking towards the city centre.

'You wouldn't have seen all of this before,' she says as I stare around. 'The city's had a facelift. And is still having one. It's certainly changed since I was living here a few years ago.'

We squeeze our way past workers and shoppers – up Collins towards Elizabeth then on to Bourke Street. A window in Myers displays a television set with a test pattern, and a large poster promising that from November 22, all Melbourne will be able to watch the Olympic Games live. Bourke Street is brimming with pennants and flags from countries all over the world as we head down to Swanston Street.

'The silhouettes and abstract shapes strung across the streets are supposed to reflect modernist art styles,' Juliette says as she looks around. 'They've painted a few buildings in pastel shades since I was last here.'

Most of the Victorian verandas have vanished. The few that remain are adorned with bare-chested male athletes flaunting their muscles and beautiful bodies in the form of sculptures and dioramas. The crowd thickens with sightseers and commuters as we approach St Paul's Cathedral and Flinders Street Station. A display board with changeable numbers on Young and Jackson's pub says *Tuesday September 23. Only 60 days to go before the opening of the Games of the XV1 Olympiad.* Sixty days? Nearly the same number of days to go for me.

'This is what I wanted you to see, Molly,' Juliette says excitedly.

A giant metal-mesh torch shaped like an ice-cream cone towers over the city, shivering and jiggling and sparkling in the sunlight. Suspended from cables, it stretches between the buildings on the four corners of Flinders and Swanston Street. Juliette indicates the spire on St Paul's and wonders if the torch is taller. It looks about eight or nine storeys high. We stare at it for a few minutes. Someone nearby says it will glimmer like a million glow-worms when it's all lit up at night. If only my sisters and the girls from the Home were here to see this. Beyond the torch structure, there are five Olympic circles on the glass panels above the clocks at Flinders Street station. Everywhere I look there are flags from countries I didn't know existed. Juliette must have noticed me staring at the backs of a group of men in red track suits who are walking past us towards Flinders Street Station.

'If you're wondering what the CCCP is on their backs,' she says, 'it stands for the Union of Soviet Socialist Republics, which means they're Russian. I believe there are about fifteen countries in the Union.'

'Does that include Catholic countries like Hungary and Poland? The ones we were always praying for at school?'

Juliette frowns. 'No. They compete separately as far as I know.'

I'm feeling a little squirmy during our return on the crowded tram and am forced to alight one block earlier. My stomach settles down almost immediately. I ask Juliette if Celie knew she was leaving.

'Not exactly, but I'll tell you something very interesting about her on our next walk,' she says mysteriously. 'Oops. I nearly forgot.' She opens her handbag. 'Andrea gave me this book for you. She said to hide it from the nuns.'

We look at each other and laugh. She must have known that boarders hid books from the nuns. That evening, a girl called Cynthia tells me that while I was out, my boyfriend called. I tell her I don't have a boyfriend. She rolls her eyes, and says she'll have him if I don't want him. When she describes him, I realise she's talking about Tony who I haven't seen since he ran away from home last year. I'm so excited. But how does he know where I'm living? Cynthia said that when Sister Leo told him visitors weren't allowed, he handed her a letter for me. I ask Hal about it, but she shrugs and says there's nothing for me. I'm furious, but there's no point in arguing with *her*.

In bed that evening, I open Andrea's present, a book called *What Every Woman Should Know*. Inside it, there's a note apologising for the delay, explaining that it was hard to get, and that it should be called *What Every Girl Should Know*. It didn't cover everything, but one of these days, she was going to write a better book. There are diagrams and descriptions of male and female reproductive organs, menstruation, intercourse, conception, birth and venereal diseases. The chapter on intercourse is the one that upsets me the most because I think of what Father Kelly did to me when I was unconscious. I'm trembling in anger and humiliation. Overwhelmed by the ugliness of it all. I'm glad I wasn't conscious when he did such a disgusting thing to me. I hate him. I can't imagine my parents and grandparents doing that unless they thought they'd be rewarded with plenary indulgences.

Two days later, the miracle happens. For the first time, I wake up without feeling the slightest bit nauseous. No headache. No dizziness. I'm full of a euphoria that follows months of illness. My death wish has vanished. I move my hands around my stomach the way the doctors do, and I feel a slight sort of fluttering. Almost instantly something inside me seems to change. I decide to look up the chapter on the foetus that I'd previously ignored. There's a diagram of what a baby looks like in the womb. I can't believe all that fits inside skinny me, or that the baby's head will fit through my hips.

From then on, I become more aware of the baby moving inside me. I think of Andrea's little Matthew. My baby brother Patrick who I took out in the pram in Ballarat. Perhaps that's why I decide that my baby is a boy. He'll be as beautiful as Patrick and Matthew. Then I realise that others will be cuddling him. Taking him for walks. I feel tears running down my face when I think of someone else doing that. Why can't it be me? This baby is mine. He's part of me. Perhaps my illness has been preventing me from thinking straight, but anyone can change their mind, can't they? Strangers will be benefitting from all the misery and illness I've suffered throughout my pregnancy. I have a sudden urge to be defiant like most of the girls around me. Now I understand why they want to keep their babies. This baby inside me is mine. Why has it taken me so long to feel maternal?

There's a girl of about twenty at the Home who calls herself Marilyn after Marilyn Monroe. Hallvard told her to change it because it's not a saint's name. 'I always do the opposite to what she says,' Marilyn says. 'I want to keep my baby, but I don't know how I'll manage.'

'I'm keeping mine, too' I tell her. 'I'm writing to ask my aunt if I can stay with her after my baby is born. I know she'll take us in.'

Marilyn looks around the room and whispers conspiratorially to me. 'Well for God's sake don't mention it to dunny-breath and the almoners. Just go along with whatever the bastards tell you and fill in the forms. After you've had your baby, whatever you do, don't sign anything. If you do, you're giving permission for the couple to steal your baby.'

I'm luckier than Marilyn. I know Maude will help me mind my baby. I can't wait to leave this place. When an almoner arrives with a form she helps me fill in, I pretend to go along with it all. It's got the names of the adopting parents on it. All I need do is sign it after my baby's birth. That night I sleep peacefully. Reconciled with my baby-to-be. Just before I fall asleep a plan begins to form in my mind.

The following morning, I write a long letter to Maude and Tony. I tell them everything that happened to me in Ballarat, and everything that's going on here in Melbourne. The Home, the hospital, Juliette, Andrea, and Doctor Rousseau. I ask Maude if my baby and I can live with her and Harry after I leave the hospital. Two days later, I'm halfway through lunch when a sixth sense tells me that Hallvard is snooping around upstairs. Mealtime must be their only chance of doing that. I tiptoe upstairs, and sure enough, there's Hallvard, just coming out of my dormitory. She would have heard the stairs creaking. She gives me a nasty look and says nothing. A few things, including my writing-pad in my top drawer, were put back in a different place. Mum's two £10 notes I'd hidden under the drawer lining have disappeared. Just as well I put Andrea's book behind my chest of drawers. I'm sure she's read my letter. I'd have sealed it up in an envelope, only I hadn't quite finished.

During my next walk, I tell Juliette about Tony calling in when we were in town, the letter I never received, and how I'm convinced Hallvard read the letter I'm posting to Maude and Tony.

'I'm also missing some money I'd hidden under the drawer lining. We're not supposed to have any, so I can't complain. Hallvard's been quite nasty to me since then.'

'Was there anything you said in the letter she wouldn't have liked?'

I shrug. 'I described what happened to me in Ballarat.'

'I'd have thought she'd be sympathetic.'

I grin. 'I told Maude to send her reply to your address.'

'She wouldn't like that!'

'And that Hallvard was such a dog, she made Mother Alphonsus look like an angel.'

Juliette laughs. 'That explains why she's been nasty to you.'

'I also asked Maude if I could stay with her.' I've decided not to tell Juliette about keeping my baby until we meet up with Andrea. 'I know she'll take me in.'

'I don't know how long it takes to recover from childbirth, but I imagine she'd be the best person to look after you.'

I pull the letter out of my pocket and Juliette gives me a postage stamp. We laugh as I post the letter because I tell her it reminds me of the boarders asking day-scholars to post their mail.

'We suspected as much,' she says, smiling. 'I think I'd have done the same if I'd been a boarder.'

It's week thirty-two of my pregnancy. Doctor Rousseau is concerned that the baby's head is too big to pass through my narrow hips. He calls in a senior obstetrician – an Honorary I think they're called, who agrees with him. They arrange to do a caesarean on November 14th, a week earlier than the due date. Dr Rousseau warns me about contractions and the possibility of my water breaking prior to my operation. Having read Andrea's book, I tell him I know what to expect, but not how nervous I am about the operation.

'You'll need to tell them at Bleak House when you're being prepped, and the time and date of your caesarean.'

I nod.

'I'm very pleased with your progress,' he says. It's probably the diet that's doing it, although we'll never really know because *hyperemesis gravidarum* can cease at any time during pregnancy.'

Sometimes, like Juliette, he speaks to me in French. He repeats it in English when I probably look a bit clueless.

'Juliette hasn't had a chance to tell you because we've only found out the details, but maman's parents are flying over from Paris next month,' he tells me slowly in French.

I understand what he's saying and nod.

He continues in English. 'They're arriving about a week before your caesarean. We'll drive them to Ballarat and stay a few nights.'

The worst thing that could happen while he's away is for me to go into early labour. I must have looked worried because he laughs.

'Don't worry. Just ask for Dr Sutherland, or one of the honoraries if you're worried about *anything*. I can be back in Melbourne in a flash! You've got weeks to go yet. I'll arrange to see you the day before we leave.' He looks at the calendar. 'That'll be Wednesday, November 6th. We'll be back by Sunday. And if I'm concerned about anything before then, I won't go to to Ballarat.'

That's a relief.

38

The Priest

They were in the front parlour.

'I haven't seen your little flower girl around at all lately, Hilton. Just the one who's sometimes with her mother,' Bob Bourke said, handing Hilton a beer.

'That's Maureen. Yes. I don't know what's happened to Molly. I haven't seen her for months.'

'Maybe they've moved. What's her surname?'

Hilton had to think for a moment. 'Harrington,' he said.

'Harrington? Kevin Harrington. I think I've seen him around.' He shrugged. 'I don't think they attend Mass together as a family, perhaps because there are babies at home. I wouldn't have a clue who belongs to whom half the time. Who knows who half our parishioners are? Most of them do their duty, I suppose, and that's it.'

'Maureen hasn't seen Molly around either.'

'His was one of the pubs the Brewery closed down, so with him being out of a job, she's probably left school. He wouldn't be able to afford the fees. She probably got a job in Melbourne.'

Hilton nodded nonchalantly, as if unconcerned.

He'd been desperate to see Molly again. Watching out for her on her return from school. Waiting to see her in the confessional. At communion. There'd been no sign of her. Meanwhile, he had another girl in mind. One who was more enthusiastic about doing the flowers than Molly had ever been.

'Sorry to change the subject, Hilton, but I've just come from the palace. The good news is that because we're building up to a thousand parishioners, we're getting another priest early next year. We'll still have O'Doherty, but at least we'll have a lighter load. Better still, word is that the new priest, Father Xavier Lawson, is one of us. A partisan.' He winked and grinned at Hilton. 'One who shares our views, you might say. Well, mine more than yours, perhaps. Although, who knows? Some like variety. Like you-know-who at St Felix's! *Capisci*?'

Hilton smiled conspiratorially at his superior. Yes, he understood. It was good news that he wouldn't need to tiptoe around the newcomer.

He was in his study sorting out a topic for Sunday's sermon when he heard a knock on his external door. How was this possible? O'Doherty wasn't around. Bob had gone off to give the last rites to a dying friend. The housekeeper, Mrs Rawlings, would have knocked on the inside door. No one else outside the presbytery knew he had his own private study. He opened the door to a well-built man of about fifty, almost as tall as himself.

'I'm Harry Norton, and this is Tony,' he said gruffly, indicating a youth of about eighteen or nineteen, who Hilton assumed was his son. 'Are you Father Kelly?'

When Hilton agreed, Harry said he needed to speak to him immediately. Before waiting for an answer, Harry pushed past him into his study, Tony following. How had this stranger known who and where he was? How dare he barge into his study! Why hadn't he rung the front doorbell? This was his private domain. His world.

'I'm here about Molly,' Harry said. 'Molly Harrington!'

Hilton frowned. 'Molly?' he said. 'The girl who used to do the flowers?'

'That's right,' Harry said. 'She said you asked her to do them last year.'

'She volunteered,' Hilton replied, wondering why this man was asking.

'Not according to Molly, but never mind. We'll come to that later. She said…'

'If you don't mind my asking,' Hilton interrupted, 'are you a parishioner? Who are you?'

'I'm not one of your flock, and I'd never want to be,' Harry replied rudely. 'Fortunately, I'm not in anyone's flock, but more to the point, I'm Molly's uncle.'

Hilton recoiled a little. 'I haven't seen Molly lately. Is she living in Melbourne? We miss her a lot.'

'Why did you invite her to the presbytery?' Harry said aggressively.

Hilton's friendly façade obviously wasn't working. He looked at the youth again. Where had he seen him before?

'What makes you think I brought her here, Mr Norton?'

'Because Molly said you did,' Harry said angrily.

Why were they here? Molly couldn't have given details to anyone about what had happened that day! She passed out. There was no way he would acquiesce to speculation and accusations on the whim of this stranger. A heathen. Someone who had no respect for the clergy. 'There was an occasion when she asked me to help her with maths when she'd got a little behind in her work. She knew…'

'Let's get this straight,' Harry interrupted. 'You asked her. She never asked you. You brought her here, didn't you?'

He was on the defensive now. 'We were in the kitchen. A very public place, what with the housekeeper and other priests…'

'I'm Molly's brother,' Tony interrupted. 'She said you brought her to this room. She'd never lie to me. We told each other everything.'

Now he could see the resemblance. The same slight curl in the dark hair, the high cheekbones that reached the deep blue eyes and long eyelashes. His skin had more of a tan.

'You were in this very room with Molly,' Tony continued. 'She said you took her to the kitchen the first time, but after that, you brought her here. She described exactly where it was.' He walked over to the desk. 'She said you had those art folios and books on your desk. And the couch and sideboard. It's as though she painted a picture of this room.'

Harry strode over to the sideboard. 'And there's the vodka and soda siphon on a tray.' All that's missing are the barbiturates.'

Hilton flinched, then recovered himself. 'You can't just barge in here making these accusations. You…'

'First of all, you denied that Molly has been here,' Harry said, his face inches away from Hilton's. 'Do you deny that you gave her alcoholic drinks?'

Hilton smiled. 'Once or twice I gave her a lemon squash. She'd been working hard doing the flowers after all.'

'And what did you talk about?' Harry continued. 'What did you do?'

Where was this going? If they were accusing him of molesting Molly, where was their evidence?

'What we discussed was very private, but if you really want to know, Molly sometimes talked about your father,' he said calmly, looking at Tony.

Tony sighed. 'Well. That's no surprise. I suppose she needed someone to confide in after I left home. But we're not talking about what you said to her, Father. It's what you did to her!'

'What do you mean?'

'You don't need to put on that innocent face. You raped her!' Harry shouted. 'Nine months ago! She's carrying your child.'

Hilton gasped, his eyes widening in disbelief. This was not possible. He'd been so careful. She was unconscious. *Coitus interruptus*. And it was only once. Nine months ago! That would be early February. Maybe late January. Just before the school year started. How could this have happened? He spoke softly to his intruders. 'What are you saying? That's a terrible accusation to make. I should call the police. Please leave my study immediately.'

There was a long silence.

Harry spoke first. 'Molly has been so ill during her pregnancy that the doctor said she could have died.'

After another long pause, Hilton finally spoke. 'I'm very sorry to hear that. But... but as well as confiding in me about her father, Molly mentioned a boyfriend she was having problems with. She said...'

'Save your breath, Father,' Tony said. 'No need for lies. When I told Molly one of my friends was keen on her, she said she wanted nothing to do with boys until she'd left school to live in Melbourne. She said that with her studies, there was no way she had time to fit in anything else. We never had secrets from each other.'

The only sound in the study was the ticking of the clock on the mantelpiece above the fireplace. 'Well,' Hilton said with a condescending smile. 'You know what young girls are like. Adolescents. Some of them are very inventive. Good at making up stories. They throw themselves at boys, even priests, and next thing... Well, you can imagine!'

Harry's eyes widened in disbelief. He clenched his fists, knuckles white with anger. 'My wife Maude wouldn't let you get away with saying that about our Molly.'

Hilton saw Harry taking one striding step towards him. The blind fury on his face. The raised fist aimed at his jaw.

39

Molly

Juliette is excited about her grandparents' forthcoming visit. She hasn't seen them for about ten years. When I think of how Mum's parents died when she was a child, I can't believe that hers are still alive. They must be in their eighties.

'We've bought an early Christmas present for all the family,' Juliette tells me as we walk around Parkville after she's finished teaching for the day. 'We've managed to get everyone tickets for the athletics at the MCG so we can watch the finish of the marathon. I can't wait to see the look on their faces. Papa and *pépère* love running!'

'And they'll be able to see the rowing when they're in Ballarat,' I say, reminded of Gabby insisting we should practise our French with the gorgeous rowers training on Lake Wendouree.

She nods and smiles. 'That'll be another surprise for them. They'll be barracking for France of course, but for maman and papa, it'll be Australia first and France second. Anyway, more importantly, you look great. Have you been okay, Molly?'

'Yes. Very well, and Doctor Rousseau thinks so too. He only needed a few minutes with me last time.'

I'm desperate for her to tell me about Cecilia.

'We'll stop off for a drink at the café and I'll tell you about Cecilia,' she says, reading my mind.

The café is near the university. We find a table and Juliette orders our drinks. Two students at the table next to us are discussing French writers. I look at Juliette, reminded of her telling us about Victor Hugo and Marcel Proust, and how every student of French should be familiar with French culture. In a flash, I'm back in Walter Mitty mode. A university student at a French lecture. I leave all the other students for dead when I discuss *Les Misérables* in French with the professor. There's a piano in the lecture theatre, so I blend myself with Cecilia, brilliantly performing the works of Debussy and Ravel. I switch to Chopin, explaining in fluent French while I play a nocturne, why the French claim him as French, and the Poles claim him as Polish.

'Andrea told me about the girl you saw on the steps at St Jude's. I knew immediately it was Cecilia,' Juliette says, breaking into my reverie. She laughs when I must have looked stunned. 'She goes there regularly to practise the organ. I wanted you to be sitting down so you wouldn't get such a shock that you'd go into labour. She's been wanting to see you, and now's the time, isn't it?'

I'm nearly jumping up and down. 'Cecilia? But how come? Why on earth would she leave St Martin's in her final year?'

'I think it would be much better if she tells you herself. Look!'

I gasp. I can't believe it. Cecilia is walking towards us. She's wearing a smart plaid knee-length summer uniform, trimmed with white collar and cuffs. Short white socks show off her Betty Grable legs, and her complexion is now quite tanned. Her straw hat is such an improvement on the convent's hideous grey felt hat, her uniform far from dowdy. A satchel is slung over one shoulder and she's clutching what is probably a music folio. She's still wearing her long, golden tresses in braids, 'like Rapunzel,' Bernice once said. We threw our arms around each other, something we'd never have done in Ballarat. Juliette stands up and kisses her in the French style, exactly how she greeted me outside Bleak House. The three of us have tears in our eyes.

Cecilia drags a chair over from the next table. 'When Juliette phoned, she told me how you were improving, and how it might be a good time to have a get together before my exams. I couldn't wait.'

I've got a million questions to ask her, but I begin with the obvious one. 'Why did you leave St Martin's?'

'It's a long story,' she begins, then looks at Juliette.

'I haven't said anything yet, Cecilia, because I thought it would be better coming from you, which is why I'm off so you two can catch up with each other. I'll be back with Andrea in about half an hour.'

Juliette stands up to leave, bends over the table, and speaks confidentially. 'Don't bother speculating as to why I left the convent. I'll tell you right now. I became disillusioned over a few things, but what happened to you two girls was *la goutte qui fait déborder le vase.*'

With that, she walks off, leaving us a little perplexed. 'It must mean something like the last straw,' I say to Cecilia.

'Except that *goutte* is drop, isn't it?'

'Yes. So it must be something like the last drop in the vase. Which makes it overflow.'

Cecilia shrugs. 'So *déborder* must mean to overflow.'

I stare at her. 'Was it something like the last straw that made you leave too, Celie?'

She nods. 'Did you realise Bernice and I didn't return after Easter?'

I had to think for a moment. 'I remember looking around for you once or twice. I wasn't taking in anything most of the time. I was away a lot, anyway. Gabby used to wonder what was wrong with me. I never told her a thing. One of these days, I'll write and tell her everything.'

Cecilia leans forward and speaks softly. 'What happened to me was nothing in comparison to what happened to you.'

When she finishes telling me, I'm all choked up and can't speak. I understand what she's been through. More than that, I'm angry. We sit there for a minute, looking at each other. Sipping our drinks. We not only have our music and former school that bind us together. There's also Juliette, the best French teacher and confidante in the world. It occurs to me that Cecilia and I have something else in common now. We are both victims. Victims of men purporting to be God's representatives on earth.

'At least you're looking much better than when I last saw you, Molly,' Cecilia says.

'I am.' I tell her about my caesarean. How kind Andrea, Juliette and Doctor Rousseau have been to me. How my spirits have lifted on my new diet. 'But I'm dying to know about your school, Celie!'

She smiles. 'Like I told Andrea, it's The Promised Land. We have extra things like excursions and competitions. Sport is during school hours, and after school as an extra, with a choice of hockey, netball and athletics as well as basketball and tennis.'

'Hockey. I always wanted to play hockey.'

'We mix with boys from Melbourne High because we're involved in a G and S operetta called *The Pirates of Penzance*, which we love.' She stops for a moment and twiddles with the straw in her glass. 'There's something else about McRob that goes beyond all that and the plethora of religion at St Martin's. I can't quite put my finger on it.'

I thought of Hallvard rifling through my belongings. 'Perhaps you're trusted more now. No one snooping around your lockers and desks. No hiding your books and altering your ball gowns.'

Cecilia laughs. 'And swapping boys around.'

'Al brought it all on herself.'

'She's her own worst enemy! I think distrust and suspicion are the dominant strains of her character. We're not treated like children at McRob. Fifth and sixth formers are trusted. *Potens Sui.* Mastery of self, the school motto says. It's based on self-discipline and responsibility to oneself and others.'

I grin. 'A bit different from *In altum oculus tollite*. When Al went on about *Raise thine eyes aloft*, or we sang it during that awful school song, Gabby and I used to pull our tunics up to our knees and sing *Raise Thy Hem Aloft*. Not too loudly, of course!'

Cecilia laughs. 'You should have told me that. Bernice and I would have had everyone doing it. Anyway, I've only been at McRob since Easter, yet I'm proud to be a student there. I sing the school song at assemblies with pride as though I've been there forever. Sometimes I wish I had another year there. I have a real sense of belonging when I walk through the school gates. We compete against other schools for sport. And debates and competitions. We cheer like crazy after we trounce University High in a basketball match. We scream at assembly when we're told that the debating team has beaten another school, especially a boys' school.'

'Alphonsus said cheering was unladylike.'

'We have Houses and inter-school competitions. Maybe pride's what it's all about. Yes. School pride and school spirit.'

I nod because I understand. It was non-existent at St Martin's. There were no Houses and the competition was academic. How could anyone be proud of a school with Alphonsus at the helm?

I notice Cecilia's music folio, reminding me that I want to hear her play the organ again. I ask her if we can call into St Jude's on our walks.

'Only if you come upstairs and say hello!'

I grin. 'We were told that we were never to enter a protestant church.'

'Andrea said she and Paul were married there. Alphonsus and Rosario must have been scandalised. A nun's brother marrying outside the church!'

'Juliette said the rule was different in France. It's not legal unless they get married at the town hall. *Le mairie.*'

Cecilia frowned. 'I remember that. They could get a blessing from the *curé* or have a Nuptial Mass later, I think.'

'Weird that it's a different rule here. Anyway, perhaps we can arrange a time with Juliette when you're practising. Like old times in Ballarat. Does Bernice ever come along?'

'No. She's got something on every day after school. Debating. A Shakespeare play with a drama group. We hardly see each other at school because it's so huge. We're mostly doing different subjects. And we're flat out now with exams coming up.'

I'm disappointed. I like Bernice.

'Never mind. We can all have a proper get together when you're feeling up to it. After our exams.'

Juliette returns with Andrea. They take our second lot of drink orders and sit down to join us. When I look across at Juliette now, I can't believe she was ever a nun. Her hair is about the same length as mine now. Just below the ears. She seems to be quite at home in Melbourne. Well she would be, I suppose, seeing that she lived and studied nearby a few years ago.

'I hope you girls have had time to chat about school,' she says.

'About how we miss Mother Alphonsus,' Cecilia grins.

Juliette laughs. 'I don't think I'll comment on that.'

Andrea asks me how I am, and I tell her I've been very well but that I'm nervous about the caesarean. She tries to convince me that in a way, it's easier than going through the pain of childbirth, the main disadvantage being that I'll be up to two weeks in hospital, and it will hurt to move or cough for a while. Two weeks seems like an eternity to me.

'The operation only takes 15 minutes with an additional 45 minutes for the delivery of the placenta and the suturing. You'll be fine in no time,' Andrea tries to reassure me. 'By the way, it's the placenta that stimulates breastfeeding. It's mentioned in the book I gave you. But it'll be different for you. They'll wrap you up.'

Different? Wrap me up? Something to do with having a caesarian, I suppose. I tell them that while I'm in hospital, I'll be turning seventeen. Seventeen on the seventeenth. Three days after my operation.

Andrea says it would be a good time for all of them to visit. 'I'll bring a birthday cake with five rings seeing that you'll be in there when the Olympic Games open.'

Seventeen sounds young to have a baby, but Maude told me that her mother, my maternal grandmother was eighteen when she married and had her first child. My mother was twenty-one when she married my father, who was nine years older. I'm still thinking of my baby as a boy, so I ask Andrea how soon I'll be able to hold him after my operation.

She stares at me. 'Do you really want to do that? They'll take care of everything. You just have to sign a form to give your approval to the adopting parents.'

'But I'm keeping him,' I whisper, aware that customers are nearby.

Andrea and Juliette give me a wide-eyed stare and exchange glances with each other. No one says anything for a minute or two. I can imagine what they're thinking.

'I've always thought it seemed quite extraordinary that anyone could go through childbirth and then give the baby to someone else,' Andrea finally says. 'We all have an overwhelming instinct to protect what's ours, but I was under the impression that you were so ill with your pregnancy, you wanted nothing to do with the baby.'

'I was. Until I started feeling better, thanks to you and Doctor Rousseau. The two of you changed my life.' I smile at Juliette. 'Well, the three of you really.' Then I look at Cecilia. 'Four, if I count you Celie. You were the one who took me to Juliette in the first place, otherwise we wouldn't be all sitting here right now, would we?'

I don't think that's occurred to any of them before. No one speaks for a moment.

'But Molly,' Andrea continues, 'have you really thought this through? You're single without any income. And there's no help from the hospital or the government. Not a penny. Or from what you've told me, your parents. And society despises single parents.'

I knew she'd bring up the practicalities. 'But look how well you've done! You told me your mother brought you up by herself.'

'Widows aren't treated like single mothers. And Mum was a qualified nurse with a small pension from Legacy. My grandparents also helped out. You'd have no income.'

'Yes I will. I'll work after a few months and Maude will mind my baby. She'll be rapt. You don't know her like I do.' I look at Juliette. 'In my letter, I asked Maude if I could bring my baby as well. Harry's always said Maude needs something to occupy her so he'll be pleased. She'll be a grandmother and a great aunt. You should have seen her with us all when she lived in Ballarat.' I look at two students ordering ice-creams, then at Andrea. 'And one of these days I'll be at the university,' I tell her defiantly.

'I don't doubt that Molly, and I'm sorry. I didn't mean it like that. I'm just thinking of you. Your welfare, and…'

'I know you are,' I interrupt her. 'But would you have given Matthew away to strangers?'

No one says anything for a while until Andrea apologises again. 'I'm sorry, Molly. You're right of course. Like I said, I thought your illness prevented you from feeling maternal.' She pauses for a moment. 'Perhaps I was thinking too of how your pregnancy came about. I must have inadvertently convinced myself that the baby would be a reminder of its father. I'm sorry. I'm no psychologist, am I?'

Well she has a point, but I think I'm over that now. Not that I'd forgive Father Kelly like St Maria Goretti forgave her murderer just before she died. I'm the opposite. If I thought for a moment that prayers did any good, I'd pray that he'd work on the chain gang after being sentenced to life, and then go straight to hell after dying from some hideous disease like leprosy. 'It's no use me thinking about him. It won't get me anywhere,' I tell them. 'I have someone else to think about now. And I have a feeling my baby's a boy. I hate saying *it*.'

They've all got tears in their eyes now. Andrea pulls out a handkerchief to wipe her eyes and nose, insisting she wouldn't have coped with what I've been through. Juliette is looking at me. Biting her lip. 'I'll help you as much as I can,' she says, taking my hands. 'You know that, Molly! With your studies. With whatever you decide to do.'

'Me too,' Cecilia says enthusiastically. 'Anytime I'm free. I've still got the album of duets. We could start playing them again next year.'

'Molly,' Juliette says when we're back at Bleak House. 'You must have said in your letter that you were keeping your baby, so Hallvard knows you've been deceiving her.'

I shrug. 'Probably, but I don't care now. She can't do anything.'

'You could easily get a job in a bank next year, Molly.' She rings the doorbell. 'They usually finish by 4pm. You could go straight to Taylors College before you go home to Maude. You'll be at university in no time at all.'

I love Juliette.

40

The Priest

His eyelids fluttered. A statuette of a saint in the corner was staring at him. Strange. The crucifix should have been on the wall to his right. Not in front of him. Then he remembered. He was in a private room in St John of God Hospital. He touched his jaw and winced in pain. What day was it? What year? Yes! 1956. Coming up to the Melbourne Olympics. He'd given his sermon on the evils of communism the previous Sunday, so it must be the second week in November. Or was it the third week? He was in so much pain, he obviously wasn't thinking clearly.

A nurse bustled into the room.

'Ah. You're awake, Father. How are you feeling now? We were worried about you.'

He felt a crunching sound in his head as he attempted to open his mouth. His voice came out as a gurgle, hurting him.

'Never mind, Father. Nod or shake your head when anyone speaks to you. Is your jaw aching?'

He nodded slowly.

'Out of ten from zero to excruciating, how bad is the pain? Don't try and talk. Use your fingers!'

He held up all ten of them.

'Not quite an invalid yet, Father,' she said smiling, as she wrote on the chart at the bottom of his bed, 'even if your jaw has been fractured in three places. It won't be long before the pain begins to fade and you'll be up and around.'

She plumped up his pillows and took his temperature. 'We'll be giving you a liquid diet for a few days because you won't be able to chew and swallow. Your bite will be abnormal. You're very lucky. The doctor has ruled out a cerebral spine injury, or concussion.'

Lucky, he thought. Lucky to be attacked by a madman?

'Sister will be giving you something to ease the pain, and an antibiotic injection. It's possible for an infection to get into the fracture site.'

She warned him not to frighten himself by looking in the mirror in the bathroom as his mouth was swollen, he had a black eye, and two of his teeth had to be removed because they were fractured. He'd have the pain and swelling for a while, and there would be bleeding from several areas in his mouth.

He thought of the scene in his study. Molly's uncle and brother. They'd said Molly was pregnant and had accused him of rape. It wasn't possible. He'd been so careful. On the other hand, he'd heard that *coitus interruptus* wasn't always reliable.

'Your mother has been waiting to see you,' the nurse said as she left the room. 'It can only be for a short time, and you mustn't attempt to talk.'

His mother gasped when she saw him, clamping her hand over her mouth in shock. 'Who did this dreadful thing to you, Hilton?'

He shrugged his shoulders and shook his head slowly. Carefully.

She began crying, in between her sobs, explaining that Father Bourke had told her what had happened and had kindly given her a lift to the hospital. 'He has to see a few patients but will be visiting you shortly,' she whimpered, delving into her handbag. 'I know it's a mortal sin if you miss saying divine office, so I reminded him to bring your Breviary. I thought we could say the rosary together,' she said, pulling out her rosary beads and sinking down on her knees beside his bed. 'I'll say it out aloud, while you say it in your mind if it hurts to speak. We'll pray for your quick recovery, and that the police find the madman who did this to you.'

The police! What could he tell them? What had that madman said before he lost consciousness? He was beginning to feel uneasy. His mother could pray her knees off, but he didn't want the police to find Molly's uncle.

'How are you, my boy?' Father Bourke said, breezing into the room in his cassock just after Hilton's mother had finished saying the rosary.

Mrs Kelly looked at her son. 'I'll go now, Hilton, so Father can talk to you. I'll see you later.'

Father Bourke stared down at him. 'I can't decide whether you look like Dracula or Frankenstein.' He paused. 'You certainly won't be wearing your dog-collar for a while.'

Hilton shrugged. He could hardly pull a face with his mouth all wired up. The black bruise encircling his eye had merged with blood, now drying on his cheeks.

'I'll be as quick as I can, Hilton. I had a call from the police this morning. They're wondering if you knew the parishioner who attacked you.'

Hilton shook his head slowly.

'You must have some connection with him! Anything to do with your little flower girl?'

Hilton stared at him, then opened out his hands in a 'What would I know!' gesture.

'You might look as though you're about to say the *Pater Noster*, but I guess you're not in the position to do that, and won't be for some time,' Bob Bourke said, sitting himself down on the chair beside the bed. 'The police have no doubt you'll be pressing charges.'

Hilton was alarmed.

'It's just as well no one else but our housekeeper knows what happened, so your position in Ballarat is safe for the time being. Safe as the confessional, one might say.'

Hilton couldn't smile. But he was relieved.

'Better make sure you've got a good story for the cops. They're usually onside with the clergy, but you never know. There could be a trouble-maker in their ranks.'

Hilton nodded. He'd think of something.

When they arrived, the policemen introduced themselves as Sergeant Kennelly and Inspector Brady. Hilton heaved a sigh of relief. At least they both sounded like Catholics.

'Now Father,' the Inspector said, after their initial shocked reaction to his face. 'I understand it will be a while before you start speaking properly without pain, so we'll try and confine our questions to simple yes and no answers so you can react accordingly. Are you happy about that?'

He nodded.

'I believe on the day of your attack, Father Bourke and Father O'Doherty weren't around, but the housekeeper heard an argument. Later, she saw a man and a youth leaving the presbytery. Did you know them, Father?'

Hilton shook his head. Slowly. The sergeant was taking notes.

'Mrs Rawlings said she became concerned when she heard the rather violent argument, so she listened at the door. She didn't want to interrupt. In any case, she said it was locked. She couldn't hear everything, but she heard the name *Molly* mentioned a few times. Molly Harrington.'

He hesitated a second, then nodded.

'Now. We will be interviewing Molly herself eventually. Difficult at the moment because she's in Melbourne.' The inspector paused. 'I believe Molly did the flowers with another lass on Friday afternoons. Is that right Father?'

He nodded.

'At any stage, since Molly began doing the flowers, did she ever accompany you back to the presbytery? Mrs Rawlings said she heard the man accuse you of doing just that.'

He shook his head.

'Mrs Rawlings is adamant that one of the men said you took Molly back to the presbytery and um, seduced her.'

'Excuse me sir,' the sergeant said. 'Mrs Rawlings quoted the visitor as saying…'

'Yes, yes. Um. He said that you, um, attacked her.'

The younger policeman was flicking through his notes. 'Raped her, is what I've got here,' he said. 'And gave her alcohol.'

Noticing his reflection in the framed image of the Virgin Mary directly opposite him, Hilton decided he scarcely needed to look shocked at this accusation. He already appeared to be in shock. Bob Bourke had been right. With raised eyebrows, wide-open staring eyes, his dark unruly hair and battered face, he looked more like the proverbial monster straight out of a horror film. He picked up a notebook and pencil the nurse had left for him. *I haven't seen her all year*, he wrote. *Molly used to do the flowers. I have no idea why this madman made such an outrageous accusation.*

The two policemen exchanged glances.

'Have you *any* idea who your visitors were, Father?'

He shook his head. Had Mrs Rawlings heard his intruders say who they were? If so, had she told the police? Perhaps he should say something. *I got the impression they were related to Molly.*

'Mr Harrington, Molly's father, certainly had nothing to do with it. He has an alibi and doesn't understand what's going on.'

The sergeant began flicking through his notes again.

'Mrs Rawlings said she heard something said about an incident occurring early this year, Father.'

It's November, Hilton wrote. *Why would anyone wait until now to make such an outrageous accusation against me? What date was this supposed to have occurred?'*

'Well that's just it, Father,' the Inspector said. 'Mrs Rawlings didn't hear everything. You're the only one who can tell us exactly what was said.'

It's a load of hogwash, Inspector, and I'm grossly offended that you should come here accusing me of such a crime, Hilton wrote. *I'm the victim here.*

'In fact, Father,' the Inspector replied. 'I'm not accusing you of anything. I am just carrying out my duty. I'm trying to get the facts together before we find your attacker and begin interviewing Molly and her relatives. It seems that whoever it was confused you with someone else, wouldn't you say, Gerry?' he said to his sergeant, who was busy writing in his notebook, and didn't bother responding.

Father Kelly picked up his pencil. *Does this mean my name will be reported in The Courier?*

'Not necessarily. I suppose the reporter could write that a priest was assaulted in the presbytery, and the police are looking for the suspects.'

Hilton was still concerned. He would discuss this with Bob Bourke later.

41

Juliette

It would be a tight squeeze in the small terrace house, but they could hardly subject their grandparents to more travelling after their long, arduous flight from Paris. Fortunately, in Ballarat, Claude and Sofia's next-door neighbours had offered their house while they were away for two weeks.

Juliette checked the mailbox, excited to see a letter from Dom. Thrilled to read in the form of a *franglais* poem that '*Dans le jardin* on Christmas Day, Unseen by the visitors*, joyeux et gais*, I will *sauter* over the wall, Wearing my habit, rosary beads, veil and all.' While Juliette couldn't wait to see her grandparents, she found herself thinking of Dom as she bustled around, tidying up and vacuuming. There would be no chance of seeing her, despite them all being in Ballarat on the next visiting day. Sunday November 10th was the feast-day of the convent's patron saint, Martin de Porres. A day of celebration. She grinned, imagining the look on Mother Alphonsus's face if she showed up to see Sister Dominique. Their last few moments of passion had been in the infirmary after the girls had gone home for the May holidays. 'You are such a wanton, Juliette,' Dom had whispered in her ear. Eventually, the two of them would share an apartment together in Melbourne, but meantime, Juliette's room at MLC into which she was moving the following year was quite spacious, with a tiny kitchenette. As a House Mistress and teacher, she could come and go as she pleased. Male visitors were a no-no, but women were welcome.

'Have you come across any suitable beaus yet?' her mother had asked last time they'd chatted on the phone. 'The trouble is, Paul's friends are all married now. Surely there must be a few eligible men around those schools where you're teaching, *chérie!*'

She tried to imagine her family's reaction if she told them she was in love with a woman. With Dom and her grandparents on her mind, she was finding it difficult to concentrate on packing her suitcase for Ballarat when the doorbell rang. A couple who looked like they were in their fifties introduced themselves as Molly's aunt and uncle, Maude and Harry Norton.

'With only a week to go before the caesarean, we thought it would be quicker to deliver my reply to Molly's letter personally, rather than send it,' Maude said, opening her handbag and handing Juliette a letter. 'Especially as we were in the area.'

'You must come in,' Juliette insisted, after introducing herself. 'I feel as though I know you. Molly has hardly stopped talking about you since her health began improving.'

'And since Molly's letter, we've been wanting to meet you,' Maude said. 'And anyone else who's been looking after her.'

'My brother Paul recognized Molly's illness as abnormal,' Juliette said as she led them into the living room. 'She's been very ill for most of her pregnancy.'

Maude's eyes were filling up with tears. 'You've all been so good to her. So compassionate! What would have happened if you hadn't been there for her?' She pulled out a handkerchief and wiped her eyes. 'Elsie only told me recently what happened, and that was because I kept on at her. She was a bit vague about it all, as only Elsie can be. She's been in a terrible state since Harry and I moved to Melbourne. I'm not even sure Kevin got the full story on Molly. His mother is dying. The brewery closed down the hotel without compensating him. He's picked up a temporary job minding someone's pub for three weeks, and that's it. It's been one thing after another. Not that it excuses how he's treated Molly.'

Juliette wanted to throw her arms around this wonderful woman who would likely be looking after Molly. 'We're all prepared to do anything to help her.'

'I told Molly in the letter I gave Tony that she could move in with us and was welcome to bring her baby, if that's what she wanted.' Her shoulders began heaving in rhythm with her sobs. 'She told me in her letter that she was never given any mail.'

'Molly told me about that. They censor the mail. Just a minute.' She went into the kitchen and put the kettle on. 'They'd have a childless couple lined up for her baby, which is why the nun in charge refused to give her your letter.'

Maude rolled her eyes. 'Typical of nuns!'

Harry nudged her.

Maude looked embarrassed. 'Sorry. I meant some of them.' She shrugged. 'Anyway, I said I'd mind the baby if she wanted to study or get a job. We've bought a pram and a bassinet, and we're doing up a room for her.'

Juliette took a deep breath. 'I'm not sure how much Molly told you, but you should know that what happened to her was not about being seduced. Molly was raped. Tricked into going to the presbytery. Unknowingly given alcohol and barbiturates in a soft drink. She was unconscious when he raped her. Out cold. He set her up. Planned it all!'

'Molly more or less said that in her letter. That bastard!' Harry said.

Maude nudged him. He looked at Juliette. 'Sorry,' he said.

'Don't be,' Juliette said. 'It's true. He's exactly what you say. A brute. Worse still, he's got away with it. He'll never get his come-uppance.'

Harry's face changed to something between a grimace and a smirk. 'Perhaps he has. Well, to a certain extent. I wasn't going to tell anyone, but I feel that you hate that... that monster as much as we do. When we received Molly's letter, I took off immediately to Ballarat to find him. With Tony, Molly's brother.' He paused for a moment. 'Anyway, to cut a long story short, we went to the presbytery. I sent the bastard sprawling on the floor when I gave him a swift upper cut that broke his jaw. And three of his teeth. I suspect he's still in hospital.'

Juliette looked at him, eyes wide in disbelief.

Maude took Harry's hand and began caressing it. 'It's paid off, that boxing your father made you do in your youth, love. Your hand is still quite swollen though.'

Juliette was looking from Harry's hand to his face, then to Maude, unsure if she believed what she'd just heard.

'I didn't go to Ballarat with the intention of doing that!' Harry said, grimly. 'It was bad enough when he started denying everything. Blind Freddy would have known he was lying like a trooper, but when he started talking about Molly as though she was a trollop, I saw red.'

They were all silent for a long moment until Juliette finally spoke. 'Well, that's the only punishment he'll get. He deserved it. You're the one who's more likely to be jailed. Not him. Have the police caught up with you yet?'

He nodded. 'The Ballarat police called in last night. That's how I know about his jaw and teeth.'

Juliette looked surprised. 'It's a wonder they didn't cart you off!'

'I was about to give him an alibi,' Maude said. 'But then Tony walked in, and they put two and two together. Well, one and one, I suppose, because the housekeeper had given them a description. She saw them on the veranda when they left.

Apparently, she began snooping near the passage door when she heard raised voices. She told the police she heard a name like Norton mentioned. And she must have heard Molly's name mentioned.'

'They nearly dragged me off on the spot,' Harry continued. 'Anyway, I wasn't too worried. Turned out, surprise, surprise, that the priest refused to press charges, but then, the police said *they* were charging me for assault. That was when I pulled out Molly's letter and showed it to them. It was irrefutable evidence. You should have seen the looks on their faces! They wanted to take it away. I refused. I said I didn't want them telling me they'd lost it. It was private property and would be used in evidence for when Molly's family pressed for rape charges against the priest. Not that Kevin would have done that! You should have seen the looks they gave each other! They told me not to leave the premises and phoned later to tell me they weren't proceeding with the charges.'

Juliette nodded. 'No surprise there!'

'The power of the scarlet cassock!' Maude said in disgust.

'*Omertà*, my Italian grandmother calls it. The great criminal cover-up by the mafia and the church,' Juliette said.

'Not forgetting the police and the judiciary,' Harry added.

Juliette headed towards the kitchen. 'We've got time for a cup of tea and scones. Paul's calling for me at midday to pick up our grandparents at the airport. We're all off to Ballarat tomorrow for three days. My parents live there.'

Maude brightened. 'Seeing that you're so busy, perhaps *we* could call into the Maternity Home and see Molly. Isn't it nearby?'

'Yes, but they'll send you packing. They don't allow visitors. Andrea and I had terrible trouble when we wanted to take Molly walking. I'll drop your letter off to her on my way back from the airport. Maybe we could arrange to meet next week when I pick up Molly.'

Maude was happy about that. After swapping phone numbers, Maude and Harry stood up to leave.

Juliette was hoping for a chance of a reconciliation between Molly and her parents. 'If only you could talk Molly's parents into visiting her in hospital.'

Maude raised her eyes to the ceiling. 'Difficult! Anyhow, they're flat out minding a pub right now.' She nudged Harry. 'We'll have to go or Juliette will be late.'

Juliette opened the front door. 'Ah. Nicely timed. Here's my chauffeur. The best obstetrician in Melbourne,' she said proudly, introducing him to Maude and Harry.

From now on, until they returned from Ballarat, Juliette knew that they would only be speaking French. Like most of their generation, her grandparents spoke no English. They looked tired when they arrived at Essendon Airport, their journey having taken three days with several stop-offs. After the usual greetings and embraces, Juliette asked them about their trip.

'The seats were comfortable enough, and we were treated like royalty, and so we should have been after what you all paid for our fares,' her grandmother said. 'I was very nervous, but we'll be forever grateful to you all, so I'm not complaining about anything.'

'Not even the noise of the engines, *mémère*?'

'Well. I suppose one gets used to it after a while.'

Their grandfather was more forthright about his first plane trip. 'It's more the smoke that drove us crazy,' he said. 'Everyone was smoking – cigarettes, cigars and pipes. *Mon Dieu*!'

'But *pépère*,' Juliette grinned. 'You used to smoke like a chimney!'

He gave a typical Gallic shrug as he rolled his eyes. 'Of course! But with as much alcohol as you wanted, half the passengers were permanently plastered. I was sure they were going to set the plane on fire when they were staggering around.'

Paul stopped the car at the Maternity Home.

'I'll explain what it's all about later,' Juliette told her grandparents. 'I'll be two minutes.'

Sister Leo answered the door. 'Molly is unavailable,' was all she said.

Juliette assumed that Molly was either resting, or at the hospital having tests. There was no way she'd leave the letter or go searching now for Molly amongst the hospital's labyrinth of cubicles and corridors.

'I'm assuming Molly's either resting or at Outpatients. Did you order any tests for her?' she asked Paul after returning to the car.

'Yes, but they're not usually done so soon.'

'Well. I've missed her. After Maude and Harry went to the trouble of calling in this morning, the letter will have to wait now until we return from Ballarat.'

42

The Priest

Following the police visit, Sergeant Kennelly returned to the hospital alone the next morning. 'I'll get straight to the point, Father,' he said. 'I dropped into the church yesterday when Maureen was there. I can tell you it was a relief not to have her mother answering the questions we'd asked her at home. Perhaps it was being in the church that prompted her memory further, because I learned quite a lot more from her, Father.'

Hilton wasn't particularly concerned. Maureen wouldn't have a clue.

Sergeant Kennelly opened his notebook. 'She was very definite about seeing you and Molly entering the presbytery via the porch door at the back last year. What do you have to say about that? My constable and I got the impression that she was telling the truth.'

With his black eye, and his mouth all wired up, Father Kelly's face was scarcely capable of showing any emotion. He slowly picked up his notebook and began writing hesitantly, getting his story together. *Yes. I remember now. Molly wanted to be excused from doing the flowers because she had hours of maths homework to do and dancing rehearsals. She said she had trouble with maths, so I offered to help her. We finished in about ten minutes in the kitchen. She was very appreciative of my help.*

'And your housekeeper was around at the time to confirm this?' the sergeant asked as he began writing down Hilton's responses.

He shook his head. Father O'Doherty had walked into the kitchen that very first time he was with Molly, but if they tried interviewing *him*, they wouldn't get very far.

'You did say Father, that Molly had never been anywhere near the presbytery.'

I'm sorry. I forgot, he wrote. *It was last year. I'm not thinking clearly right now. I'm in terrible pain.*

The sergeant copied what Hilton had written into his notebook and stared at him for a moment. 'On another occasion, Maureen said you asked her if she'd be alright on her own. She saw Molly following you out of the church and didn't see either of you again that afternoon. There would be no reason for her to make up such a story, Father, so can you explain that?'

Hilton was scowling under his mane of dark hair. His distorted face. *What did Maureen say?*

'I'm asking the questions here, Father,' the sergeant said a little tersely.

He flinched. He hadn't handled that very well at all. Surely Maureen hadn't seen them going to his study. He'd take a risk. *Maureen's a bit slow on the uptake sometimes. That's why I was asking what she said. In any case, Molly wasn't feeling well that day, so I sent her home.*

'Okay,' Sergeant Kennelly sighed. He began writing in his notebook again, then flicked to another page. 'So, Molly never went near the presbytery on any other occasion?'

He shook his head.

The sergeant stared at a page and looked up. 'Are you absolutely sure Molly never went near the presbytery again, Father?'

His hands were clammy. Did the sergeant have a smug look on his face, or was he imagining it? He was in a predicament now. Had Maureen seen the two of them entering his study? Or worse still, a passer-by! Could he risk telling another lie?

He was about to shake his head when Sergeant Kennelly explained that Maureen might be considered a bit slow, but her memory couldn't be faulted.

'Maureen clearly remembers the Friday before school was due to start back this year, because she was upset that Molly wouldn't be returning to do the flowers again. She said she loved chatting to Molly.'

Father Kelly nodded.

'Maureen remembered you asking her if she could do the flowers by herself. Do you remember that Father?'

He nodded, frowning. Uneasy.

'So Molly went home, Father?'

He nodded.

Sometimes she couldn't come, or she left early, he wrote. *That might have been when she told me she wouldn't be returning to do the flowers again.*

The sergeant consulted his notes again. 'Maureen has quite a different picture from you, Father. She said that she was arranging some small vases of flowers for the pedestals. The first one she did that day was for the statue of St Joseph near the side entrance of the church. She said she glanced up and noticed you and Molly entering the presbytery via a side door opening onto the veranda. I quote. "I thought it was strange because Father Kelly told me Molly was going home." Unquote. Can you explain that, Father? We have no reason to believe Maureen was lying.'

Now he was beginning to panic. What could he say to this?

'What concerns me Father, is that you seem to have forgotten about that visit too. What was that one all about?'

He hesitated. His hands were so clammy now that his pencil was slipping in his fingers. Should he say Molly was only with him for a minute or two, and then left, or did the sergeant have another card up his sleeve? He began writing. *Molly asked to speak to me privately. I took her there so that no one would interrupt us. She was very upset. She told me about the problems she was having with her father. He didn't like the idea of her having a boyfriend. She said her father was accusing her of getting up to no good with him.*

'And was she?'

This sort of counselling is like the confessional, so I can't talk to you about it, Sergeant. Molly wouldn't want me repeating any part of our conversation.

Sergeant Kennelly nodded and sighed. 'Well, Father,' he said. 'You may not want to tell me what was said or what really happened. I can see that you're in pain, but it's pretty incredible to me that you could not remember Molly going to the presbytery at all when you were first asked.' He continued writing in his notebook. 'One more question, Father. Where does that side door that you both entered lead to?'

To a study.

'Your own study, Father?'

He blinked, unsure what to write. *Mainly*, he wrote.

'Well, that sort of detail will probably be more relevant at a later date.'

Oh God! What did he mean by that?

Sergeant Kennelly looked straight at him. 'Did you ever give Molly an alcoholic drink, Father?'

He shook his head so vigorously, it hurt. He avoided Sergeant Kennelly's eyes.

'Any drinks at all Father?'

Sometimes I gave her a lemon squash, he wrote.

'Sometimes?'

He nodded.

'Hmm,' the sergeant said, writing in his notebook. 'Sometimes.' He slammed his notebook shut and looked at Hilton. 'Molly is apparently living in Melbourne now, and we'll be contacting her after we speak to Mr Norton, her uncle, whose name Mrs Rawlings mentioned. But while you're here, you might like to think a little more about what else was said, Father. Mrs Rawlings said your visitors were there for at least twenty minutes. All I can say is that you'll need to come up with something better for the judge than the string of contradictions you've given me today, Father.'

Hilton opened his eyes wide. His fingers were so moist, he had to wipe them on his pyjamas before he wrote *I don't understand what you mean*.

'Your assailants were angry. When we find them and they're charged with assault, they may counteract with a charge of sexual assault against you on Molly, Father. I'm not sure what's really going on here, but I've got a feeling they won't be scratching for evidence, even though the parents seem vague about their daughter's circumstances and where she's even living.'

It cannot involve me, Father Kelly wrote confidently.

'The church may be exempt from many things, Father, but if you're called to give evidence, you will have to go before the court. You won't be able to change your tune as many times as you did today.'

He couldn't believe what he was hearing. Surely Molly's family wouldn't give evidence against a priest! His life would be ruined. If he'd been able to speak or show disdain on his damaged face for this cocky little sergeant, it would have been palpable. He felt that the inspector would have handled all this much better and might not have even allowed this line of questioning. Bob Bourke would sort this out.

43

Juliette

Had she not been booked for a week's relief-teaching, Juliette would have gladly stayed on in Ballarat for a few more days. She'd also promised to call in on Molly after school on Monday, the day before she was due to go to the hospital.

Juliette had been to the Home often enough to know that the long corridor with its polished wooden floor and high ceiling echoed every syllable. When Sister Leo told her once again that Molly wasn't available, Juliette raised her voice, her politeness beginning to fray around the edges. Was she at Outpatients? Was she upstairs resting? Sister Leo's face remained blank. Two girls in the passage were staring at her. With a bit of luck, Molly might hear her from upstairs or down the back in the living area.

'This time I demand an answer, Sister. I'm not leaving until you tell me what's going on!' she shouted.

The building suddenly became quiet. Juliette decided she wanted the whole street to hear what she had to say. The Royal Women's Hospital opposite. Let's face it, she wanted all of Australia to acknowledge how shamefully society treated girls who were uneducated about their bodies. Girls who were unable to resort to hastily arranged marriages or abortions or family support. For the last few years, Juliette had learned to control her feelings. To remain calm. To be submissive. Never assertive. Now she would liberate those emotions. 'There's something else, Sister,' she said in her most authoritative voice. 'When Molly's brother called in recently, he handed you a letter from their aunt. Why didn't you give it to her?'

Something flickered in Sister Leo's eyes, but her silence said it all.

'One of the girls can confirm it. Sister Hallvard told Molly the letter didn't exist. No one has the right to withhold any of the girls' mail from their relatives, or to go through their private belongings! It's about time you started treating these girls like human beings.' She was almost shouting now. 'I demand to see Sister Hallvard.'

'She has a visitor!' Sister Leo said quietly.

Ah! Finally Juliette got it. Having read the letters, Hallvard assumed Maude and Molly were scheming and conniving to keep the baby. Hallvard would be trying to wear Molly down. Insist that society would ostracise her. Keep Juliette away from her. Molly would never change her mind. She'd pretend to go along with it all. Well. Would one more day make much difference? She'd be at school when Molly was admitted the following day, so Paul could give her the letter.

'I got the same treatment at Bleak House again today,' Juliette told him that evening. '*Molly is unavailable.* You'll have to give her the letter tomorrow.'

Paul arrived home the following evening to say that after his last delivery, he'd called into the ward to see Molly, but they told him she hadn't shown up. 'A few minutes later, around 6pm, I knocked on the door at Bleak House to see what was going on, but no one answered. The place was dead!'

'Ah!' Juliette said. 'The Angelus. *The knell of parting day.* All the nuns would have been in the chapel. No one answers the door after 6pm.'

'You mean firemen could be hammering on the door because the place is burning down and they won't answer?'

Jeanne shrugged. 'Possibly!'

The following day, when Molly didn't show up at the hospital for her caesarian, Paul arranged to meet Juliette at the Home.

'Molly is unavailable,' Sister Leo said again.

'She was booked for pre-op yesterday and a caesarean today Sister,' Paul said angrily. 'I need to see the nun in charge to find out what's going on!'

'I'm sorry,' Sister Leo said. 'She can't be disturbed.'

She was about to close the door, but Paul, closely followed by Juliette, strode past her down the passage. 'Molly is my patient,' he said angrily. 'And I'm going to call the police if I don't get any answers. I'm concerned for her whereabouts, and her health. It's imperative that she has a caesarean immediately. I'm her obstetrician. What's going on? I need to see her.'

'It's all been taken care of,' Hallvard said, stepping into the passage with a smile that Juliette decided was as false as her teeth. 'She went to St Vincent's last week. She's our responsibility and we have the final decision as to where she goes to have the baby.'

Last week? When they were in Ballarat? They were furious, but it was Paul who let fly first. 'What's this all about? Surely not religion! I know Catholics are expected to give up health, happiness, and life itself rather than have dominion over their own bodies and lives. Has the Pope invented more bloody rules? Or has Archbishop Mannix declared that Catholics are obliged to attend Catholic Hospitals now as well as Catholic schools?'

Juliette nudged him, embarrassed by his vitriolic tirade.

'Have you ever heard of common courtesy, Sister?' he said coldly to the nun. 'I'm her obstetrician and no one bothered to inform us that you'd terminated our services.'

Sister Hallvard looked a little embarrassed. 'Well. I'm sorry Doctor. It must have been overlooked.'

Juliette knew she was lying, regretting immediately she'd mentioned they'd be in Ballarat for a few days.

'Why? Why did you do this, Sister?' Paul continued. 'You use our services, our diagnoses, and send our patients elsewhere when it suits you! Have you informed Molly's parents?'

'I've tried phoning but there was no answer. I also wrote but they didn't reply. A few months ago, Mrs Harrington signed papers to the effect that Molly was entirely in our care until she went to the hospital to have her baby.'

'I tried contacting them too, Paul,' Juliette said. 'Maude said they're minding a hotel.'

'Well, that's beside the point,' Paul said angrily, storming off, Juliette trailing behind. He had to return to the hospital.

When she phoned St Vincent's Hospital, the receptionist insisted that there was no record of a Molly or Margaret Harrington. Once again, she went to the Home, where Sister Hallvard insisted that Molly had definitely been taken to St Vincent's Hospital by ambulance. Juliette decided she was telling the truth and caught a tram to the hospital. The receptionist was adamant. There was no Molly or Margaret Harrington at the hospital. When she returned home, she rang every private hospital in Melbourne in case Hallvard had got it wrong.

'I've just thought of something,' Paul said when they were rushing off to work the following morning. 'My colleague Brian Donovan. He's a cardiologist at St Vincent's.'

'I remember him. You introduced him to me when I was studying down here.'

Paul grinned. 'He was absolutely smitten with you. I'll phone him to see if he can find out anything.'

When he arrived home, he said that Brian was flat out but was looking into it. By the time he rang that evening, Juliette was seized with a desperate foreboding. A sixth sense of apprehension filling her whole body like a dead weight.

'He said it would be better to talk face-to face so he's calling in here tomorrow morning. I told him it was urgent, but he said he couldn't make it tonight. And wasn't Saturday better, seeing that we were all at home?'

'There's no way I could discuss what I'm about to say over the phone,' Brian said the next morning, after apologising for not calling earlier. 'I had an emergency, and I couldn't phone you from the hospital because you know what switchboard operators are like if they've got nothing better to do. Better to drop in seeing that I haven't seen you for ages.' He looked at Juliette and smiled. 'Nice to see you after all these years, Juliette.'

She nodded, unsmiling. Angry that he'd taken his time to get back to them.

'I'll come straight to the point,' Brian said. 'Is the father of this girl's baby a priest?'

Their eyes widened in surprise.

Andrea was the first to speak. 'Why on earth are you asking us that?'

'There's a ward in St Vincent's which is very hush-hush. It was set up by a nun called Sister Fabian following a request from Archbishop Mannix. We're not supposed to know about it of course but those of us who do call it the *sub rosa* ward. The word is, and I quote from someone who was around when it was set up *for those in situations created by clergy unable to maintain their vows of celibacy*. Mannix's exact words apparently.'

They were so surprised they could say nothing for a long moment.

Then a spike of anger shot through Juliette. 'It's *omertà* again.'

Andrea frowned. 'What do you mean?'

'*Omertà*! The Mafia code of silence about criminal activity and refusal to give evidence to the police. *Mémère* used to talk about how it happened in Italy, didn't she Paul?'

'I couldn't ask you over the phone if the father was a Father, so to speak,' the cardiologist laughed. 'Like I said, we're not supposed to know about it, let alone discuss it. You know. Scandal and all that.'

'Yes,' Andrea said angrily. 'You can't have scandals!'

The cardiologist shrugged. 'Well. You know how it is. Once a priest, always a priest.'

'I know the motto,' Andrea said. 'Their behaviour is condoned rather than condemned.'

'Molly is nearly seventeen,' Juliette added, now emboldened by Andrea's outburst. 'She's neither a temptress or a seducer. She was raped by a priest. No one else knew she became pregnant to that monster except us and Molly's parents.' Well, maybe Hallvard was a possibility.

'And her doctor in Ballarat,' Paul added.

'I'm really sorry to hear that,' Brian said sympathetically. 'But whoever arranged for her to go to St Vincent's must know the details of her pregnancy.' He shrugged. 'Mind you, I'm just guessing that's what's happened. I know everyone pretends the ward doesn't exist. The babies are adopted by infertile couples. No questions asked.'

Andrea looked at Juliette. 'We're going there right now,' she said standing up to leave.

'They won't let you in,' Brian said.

'Yes they will,' she said angrily.

He told them how to find the ward. 'You didn't hear it from me.'

44

Molly

I've been putting on an act with Hallvard. Just to keep her happy. She tried to get me to sign a paper with the names of the adopting couple on it, but I know what she's up to. Andrea and Juliette told me not to sign anything.

It's Wednesday, November 6. Eight days to go before I'll be holding my baby in my arms. I can't wait! Dr Rousseau saw me this morning and says I'm doing very well. He's leaving tomorrow for Ballarat but will be back by Sunday. Meanwhile, he said if I have any worries, he'll be back in a flash.

I'm drifting off to sleep when I awake to find Hallvard shaking me. She orders me to put on my dressing gown and to go downstairs. I'm feeling dazed and confused, but I'm not about to ask *her* what's going on. Before I realise what's happening, I'm whisked off in an ambulance.

'Has there been a change of plan?' I ask an attendant sitting in the back with me. 'Has Doctor Rousseau decided to do the operation earlier?'

He shrugs and says he has no idea.

'I think there's been a mistake,' I insist, 'because I saw Doctor Rousseau this morning. He would have told me if there'd been a change of plan.'

'We just do as we're told, love. No questions asked!'

It seems to take ages to get to the Women's Hospital. After all, it's just across the road from the Home. Perhaps they have to go around the block to a special entrance for maternity.

I'm put in a wheelchair when I arrive and taken along a darkened corridor to a single room. A nurse tells me the toilet is next to my room, then a few minutes later, gives me an injection after tucking me into bed. When I wake the next morning, I touch my stomach, thinking I might have already had the caesarean. No soreness anywhere and my stomach is still huge. The sides of my bed have metal barriers like a cot. I slide off the bed, carefully lowering myself to the floor. There's a crucifix on the wall in front of me. In the corridor, I recognize a statue of St Vincent wearing the familiar monk's robe with clerical cap, one arm cradling a baby, his other arm wrapped around a young child. I stare at the statue, confused. Why am I in St Vincent's Hospital? A nun suddenly appears, and orders me back to bed, ignoring my questions. It seems I can never get away from nuns. A nurse brings me a cup of tea and I ask why I'm not at the Women's, but she shrugs and says she has no idea.

'You must only get up to go to the toilet,' she says. 'You mustn't wander around!'

I'm so confused. I can feel tears building up inside me. I need to go to the toilet. When I'm washing my hands, a very pregnant girl who looks younger than me opens the bathroom door.

'Are you alright?' she whispers.

'I don't understand why I'm here,' I tell her. 'I'm booked to have a caesarean with Dr Rousseau at the Women's Hospital next Wednesday.'

'We're in a special part of St Vincent's, but they don't tell you anything so don't bother asking. The girl in the room on the other side of mine has been here before.' She laughs. 'She still hasn't worked out what's causing it. We have private rooms because they don't like us talking to each other.'

Private rooms? Probably because our shame can be quarantined from joyful, virtuous parents. The girl stops speaking when footsteps approach in the corridor. 'When is your baby due?' she whispers after the footsteps disappear.

I explain about the caesarean, but I don't think she understands the slightest thing about childbirth, only that she's going to be induced and is as ignorant as I am of the procedure.

'Are you keeping your baby?' I ask her.

She looks at me like I'm crazy. 'They'll sell it to a posh couple who can't have kids and good bloody riddance.'

I can remember that feeling. 'Will you be seeing your baby's father again?' I ask her.

'Father?' she snorts. 'Father Shelton? That bloody creep. I don't want him anywhere near me. He'd visit our house and pretend he was friendly with my family. When I tried telling my parents he was touching me they wouldn't believe me. He'd take me places in his car. I didn't want to go. He was a priest, so I could never be given absolution unless I obeyed him. When he started sticking it inside me, he threatened that if I told anyone, he'd tell them I was making it up because I had a boyfriend. I've never let any boy put it inside me, but I knew they'd believe him. Who believes a fourteen-year-old? Then this happened,' she said pointing to her stomach, 'so I knew it had something to do with him.'

'But surely your parents believed you?'

'No. I had a boyfriend, so they thought it was him. I ended up here after I became a domestic for some lah-de-dahs in Toorak. Probably the ones adopting the baby. They'll pretend it's their own. They pay the hospital a fortune for babies.'

I realise that by comparison I'm lucky. I have the two Dr Rousseaus, Juliette, Maude, and Cecilia on my side. Tony too. Juliette should have Maude's reply to my letter by now and will be here soon to explain what's going on.

They give me a slice of toast and a cup of tea. In the afternoon, I'm wheeled into an operating theatre. I stare up at the faces, desperate to see the brown eyes above the white masks. The dark curls. The olive complexion. I listen for a soft French accent. I tentatively ask if Doctor Rousseau will be doing the caesarean.

'Rousseau? From the Women's?' he says to another doctor as though I'm not there. 'Why him? I thought it was always pot-luck for public patients! They change doctors more often than we change our underpants!'

These doctors seem to have an air of superiority about them. I'm panicking now. Where is Doctor Rousseau?

'This'll be all over in no time, love,' someone says stretching a mask over my face.

I hear their conversation as I start drifting into unconsciousness. One of the doctors says it's a shame I'll never look virginal again. I'll be damaged goods with that scar. Anyone who thought of marrying me would know immediately what I'd been up to if I wore a bikini. They laughed.

I wake up in my cage-bed, staring at white walls, a white ceiling. I can't think clearly. My brain seems to have left my body. It's as if my body knows something my mind doesn't. Everything is a blur and I'm in excruciating pain when I try to move. Doctor Rousseau must have been delayed in Ballarat.

'I want to see my baby right now,' I tell the nurse.

'Caesareans are major operations,' she tells me. 'Now don't worry. Everything has been taken care of.'

'Did I have a girl or boy?'

She doesn't know. 'You won't need to use your bowels for a few days, love, but all you have to do is to press this call button so I can help you with a bed-pan. You must try not to move suddenly. Or cough or laugh.'

Laugh? I try to think of the last time I laughed. Was it when I was at the café with Juliette and Cecilia?

'I don't understand why no one has called to see me,' I murmur.

'Visitors are not allowed in this ward,' she says with certainty.

My tears turn into sobs. Each sob stabs my stomach like a knife, but I can't stop myself. A nun gives me an injection 'to help with the pain,' she says firmly. It's not the pain I'm crying about.

When I awake, I'm not sure what day it is. What time it is. All I know is that it's dark. I press the call button and tell the nurse that I must see my baby now because I must feed him. Andrea said my milk wouldn't come through for three days, but the baby should start sucking the colostrum immediately after the caesarean, and preferably several times a day to stimulate the milk supply. But the nurse doesn't bring my baby. Instead she gives me an injection, then proceeds to wrap tight binding around my breasts. Andrea said something about wrapping me up. I'm panic-stricken now. 'Did my baby die?' I ask the nurse. I'm sobbing again, pleading. 'Please tell me. Please don't lie to me. I need to know.'

She looks at me, biting her bottom lip. I can see she's sympathetic.

'No. He… he didn't die.'

Ah. My baby is a boy like I thought. 'Is there something wrong with him?'

'No.' She shrugs. 'I'm sorry. I don't think so. I wasn't given any details.'

I'm calling him Julian, after Juliette. I have to find him. I've never heard the cries of babies in this ward. Not even a whimper. The nurseries must be on another floor.

I have no idea what time it is. All I know is that it's dark and quiet. A pale light is filtering in from the window when I push myself up from the pillows. I slide down past the rail on the side of the bed closest to the door. Every movement feels like someone is stabbing me in the stomach. I swing my legs around slowly, grabbing the metal rail and gradually pushing myself upright. My bare feet touch the cold linoleum floor. Every stitch in my stomach pulls with every step as I open the door to teeter along the darkened corridor away from the nurses' station. When I take the lift to the next floor up, I'm in so much agony I think I'll faint. Perhaps they'll find my body in the lift the next morning. I can hear babies crying on this floor. There's a nurse on duty when I examine the list of mothers' names near a door. She doesn't see me. My name's not there anyway. I find another nursery further down and a nurse asks me what I'm doing out of bed at this hour. I gasp that I want to see my baby. She gives me a strange look and asks me my name. My baby isn't in this ward, she says, as I begin to slump down to the floor.

'From now on, you must get on with your life,' a nun tells me the next day when I find myself back in my bed.

'I will, as soon as you give me my baby.'

'The baby is not yours,' she says. 'We've found a lovely Catholic couple who will be taking him home.'

'But he *is* mine,' I scream at her. 'He was inside me for nine months so he *must* be mine. My aunt's going to help me mind him. Where is he? I want him. You can't have him.'

My words push against the stitches in my stomach. The pain is overwhelming. Any moment my innards will begin to squeeze out through my stitches, but I don't care. Despair is seeping into my soul. I see Hallvard pulling her lips back to her teeth like a snarling dog. I hear her yelling at Gina. Her child will be called a bastard. Gina yelling back that Hallvard can't bloody-well order her around because she's over twenty-one. 'And if anyone's a bastard it's you Hallvard.' Her swearing and what I learned to ignore at the hotel must have trickled into my subconscious because now it emerges into a torrent of profanity and impiety.

'You're a piece of shit,' I scream at the nun. 'You're all bitches and a bloody disgrace to the nursing profession. You call yourselves Sisters of Charity. Sisters of Charity? Sisters of Barbarity, more like. You're a pack of bastards.'

The nun smiles condescendingly, and before I know what's going on, cold eyes are jabbing cold steel into my arm.

'I haven't signed any forms to give up my baby, so give him to me. He's mine,' I sob. 'Why did you take him,' I keep repeating until everything begins to blur around me. I'm Alice, shrinking into a room. Into my bed. Drifting on a cloud.

I don't know what day it is when I wake up. My stomach's killing me. Every time I try to get out of bed, I think I'll faint. I'm back in the presbytery, with a fog in my brain that makes everything seem far away and confused. Father Kelly is walking towards me with a syringe in a glass of lemon cordial. Are they watching me, these witches who think they're my guardian angels? Strange shadows pass back and forth along the corridor, dark demons stalking my mind. Ghost-like figures in white gowns and masks encircle me. Throwing a ball to each other. The Ugly Duchess grabs it and flings it to me. I catch it, but it transforms into a baby. My baby. I run down a maze of endless, winding corridors with him, trying every door. They're all locked. I keep running until I trip and slide along a floor smothered in blood. I wake up to find that I'm drenched in milk. It oozes through the bandages wrapped around my breasts, soaking my night-dress. I cry because my breasts are swollen and hurting. The pain in my stomach is excruciating. I cry because I want my baby. I want to see my friends. Juliette. Cecilia. Doctor Rousseau. They give me another injection.

There's a shadow hovering above me like a cloud. I try to fight it but I'm powerless. It's gradually lowering to envelop every part of my being. Fear is clutching my insides. The future I've built for myself is disintegrating. All my dreams gone forever. Everyone is convinced that my child belongs to someone else. That I don't deserve him. Perhaps they're right. They'd be here by now if they were on my side. I should never have agreed to do the flowers. To have gone to the presbytery. Did God punish me with that awful illness I had for so long? I should never have let Father Kelly touch me. He's a man of God. Infallible. They think I encouraged him. It's my fault. It explains why no one has been to see me. They've all been leading me on. They sent me here because Catholics have their own rules, don't they? Separate from the rest of the country. No almoners to argue with here. No forms for me to sign. My fate has been decided.

There is nothing left for me now. They're all ashamed of me and of what I've done. I twist the ring on my finger. Why didn't Juliette take it back before they all went off to Ballarat if she was never going to see me again? They were all so kind to me, yet they don't want me now. What about Maude's reply to my letter? Maude was always on my side, but then, so was everyone else. How many days were they going away for? Three? Or was it four? They should be back by now. Why did they allow me to come here? There's no one now. No Juliette, my wonderful teacher and friend. No Cecilia, who promised to play duets with me once again. No Tony or anyone else in my family. No Andrea and Paul Rousseau, the best doctors in Melbourne. No Maude to become a wonderful grandmother. And worst of all, no baby Julian to love and to hold. Where is everyone, I scream. They give me another injection.

How long have I been here? One day is blurring into another. They keep giving me injections. I refuse to eat. I think my birthday's been and gone. Or is it today? Andrea and Juliette said they'd visit me on my birthday. With Cecilia. We'd have a birthday party. A tea-party. Like the Mad Hatter's. Except that I'm the Mad Hatter now and no one is coming to my tea-party. No one is coming to see me again. They were full of smiles the last time I saw them all. Why didn't I notice their smiles were false? Smiles of pity. They've all forsaken me. Like God forsaking Jesus. *My God, my God, why hast Thou forsaken me?* I know how he must have felt.

They think I've given in to them. That I've calmed down because I'm silent. Inside I'm screaming. I hate them. I think the tablets they're giving me are to dry up my milk. They don't work because my breasts are killing me and I'm leaking pints. Does everyone feel like this after a caesarean? My brain fuzzes and spins after the injections. When I stand up to go to the toilet, I'm dizzy and a wave of nausea rises through my body. I feel as though someone is wrenching the stitches from my stomach, but I tell them I'm fine. My guardian angels are not keeping watch over me as much as they should.

I'm allowed to walk to the toilet for exercise. I pretend I'm not hurting, but every step pulls on every stitch. My feet seem to be dragging through sand. I limp down the corridor away from the nurses' station towards the lift. I have no idea what day it is. What time it is. They don't see me pressing the button for the lift. I reach the top floor without anyone noticing me. A few nurses are wandering around, out of focus. I'm wincing with every step but now I have this weird sensation that I'm floating. That I'm gliding into oblivion. My numbness is blurring everything around me. The walls are dipping and swaying as though I'm in a boat. I hear blurry strains of pop music coming from a room. Nurses laughing. Someone on the telephone. A baby crying. No one can see me. No one needs to rule my life now. To bother about me. I'm in control of my own destiny. A woman is lying on a bed in a single room with an open window. I float into the room and am drawn to the light from the window. I begin leaning out. I see cars whizzing by in a blur. Trams. I lean out further. The woman starts screaming.

I'm Alice.

I'm falling.

Falling.

Epilogue

After their frantic rush to the hospital, Juliette and Andrea had no difficulty finding the ward from Brian's instructions. 'I'm Doctor Rousseau. I've come to see Molly Harrington,' Andrea told a nurse, who directed them to an office, where they were told to wait for Sister Claire. Juliette stared vacantly down at the trams and cars on Victoria Parade; a photograph of the nun who founded the Order; a statue of St Vincent. Despite the stuffy office and November heat, she felt a chill, her thoughts beginning to choke her. Was there a problem with the birth? The caesarean which she assumed they did last week? Was Molly ill? Did the baby die? If she'd been forced to relinquish the baby, there must be a clause stating that Molly could change her mind within a certain time. Fear was wrapping itself around her, her stomach clenching up. Her hands were cold and clammy, and she was beginning to shiver.

'I'd rather you start the talking,' Andrea said to her. 'You're more used to containing yourself with nuns. I'm too angry with them for kidnapping Molly. I feel like I'm going to explode.'

Fifteen minutes later, a nun entered the room and introduced herself as Sister Claire. She apologised profusely for keeping them waiting. Juliette didn't want this. She'd been hoping for a semblance of outrage from the nun for violating this sacrosanct area of the hospital. But the nun looked uneasy. Agitated.

Juliette stepped forward. 'I'm Juliette Rousseau, and this is my sister-in-law, Doctor Rousseau. We're Molly's friends. My brother is Molly's obstetrician at the Women's Hospital. Paul expected to do her caesarean there this week until someone arranged for her to come here last week without informing us!'

Sister Claire indicated the chairs. 'Please sit down,' she said.

'I'd rather not, Sister,' Juliette said. She felt her fingernails biting into the palms of her hands. 'We'd like to see Molly immediately. It's her birthday today.'

The nun clasped her hands together, looked from one to the other sympathetically, then took a deep breath. 'I'm sorry,' she said. 'There's no... no easy way to break bad news. I'm sorry to tell you that Molly is dead.'

It was as though Juliette hadn't heard. For a long silence she stood there. Staring at the nun. Mouth open. 'No!' she said finally in disbelief, her voice choking up. '*Mon Dieu*! She couldn't be! She's too young. She's still a child. What happened? What did you do to her?'

She gulped, forcing herself not to cry. To scream out. It was the Catholic thing, wasn't it? The Catholic rule. Molly had gone into early labour and someone had decided that it was too late for a caesarean. With Molly's narrow hips, the baby couldn't be born naturally so they'd killed Molly to save the baby. Hallvard must have decided the Women's Hospital would have saved the mother before the baby. Paul, a top obstetrician, would have saved both of them. It was all to do with the church's monstrous proclamation about making way for the new life. All Catholics knew that. Women must suffer the consequences even if they had ten other children waiting for them at home. A rule as hideous as the Jehovah's Witnesses who didn't allow blood transfusions.

Sister Claire started to speak but Andrea couldn't contain herself and leant across the desk, pointing her finger in the nun's face. 'You killed her! She went into early labour. By the time she got here, it was too late for a caesarean, wasn't it? You killed her!'

Juliette threw her arms around Andrea, sobbing and gasping into her shoulder. 'Poor Molly. Poor Molly. That beautiful girl.'

'They killed her,' Andrea kept repeating in a choking, almost incoherent voice.

Juliette, head in her hands, slumped down so hard onto the chair, it skidded on the floor.

'The caesarean went very well,' Sister Claire said. 'Molly was brought here about a week ago. She died this morning.'

Juliette and Andrea looked at the nun in astonishment. Andrea sat down, taking Juliette's hand in hers. 'Whoever operated on Molly is not a patch on my husband. He wouldn't have let her die. Paul was aware of all the problems with Molly's pregnancy. Your lot weren't. You snatched her away.'

'I'm afraid Molly killed herself, Doctor,' Sister Claire said with conviction. 'She jumped from a window on the top floor.'

Andrea and Juliette exchanged glances. Open-mouthed. They said nothing for a minute.

'Why would she do such a thing?' Juliette murmured to Andrea between sobs. 'It doesn't make sense.'

'You must understand that she was very depressed. We thought she was getting over it but…'

'Depressed?' Juliette gulped, almost choking on her sobs. 'Are you sure we're talking about Molly? Molly Harrington? Depressed? What happened to change her? Did her baby die?'

Sister Claire looked uncomfortable. 'No. He's very well.'

He. Molly was right. She thought her baby was a boy. Then another thought occurred to her. 'You didn't steal him, did you?' Her voice was choked up. Accusatory.

'You must understand that the poor child…'

'A child old enough to have her own child to be stolen and auctioned off to your highest bidders,' Andrea snapped. 'I've heard you do that!'

'Molly was very depressed. Her behaviour…'

'Save those platitudes for someone else, Sister. Not for me. Or Juliette and anyone else who has known Molly for longer than you or anyone here. Molly was not depressed, especially during her last few weeks, and I'd be willing to swear it on oath in court. Not that justice will ever prevail. *Omertà* will see to that.' She paused to get her breath for a moment and looked at Juliette.

'I taught Molly in Ballarat,' Juliette gulped, wiping her nose, tears streaming down her face. 'Molly said she'd be living with an aunt in Melbourne and was keeping her baby. She… she was going to be a mother and a teacher,'

'These were difficult circumstances. Not like other…'

'Did she see her baby?' Andrea demanded.

'Like other babies from this ward, he… he was adopted.'

Andrea looked at Juliette. 'You may not have heard about illegal adoptions Juliette. It happens here and a few other hospitals.' She turned to the nun and spoke coldly. 'It was illegal of course Sister. Molly wouldn't have signed anything. She was definitely keeping her baby.'

With thoughts of her beautiful little nephew, Juliette's tears began flowing again. Imagine if someone had kidnapped Matthew after he was born. She thought of the last time they'd all met up in the café. Molly describing the style of dress she'd like to wear as soon as she got her flat stomach back. Swooning over Cecilia's music when they'd gone to St Jude's. Her face lighting up when she spoke of her brothers and sisters. Her favourite aunt, Maude.

'Do you know what I admired about Molly more than everything else?' Andrea shouted in rage at the nun. 'She was seriously ill for most of her pregnancy, but she was desperate to keep her child, despite being raped by a priest!'

The nun looked shocked. 'We weren't told that, but surely that's the very reason why she was depressed and committed suicide. You can't blame her hospitalisation here.'

'Molly was definitely not depressed for the last eight or nine weeks of her pregnancy. Before you kidnapped her!' Andrea paused for a moment. 'No doubt you gave Molly stilboestrol to dry up her milk. You and I know that the double dosage they hand out like sweets to single girls causes painful engorgement of the breasts.'

Juliette had no idea what Andrea was talking about, but she trusted every word her sister-in-law said. Sister Claire certainly wasn't denying it.

'Not enough on its own to make Molly depressed. She coped with pain,' Andrea continued. 'Molly died because of how you treated her. Then there's the pentobarbitone. You dole it out to unmarried mothers who want to keep their babies. I'm not going to list all its side effects, but you and I know it's dangerous, Sister. It can send you crazy. Put that with letting Molly think we'd all abandoned her was what caused her death.' She stood up to leave, sobbing now, and tugging Juliette by the arm.

'I'm sorry you feel we're at fault Doctor, but others think differently.'

Differently? Juliette knew that during the last few months, she'd learned to think differently. To act differently. No longer did she have to be submissive to a narrow-minded superior. No one owned her now. She felt the fury building up inside her. Emboldened by Andrea's tirade, she leant over the desk. 'You told Molly she couldn't keep her baby, didn't you? You abducted him! Or did you tell her he'd died? I've heard you do that! You kidnapped Molly and stole her child. Why was she brought here? Why wasn't she allowed to have her child at the Women's Hospital? I'm not leaving here until you tell me, Sister.'

The nun sighed. 'It's the church's policy that when a priest fathers a child, the baby must not be returned to... to...'

'To its rightful owner,' Juliette interrupted, her anger overwhelming her anguish. 'The child's mother. It will create a scandal, will it?'

'It's better if no one knows that a priest fathered the child. In any case, single girls...'

'Ah. Church protocol. Once a priest, a priest forever. I'm familiar with the dictums. The priests can break the rules, but their victims are punished. The façade of purity must be upheld. Their vow of celibacy can be interpreted any way you like.' If she believed in the concept of a soul right now, she would have added that power had corrupted their souls.

Andrea suddenly banged her fist on the desk. 'And I can tell you from experience Sister, that with your help, the women or girls in your secret ward will have had their lives ruined forever. One doesn't need to be a psychologist to know that.'

'And I can tell you with certainty, Doctor, that none of us approve of what these priests get up to, but we can do nothing about it. I don't know how you found out about this ward, but I'd appreciate it if you make no mention of it to anyone.'

'Why, Sister? Surely you can see that it's shameful. And you are complicit in the whole thing.' Andrea's voice was just a breath now. 'Archbishop Mannix and those he is protecting will live and die with their names and reputations intact. But not the girls and women in this ward. They're punished for the rest of their lives. I'd be mad not to mention this outrageous crime to anyone. I'll be telling the world about it. In fact, I'd like to submit an article to the Medical Journal.'

She grabbed Juliette's arm and they left the room. 'Not that any of those conservative bastards would ever publish it.'

Red-eyed and tearful, they set home in silence, ignoring the looks they got on the tram. Juliette felt that she would have a layer of guilt smouldering under her skin for the rest of her life. Molly died surely believing they'd abandoned her. A few hours earlier and they'd have made it in time. If only she hadn't gone to Ballarat with her grandparents. No. That wouldn't have made any difference. Paul had seen Molly the day before they left. She'd cancelled their walk, planning to see her the following Monday. She should have been more assertive when Sister Leo said Molly was unavailable the first time. Should have demanded to see the Registrar, instead of waiting around for Brian to call. *If only*. 'If only I hadn't taken you to that exhibition and talked you all into emigrating,' her father had said when she told the family she was entering the convent. The world was full of *if onlys*.

'There were a lot of other questions we should have asked her,' Juliette said after they got home. 'You can't think straight when you're stressed. They must have worked it all out at the Home. I told Sister Leo we were going away and wouldn't be returning until Sunday. They would have done the caesarean while we were away.'

Paul snorted. 'And then stuffed us all around during the week.'

Juliette knew she'd have to phone Maude, but she kept putting it off. In the end, it was Maude who had phoned her, so distressed she was hardly coherent. Between their sobs, it emerged that it had taken the police hours to find the Harringtons. They'd been acting as relief managers at a hotel on the outskirts of Ballarat. Maude phoned again the following Monday, her voice choking with emotion.

'Kevin has tried every Catholic church in and around Ballarat to arrange a Requiem Mass. Not one priest, including his brother Michael, will contravene the church ruling on suicide. Elsie's not coping and won't be attending the funeral no matter where it is. In any case there're the other children to mind. They still don't know about Molly.'

'Leave it to me, Maude. I'll see what I can do from here. In any case, you should remind Molly's parents that it would be expensive to transport Molly's body to Ballarat, and they may not want anyone there knowing the circumstances of her death. Even if the church allowed it, Father Kelly himself could end up doing the Requiem Mass.'

Maude gasped, becoming so upset, Juliette couldn't understand what she was saying. She promised to call Maude back later. After phoning several Catholic presbyteries in Melbourne and calling into the nearby Sacred Heart Church in Rathdowne Street, Juliette couldn't find one priest who was prepared to contravene the church ruling. Suicide was a mortal sin. The chaplain at St Vincent's was sympathetic enough but refused. All she really needed now was to tell Dom what she was going through. To fall into her arms. For Dom to comfort her and talk about Molly. Her tears welled up again when she remembered Molly insisting she couldn't possibly choose *Demain, dès l'aube* for the *Alliance Française* poetry competition this year.

'*C'est trop triste, ma soeur.*' Molly had insisted. 'By the time I got to the last two lines with Victor Hugo putting flowers on his daughter's grave — *et quand j'arriverai, je mettrai sur la tombe, Un bouquet de houx vert et de bruyère en fleur* — I'd be crying my eyes out in front of the adjudicators. It's so sad!'

Andrea's mother was about to take her grandson for a walk back to her place. 'We'll go via St Jude's today,' she told Juliette. 'The Church of England is closest to the Catholic church. Reverend Newman might agree to holding the funeral service.'

She returned an hour later to say that the vicar was scandalised by the church's attitude to a member of its own flock. 'He wasn't happy about officiating at a funeral service for someone who's not in his parish. But when I gave him the circumstances of Molly's suicide, he phoned a senior colleague, who he quoted as saying "If there's a body, it's got to be buried. It's not as though you're going to be executed or excommunicated. When it all boils down, conscience overrides bureaucracy. And as someone once said to me, didn't Jesus himself commit suicide? He could have saved himself." So, to cut a long story short, Juliette, he'll do the service.'

It was arranged for the following Thursday morning at 11 o'clock, coincidentally, the same day the Olympic Games opened. November 22. Juliette decided that they needed more answers relating to Molly's death. She arranged to meet Andrea, Tony, Maude and Harry outside the Home an hour before the funeral. She felt a sense of collaboration with the family now. Maybe their united anger would lessen their self-reproach. Appease their grief a fraction.

'I'm sorry,' Sister Leo said when she answered the door. 'The almoner has just arrived so the parlour is unavailable. It's not a good time. Sister Hallvard is busy right now.'

'And so are we because we have a funeral to attend, Sister,' Juliette said curtly as she stepped into the entrance past her with the others close behind. 'We've only got a few minutes, so we'll stay right here until she sees us.' The door into the large room at the end was open. Girls whose pregnancies must have ranged from five months to almost full term were plodding around to and fro – sweeping, dusting, carting fresh flowers into the chapel and polishing the floors and bannisters. There were no sounds of fun and laughter here. No babble of girls in the throes of a joyful pregnancy. They could all be heading for the gallows. Two teenagers were lugging a large laundry basket through a door via the dining room from which the noise of clattering dishes echoed down the passageway.

Sister Hallvard suddenly appeared, and nodded to Juliette who introduced her to Maude, Harry and Tony. Did she detect a glimmer of remorse in the nun's face? A trickle of sympathy? Perhaps there was an element of discomfiture in her eyes. She told them she was sorry to hear about Molly's death. They stared at her, saying nothing. She indicated her office, perhaps fearful of others overhearing their conversation.

'We'd rather speak from here, Sister,' Juliette said, pausing until all the girls were quiet. 'We've only got a few minutes.' She looked around at the girls. 'I know you can all confirm that Molly's health improved, thanks to her change of diet and other factors. She became a different person, despite being raped by a priest.' There was a collective gasp from the girls. Juliette turned to Sister Hallvard. 'You arranged to have Molly carted off in an ambulance to St Vincent's like the police bundling a drunk into the Black Maria. You didn't notify anyone. You knew St Vincent's arranged illegal adoptions for priests' offspring.'

She paused to get her breath. The building was so quiet they could hear the clock ticking in the parlour. The girls stood stock still. Sister Hallvard said she had to go, but Andrea started up. 'Molly is dead now because of your collaboration with that secret ward. I know all about it. It's as top secret there as… as…'

'As the Petrovs' home address,' Harry muttered.

Maude was wringing her hands. 'Poor Molly' she sobbed. 'I had no idea she was so ill during her pregnancy. I would have looked after her. I hope you did, Sister!'

Juliette was flushed with anger. 'You knew a priest fathered Molly's baby, Sister, because you read Maude's letter and the one Molly was about to post to Maude. The letter explaining how Father Kelly drugged and raped her while she was unconscious.'

There was no reaction from the nun, but more gasps from the girls.

'No one in Australia is supposed to know that priests go astray, are they Sister?' Maude joined in. 'I could tell you a few stories that would make your hair sprout through your veil Sister. I grew up in a back street behind a presbytery. The comings and goings that went on there! Do you know what we discovered? The church keeps its garbage. They cover it up!'

Sister Hallvard was on the defensive. 'In fact, you're wrong. I'm not at liberty to say who arranged for Molly to go to St Vincent's, but it wasn't me.'

'Perhaps not arranged from here, but you instigated it Sister!' It was time to lambaste Hallvard. Juliette had never liked this woman. 'Molly knew you'd been rifling through her things. You even took her money. After you read the letter she was about to post, you realised she was going to keep her baby.'

It was Andrea's turn. 'That was the final nail in the coffin! Literally! Not only was Molly keeping her baby, but it was a priest's baby. You collaborated! You informed the Bishop! The Women's Hospital may coerce single mothers into relinquishing their babies, but they don't permit illegal adoptions like St Vincent's.'

The nun flushed. 'Girls are not permitted to... to keep those babies,' she said coldly.

Juliette gave her a scathing look, pushed past her and headed towards the front door. The others followed, except for Maude who lingered behind.

'One more thing Sister,' Maude said shouting tearfully for everyone to hear. 'Your actions and others in the church brought poor Molly to this act of despair. You dare to talk so calmly about her death when you were cold-heartedly complicit in it. None of us here who cared for Molly will ever forgive you for what you've done.' She moved forward and raised her arm as though she was about to strike Hallvard. Instead, she jabbed her finger in the air, and pointed it towards the nun's face, forcing her to take a step backwards. 'Mannix and the Bishop and all his yes-men are responsible for Molly's death. Power has corrupted their souls.' She paused for a moment. 'If they ever had one! As for you, Sister, you might just as well have pushed Molly out the window yourself.'

It was a scorching ninety-five degrees. Inside St Jude's was cooler, except for the gallery, always warmer than the nave. Cecilia and Bernice were wearing their MacRob Girls' High plaid summer uniforms with straw hats. They were devastated and angry over Molly's death. Cecilia was upset that she couldn't think of an appropriate piece of music for Molly. The sort Molly liked to play. One that would not be too out of place at the end of the service. She was playing a Bach Chorale, while Bernice was trying to identify her former teacher among the few mourners trickling towards the front of the church. 'That tall man with the dark curls must be Doctor Rousseau, Celie. I remember Jeanne describing him in French conversation. *Mon frére est médecin. Il est grand avec des cheveux noirs bouclés.*'

Cecilia's view was hazy from the console mirror. It wasn't easy to see the women's faces, because like them, they were wearing hats. Two elegantly dressed women in black sheath dresses were walking ahead of him.

'Oh my God! That's her, Celie. Juliette! The taller woman in the cloche hat. Can you see her in the mirror? She looks stunning in those high heels. Nothing nunnish about her now. She's like Cyd Charisse, isn't she?'

When Cecilia had first told Bernice about their former French teacher, they'd discussed her birth name. Bernice had asked if it was pronounced the French way with the soft J like in Jeanne. No, she'd replied. The Australian way, like Julie.

'She's gorgeous,' Bernice said. 'She'll have no trouble finding her Romeo. They'll call her Mademoiselle Rousseau at MLC I suppose. It sounds so chic.'

Everyone was seated. Cecilia's eyes were drawn to the mirror as though waiting for the happy bride to appear. All she saw was Molly's coffin. Molly's broken body lying inside it. The litany of atrocities that had led to her death. Juliette had explained what had happened when they were making the funeral arrangements. Now it was boiling up inside her to the point where she had to stop herself from playing the Chorale aggressively. To moderate the music to suit the surroundings. Everything was churning around in her mind. The priest at the presbytery. The Maternity Home. Molly's cruel treatment by those who were supposedly her carers. The staff at two of Melbourne's top hospitals. Then there was the church with all its rules! Its paranoia about scandal so excessive that it protected criminal priests who preyed on the innocent. No one need convince her about who caused Molly's suicide. Then even in death, the church had abandoned her. Surely people who are suffering and tormented don't think about what's right or wrong when they commit suicide! She'd said as much to Bernice's father who replied that churches had you believing Jesus could walk on water and turn it into wine but couldn't see that he didn't bother saving himself when he had the chance. What was that if it wasn't suicide? The church was full of contradictions!

The Harringtons and Reverend Newman had compromised. Protocol would prevail. The tradition of hymns in the Anglican funeral service was dispensed with, hymns never being sung at Catholic funerals. Cecilia would play at suitable intervals throughout the service, but nothing too grandiose. Definitely Mozart's *Ave Verum*. Serene and relaxed. Soul-stirring and uplifting without being too mournful. Molly had asked about it after she'd played it at the High Mass in Ballarat when they first became friends. Now she was playing it for Molly, but this time, Molly was lying before the altar in a coffin. Three weeks ago, she'd played it for Molly right here with Juliette, where Bernice was standing now.

Reverend Newman recited the twenty-third psalm and three antiphons in thanksgiving for the life of the departed, followed by the prayers for the burial of the dead. After some persuasion, he'd agreed to Paul saying a few words about Molly on behalf of her family. The Lord's Prayer would end the service.

'It looks more like a school hall,' Bernice whispered. 'Molly's relatives will be feeling so uncomfortable when they look around. They'll be wondering why there's no crucifix. Just that empty cross. And the vicar wearing a black suit and clerical collar.'

'He'd look a bit weird here in a lacy amice and black and gold chasuble.'

'The altar's so bare. It looks like a refectory table. But I love that psalm. *The lord is my shepherd*. It's beautiful. I wish we had something like that. A bit of an improvement on a cold Latin Requiem with all the sanctus bells and pomp and pageantry.'

Cecilia agreed. The scene might look as bare as Mother Hubbard's cupboard, but there was something warm and comforting about the English language. It compensated for the lack of ornaments and finery.

'When it comes to religion, I'm leaning towards Dad's side now,' Bernice continued. 'He says he doesn't like being labelled, but I can think of him as a fence-sitting spiritualist.'

'I'm so angry with the church right now, the C of E looks more appealing. It's the music that draws me in.' Cecilia wanted to accompany a top choir one day. She remembered Sister Katerina saying that the best choral works in the world were religious because true belief was surely inspirational.

Reverend Newman was reciting the prayers for the burial of the dead:

I am the resurrection and the life, saith the lord ...

I know that my Redeemer liveth

Where had she heard those words? *I know that my Redeemer liveth.* Yes. During a duet practice when they'd been discussing composers, Molly mentioned her favourite aunt singing it around Christmas time. They'd giggled when she said her accompaniment would have made Handel cry in his coffin, wherever that was. Molly's adored Aunt Maude was here today. 'Quick. I want *I Know That My Redeemer Liveth.* It's in *The Messiah*,' she told Bernice who found the score on a shelf.

Molly would have chosen it more for her aunt rather than for herself. Wasn't it sung at this time of the year? Amidst all the advertisements for the Olympic Games, she'd seen posters for *The Messiah* outside St Paul's and the Melbourne Town Hall. Earlier in the year, Cecilia recalled how they'd talked about Melbourne and their Christmas holidays. How Molly sometimes visited the convent in Albert Park, her aunt cross-examining them in the parlour for hours, desperate to know what was going on in the outside world. All the while, Molly said she suffered from Sea Fever. Across the road from the convent was a beautiful beach inviting her for a swim.

Cecilia tended to block out images of large expanses of water. While sun, sand and water might be an intoxicating combination for others, her anguish remained silent under the waves at St Kilda and Brighton Beach when she went there with Bernice's family. She was always reminded of that day. The dam. Her two little brothers floundering around inside the car. Desperate to get out. The darkness closing in on all sides. Water flooding their little lungs. The two tiny coffins. Her father's enduring guilt. Now Molly's coffin. There was no greater reminder of your own mortality than looking at a coffin and imagining that it could have been you. Why were all these harrowing memories resurfacing? Did families ever cease their lamentation? Perhaps there were things in life you could never get over. Some people you would never stop missing. She recalled the first verse of an elegy they had memorised for Sister Isobel.

Music I heard with you was more than music
And bread I broke with you was more than bread
Now that I am without you, all is desolate
All that once so beautiful is dead

Paul Rousseau walked to the front of the church and stood before the lectern. 'I've been asked to speak on behalf of Molly's family, her relatives and friends Cecilia and Bernice, my sister Juliette, and my wife Andrea,' he said with a soft French accent as he looked directly at the mourners before him. 'Most of you here, of course, have known Molly much longer than the short time she was my patient at the Royal Women's

Hospital.' He paused for a moment and looked around the small group of mourners, '*My* patient,' he emphasised. '*My* patient before she was suddenly taken from the Maternity Home to St Vincent's without our knowledge. *My* patient, who after she left my care, was subjected to outrageous psychological trauma,' he said, trying to control his anger. He paused again and took a deep breath. 'As my patient at the Women's, Molly was uncomplaining despite her terrible headaches and nausea and vomiting, which some of my colleagues mistakenly referred to as anxiety and guilt. It was no such thing. *Hyperemesis gravidarum* is a very rare and physically debilitating condition, with all of those symptoms I mentioned, including weight loss. It is usually ongoing right throughout... throughout confinement. Women have died from this terrible ailment. It was only a few weeks before the end of her life, in fact, after we changed her diet, that Molly began to recover. Her *joie de vivre* returned. She began to smile and chat about her family, particularly her future.

'Molly's Aunt Maude has told me of her many talents. How she loved to dance with her sisters and entertain with her musical skills. Tony recalled hotel customers saying the only reason they didn't go to the neighbouring hotel was that they preferred a singalong with Molly at the Barkly. He also told me some humorous stories about Molly which I'm sure he'll share with you later back at our house.'

The two girls stood back from the balustrade. Cecilia was biting her lip, tears beginning to fill her eyes again. She recalled the first time Sister Angela had given them the piano duets. Molly dancing around to one of them. How during breaks between practices, they'd swap stories about their home lives. Cecilia describing the farm in Kingston. Her parents and sister. Her two little brothers and how they'd drowned. Molly, proud that her mother had been a singer and dancer. Her beloved Aunt, Maude. But how could her uncle – a priest on her father's side who Molly loved – refuse to have anything to do with her funeral? Such heartlessness was something she'd never understand. They'd laughed when Molly said she sometimes imagined Alphonsus storming into the piano room at the hotel to accuse her of socialising with the riffraff or committing blasphemy when she jazzed up the hymns for 'the religious loony.' Sometimes they'd talked more than practised, but Cecilia loved hearing Molly's stories. With Molly dancing and playing all those tunes for the customers, pub life had sounded more exciting than boarding school. If only she could think of an appropriate piece of music to play for her at the end of the service.

'Molly's ear for music obviously carried over to her skill in foreign languages,' Paul went on. 'When I occasionally spoke to her in French after her health began to improve, she sounded more like a native rather than a schoolgirl learning a new language. My wife, Andrea, and my sister Juliette tell me that Molly was always very modest about her talents, both in language and music. During their walks around Carlton and Parkville, she expressed her admiration for Andrea's work as a doctor working with the under-privileged, particularly girls and women. Molly's own ambition was to become a teacher of languages. She told me once that if she could be half as good a teacher as Juliette, she'd be over the moon.'

Paul took a deep breath, looked again at his notes, then towards his sister. 'At school, Molly was awarded prizes for French and German. Juliette taught her in Ballarat and was lucky enough to hear her practising duets with Cecilia, another talented musician,' he said with a half-smile, nodding towards the organ gallery. 'Juliette said Molly played anything by ear, including the French melodies they learnt in class.'

The penny dropped for Cecilia. That was it! The French melodies! They'd both agreed that *La mer* was their favourite French song. One lunchtime Cecilia had asked Molly to play it, which she was doing when Sister Jeanne walked into the classroom to prepare a lesson. Jeanne asked Molly to play it again and sing the English lyrics with Cecilia. 'Well,' Jeanne had said. 'Interesting that the English version is about mourning for a lost love, whereas the French is an ode and homage to the changing moods of the sea. It's my favourite Trenet, although *Les feuilles mortes* – Autumn Leaves – is my favourite French song.' She'd lent her Trenet album to Cecilia so that she could memorise *La mer*.

The mourners recited *The Lord's Prayer*. Cecilia mouthed the words in automatic mode, her brain and lips not synchronised. *La mer* would bind the three of them together. Her, Molly and Juliette. The English version of mourning for a lost love was appropriate enough, the original *La mer* surely a metaphor for a hymn. Spiritual in that it was synonomous with nature. The sea shimmering with silver. The rain. The gulfs. The sheep and the birds. The ponds, the reeds.

'I know what to play for Molly now,' Cecilia said to Bernice. Her voice was choked, husky. 'I know it from memory. Change the stops whenever you like.'

It was all she could do now to stifle her sobs. A few bars in, Cecilia was distracted by the thought that from today Molly would be all but forgotten. Her death would never be avenged. An epitaph was forming in her mind. *Here lies Molly. Callously treated by society. By the church. Deprived of her loving family and friends. Denied a promising career. A chance to make beautiful music and entertain. Above all, denied a chance to love her tiny child.*

How could she keep Molly's memory alive? How could she prevent others afflicted by society's prejudices and narrow-mindedness from suffering like Molly? Andrea, as a doctor, had told her how people can make changes. Why couldn't she? Would it be possible to consider a career in medicine despite the possibility of getting a scholarship in music? She'd grown up thinking of girls becoming nurses rather than doctors. Music would always be in her life. She could accompany soloists, choirs. Join a chamber group. She recalled Sister Dominique begging her to continue with science. Why hadn't she listened? Deep down she knew why. She wanted top marks in the subjects that came easily to her. With a renewed sense of optimism, she decided to talk to Andrea and Juliette. Like Andrea, she would be guided by her own conscience rather than those with no sympathy for girls in Molly's circumstances. She would have independent opinions in an era when women didn't have a voice. Daniel would help her with maths and science if she returned to MacRob to repeat Matriculation. She was qualified to teach piano. She could earn her keep. Have private students. Maybe play for weddings. Now her grief seemed to be radiating energy. Motivating her. Molly would be her inspiration. A memorial to a friend callously deserted by the church to protect her attacker.

Her shoulders were heaving. Every few bars she wiped her eyes with the back of her hand. The keys blurred, merging with her tears. She was playing by touch now. Fumbling. Feeling for the keys like a blind person. She felt the tremulous tones of the organ enfolding her as she took deep breaths, trying to control herself while tears streamed down her face. The lyrics drifted through her mind. The ones they had sung in the classroom that day for Juliette, Molly accompanying.

Somewhere, beyond the sea
Somewhere waiting for me
If I could fly like birds on high
Then straight to her arms I'd go sailing.

She felt Bernice nudging her and followed her eyes to the top of the stairs to where their former teacher was standing with a half-smile on her face. Juliette put a finger to her lips and walked towards the organ. She stood behind Cecilia, placing her warm hands on the shoulders of the only person who understood the significance of the music, and began singing softly:

'*La mer, qu'on voit danser*
Le long des golfes clairs
A des reflets d'argent, la mer
Des reflets changeants sous la pluie'

Acknowledgements

I am forever indebted to my husband Colin, my literary and scientific advisor and 'techo support' who pushed me into writing this book when I wasn't sure which road to take after I retired. Thanks also to my sister Elizabeth for her memories, suggestions, and edits. Perhaps I wouldn't have persisted without my good friend Wendy Taylor, who was so patient and encouraging, editing several of my early raw attempts at this, my first novel. Thanks also to Ed Highley for referring me to my manuscript assessor and advisor, Kaaren Sutcliffe, who set me on the right path to writing a more professional literary narrative. Many thanks also to my good friends – Monica Hingston for her help with my synopsis, Sandra Favre for checking my French, Lorraine Clarke for checking my medical references, and Jean-Pierre Favre for his cover design.

www.ingramcontent.com/pod-product-compliance
Lightning Source LLC
Chambersburg PA
CBHW030549260626
47157CB00006B/2248